MW00955157

A Pair of Sparkling Eyes

A Pride and Prejudice Variatation

Andreea Catana

Copyright © 2024 ANDREEA CATANA

This is a work of fiction.
Names, characters, places, and incidents for this specific book are products of the author's imagination or are used factiously. Any resemblance to actual events or person, living or dead, is entirely coincidental.

A PAIR OF SPARKLING EYES
Copyright © 2024 by ANDREEA CATANA
ALL RIGHTS RESERVED, INCLUDING THE RIGHT TO REPRODUCE THIS BOOK, OR PORTION THEREOF, IN ANY FORMAT WHATSOEVER.

No part of this book may be reproduced, or stored in a retrieval system, or transmitted in any form or by any means, electronic, mechanical, photocopying, recording, or otherwise, without express written permission of the publisher.

ISBN: 9798343277968

Cover design by: ANDREEA CATANA
Library of Congress Control Number: 2018675309
Printed in the United States of America

Contents

Chapter 1

The young girl stared at the impressive building in utter silence — something that rarely happened, if ever — her brown eyes widened in complete admiration.

"It is so pretty, Aunt! And so large! A hundred times larger than Longbourn," she exclaimed enthusiastically as she held tight to the hand of an elegant young lady next to her, who was equally lost in awe.

"Not quite a hundred times larger, Lizzy, but almost," the lady answered, brushing her hair out of her face. "I am so glad we came! Pemberley is even more beautiful than I remember. Is that not so, Mr Gardiner? Do you find it agreeable?"

"Indeed I do, my darling. I am happy to be here at last." The gentleman behind them gazed up in wonderment at the sprawling house. "I was starting to tire of listening to you talking about the park, the woods, the lake, and the views. But now I must admit that I have never seen a place more beautifully situated. You were right to praise it so."

Lizzy turned to him seriously. "Uncle Edward, Mama says that since you are now married, you should always listen to Aunt Madeleine and never question her. And Mama says she knows best as she is your elder sister."

"I would never dare to contradict your mama," the gentleman answered with equal seriousness.

"I listen to Jane too, because she is older than me," the girl added, then corrected herself. "Well, I do not listen to Jane all the time, as I am obstinate and disobedient. Mama says so."

Edward Gardiner and his new wife Madeleine laughed at the sweet sincerity of his favourite niece, Lizzy, the second daughter of his sister Fanny Bennet's five. Married for six months, Edward Gardiner had at last indulged his wife's desire to visit Derbyshire — the place where she had grown up. The opportunity for such a visit had been unexpected. The Bennet daughters, with the exception of Lizzy, and Mrs Bennet were all bedridden with a terrible cold, and Mr Bennet could hardly supervise a healthy and energetic child of ten as well as bear the constant whining of the other five members of his family.

"Come, we should go to the back entrance," an older woman interjected from the carriage with a sign of urgency on her face. "We have a fixed appointment, and it would not do for Lady Anne to have to wait. We cannot be a single minute late."

"Of course. I shall take you to the door, Mrs Clarke. When should I return to fetch you?" Mr Gardiner enquired.

"Aunt Honoria, dear Edward, just as Madeleine calls me. After all, I am your great-aunt now too."

"As you wish, Aunt Honoria. It would be my pleasure." He bowed ceremoniously with a little smile on his face.

"Good. Now, you do not need to return. Mrs Reynolds, the housekeeper, will send us back to Lambton in a carriage as soon as we have completed our task here," the lady explained, eager to set foot on the ground.

Mrs Clarke's advanced age and her recent illness made her unsteady on her feet, so she immediately grabbed her niece's arm, stepping inside the mansion hesitantly. Behind them, a couple of servants were carrying two large packages from the carriage.

The ladies walked down a long hall, and the echoing of their steps impressed young Lizzy even more. She continued to hold her aunt's hand even tighter, looking around, astounded by the elegance, the significance of which she could not fully understand but perceived as being special. So much richness she had never seen, nor had she ever imagined.

"Mrs Clarke, how kind of you to have come. You feel better, I trust?" a woman of gentle features said as she approached, followed by two maids.

"Mrs Reynolds, good day," Mrs Clarke answered. "I feel a little improved, but my feet and my back are still aching. One cannot fight old age, and seventy years are not easy to carry."

"But I am pleased to see you looking better than last week." The compliment was received with a slight smile. "And who are your lovely companions?" Mrs Reynolds directed her attention to the two other ladies accompanying Mrs Clarke.

"This is my great-niece, Madeleine Gardiner. She is visiting Derbyshire with her husband, and she was kind enough to accompany me today for the fitting of the first three dresses. Mrs Norbert remains at the shop, working on the rest."

The eyes of the housekeeper fixed on the little girl who was standing in front of Mrs Gardiner.

"And this is my niece, Elizabeth Bennet," Mrs Gardiner said, as Lizzy curtseyed properly. "I hope you do not mind that I have brought her with me."

"No, not at all, my dear. Pemberley needs some cheer," she added with sadness in her voice. Addressing Lizzy directly, she said, "Do you like Pemberley?"

"Very much so, Mrs Reynolds. I have never seen anywhere more beautiful than this."

"I am glad you approve of it. It is a magnificent estate. And it is a good home to those that live here, although..." Mrs Reynolds's voice trailed away, the lady clearly realising it was not proper to speak of her employers' lives to others. "Allow me to lead you to the mistress's apartment, Mrs Clarke. She has been waiting for you. When you have finished, we shall have a cup of tea and some biscuits," the housekeeper added with kindness in her voice.

As they walked at a slow pace to accommodate Mrs Clarke, Lizzy's attention was drawn to the windows. It was a sunny summer day, and from afar, a child could be seen playing under the supervision of two women. A couple of puppies were barking happily around her. Lizzy withdrew her little hand from her aunt's and moved closer to one of the windows, staring out curiously.

"Lizzy, come here," Mrs Gardiner whispered, alarm in her voice.

But Lizzy remained at the window, looking out with delight at what seemed to be a jolly scene.

"Who is she?"

"Lizzy!" Mrs Gardiner exclaimed, blushing. However, her relief came quickly when the housekeeper smiled.

"That is my young mistress, Miss Georgiana Darcy, with her governess and her nanny," Mrs Reynolds said.

"Are there many children here at Pemberley?"

"Just Miss Georgiana and her brother, Master Fitzwilliam. He is her senior by several years. But he is not at Pemberley currently. He has accompanied his father to town. You see, he will inherit the estate one day, and he has been very eager to learn about its management from his father." The housekeeper continued with an explanation that seemed to be more for Mrs Gardiner than for little Lizzy, whose attention was still fixed on the scene in the garden. Mrs Reynolds turned her gaze towards the group on the lawn, then spoke again to the ladies.

"Perhaps Miss Elizabeth would rather go out and play instead of waiting for you in a chamber? One of the maids could take her there."

"Yes, I would like that very much!" Lizzy said enthusiastically before the other ladies could reply.

Mrs Gardiner was slightly hesitant. "Are you certain it will not disturb Miss Darcy?"

"No, not at all. She will be happy to have company closer to her age. There are rarely young visitors, especially young girls at Pemberley," Mrs Reynolds said, admitting the real reason for her proposal. "Besides, to be honest, Lady Anne is not feeling well. Her apartment is not the proper place for a child."

"Please, Aunt Madeleine," Lizzy begged, encouraged by the housekeeper's words.

"If a maid could accompany her there and someone will

closely supervise her, it is acceptable. Lizzy, you must promise me you will be careful and will do what you are told. I trust you to be wise and well behaved."

"I shall, Aunt, I promise! I only wish to play with the puppies. I shall bother no one else. Not even Miss Darcy if she does not want me to."

"You must not worry," the housekeeper said. "Miss Georgiana is playing under strict supervision, as she is only five years old. There will certainly be no danger for Miss Elizabeth."

"Oh, but I am much older!" Lizzy declared. "I am ten years old, which is twice as old as Miss Georgiana. My sister Lydia is five years old as well, so I know how to play with little children. I am quite grown up!"

Mrs Reynolds' smile broadened in front of the girl's liveliness, and she made a small hand movement towards one of the maids. "Miss Elizabeth seems to be a very clever girl. I am sure she and Miss Georgiana will enjoy each other's company."

Lizzy nodded and, despite her aunt's lasting reluctance, agreed to take the maid's hand and follow her to the gardens.

The governess and the nanny both received Lizzy with surprise and aloofness, as very few children were allowed near Miss Darcy. Miss Georgiana herself stepped back, seeking protection from her nanny due to the uniqueness of the circumstance.

The two women proceeded to question the maid about Lizzy's identity and then ask the girl her about her family and the reason for her presence there. While slightly intimidated at first by the two ladies' severe voices and expressions, Lizzy's spirits became playful soon enough, and she lost no opportunity in answering in an animated and confident tone. The two puppies, however, had fewer reservations towards the newly arrived girl, running eagerly towards her. Lizzy knelt on the grass at once, laughing as they licked her face, which made Miss Georgiana smile for the first time.

Only a few minutes were needed before Miss Georgiana's

curiosity and interest led her to approach Lizzy. Once the strangeness had dissipated, the two girls played together under the reluctant approval and strict observation of the women, as well as their demands that they should behave in a certain manner. But the girls paid no attention to anything except each other and the puppies.

***

Lady Anne Darcy's apartment was as impressive and elegant as one would expect. Mrs Reynolds announced the presence of the ladies, and they entered together with the two male servants carrying the packages, who immediately departed.

Mrs Gardiner, although no stranger to people from high society, felt intimidated and nervous. As a child, growing up in Lambton, she was well aware of the reputation of the Darcy family of Pemberley and had even seen Lady Anne a few times — always looking vibrant, elegant, and poised.

Her recollections, however, were far from the image in front of her: a woman still young, dressed in a silk gown and robe, her brown hair falling over her shoulders. Her features were flawless by the standards of beauty, but there was a paleness that emphasised her blue eyes, from which light and life itself seemed to be missing. She was very thin, almost ethereal, sitting in an armchair by the window. In a corner, a gentleman of middle age with a grave countenance, introduced as Lady Anne's physician, was packing his bag. She appeared not to have heard Mrs Reynolds's introductions at first, so the housekeeper spoke again.

"My lady, Mrs Clarke is here. Her great-niece Mrs Gardiner has accompanied her to help."

"Please come in," the lady's low voice invited them. "Mrs Clarke, I am sorry you have had to come all the way to Pemberley, but I have not been feeling too well recently, and some of the dresses must be ready by the end of next week. Of course, you and Mrs Gardiner will be properly compensated for your effort."

"Your ladyship, coming to Pemberley has always been a pleasure, and you must know we would do anything to help," Mrs Clarke said, stepping forwards with some difficulty. "As for compensation, nobody has ever complained about your generosity."

Moving closer, Madeleine Gardiner was even more impressed by the lady, and she watched her with an aching heart. Lady Anne turned to the window after bidding farewell to her doctor, who exited the room after greeting the ladies.

"Mrs Reynolds, who is the young girl playing with Georgiana?"

"Her name is Lizzy, my lady. She is Mrs Gardiner's niece. I took the liberty of allowing her to play with Miss Darcy. I hope you do not mind."

Mrs Clarke added quickly, "The girl's father is a gentleman from Hertfordshire."

"How lovely. Georgiana is running and rolling in the grass," Lady Anne continued in a subdued tone.

"I hope you do not disapprove of it, your ladyship," Mrs Gardiner said, unsure what Lady Anne felt. "Lizzy can be quite animated and energetic. She might be too much at times."

"Oh no, not at all. It is so lovely to watch my daughter playing like any other child. My son is more than ten years her senior, and so are most of her cousins. Poor Georgiana is too shy and too well behaved for her age. I believe she could do with some energy and liveliness."

With much care, Lady Anne was helped to stand by her maid, another servant, Mrs Reynolds, and Mrs Gardiner. She appeared weak, but she tried to bear the trying on of the dresses stoically. However, she stopped after the first two and declared it was enough for that day. The encounter had lasted less than an hour, but both Lady Anne and Mrs Clarke looked exhausted.

"We shall return again the day after tomorrow," Mrs

Clarke said. "By that time, I shall have both these gowns finished."

"Thank you." Lady Anne forced a smile. "Mrs Gardiner, how long are you staying in Derbyshire?"

"A fortnight, your ladyship. That is what we have planned."

Mrs Clarke and Mrs Gardiner curtseyed to bid their farewells, but to their amazement, Lady Anne said, "Mrs Gardiner, if it is no imposition, would you be so kind as to bring your niece again when you next come with Mrs Clarke?"

"Of course, my lady! I am sure Lizzy will be delighted." The brief exchange appeared to have fatigued Lady Anne extensively, and one of the maids hurried forwards to help her settle back into the armchair and place her feet on a stool. The visitors, understanding the need to allow her to recover with dignity, left her presence at once.

As expected, Lizzy was reluctant to leave Miss Georgiana and her puppies so soon. With amusement and some concern, Madeleine Gardiner noticed spots of dirt on Lizzy's gown — which was quite expected — but also on Miss Darcy's, whose cheeks were crimson and whose hair had escaped from its pins. Both girls were in high spirits, animated by the fresh air and movement. The governess, who was much alarmed by such agitation, adjusted Miss Georgiana's bonnet, but the girl seemed more interested in her new companion than in making herself presentable.

The promise to meet again in two days made the separation easier, and on the way back to the inn in Lambton, Lizzy spoke of little else except Georgiana and her puppies, counting the hours until she could return.

For Mr and Mrs Gardiner, the conversation over dinner — as soon as Lizzy had been sent to her chamber — was engaging but rather sad. The couple shared observations and reports and reached the same painful conclusion: Lady Anne's health was a reason for immediate concern.

"My aunt Honoria has been making gowns for the Darcy

family and servants since long before Lady Anne came to live at Pemberley. In the last few years, the lady has spent most of her time in Derbyshire, so my aunt has had the privilege of becoming her main seamstress. Mr Darcy was the one who invested in my aunt's little shop and encouraged her to hire as much help as she needed."

"Yes, Mrs Clarke mentioned it to me," Mr Gardiner said. "A customer as illustrious as Lady Anne must have led to a huge increase in business."

"Yes, but my aunt does not care much for that. At her age, she passes most of the work to her granddaughter. Aunt Honoria is mostly interested in pleasing Lady Anne."

"From what I have heard, the people of Lambton are extremely fond of the lady. It is such a tragedy that she has taken so ill."

"Aunt Honoria says the lady's health has been declining for the last three years, and none of the doctors brought in by her husband have been able to help. They have spent the summer months at the seaside every year and purchased medicines from all over the world, but it has mostly been in vain."

"How very unfortunate, my dear. May God watch over her."

"I cannot help but think of her family too. How they must suffer. Though I am sure everyone is putting on a brave face. A daughter so young — imagine! You know, I admire her so much. She strives to create the illusion of an ordinary life for the sake of her family. She does not need the dresses Aunt Honoria is sewing for her — that is evident — yet she is continuing to do all the things she has always done. Being the mistress of Pemberley."

"But I hear she has a son as well."

"Of course, my dear. I have been told he is studying at Cambridge and resembles his father very much — both in appearance and in character. He must be eighteen now. Aunt Honoria speaks highly of him too. He is seemingly intelligent, diligent with his studies and his duties, and very fond of his parents and little sister. Everyone has a high opinion of him I have heard, which is quite a rare thing these days."

"Quite a family, the Darcys!" Mr Gardiner declared. "I am surprised they are not titled, though."

Until they retired for the night, the discussion continued, mostly centred around the Darcys, and the tiring day finally ended with a glass of port.

The following day, the Gardiners had the extraordinary surprise of being visited by Mr Darcy himself, who had come to make their acquaintance. The master of Pemberley — tall, handsome, and impressive in figure and manner — intimidated everyone at the inn, including the Gardiners and young Lizzy. The girl immediately hid behind her aunt when the gentleman entered — a very rare response on her part.

"Both my wife and my daughter were delighted with the visit from you and your niece, Mrs Gardiner," Mr Darcy said. "I believe it is the first time they have shared the same pleasure in anyone's visit."

His voice was deep and grave, but his expression was friendly enough.

"We were honoured and happy with the chance to see Pemberley, sir," Mrs Gardiner answered sincerely.

"I understand you grew up in Lambton. I must admit I do not recall you."

"Oh, I am sure you would not, Mr Darcy. I left when I was Lizzy's age, and I do not believe we ever exchanged a single word," Mrs Gardiner said.

"I see. Miss Elizabeth, do you enjoy travelling with your uncle and aunt?" the gentleman enquired.

She nodded, glancing at her uncle.

"Do you have any brothers or sisters?"

"I have four sisters," she said quietly.

"How lovely. I am sure you miss them. Would you like to come and play with my daughter again?"

"Of course!" Lizzy said with increasing determination. "I

promised Georgiana that I should come again tomorrow, and I must keep my promise! Papa says a gentleman's daughter always keeps her promises!"

"I could not agree more, Miss Elizabeth," Mr Darcy declared. "Then it is agreed. We shall be very happy to have you at Pemberley again. My Georgiana has talked extensively about you, much to my wife's joy. Mrs Clarke," Mr Darcy went on to address the seamstress, "Lady Anne has told me that you are in need of…"

The rest of the conversation was lost on Lizzy, who could hardly contain her eagerness to see her new friend again. Although Mr Darcy's presence at the inn lasted no more than a couple of minutes, his call impressed and puzzled the Gardiners, as well as Mrs Clarke. Despite the universally high opinion of Mr Darcy, he was not known as a friendly man, nor one who sought the company of strangers. One thing they all agreed on was that he loved Lady Anne and Miss Georgiana very much, and he was eager to do for them whatever provided them relief or happiness.

Regardless of the gentleman's reason for such amiability, the next day when Lizzy arrived at Pemberley, she and her aunt faced another surprise. The girl was invited to Lady Anne's apartment and introduced to the mistress of Pemberley herself. Georgiana was seated next to her mother, solemn as a young lady ought to be, though her joy of seeing her friend once again was visible on her face.

Her ladyship kindly asked questions, to which Lizzy replied with some restraint but honesty. The conversation was short, and afterwards, the girls were invited to go and play. Lady Anne seemed pleased to see her daughter content, and for a while, even her pale countenance showed some colour. When it came to the hour of parting, Lady Anne demanded to speak to Lizzy once again.

"You have such bright eyes, my dear. One can easily see your soul and your spirit in them."

At the age of ten, Lizzy hardly understood the meaning

of the lady's words, but the gentle voice and the little smile indicated it was something good. She thanked Lady Anne and attempted a curtsey, which was rather clumsy but charming nevertheless.

A few days later, Lizzy found she was already familiar with the Pemberley halls and gardens as she and Georgiana followed and chased the puppies from place to place, filling the rooms with gaiety, dispelling the sombreness of the house for a few hours.

On one occasion, however, they were suddenly interrupted by the appearance of a young boy, who was several years older than Lizzy. The boy cast a superior gaze at Lizzy and, after seeing her dirty shoes, looked away in disgust. His attention turned instead towards Georgiana, who seemed delighted to see him. The boy's countenance changed immediately into a friendly smile, and he beckoned her to come towards him. Lizzy watched them, intrigued but not making much sense of what was happening.

"Did you take it?" the boy whispered. Georgiana nodded and pulled something from her pocket. "I hope nobody saw you…"

"No, I swear."

The boy looked at what Georgiana had given him with a frown.

"Can you get more, do you think?"

"I can get more."

"Good. You are a clever girl, Georgiana. Remember, you must keep it as our secret! Do not tell anyone."

"Yes, Brother, it is our secret."

"Our very special secret," he said, then walked away with not a single glance towards Lizzy. As soon as he departed, Georgiana returned to her friend.

"Who is he? Is he your brother?" Lizzy asked. Even at her tender age, she could comprehend that she had witnessed something suspicious.

"Oh no. Fitzwilliam is not here. He is in London."

"Oh...but you called him brother. Then who was that?"

"That is George. My father's godson. But George is like a brother to *me*," the girl whispered, as the two walked out into the gardens.

"What did you give him? And what is the secret?" Lizzy insisted out of childish curiosity.

The girl's blue eyes shadowed, and she frowned.

"I cannot tell you that, Lizzy. I promised I would not say." She took a deep breath and smiled, holding out her hand. "Come. I must show my kittens to you. Nanny Morris has them in a basket. She says we can play with them when they are older, but I am sure she will not mind us visiting them."

Lizzy saw the young man again on several different occasions over the following weeks, but he continued to pay no attention to her, not once asking Georgiana anything about her. Soon, Lizzy began to understand that he was making Georgiana remove items of value from the household and give them to him without anyone else's knowledge. While she witnessed it only in a few instances, it was clearly a habit the two shared. But, since her new friend had said it was a secret, Lizzy did not betray it either.

Upon a subsequent visit, when Lizzy arrived with Mrs Gardiner and Mrs Clarke, she was already familiar with the grounds, and she sprung down directly from the carriage, running towards the lawn at the front of the house. Georgiana, with her nanny and her governess as well as her two puppies, was at the edge of the lake, which was her most favourite place. To Lizzy's surprise, she was riding a pony, with George holding the reins. They appeared to be at ease with one another, while the two older ladies were much engaged in a conversation on a bench a little way away from them. Spotting Lizzy's presence, Georgiana waved to her and asked George to release the reins so she could show off her riding skills.

The puppies ran towards Lizzy, then back to Georgiana, barking joyfully, which seemed to annoy George greatly. Lizzy knelt to hug one of the puppies, and at that moment, a loud whistle, followed by what sounded like the lash of a whip, was heard, startling the pony. The animal broke into a gallop, racing frantically away along the edge of the water with one of the dogs chasing him.

Georgiana was quickly jolted from her seat, and she fell into the mud before rolling several times and plunging into the lake. The two women, who had only just noticed the commotion, ran towards her, screaming for help. George approached the edge of the lake also but remained unmoving, watching in amusement as Georgiana struggled in the water, gasping for air.

Two male servants heard the noise and came running, but before anyone else could reach them, Lizzy threw herself into the lake, grabbing Georgiana with both hands. She kicked the water wildly with her legs, unable to touch the bottom, her hands busy holding the little girl. Their gowns, heavy with the muddy water, were pulling them both down, and Lizzy fought with all her strength to keep them afloat. Georgiana was frightened, and that made Lizzy's struggle much harder.

"Georgiana, do not move," Lizzy cried in vain, struggling for air, as she felt herself pulled downwards once again. Her effort was considerable for someone of her age, but she kept a firm hold on Georgiana's arm, despite the girl's frantic movements, which pushed her head under the water over and over.

It seemed like an eternity until the two servants arrived at the edge of the lake to pull both girls to safety. Georgiana began crying almost immediately in the arms of her governess, as Lizzy attempted to regain her breath and remove all the hair that was stuck to her face. As she stood up, all her limbs shaking, she saw George make a strange face that seemed to express his discontent at such a conclusion; however, once more people began to approach from the house, his expression changed to one of sadness and concern, and he moved to comfort Georgiana, pulling her into his embrace.

The girls were at last carried inside the house with much

care, despite Lizzy's insistent claims that she was perfectly well.

"We must thank God that everything turned out so well," Lady Anne's physician said once he had examined the girls in Georgiana's chamber. "Miss Elizabeth, it seems you saved Miss Georgiana's life today. You showed great courage. The greatest I have ever seen. I shall tell Lady Anne the happy news at once. She must be worried sick, and such torment is the last thing she needs."

Lizzy could not conceal her proud smile at such praise, and Georgiana, still trembling, hurried to embrace and thank her. Lizzy returned the affectionate gesture, holding the girl tight, while all the adults were fighting tears.

The rest of the day passed without further agitation at Pemberley. Towards the evening, once they were fully bathed and cleaned, the girls were taken to Lady Anne, who wished to be certain they were both well. The lady suggested, then insisted, that Lizzy be under the doctor's supervision until the next day — something that neither Mrs Gardiner nor Lizzy herself considered necessary. As the discussions went on, Lady Anne asked Mrs Gardiner to allow Lizzy to remain at Pemberley overnight, a suggestion that thrilled both Lizzy and Georgiana but left Mrs Gardiner doubtful.

"I assure you, Mrs Gardiner, that Lizzy will be treated like family. She will have her own room, and her maid and the doctor will be here to care for her if necessary."

It was only Lady Anne's sincere concern and her obvious tiredness that induced Mrs Gardiner to accept in order to avoid further debate. Therefore, a note was sent to Mr Gardiner at the inn, together with Mr Darcy and Lady Anne's thanks and gratitude.

For Lizzy, spending an entire day and night at Pemberley, staying in an elegant room three times larger than the one she shared with Jane at Longbourn, being assisted by a maid, and having a formal dinner with Georgiana was half amusing, half intimidating. However, she did enjoy the conversations with

Lady Anne and Mr Darcy, who showed nothing but kindness towards her. When the evening ended, Lizzy felt she knew all there was to know about the family.

They were excellent people whom she admired greatly, and as she was returning to her chamber later that day, she thought that if Master Fitzwilliam had been at Pemberley, she would have liked him greatly too. After all, she had heard many good things about him; words of praise were not spared when the young Darcy's name was spoken in conversation. The opinion was unanimous. Fitzwilliam Darcy was going to be a great man, a kind and caring soul, with no affectations or arrogance. He would be a great friend, a great brother, a great son, a joy for everyone to be around.

Lizzy accepted all this as fact.

Due to all the attention, activity, and novelty, Lizzy, however, found it difficult to find sleep that night. The doctor came to examine her before she retired, and she took some time to become accustomed to the unfamiliar bed. Then, around the hour of eleven, she felt her throat was dry. The maid, who had been assigned to assist her, had left, undoubtedly summoned by other business of the household, so Lizzy opened the door to her chamber, hoping to find help in the hall.

Instead, she came face to face with George, who was just leaving a room nearby and mumbling a curse while pushing something into his pocket. When his eyes met Lizzy's, he stopped for a moment, glaring at her defiantly.

"What are you doing here?" she asked.

"Me? What are *you* doing here? And how dare you question me? I have lived at Pemberley all my life, unlike you."

His words were dismissive, and Lizzy felt her temper rise. "I saw you."

"You saw what?" George said, for the first time with interest and maybe a little bit of panic in his tone.

"I saw you putting something in your pocket. What is it? Did you steal something? Or did you trick a little girl into stealing it for you?"

The boy's expression changed to one of ire, and he stepped towards her.

"How dare you talk to me like that! You are a little nothing."

Lizzy put her hands on her hips, ready for a confrontation.

"I might be a little nothing, but you are a big something! And I know you have deceived Georgiana. You are sneaking around. I saw you put something in your pocket!"

"So what? I do not have to tell you anything! You are nothing but a servant's niece. You should not even speak to me!"

"Your father works for Mr Darcy, so you are a servant's son! Besides, I am a gentleman's daughter, and I do not lie or steal!"

"And I am Mr Darcy's godson! He allows me to do anything I want!"

"Does he? Well then, I shall tell him what I heard of your conversation with Georgiana and see what he has to say!"

"Do not dare! You will regret it if you speak to my godfather. Do you think you mean something to him because you saved Georgiana? He will never believe you over me and will throw you out of the house like the little liar that you are!"

"At least I saved Georgiana, while you stood there like a fool and a coward! Your soul is wicked! I saw you! You were not even brave enough to enter the water. I bet you cannot even swim!"

"I can swim, you ninny, but why would I put myself in danger, since the servants were coming regardless? You were a fool to risk your life! You could have waited a little longer, and someone would have pulled Georgiana out. You think you were brave, but you were a simpleton."

"Simpleton or not, if you do not stop your so-called secret with Georgiana, I shall tell Lady Anne. Or I might even tell Mr Darcy!"

George's face flickered with anger, which turned into a smirk.

"And how will you do that?" he asked superciliously. "You will be gone in a day or two and will very likely never set foot at Pemberley again. I shall always be here, and I shall always have my godfather. He knows me better than he knows you."

Lizzy knew it to be true on some level — what reason did the Darcys have to believe her. Still, she would not accept defeat, and when she spoke again, she strove to do so with great conviction.

"Leave Georgiana alone! Or I promise I shall tell anyone who will listen that you are taking things from this house. Someone will believe me."

He brought his head close to hers. His thin lips were twisted into a cruel smirk, but in his green eyes and in the small crease between his brows, Lizzy could see a hint of fear. "You are an insolent, headstrong doddypoll! Do not threaten me, or you will be sorry!"

"You can call me names. I do not care! Leave Georgiana alone or I shall tell on you!" Lizzy concluded, but the young man had turned his back and left, cursing again loud enough for Lizzy to hear him. Soon he was gone from her sight, and Lizzy returned to her room, determined to tell Lady Anne the truth of what she knew. Her friend Georgiana deserved it.

In the morning, Lizzy was woken by Georgiana's governess with the news that Lady Anne was waiting for her in her private apartment. She prepared herself eagerly, as she had things of her own to tell the lady. She knew she was right to do so, and on the way to Lady Anne's chamber, she rehearsed in her mind what she must say in order to be believed.

However, when she entered the chamber, her ladyship was resting in her bed with the doctor standing next to her and her personal maid and Mrs Reynolds watching over her every move. Lady Anne looked weaker and paler than the previous day, despite the large smile on her face, and Lizzy's little heart beat faster with worry.

"Come here, Lizzy," the lady invited her, suggesting she sat on the bed. Lizzy hesitated, but Lady Anne smiled gently. "Do not be afraid, my dear," she said softly. "I shall not keep you long. There is something I would like to give you."

Mrs Reynolds handed her mistress a small box, and with trembling hands, Lady Anne opened it to reveal a necklace with a small cross filled with little red stones. Lizzy's eyes opened wide in wonder.

"My mother gave this necklace to me," the lady said in a warm yet weak voice. "I believe rubies are appropriate for your strength and brightness. Georgiana has one similar, only with sapphires."

The gesture would have left anyone speechless, and Lizzy struggled to know how to respond.

"Lady Anne, I cannot accept it. It is too much. Mama says I am too young to wear jewels. And besides, I must tell you something I have found out..."

The lady stretched out her hand to caress Lizzy's hair, which made the young girl pause from speaking her mind.

Lady Anne spoke gently, "Please allow me to speak first. You are a generous soul, my dear, and I wish you to have this. I shall give it to your aunt to keep for you until you are a little older. This is to remind you of your courage. And Georgiana, of course. God brought you into our lives."

The lady's voice made Lizzy tremble, and tears filled her eyes, which only happened very rarely. She suddenly understood the meaning of this early morning encounter — a sort of farewell that pained her heart. "My lady," she suggested hopefully, as she gently took Lady Anne's hand, "maybe *you* could keep it and give it to me when I am older."

Lady Anne averted her eyes for a moment, trying to conceal her own tears, then turned to Lizzy again, the eyes of both glistening.

"That will not be possible, I am afraid. I shall give it to your aunt when she comes to visit. I am so sorry if I have upset you, Lizzy. All is well. Do not worry."

"You are not well, Lady Anne…"

"I am not, my dear. But I am not afraid, for God is with me. Please, do not be sad. All will be well." Her hand once again caressed Lizzy's face, and her eyes rested on those of the child, who was now trying to appear brave. "You have kind eyes, Elizabeth Bennet. I only hope you never allow them to lose their sparkle."

For a moment, the two looked at each other, and the girl's little heart beat so strongly, as if to compensate for the lady's weakness. She knew she could not tell her anything that would displease her, even if it meant allowing George to win. Lizzy took Lady Anne's cold, thin, pale hand and kissed it, while she felt the other hand tenderly stroke her hair.

"Lizzy dear, please return to Georgiana now. I am sure she is expecting you," Lady Anne eventually pleaded, and Lizzy obeyed. From the door, she turned and gazed at the lady once more, but Lady Anne had already closed her eyes from exhaustion.

Never in her entire life had Lizzy Bennet felt such a heavy burden on her shoulders and such an ache in her heart as in the moment when she left Lady Anne Darcy's chamber.

Mr and Mrs Gardiner arrived later that day and talked to Mr Darcy and Lady Anne. Due to the circumstances, Lizzy was allowed to remain at Pemberley for three more days, and Georgiana's joy was a sweet reward at that sad time. The two girls spent every minute together, praying and comforting each other, but Lizzy never saw Lady Anne, Mr Darcy, or George again.

Four days after her meeting with Lady Anne, Lizzy returned to the inn. Guests were expected at Pemberley: the Matlocks, Lady Catherine de Bourgh and her husband, and even the young master Darcy arriving earlier than planned with his cousin.

When the devastating news of Lady Anne Darcy's death arrived, it fell like a dark shadow over Pemberley, as well as over Lambton. Lizzy and the Gardiners cried over the painful loss as though Lady Anne had been part of their family, but they never saw any of the Darcys again before they left Derbyshire. Despite Lizzy's pleas and even tears, she had no chance to see Georgiana again, as tragedy had closed Pemberley to everyone but family, and the desire of the two little girls to see each other was inconsequential to Lady Anne's family under the circumstances.

As time passed, Lizzy asked often about Georgiana, and Mrs Gardiner provided her with news from Lambton from time to time. The death of Mr Darcy, a few years later, was received with the same grief and sorrow, and the Gardiners and Lizzy knew that their ties with the family from Pemberley were now completely cut.

While she never forgot her little friend or Lady Anne, Lizzy — Miss Elizabeth Bennet of Longbourn — never had the opportunity to cross paths with Miss Georgiana Darcy again. She wore the necklace only a few times, in the privacy of her room mostly, keeping it locked in a drawer, like a treasure she was not prepared to share with the world — just like her bittersweet memories of her time spent at Pemberley.

Chapter 2

The Meryton assembly room was crowded, barely accommodating all those in attendance. The uproar of voices mixed with the sound of musicians preparing their instruments made it difficult to carry on a reasonable conversation, but there were some who were desperate enough to make themselves heard over the din. The occasion required it. In the last few days, one subject had dominated the conversation — Mr Charles Bingley, the gentleman who had let Netherfield Park, was expected to attend the assembly.

To those who had made his acquaintance — including Mr Bennet — Mr Bingley had left a most favourable impression. He was a pleasant-looking young gentleman with amiable manners and a lively disposition, and most importantly, he had an income of four thousand pounds a year — a sum that would give any mother of young daughters hopes that he might be looking for a wife.

The six Bennet ladies were more fortunate than most, for they had caught a glimpse of Mr Bingley when he had briefly called on Mr Bennet. Mrs Bennet had even invited the gentleman to dine at Longbourn, but unfortunately, he had declined due to business necessitating his return to London. That fact caused much distress and displeasure, particularly for Mrs Bennet, who feared Mr Bingley was the type of man who liked to flit from one place to another and would not settle at Netherfield as he ought to. That evening, however, Mr Bingley was expected to join the assembly, together with a large party that included his sisters and some friends.

Mary Bennet, the middle of the five sisters, sat at the side of the room, away from conversations, watching people with a reflective and philosophical air. Kitty and Lydia, the two youngest of the family, wandered around the assembly room most amused, laughing and talking louder than most, seeking to draw attention to themselves. Mrs Bennet, however, found it imperative to keep her eldest daughters near her in the hope they might be among the first to be introduced to Mr Bingley.

"Oh, dear Lord — look, Mr Bingley! He has arrived!" she whispered in awe as the room quieted at the entrance of an elegant party of young people. "What a handsome gentleman! And what a lovely smile he has! I see there are only two ladies and two gentlemen with him. Lady Lucas claimed he would bring twelve ladies and seven gentlemen. She always pretends to be knowledgeable but, in truth, knows nothing! More gentlemen would have been appreciated, as there are certainly enough young ladies in this room."

Amused, Elizabeth exchanged a furtive smile with her older sister, Jane, who had been pushed to the front by her mother and was clearly much more visible to anyone passing them by.

"Oh!" Mrs Bennet exclaimed with some disappointment, seeing Sir William Lucas approaching Mr Bingley's party. "If only Mr Bennet were here to introduce us. Sir William is already seeking an advantage for the evening."

Since Mr Bennet was safely ensconced in his library at Longbourn and could not be employed to make the introductions, Mrs Bennet sighed in frustration and urged her daughters to straighten their postures, in the hope of them being noticed. Sir William continued to talk to the party of illustrious guests, welcoming them with exaggerated formality and sweeping gestures, which only served to increase Mrs Bennet's impatience. At last, he introduced them to his wife, his son, and his eldest daughter — Miss Charlotte Lucas.

Mrs Bennet's agitation grew at the prolonged introduction. "Well! That grasping Lady Lucas! She would die just to snare a man for her daughter Charlotte, who is already a spinster. As if Mr Bingley would even look at her! She is very plain and has no charm at all!"

"Mama!" Jane whispered, mortification written on her

features. "Please do not say such a thing. Charlotte is a wonderful friend to Lizzy and me. She is educated, wise, steady, and always polite."

Mrs Bennet rolled her eyes. "All that is true, Jane, but she is also plain and lacks charm, just as I said. If only I could find someone to introduce us to Mr Bingley!"

"Mama, I beg of you not to attempt anything improper!" Elizabeth pleaded. "Mr Bingley is acquainted with Papa, and he has already visited us. He will request an introduction if he wishes for one."

"Hush, Lizzy, do not bother me, I am thinking! If only your father was not so stubborn and had accompanied us this evening for the sake of his daughters' futures instead of making my life that much more difficult," Mrs Bennet replied, casting her eyes around the room, only to observe Mrs Long, who was greeting Mr Bingley. The lady curtseyed to the gentleman before moving towards Mrs Bennet's sister, Mrs Phillips, and became much engaged in telling her something in great confidence. Overcome with curiosity, Mrs Bennet abandoned her daughters, determined not to be left out of any meaningful gossip regarding the guests.

Elizabeth watched the entire scene with her usual inclination for amusement. While Mr Bingley seemed genuinely pleased with the gathering, the ladies — although fine and fashionable women — looked around with an air of apparent disapproval and superiority. One of the gentlemen seemed either irritated or tired, while the second — tall and handsome with an impressive posture — showed little more than a frown. His gestures were reserved, and he nodded more than spoke to those who were introduced to him. His quiet, distant presence was rather provoking, but his figure looked somehow familiar to Elizabeth, although she was certain she had never seen him before.

Mrs Bennet eventually returned to her eldest daughters, this time together with her sister, and addressed them with an air of conspiracy.

"My dears, you will never guess what I have found out. Do you see the gentleman accompanying Mr Bingley?"

"Which one, Mama?" Elizabeth asked, amused by her mother's secretiveness.

"Oh, there is only one who matters. The other is married already — he is Mr Bingley's brother-in-law, Mr Hurst. The tall and handsome one — look, look at him!"

"What should we look at, Mama?" Elizabeth continued, holding back a laugh.

"At a man with ten thousand a year! I doubt you have seen one before or you will again any time soon. Can you imagine? His wealth is more than double that of Mr Bingley! How fortunate this is for you!"

"For us? What do you mean, Mama? Will he share his ten thousand a year with us?"

"Lizzy, stop mocking my words!" Mrs Bennet scolded through her teeth while casting a smile at a lady passing them by. "With how you behave, I would not be surprised if you never marry! You have nothing but a sharp tongue, a headstrong mind, no dowry, and no connections, and not enough beauty to compensate for all those things!"

"Forgive me, Mama. I do not mean to sound insolent. But it is rather amusing that you would think two affluent gentlemen might ensnare my interest to such a degree to prevent my capacity for independent thought. As for marriage, I hope Jane will make a happy one. She is the most deserving of us all."

"I wish for all five of you to make good marriages, but I shall not deny that Jane has the best prospects. She is the most beautiful and has the sweetest disposition, and gentlemen are foolish enough to prefer those traits above others. You may be the cleverest, but you resemble your father too much, Lizzy. And traits that are acceptable in a man are unappealing in a young lady, mark my words."

The long lecture at a dance was unusual even for Mrs Bennet, but it showed her disquiet and her obsession with attaining her goals for the night.

"I promise to conceal my 'unappealing traits' for tonight, Mama," Elizabeth said with feigned obedience. "But you must agree that the manners of the gentleman with *ten thousand a year* are also unappealing. He is so disdainful of everyone that I wonder why he even came."

"Well, Lizzy, you are virtually penniless, and your manners are not always impeccable either," Mrs Bennet continued. "You only stopped climbing trees a couple of years ago, and you still wander through the fields by yourself, with your gown five inches deep in mud."

Elizabeth was already exceedingly amused. Such conversations between her and her mother never failed to divert her.

"That is fair, Mama. I cannot deny my flaws. But speaking of this gentleman — I have a strange feeling that I have seen him before."

"I doubt it, Lizzy," Mrs Phillips interjected. "Where could you have seen such a gentleman?"

"May I ask which gentleman you are talking about?" Lady Lucas asked. She had approached unnoticed, and her intervention surprised the others.

"Lizzy said Mr Bingley's friend looks familiar to her, but she is probably wrong," Mrs Bennet explained, annoyed that Lady Lucas had interrupted them.

"You mean Mr Darcy? Oh, I doubt that very much!" Lady Lucas replied with an air of superior knowledge on the subject. "He has never been to Hertfordshire before, I was told. Sir William mentioned he spends his time between his London townhouse and his large estate in Derbyshire."

Lady Lucas's words gave Elizabeth thrills of joy and disbelief. She had not heard the name that had marked her childhood for more than ten years, and her heart pounded with strong emotions. Could it be true? Or was it a mere coincidence? Either way, the sudden recollection of Lady Anne and Georgiana, and the memory of a bittersweet summer in her childhood, warmed her with delight.

"You say his name is Mr Darcy. Are you sure?" Elizabeth asked, enchanted, and Lady Lucas frowned with displeasure.

"Of course I am sure, Miss Eliza. I have just made his acquaintance, and Sir William has spoken to him and to Mr Bingley several times. His estate in Derbyshire is vast.

Pemberley is its name. It seems he was the one who suggested Mr Bingley choose Netherfield over several other proprieties."

"Well, thank God for that!" Mrs Bennet interjected. "Let us hope he is at least half as amiable as he is rich."

Usually, such dialogue would have diverted Elizabeth, and she would have answered with wit and jests. But the overwhelming memories of her childhood and the sadness of the loss she could still feel were too strong to allow other feelings. Although some of her recollections were unclear, lost in a mist due to her young age when the circumstances occurred, she did remember little Georgiana as well as Lady Anne and Mrs Reynolds speaking well of the young master Darcy.

Time could not have changed him that much, could it?

She even remembered his long and difficult name. Fitzwilliam. Apparently Lady Anne's maiden name. Elizabeth wondered why such seemingly insignificant details returned to her mind after such a long time. Was it possible that Georgiana might remember her too? It was very unlikely, but not impossible. And since her brother had appeared in the neighbourhood, she had the chance to enquire after her friend and at least hear some news — hopefully all good — about her.

Elizabeth studied Mr Darcy's person with renewed interest; of course he seemed familiar to her, as he very much resembled his father. What a wonderful surprise that night at the assembly had brought her! She kept her gaze on him, hoping for a glance back, a gesture, anything that could start a conversation. Mr Darcy, however, seemed to be as untouched by any of the activity in the room as he had been on first entering it. Elizabeth studied him some more. She found him pleasant to look at; there was something entirely appealing to her about him. She watched him briefly address the young woman next to him — presumably one of Mr Bingley's sisters — and in this short interaction, she noticed the pleasant way in which his countenance changed while giving his approval. Yes, there was something very appealing about his mouth — a masculine assuredness in the set of his jaw. She blushed slightly, not even sure why she had responded in such a way. In watching him give a short smile to his companion, Elizabeth smiled to herself also as she admitted to agreeing with her mother: if her father had been there, an introduction to him would have been easy and quick.

Eventually, Mr Bingley, accompanied by Sir William, came in their direction, and while Mrs Bennet tried to keep her composure, warning her eldest daughters to 'be charming', Elizabeth noticed Mr Darcy following his friend. She was suddenly thrilled yet nervous, as if she was facing a long-awaited reunion only one party had the remembrance of. Elizabeth unconsciously straightened her back, and a nervous smile — very much unlike her — appeared on her face.

Mr Bingley stopped in front of the Bennets with an expression of utter delight on his face. With formality and self-importance, Sir William performed the introductions. Mr Bingley's smile widened once his gaze found Jane — whom he declared he had heard much of — and he began speaking to Mrs Bennet with so much ease that anyone would have thought they were old acquaintances. Much to Elizabeth's disappointment, however, Mr Darcy only acknowledged them with a slight bow. Elizabeth rubbed her hands against her dress uneasily, to ease her agitation.

"I had the pleasure of making Mr Bennet's acquaintance a few days ago," Mr Bingley said, "and I had hoped to see him again tonight."

"Mr Bennet is busy with other business tonight," Mrs Bennet said clumsily. "But I am sure he will visit you when he has the chance. Meanwhile, I hope you will accept our company and our willingness to amuse you. My daughters, especially Jane here, are wonderful dancers."

Jane blushed violently. Mr Bingley, on the other hand, seemed delighted.

"Excellent! I am looking forward to dancing with your daughter— That is, if Miss Bennet is not otherwise engaged, I would be honoured if she would grant me the favour of the next set."

Jane blushed for a second time with even more becoming demureness and while curtseying, said, "I am not engaged. It would be a pleasure, Mr Bingley."

Mrs Bennet threw a triumphant glance to the other ladies, then she noticed Mr Darcy looking somewhat lost, and she seized a perfect opportunity, addressing him directly.

"Mr Darcy, I hope you are equally desirous to dance, and there is no better time than this. You will hardly find better company or—"

"Forgive me, madam, but I rarely dance. It is a diversion that I truly dislike," he declared sternly, then bowed and stepped away.

Mrs Bennet seemed stunned, glaring after him in disbelief. Mr Bingley apologised and hurried after his friend. Mrs Long and Mrs Phillips looked dumbfounded, while Lady Lucas witnessed the scene with a smirk.

Elizabeth was dumbstruck by Mr Darcy's apparent coldness and impoliteness — so opposed to her every expectation. She tried to conceal her disappointment, but her mother made no such effort.

"Well! That was certainly unexpected! And rude! I have never heard such an answer from a gentleman at a ball in my entire life!"

"It was rather unpleasant," Mrs Phillips agreed.

"Rather? Very much so!" Mrs Bennet continued. "Mr Darcy might be rich and important, but his behaviour is very ungentlemanly, particularly in a ballroom! What a difference between him and his friend! Mr Bingley's character surely compensates for his smaller fortune."

Mrs Bennet became more irritated, and her tone showed as much. Jane panicked and gently touched her arm. "Mama, let us assume Mr Darcy is in a poor disposition tonight. I am sure he had no intention of offending us."

Elizabeth was much too confused to speak, and only when Jane said her name a second time did she regain her composure enough to say, "Jane might be right, Mama. As you know, Papa also loathes balls and parties. If he did not, he would be here with us now."

"If he was, I am sure he would put Mr Darcy in his place!" Mrs Bennet went on, and her sister and friends nodded.

Fortunately, the music began soon after, and Mr Bingley came to claim Jane's hand, so Mrs Bennet's ire immediately soothed. But she did not forget nor forgive so easily, so she continued to speak to the other ladies, sharing her vexation.

Soon enough, others in the room joined Mrs Bennet in her disapproval of Mr Darcy. While at first the gentlemen had pronounced him to be a fine figure of a man, and the ladies had declared he was more handsome than Mr Bingley, as the evening progressed, his manners were seen as so disagreeable that it turned the tide of his popularity. He was pronounced determined to be proud, above his company, and above being pleased; and despite his large estate, great fortune, and tall and fine figure, he was declared to be beneath his amiable friend.

Mr Bingley was lively and unreserved, danced every dance, admired the company, and already talked of giving a ball himself at Netherfield — delightful qualities that made him everyone's favourite.

Mr Darcy danced only once with Mrs Hurst and once with Miss Bingley and spent the rest of the evening walking about the room, speaking occasionally to one of his own party and neglecting the rest, who quickly decided his character. He was the proudest, most disagreeable man in the world, and nobody desired to see him at another ball ever again — Mrs Bennet being one of his most severe critics.

Oddly, after her initial shock had subsided, Elizabeth began to feel pity for him, while she continued to watch him with increased curiosity. He looked utterly uncomfortable, and during the two sets that he danced with his friend's sisters, he showed good dancing skills but no enjoyment at all. There were times when he caught her gaze, and in those moments, he appeared even more miserable, making Elizabeth wonder why he had not ended the torture and simply returned to Netherfield.

Due to the scarcity of gentlemen, Elizabeth was obliged to sit down for two dances, and she employed her time watching the rest of the attendees. During part of that time, Mr Darcy happened to be standing a short distance from her. She was partly hidden by a column, but she contemplated the idea of making her presence known. She wondered whether this might be an opportune moment to speak to him, at least a few words to acquaint him with her connection to his family so she could enquire more on another occasion. But before she could act, Mr Bingley left the dance for a few moments to press his friend to join it, and Elizabeth unintentionally heard their conversation.

"Come, Darcy. I must have you dance. I hate to see you standing about in this stupid manner. You had much better dance."

"I certainly shall not. You know how I detest it, especially among strangers. At such an assembly as this it would be insupportable."

"I would not be so fastidious as you are for a kingdom!" cried Mr Bingley. "I never met with so many pretty girls in my life before, and the entire company is generally pleasant."

"You are dancing with the only handsome girl in the room," said Mr Darcy, nodding towards Jane and making Elizabeth smile to herself.

"Darcy, she is the most beautiful creature I ever beheld! But there is her younger sister. You saw her earlier and were even introduced to her. She is very pretty as well, and I dare say very agreeable. Why not ask her?"

"The sister you mention is tolerable but not handsome enough to tempt me. I am in no humour to give consequence to young ladies who are slighted by other men."

"Darcy, you are being ridiculous, truly. Come, do tell me what you have against her."

"I certainly am not, Bingley. This person, this...*young lady*..." he enunciated in a tone that conveyed the exact measure of his discomfort, "this young lady you mentioned has been staring at me the entire evening! It is most disturbing. I imagine men of wealth and good connections are rarely seen in this town, and when one does happen to appear, they are hunted like prey! I can only imagine how the younger Miss Bennet would act if I asked her to dance, since she has been obsessively looking at me when we have barely said two words to each other."

"I am sure you are wrong, Darcy. I noticed nothing of the kind!"

"Bingley, you had better return to your partner and enjoy her smiles, for you are wasting your time with me."

Bingley followed the advice and left. On the other side of the column, Elizabeth was suffocated by offence, embarrassment, and anger — so hurt that she did not know how to respond. Mr Darcy walked off, and when he turned his head, he noticed Elizabeth and likely realised she had heard him. He looked slightly uncomfortable, but then he straightened his shoulders, looked away, and stopped near another column across the room from her, while Elizabeth was still disquieted, hardly believing her ears. How dare he? She had been such a fool to invest her former affection for his family in this horrible, arrogant man, who deserved no cordial feelings and no respect.

The music continued, and by the end of the set, Elizabeth had regained some of her composure. When her friend Charlotte Lucas resumed her seat after dancing, Elizabeth moved to join her, determined to share Mr Darcy's incivility so they could amuse themselves together. As she crossed the room, she noticed Mr Darcy was still alone, and she paused, unsure, hesitant, until the impulse of the moment was stronger than her reasoning. She walked towards him, observing as she approached his growing confusion and anxiety, and she assumed he was likely questioning her intentions.

When she was close enough to avoid being heard by others, she smiled and said, "Mr Darcy, rest assured I had no intention of hunting you. Indeed, I find no pleasure in such prey. My curiosity and interest — for which I apologise — was roused by the fact that I was fortunate enough to meet your family a long time ago, and I hoped for a pleasant meeting with another Darcy. I was deeply grieved by the news of your parents' deaths, and I wished to present my condolences and to enquire after Miss Darcy. However, I shall refrain from disturbing you further. Besides, if not for your name, I would not have imagined you could be related to them, since you do not resemble them at all, at least not in nature and manners."

With that, she bowed her head, turned, and left, satisfied to notice out of the corner of her eye Mr Darcy's incredulous and dumbfounded countenance.

As she walked towards her friend Charlotte, Elizabeth decided not to recount the small and unpleasant incident after all. She considered her rebuke of Mr Darcy to be enough chastisement for the time being. Despite his awful rudeness, she could not forget that the uncivil man was still the son of Lady Anne, and shaming him would mean hurting her memory also.

"My dear Eliza, did my eyes deceive me or did you speak to Mr Darcy? What on earth about?" Charlotte asked directly with no little astonishment.

"I certainly did, but the conversation gave little pleasure to either of us, and it is not worth mentioning."

"Nobody has spoken to him directly, except for his friend. That is why I was surprised."

"I assure you I would have avoided addressing him too if it were possible. But I overheard him making some remarks about me that needed immediate clarification."

Charlotte smiled and shook her head. "Dear Eliza, I hope Mr Darcy did not become acquainted with your usual sort of clarification. The poor man has only just arrived in Hertfordshire."

"Do not be concerned, Charlotte. Mr Darcy is certainly not a man to be pitied."

As she spoke to her friend, Elizabeth noticed — and even more, she felt — Mr Darcy's insistent gaze upon her. Several times she looked back at him, only to prove she was not intimidated. But she remained peevishly offended. Upset with herself for her hopes of a friendship with a man who had no other quality except his name. And his handsome features, of course, which were all ruined by his manners. Poor Georgiana; how unfortunate for her to be forced to live with such an unpleasant brother who probably rarely had a kind word to say to her.

As a new set was forming, Mr Darcy walked in her direction, and Elizabeth turned her head deliberately, showing she was paying him no mind. Still, he bowed, saying, "Miss Bennet, please forgive my boldness, but would you be so kind as to grant me two minutes of your time? There is something I must ask you."

Surprise was apparent on Charlotte's face, but Elizabeth kept her composure and showed indifference when she replied.

"I am afraid that will be impossible, Mr Darcy. We are at a ball, and I am ready to dance the next set. I am in no mood to ruin my pleasure of dancing with other activities that might not be tolerable enough to tempt me. I would be happy to listen to what you wish to ask me on another occasion, if your interest can be sustained that long."

Her impertinent response stunned him into silence for a moment, while Charlotte gasped and only stared wordlessly. Although no stranger to her friend's audacity, addressing a man such as Mr Darcy in such a way was difficult for Charlotte to comprehend.

After a moment of confusion, Mr Darcy continued. "Then, would you do me the honour of dancing a set with me? The next one, perhaps?"

"I am sorry, but I am engaged for the next set. I am not sure that I have any more available this evening," Elizabeth concluded, and Mr Darcy's expression became even colder, while Charlotte blushed next to her.

Elizabeth was pleased with her retaliatory offence that provided her with a satisfying victory over the arrogant and rude man. But then, as he bowed again and departed, Charlotte's distressed countenance made her reconsider her position. If she was to be honest, she was no better than Mr Darcy, neither in character nor in manners. He had offended her in the presence of his friend, while she had been equally uncivil to him — in her words but especially in her tone and expression — in the presence of *her* friend. Revenge was sweet only briefly until remorse overcame it. Surely Lady Anne would have been displeased with her son's behaviour, but also with Elizabeth's.

When Charlotte's brother came to claim her hand for the next set, Elizabeth excused herself for a moment and took a few steps towards Mr Darcy, who was standing alone near a column.

"Mr Darcy," she said, trying to control her voice, "I believe we should not speak of any important matter tonight, since our mutual first impressions were far from good, and there is little chance of a favourable outcome to this situation. But, as I said, I shall gladly answer any enquiry you might have when we next meet."

Although he had clearly expected another confrontation, the change in her tone and her softened countenance seemed to relieve him, and he genuinely accepted her offer of a truce. He bowed, she curtseyed, both with proper civility, and she walked away to where Mr John Lucas was waiting to lead her into the next set, while he remained standing where she had left him.

They did not speak again for the rest of the evening, but their eyes met often, and his gaze — changing from cold arrogance to puzzlement, then to curiosity and interest — rested on Elizabeth many times.

Once she shook off the anger and her wounded vanity, Elizabeth's spirits rose, and she felt more like her usual self. She tried to enjoy herself in the company of her dance partners, to engage in conversation, and to watch her sister Jane being the object of Mr Bingley's obvious admiration. As for Mr Darcy, of one thing she became certain: he was unpleasant, arrogant, and loathed dancing not just with her but with everyone else — and that made his initial offence easier to overcome.

If she had not heard him speaking to Mr Bingley, and if her expectations of him had not been so high, she would have decreed that he was an arrogant, haughty, irritating man and disregarded him completely. But as it was, she could not help thinking of him throughout the rest of the assembly and even later in the comfort of her own house.

Once they returned to Longbourn, Mrs Bennet apprised Mr Bennet of every particular of the evening, with many tormenting and tiresome details, repeating how Mr Bingley danced two sets with Jane and how much he seemed to admire her.

"But his friend, Mr Darcy! Such a horribly rude man! Tall and handsome he might be with his ten thousand a year, but he is not worthy of our interest. He barely spoke two words when we were introduced, and he did not dance a single set nor speak to anyone except his friends. Lizzy, did you speak to that horrible man? I believe I saw you talking to him. What did he want? What did he say to you?"

"I did exchange a few words with him, Mama," Elizabeth admitted. "But nothing of consequence, I assure you."

"I assumed as much," Mrs Bennet replied, then she continued to talk about the ball until her husband claimed tiredness and withdrew to his room, forcing his wife and daughters to do the same.

In their shared room, Jane found the courage to open the discussion about Mr Bingley. Elizabeth listened to her sister with only half her attention. The rest of it was on Mr Darcy, wondering when she would see him again and how their second meeting would unfold after the disastrous first experience.

Chapter 3

At Netherfield, Darcy looked at the two open letters on the desk — one from his sister, Georgiana, the other from her companion, Mrs Annesley. He was finally enjoying some privacy, hidden in the library, away from his friend's sisters, Miss Caroline Bingley and Mrs Louisa Hurst. Bingley was out, likely visiting the Bennet family again, as he had declared he would, despite the idea being strongly objected to by his sisters.

It was only one of the assembly's unpleasant consequences. Since that disquieting night, there had barely been another subject of conversation at Netherfield beyond Bingley's approval of the people in the neighbourhood and his particular admiration for Miss Jane Bennet, mixed with his sisters' contrary opinions.

Darcy's mood was so low that he had no interest in the subject. He did not take Bingley's attraction to the lady seriously, considering he had seen his younger friend bewitched many times. Bingley's amiable nature made him blind to people's flaws, and any pretty lady showing him some interest would be successful. Luckily, Bingley was also a deeply honourable gentleman, so, although he enjoyed being the centre of attention, his admiration for a lady would never induce him to cross the boundaries of decorum.

Dancing two — or was it three? — sets with Miss Jane Bennet had been an obvious gesture of partiality, and calling on her family would only add to the rumours that were undoubtedly circulating already. However, after several attempts to convince Bingley to see reason on the morning after the assembly, Darcy had abandoned the endeavour. He was too tired and too immersed in his own problems to waste any more effort on such an insignificant matter.

His mind was rather perturbed by the second Bennet daughter, who had challenged him beyond the edge of his tranquillity. He had regretted his rude remark regarding her the moment he realised she had heard it. He had no intention of offending a young woman — neither his nature nor his education would allow him to do so. His words, as harsh and hurtful as they had been, were meant to be heard by Bingley alone.

It had been true — he had been in no disposition to dance at the assembly, and Bingley's insistence had irritated him. Also, his concern about being watched with too much interest was genuine, based on his own observations and past experience. How could he even have imagined she was curious about him due to her previous knowledge of his family? Who would have believed such a coincidence? Miss Elizabeth looked young — she must have been a child when his mother died. How was it possible that they were acquainted? In what circumstances? She could not have befriended Georgiana, since his sister had been an infant at the time, and she had no friends outside the family. In what way was the daughter of an insignificant gentleman from Hertfordshire connected to his family in Derbyshire?

Miss Elizabeth's behaviour intrigued Darcy almost as much as the connection itself. She possessed a self-confidence rarely seen in a woman of her age and situation in life, and a boldness — which was rather appealing if he were to be honest — that was clearly displayed in her eyes as well as in her posture.

She was not a flawless beauty based on society's rules and expectations. But she was pretty — certainly more than tolerable, as he had claimed — though he had only realised that later. She was the first woman he had known who had possessed the audacity to scold him, although they were barely acquainted, which at first he had been inclined to see as rudeness. She was also the first woman — as far as he recollected — who had refused to dance with him after such a public invitation.

She had granted him a concession by agreeing to answer his questions on their next meeting, and in doing so, she had practically demanded that there be a second meeting — one that would please her enough to satisfy his curiosity. Was she too impertinent? Too condescending? Too daring? Or a fool, perhaps? Should he continue their acquaintance or just forget her? After all, even if she had met his family in the past, why should he care? Surely she was not in possession of any secret that might affect him, he mused, smiling to himself. Very likely her acquaintance with his mother and sister alluded to a brief encounter in which they had exchanged a few words. Was it worth the effort of another meeting with her, considering he would return to London soon?

At that point, tired of all his musings, Darcy's attention returned to the desk and the two opened letters.

He read Georgiana's first, with interest but also concern. The letter was written impeccably and elegantly. He had made his sister promise to write to him often, and he had promised to do the same. As always, Georgiana had kept her promise. But her letter was impersonal, the words sounding like they were hiding more than they were revealing. While Georgiana never mentioned sadness or pain, Darcy could feel they were still vivid in his sweet sister's heart.

Dear Brother,

I beg of you not to worry about me. While you are away, I am employing my time visiting my aunt and Lady Amelia, playing the pianoforte, or reading. Mrs Annesley is the most reliable and pleasant companion anyone could wish for. So please stay in Hertfordshire as long as you like or as long as Mr Bingley needs you. I miss you, but I shall be happy if I see you at Christmas.

Until then, I am looking forward to receiving letters from you as often as you can spare a few minutes to write to me.

Your loving sister,
Georgiana.

While her letter did not say as much, Darcy felt like his sister wished for him to be away for a while. Perhaps she needed time without him; perhaps his presence was a reminder of the failed elopement planned with that scoundrel Wickham. She seemed to prefer the company of their aunt Lady Matlock and her daughter-in-law, Lady Amelia — the viscount's wife.

Georgiana missed him, but she preferred his absence. Perhaps he was not a good enough brother to give her the comfort she needed and deserved. Regardless, she clearly did not wish him to be near her, and he knew he should reconsider his hasty return to London.

After that, he read Mrs Annesley's letter, and his worries increased. The lady — whom he had carefully chosen after the betrayal of Mrs Younge — expressed once again her admiration for Miss Darcy and her dedication to her studies, as well as her worry for her tendency to spend too much time indoors. Yes, Georgiana was hiding from the world. She had always been shy — too shy — and felt awkward in the company of strangers. He knew the reason but could not find the remedy.

"Darcy, what are you doing here all alone?" he heard Bingley's voice calling.

"I am reading a letter from Georgiana. I am surprised you have returned already."

"I have been gone for quite some time, Darcy. Besides, in a few hours, Miss Bennet will come to take tea with Caroline and Louisa. I understand her sister Elizabeth will join her."

"Is that so?" Darcy replied, concealing his puzzled expression from his friend.

"Yes. I need to send some papers to my solicitors by express, so I must go into Meryton. Since I shall be nearby, I intend to escort Miss Bennet and Miss Elizabeth to Netherfield in my carriage. I understand their father needs the horses on the farm."

"How interesting. I imagine everybody knows everything about everyone in such a small place. Gossip spreads easily. Which is precisely why you must be cautious about any rumours that might be spread due to your actions, Bingley."

"Yes, yes. I am cautious enough, Darcy. I hope my actions are always respectable and proper. Would you not agree?"

"I do agree, Bingley. And yet, even proper and respectable actions might cause harm if they give rise to expectations that cannot be fulfilled and hopes that are to be dashed."

"Darcy, you are always too serious and grave! Will you not join me in Meryton and then at Longbourn? I have found Mr Bennet to be a very pleasant gentleman. He seems very fond of books, which is an interest he shares more with you than with me."

Visiting Longbourn was something Darcy had not considered, and his first impulse was to refuse.

"I shall," he heard his own voice answering on an impulse he could not comprehend.

"Good! Excellent! Mrs Bennet has invited me to dine at Longbourn one of these days. Caroline and Louisa have declined any interest, but you may come with me if you wish."

"Bingley, let us take one step at a time. I shall call at Longbourn with you today, but that is all. I cannot commit to any other engagements."

"As you wish. You should know that Mrs Bennet was not impressed with your manners at the assembly, and neither were half of the attendees. But I tried to sketch your character in a favourable light. Not that their opinion would mean much to you."

"You must not worry, Bingley. Since I agreed to this call, I shall present myself with my best manners," Darcy replied, half in earnest, half jesting. Surprisingly, even to himself, there was at least one person's opinion that he cared about at Longbourn.

***

At Longbourn, the hour of Jane's visit to the Bingley sisters approached with much agitation on Mrs Bennet's part as she prepared her eldest daughter with the care appropriate for a more solemn occasion than a friendly call upon a neighbour. Elizabeth was mostly left to herself, as her future — according to her mother — would in no way be affected by the visit. No one knew of Elizabeth's own discomfort as she tried to guess how Mr Darcy would behave upon seeing her again, or how she would be forced to reserve her opinions and, more importantly, her tongue. She was determined not to allow him to intimidate her, just as she was not willing to give him the satisfaction of thinking ill of her.

As Mrs Bennet had hoped, the gathering clouds suggested that heavy rain was likely. Mr Bennet had ordered the carriage to take his eldest daughters to Netherfield, but shortly before their departure, an unexpected visit changed their plans entirely. Mr Bingley called again, this time accompanied by Mr Darcy, causing a real disturbance at Longbourn.

Despite her declared aversion to the man, even Mrs Bennet seemed impressed by Mr Darcy's appearance.

She invited the two gentlemen in, then called her husband from his library.

"Forgive us for intruding," Mr Bingley said, "but we happened to be in Meryton, and since we were nearby, I thought we could escort Miss Bennet and Miss Elizabeth to Netherfield if that is agreeable to you. Of course, my carriage will also bring them back home later."

"Oh, my dear Mr Bingley, this is more than agreeable! How generous of you! Jane, thank Mr Bingley — is he not the most generous of men?"

"Mama…" Jane whispered, her face flushed and her eyes on the floor.

Elizabeth, deeply embarrassed herself, glanced at Mr Darcy. He showed some discomfort and did not meet her eyes, standing silently.

Mr Bennet entered the room, greeting the two gentlemen with apparent surprise and interest. Mr Darcy bowed properly, while Mr Bingley performed the introductions. Mr Bennet invited the gentlemen to have a drink with him in the library, but his wife interjected decidedly, much to Elizabeth's mortification.

"Dear Mr Bennet, I am sure they are in a hurry to return to Netherfield. Miss Bingley and Mrs Hurst must be waiting for Jane. They cannot delay further!"

Mr Bingley looked between Jane and his host, evidently undecided, then, to Elizabeth's complete surprise, Mr Darcy spoke up.

"We are in a hurry indeed, but I trust a drink will not delay us too long. I admit to being incapable of refusing any invitation that involves a library."

"That is true," Bingley said. "Even at Netherfield, Darcy spends most of his time in my library."

"Then allow me to lead you to it," Mr Bennet said. "I pray you will not be disappointed, Mr Darcy. My library is much smaller than the one at Netherfield and even more inferior when compared to yours, I imagine."

"When it comes to libraries, I do not judge them by the size of the room but by how much they express a love for books," Darcy replied, following Mr Bennet. He had no chance to notice how his hoarse and deep voice affected Elizabeth, nor her intrigued gaze staring after him.

As decided, the gentlemen remained in the library for less than half an hour, during which time Mrs Bennet was highly agitated, sending Mrs Hill, the housekeeper, on numerous occasions to confirm that the gentlemen were satisfied. Mrs Hill returned each time to inform her mistress that they required nothing further, and when the gentlemen themselves returned to the drawing room, they all appeared to be in good spirits.

Since the hour was growing late, there was no time for further discussion. Mr Bingley escorted Jane and Elizabeth to his carriage, with Mr Darcy walking behind them. Before stepping into the equipage, Elizabeth turned to see all the remaining Bennet ladies watching them leave from the drawing room window, each with a different expression on their face; Mr Bennet was also observing them from his library, and he raised his glass and an eyebrow at his daughter.

When the carriage started to move, the rain also began. Elizabeth mused that Mrs Bennet would be rejoicing, hopeful that the weather would keep Jane and Elizabeth at Netherfield for a night at least.

Inside the carriage, there was a rather awkward silence, the sound of the rain loud enough to make conversation difficult. Some shy glances and smiles were exchanged between Mr Bingley and Jane, with Elizabeth and Mr Darcy barely looking at each other. When the carriage arrived at Netherfield, the rain still pouring heavily, Mr Bingley leapt out first, stretching his hand out for Jane and solicitously ushering her into the house.

Elizabeth prepared herself for what was to follow. Mr Darcy had also exited the carriage, and he looked briefly at her saying only, "Miss Elizabeth…"

With no other choice, and without looking at him, she took Mr Darcy's offered hand. It was a shock for Elizabeth to feel the contrast between its heat and the cold autumn rain, and her feet slipped on the step, causing Mr Darcy to grab her by the waist to prevent her falling.

"I am well, sir," she said, though she was not sure her words were audible despite the gentleman standing only a few inches from her. The wind was driving the rain directly into her face, and she grimaced at how terrible she must look with her hair stuck all over her cheeks.

"Take my arm, Miss Elizabeth, and we shall be out of the rain in a moment."

Mr Darcy turned his head to the house, indicating the entrance, and Elizabeth did not hesitate to place her hand on his arm and run alongside him up the steps.

Chapter 4

Neither Jane nor Elizabeth were looking their best when they were introduced in the drawing room. In just the short distance from the carriage, the rain had done much damage to their appearance, and maids were called to bring towels, while tea was waiting to be poured.

"My dear Miss Bennet, how lovely to see you again!" Miss Bingley declared. "And Miss Eliza — how kind of you to accompany your sister. Have you ever visited Netherfield before?"

"Thank you. We are grateful for your invitation, Miss Bingley," Jane said. "Yes, we have visited Netherfield often in the past. Our parents were good friends of the owners, Mr and Mrs Norfolk, before they moved to Bath."

Miss Bingley's lips pinched together, and she did not appear happy with the news. "Do not thank me. We are pleased to have some entertainment, as life in the countryside is so dull. I do not wonder that the Norfolk family moved to Bath. It cannot compare to Meryton. I truly cannot understand how you bear it!"

The comment, offensive under a veneer of amiability, caused Elizabeth to frown. She had not had much time or interest in sketching the Bingley sisters' characters at the assembly, beyond noticing their elegant gowns and distant, arrogant behaviour towards most of the neighbourhood. They had been attentive and polite to Jane, though, and for that, Elizabeth was ready to approve of them. However, the very beginning of the visit changed her mind completely.

"We have lived here all our lives, so we are accustomed to

it, Miss Bingley," Jane responded.

"I find country living very charming!" Mr Bingley interjected. "If one happens to have pleasant neighbours, one might be content to live in the country all the time."

"If one has never had the opportunity to experience life in London, one cannot make any comparison and therefore may simply enjoy the country because they know of nothing else. Do you ever go to London, Miss Bennet?" Mrs Hurst enquired.

"We do. My uncle and aunt have often invited Lizzy and me to visit them."

"Have they? How lovely. And in which part of town do they live?"

"In Gracechurch Street," Jane said, showing increasing discomfort. Mr Bingley seemed disquieted too, while Mr Hurst was enjoying his drink, and Mr Darcy watched silently, holding his glass.

"Where precisely is Gracechurch Street?" Miss Bingley continued.

"Near Cheapside," Jane answered, and the Bingley sisters exchanged appalled and amused glances.

"I have never been to that part of London," Miss Bingley admitted.

"Neither have I," Mrs Hurst supported her. "We have no business there."

"My uncle and aunt have a lovely home," Elizabeth interjected. "We feel privileged every time they invite us."

"What is your uncle's situation, may I ask?"

"He is in trade. But he also studied to become a lawyer."

"How interesting," Miss Bingley said, barely concealing the disdain in her voice. "Mr Darcy also has an uncle who went into the law, except that he is a judge."

"My father was also in trade," Bingley said. "Such an excellent, hardworking man! A real gentleman to look up to!"

"I could say the same about my uncle," Elizabeth replied with a smile of gratitude towards Mr Bingley for his timely intervention which stopped his sister's insolence.

The admission of having a relative in trade — although hardly a secret to anyone present — made Miss Bingley's face colour, and she gulped some tea, exchanging more glances with her sister.

"What terrible weather!" Mrs Hurst turned the conversation to a more neutral subject. "The time is still early, but the darkness makes it feel like late evening."

"Precisely," Miss Bingley said. "Speaking of time, we were expecting you earlier. Did something happen to your father's carriage, since you were conveyed here by Charles? I was not even aware that my brother would visit you today."

The rudeness in her words and especially in her superior tone made Elizabeth cringe. She congratulated herself on her decision to accompany Jane and not allow her sister to face such rudeness alone. She was ready to provide an equally harsh reply when Mr Bingley interjected again.

"Miss Bennet and Miss Elizabeth were ready to depart in their father's carriage at the established hour. I suggested calling on them and escorting them here. It was my pleasure and my decision, so any fault for the delay is mine."

"I must also admit to my share of the blame," Mr Darcy intervened in a distant tone. "Mr Bennet invited us to join him for a drink, and I insisted on accepting."

"But are you even acquainted with the Bennets, Mr Darcy?" Miss Bingley enquired with reproachful puzzlement.

Elizabeth saw Mr Darcy's shoulders straighten in a gesture that betrayed his displeasure.

"What difference does that make to you, Miss Bingley?" Mr Darcy asked icily. "I am not accustomed to justifying my decisions, nor to requesting approval for my actions. I trust it is a gentleman's prerogative to choose his drinking companions, whether they are new acquaintances or old. Would you not agree?"

"I agree," Mr Hurst interjected unexpectedly. "Upon my word, this argument is a complete waste of time. Let the men drink, and you ladies enjoy your tea and make everybody happy."

Miss Bingley and Mrs Hurst looked angered by such a rebuke, while Elizabeth could hardly conceal her amusement. However, a moment later, she became utterly disconcerted when she heard Mr Darcy addressing her.

"Miss Elizabeth, speaking of your father, we discussed a book that he would like to read, and I believe I have seen a copy in Bingley's library. He said it was one of your favourites too, and I would be happy to help you find it for him if you wish to."

Elizabeth was momentarily lost for words at such a bold suggestion. She had hoped for a private moment with Mr Darcy to explain her prior connection to his family, but to ask her to join him in the library, away from the others, was a barely proper gesture.

She met his gaze and held it briefly, then stood up.

"That is very kind of you, Mr Darcy."

"If you are familiar with Netherfield," Miss Bingley interjected, "you must be well acquainted with the library too, Miss Eliza. I am sure you are capable of finding the book by yourself."

Elizabeth did not even attempt to be polite as she replied, "I am, but since Mr Darcy has been so generous as to offer me his company, I shall gladly accept it. It will be my pleasure to benefit from his support."

As though he understood her intention, Mr Darcy answered, "The pleasure is mine, I assure you, Miss Elizabeth. Allow me to escort you."

They left the room together, and Elizabeth could feel the Bingley sisters' cutting gazes stabbing her from behind.

They walked towards the library, and before they entered, Mr Darcy stopped, and she did the same.

"Miss Elizabeth, I beg you to excuse my deception. As you probably imagined, I lied in order to steal a few moments of your time. I hope it was not too much of an imposition."

"Mr Darcy, any time away from Miss Bingley is most

welcome—" She paused and took a breath. "I apologise for being so hard on your friends, but I feel like Mr Bingley has received all the kindness and amiability in that family."

"Mr Bingley is my friend. In truth, I cannot argue with your assumption. Would you like to enter the library?"

"Certainly. Besides, we must return with at least one book, or else we shall have to spend the rest of our visit in arguments and explanations."

He opened the door and entered but remained standing.

"Before we go any further, I must apologise again for my rudeness at the assembly. I was in very low spirits, and I only attended because Bingley insisted. Regardless, there is no excuse for my incivility. I assure you it is not my habit to offend young ladies whom I am not acquainted with, even in my foulest of moods."

She laughed. "Yes, I have noticed that you not only offend strangers but also your friend's sisters. But I cannot fault you for that."

He seemed disconcerted by her statement, and she realised she must soften her tone to avoid turning their second meeting into another disaster. After all, she wished to speak to him about his family likely as much as he did. And from what she had seen that day, she was not completely opposed to his behaviour. He had shown enough civility to her family and enough censure to Bingley's sisters to gain some sympathy and approval from her.

"However, if we are to apologise, it is my turn to do so too, Mr Darcy. I am not in the habit of being impolite to gentlemen I have just met or refusing to dance or have a conversation at an assembly. Not even in my foulest of moods," she said, mirroring his words and allowing herself to laugh to show her amusement.

Her open laughter and teasing clearly caught Mr Darcy off-guard. He looked awkward, and she took pity on him.

"Come Mr Darcy, let us try to show each other the better side of our manners and education, shall we? Please feel free to ask me whatever you want to know."

"I shall gratefully accept your generous offer of a truce, Miss Elizabeth. I admit to being extremely curious in regard to your connection to my family. Would you be so kind as to share the circumstances?"

"Gladly, sir. Ten years ago, I visited Derbyshire with my aunt, Mrs Madeleine Gardiner. The aunt who lives near Cheapside," she said meaningfully.

"I feel the need to apologise again, this time for Miss Bingley and Mrs Hurst's rudeness," he said, but she stopped him with a gesture.

"Do not worry. It was not your offence to apologise for. My aunt grew up in Lambton and herself has a great aunt, Mrs Honoria Clarke, who was still living there at the time."

Mr Darcy stared at her with increasing curiosity. "Truly? What an astonishing coincidence! Lambton is only five miles from Pemberley, my home. Mrs Clarke was my mother's seamstress for years. I remember her from my childhood."

"Precisely. That summer I joined Aunt Clarke and Aunt Gardiner at Pemberley several times while they fitted Lady Anne for new gowns. As a child, I played with Miss Darcy, although she was much younger than me. I met Lady Anne too, and I was rewarded with her graceful kindness. Sadly, that was the summer Lady Anne died…"

"Yes…it was ten years ago this past summer," Mr Darcy replied, his voice strangled with emotions.

"Indeed. It was tragic news that greatly affected me and my aunt and uncle. I can only imagine how much you and Miss Darcy suffered. I know it is too late, but please accept my heartfelt condolences for the deaths of both your parents. Such remarkable people, gone so soon, at such a young age. What a terrible loss for you and for everyone who knew them."

Mr Darcy sat, clearly overwhelmed by emotions, disregarding the fact that she was still standing.

"Thank you, Miss Elizabeth. It was a tragic loss indeed… More than I can say…"

"I am afraid to imagine how much Miss Darcy suffered, being still a small child. I have often thought of her and prayed for her. My aunt has asked for news about her over the years. Mrs Clarke was a close friend to Mrs Reynolds, but sadly she also died a few years ago."

"Yes…" he mumbled.

"I hope Mrs Reynolds is in good health. She was much younger than Mrs Clarke. Is she still at Pemberley?"

"Yes…Mrs Reynolds is still our housekeeper. She is part of the family. Yes, fortunately she is in good health."

"I am glad to hear that…"

"You have not seen my sister since she was five years old?"

"I have not. Your relatives would not allow me to see her again. They did not approve of a friendship with someone so far below your family. I understand that. I just hope she is well. I have thought of her often and hoped to meet her again one day. Of course, I am sure she does not remember me, since she was so young," Elizabeth concluded with fondness and a lump in her throat.

Mr Darcy watched her, his brow creased and sadness in his eyes.

"She is well. Thank you for thinking of my sister, Miss Elizabeth."

"I do and quite often…"

The silence became heavy and deep, and their shared gaze became almost unbearable. With trembling hands, Elizabeth opened the reticule she was carrying on her wrist and searched inside it.

"I have something to show you. I always carry it with me, though I never wear it in public. It is something that Lady Anne gave me," she whispered.

Mr Darcy's eyes lowered to her hand, closed in a fist, hiding something. Her fingers slowly opened, revealing the necklace. He stared at it with a frown on his face, a look of incredulity slowly spreading across his features.

He looked from Elizabeth to the necklace, then back again. Then he took it gently, his fingers touching her gloved palm. He held it up to the light, and his frown deepened, then he finally spoke, barely audibly.

"My sister has one almost identical, only the stones are different. This one belonged to my mother."

"Yes, I know. Lady Anne told me when she gave it to me. She told me to wear it, but I have never found the right occasion," she said, her voice as weak as a whisper.

Mr Darcy closed his fist around the necklace as if he intended to keep it. Elizabeth looked at him, disconcerted, and the heavy silence returned.

"May I have it back, please?" she whispered after a while, and he seemed to regain some composure and nodded.

With obvious reluctance, he opened his fist so she could take it. This time, her fingers touched his palm, and the sensation overwhelmed them both, adding to the tumult of other emotions already enveloping them.

"I believe we should return to the drawing room. We have been gone for long enough," he eventually said, gesturing to the door.

"Mr Darcy, the book?" she reminded him.

"Oh yes, the book. Would you please choose one? Perhaps something you would like to read?"

"I...let me see... Some poetry would be lovely," she said while placing the necklace back in her reticule and closing it carefully.

"My sister loves poetry too," he said, his words still unsteady. "And music. Please chose any book you like, Miss Elizabeth," he repeated.

Several minutes later, they re-joined the others in the drawing room, Elizabeth holding tightly to a book and her reticule. After that, the visit lasted less than another half an hour. When it was over, Mr Bingley offered to escort the ladies home.

***

Mr Darcy bid the guests a proper, polite farewell but did not join them. As soon as they left, he refused to be engaged in conversation and excused himself, then hurried back to the library and started to write a letter which he sent that very evening by express.

Chapter 5

The encounter with Mr Darcy felt like a heavy burden on Elizabeth's shoulders. Without knowing the precise reason — after all, the conversation had been polite, even friendly — she sensed that it had affected her, as well as Mr Darcy, more deeply than she had expected.

Fortunately for her, the wave of enquiries from their mother was directed entirely towards Jane and centred around Mr Bingley, so she had time to examine her own thoughts. However, she did not entirely escape from Mr Bennet's scrutiny and questioning.

"How was the visit, Lizzy?"

"It was pleasant enough, Papa."

"Did you and Mr Darcy resolve your disagreement?"

"We did. He was curious about my connection to his family, and I related the circumstances to him."

"I am glad to hear that. I confess I liked the fellow well enough, but it must be because I was only in his company for half an hour, and men have no time for rudeness when they are enjoying a drink."

Elizabeth replied with a little smile. "To be honest, he was rather harsh with Mr Bingley's sisters too. But I certainly cannot fault him for that. They very much deserved it!"

"Well, well, that sounds rather harsh in itself, but I confess, I have no interest in Mr Bingley's sisters. What did Mr Darcy say about your story?"

"He was surprised, of course. Apparently, he has fond memories of Mrs Clarke. He said that he grew up with her around."

"How nice of him. I would dare to presume he has a good heart. A young master remembering a seamstress is not common."

"You might be correct. I have had little opportunity to examine Mr Darcy's heart yet. He seemed puzzled and doubtful when I showed him the necklace. He remembered it belonged to his mother, and his sister has one that is similar. I assume it was quite expensive, and perhaps he wondered why it was in my possession."

"Did you not tell him the reason that prompted Lady Anne to give it to you?"

"No, Papa. How could I have told him such a thing at our second meeting? It would certainly not do. If he enquires further, I shall tell him. But if he already doubts me, he might question the truth of my narration entirely."

"Do you *know* that he doubted you, or is that just your assumption? Are you not a little too hasty in thinking the worst of him because he did not find you pretty enough?"

Elizabeth felt the sting of Mr Bennet's tease, despite the light tone and the eyebrow arched meaningfully.

"I admit I might have been hasty in my judgment. Regardless, a man should not be easily forgiven for refusing to dance at a ball where gentlemen are scarce. It is a capital offence!"

"You frighten me when you speak like your mother, although I know you are only jesting, Lizzy," Mr Bennet concluded just as they heard the bell ring for dinner.

While they ate, the subject of the conversation moved from Mr Bingley to the handsome officers of the regiment of militia encamped in Meryton. Elizabeth hardly participated in the discussion, and Mr Bennet rolled his eyes and sipped his drink more often than usual.

"I have some news too," he interjected when there was finally a pause in the conversation. "I have recently received a letter informing me of the arrival of a particular guest. No, do not attempt to guess. I already have a headache."

"Do tell us, Mr Bennet!" his wife cried. "Who could this particular guest be? What did they say in the letter?"

"The guest is my cousin, Mr Collins. Yes, the very one who will inherit Longbourn once I am dead and may throw you out of the house as he pleases."

"My dear Mr Bennet, do not speak of that horrible man! How dare he? What does he want by coming here now?"

"I cannot answer that question. He wrote that he wishes to make peace between our families and is eager to meet his cousins. He sounded reasonable enough, but he might also believe I shall die soon and wishes to view his inheritance."

"Papa!" Elizabethan chided. "This is not a matter to joke about!"

"Yes, it is, Lizzy. I look forward to meeting him. From his letters, I expect him to be delightfully ridiculous. His pompous writing is highly entertaining."

"But where does he live? What does he do?" Mrs Bennet enquired.

"He is a clergyman and has been granted a living somewhere in Kent. Apparently, he is fortunate enough to have a very influential patroness, who is supporting him. He expressed his gratitude for the lady in every other line of the letter, though her name is unknown to me."

"Do you at least know him, Papa?" Elizabeth asked.

"Barely. I remember meeting him a long time ago when he was very young. He must be around five-and-twenty now."

"So young?" Lydia asked. "Is he handsome too?"

"Lydia, as I just said, I met him when he was a young boy. How could I know if he is handsome twenty years later?"

"But is he married?" Mrs Bennet continued.

"I am afraid I must disappoint you again, since I have no answer to that either. However, you will be able to satisfy your curiosity in three days' time, when he arrives."

"Three days? And how long will he stay at Longbourn?" Mrs Bennet insisted.

"I do not recall. I shall allow you the pleasure of asking

him directly. I am anticipating a diverting time, regardless of the length of his visit," Mr Bennet concluded.

"I only hope he will not interfere with Mr Bingley's visits. He has promised to dine at Longbourn this week. Hopefully, it will be before that Mr Collins makes an appearance. In fact, I shall settle the date tomorrow. Mr Bennet, you must write to Mr Bingley early in the morning and invite him to dinner the day after tomorrow."

"I have no desire to do such a thing," Mr Bennet said. "You may write to him yourself, Mrs Bennet, and sign it in my name."

The discussion continued in the same manner, and Elizabeth grew tired of it. As soon as the meal ended, she retired to her chamber, claiming tiredness.

As she recollected her conversation with Mr Darcy, she realised the only things he had told her about Georgiana were that she liked poetry too and that she was well. But something in his voice and in his countenance worried her, and she blamed herself for not probing more on the subject. But even if she had, would he have revealed more to her than he had already willingly done? She told herself that the best plan was to wait before enquiring further. Fortunately, their second meeting had gone significantly better than their first, and there were reasonable indications that their acquaintance would continue to improve.

***

Darcy woke up at his usual hour, although he had barely slept. His mind was too perturbed by all his thoughts in regard to Miss Elizabeth's story. The coincidence of her having an aunt who had grown up in Lambton and was related to Mrs Clarke, as well as her having met his mother and sister, could have been a lovely, delightful one. However, her being in possession of his mother's necklace had cast a dark shadow over it. It was a special, valuable object, made for his mother, and later, she had commissioned a replica for her daughter. Why would she give it to a girl so wholly unrelated to her, whom she had met by chance? If, for some reason, she had wished to give the young girl a gift, it could have been something else with less sentimental significance. Surely there was more to the story. Troubled and curious, he had written to Mrs Reynolds and to his aunt Lady Matlock, hoping they remembered something that might clarify the undisclosed parts of Miss Elizabeth's narration.

That lady and her history with his family added to his worries regarding Georgiana. Since the night of the assembly, he had thought of Miss Elizabeth so often that it troubled him. It had become disquieting and irritating, and it was the last thing he needed.

Bingley had received a dinner invitation to Longbourn that included his sisters and Darcy. Miss Bingley and Mrs Hurst had refused it immediately, and Bingley's hopes had then turned to his friend. Despite their previous conversation on that subject, Darcy had declined too.

Mrs Bennet and the youngest daughters were tiresome. Almost as tiresome as Bingley's sisters. The difference was that, at Netherfield, he could remove himself from their presence when he wished to — a liberty he did not have at a dinner party. But that was not the reason for his refusal.

While he had enjoyed Mr Bennet's company, as brief as their encounter had been, and was disconcertingly enchanted by Miss Elizabeth, he felt it was too much to be in her presence again so soon, when his thoughts on her were so tangled.

To Bingley, he expressed his refusal in cautious, polite, and considerate words, asking his friend to convey his apologies to the Bennet family, insisting he had to complete some business letters. Bingley did not believe him, and probably the Bennets would not either, but it was a risk Darcy willingly accepted. To his surprise, Bingley's insistence was not as great as on other occasions. He was likely so happy at the prospect of seeing Miss Bennet again that he did not care who else was in attendance.

If he was to be honest with himself, he would admit to an eagerness to see a certain Miss Bennet too. But he had to exercise some control over his desires.

The following evening, while Bingley was enjoying his time at Longbourn and Darcy was dining alone in his room at Netherfield, a letter arrived. He recognised Lady Matlock's handwriting and opened it impatiently.

My dear nephew,

I was pleased to receive your letter but also surprised and puzzled. Whilst I can see the matter is important to you, I fear there is not much, if any, that I remember.

I vaguely recollect some discussions about a girl who befriended Georgiana ten years ago — the niece of some shop owner from Lambton. It was the same month as your dear mother's death, and we all tried hard to protect Georgiana from completely understanding what was happening. Your father, or perhaps Mrs Reynolds, suggested inviting the girl to distract her, but Georgiana's governess at the time — Mrs Richmond I believe was her name — opposed it, as she believed the girl to be inappropriate company for Georgiana. This is all I can remember. I also asked your uncle, but he knows nothing about the subject. Now that you have asked about it, I admit to being intrigued in regard to the reason for your interest. Do tell me more. I am curious to know.

Do not worry, I shall not mention anything to Georgiana, as you requested. I did tell Richard, however. I know he is your favourite cousin, and you keep no secrets from each other. As you may imagine, Richard is also ignorant of the subject and equally curious about it, so we expect further news.

Your loving aunt.

Darcy put down the letter with a deep sense of dissatisfaction. He had hoped that his aunt's reply would shed some light on the past, but those hopes were shattered. His first impulse was to search for Mrs Richmond's whereabouts. She had left Georgiana five years ago, the year his father died, to be closer to her daughter in Bath, but he had no other knowledge of her.

He poured himself a drink and savoured it to calm himself. The best course was to wait for Mrs Reynolds's reply and to decide on further action afterwards. In the meantime, he could not decide whether he should remain at Netherfield or return to London. Neither his heart nor his mind was clear in that regard.

Chapter 6

Mr Bingley arrived for dinner at the perfect time and was received by at least two overjoyed ladies. Elizabeth admitted to herself that she was deeply disappointed by Mr Darcy's absence. The excuse offered by Mr Bingley that his friend was too busy was easily accepted by Mrs Bennet and her other daughters, who cared little for the gentleman. To Elizabeth, it was just a poor excuse to justify his unwillingness to be in their company again.

It all became clear to Elizabeth: Mr Darcy could amend his manners to be civil if and when he chose, but in essentials, his feelings remained the same. She was determined to cease thinking of him and abandon any expectations in regard to him. If she wished to find out more about Miss Darcy, she could ask Mr Bingley, who must have some knowledge about his friend's sister. Miss Bingley had mentioned Georgiana's name several times, praising her accomplishments, so they must be on friendly enough terms to provide her with sufficient details.

For Mrs Bennet and her daughters, Mr Bingley was a most delightful presence, and the dinner was a success. The gentleman showed his admiration for Jane quite obviously, causing Mrs Bennet to treat him with excessive amiability and Jane and Elizabeth to blush with embarrassment.

"I hope you do not intend to return to London soon, Mr Bingley."

"No indeed, Mrs Bennet. I have no plans to leave Hertfordshire at present."

"Then perhaps you might give a ball soon!" Lydia

suddenly intervened, paying no attention to her eldest sisters' reproachful glares.

"A ball would be lovely!" Kitty supported her. "Especially with the regiment in Meryton and so many officers we might dance with!"

"Do you think the neighbourhood would approve of a ball?" Mr Bingley enquired, mostly of Jane.

"Certainly, if it is not too bothersome for you," Jane answered shyly.

Mr Bingley's smile broadened even more. "Not bothersome at all, I assure you. We shall have a ball as soon as my cook can make enough white soup!"

"You must invite all the officers," Lydia continued.

"Of course, Miss Lydia. In fact, since I am not so well acquainted with the neighbourhood, I would appreciate it if Mrs Bennet and Miss Bennet would suggest a list of guests."

The compliment did not go unnoticed, and Jane's cheeks crimsoned with delight.

"We would be happy to," Jane whispered.

"Very happy, indeed!" Mrs Bennet exclaimed. "We know all our neighbours, and we could write a guest list in no time."

"But I am sure your sisters will wish to look over the final list, Mr Bingley," Jane added.

"How considerate of you, Miss Bennet. However, I doubt my sisters will have much interest in the ball. But I shall ask their opinion, of course."

"What about Mr Darcy?" Mr Bennet asked with a glimpse of amusement in his eyes.

"Darcy?" Mr Bingley shrugged. "He never has much interest in balls. I doubt he will even attend. He might choose to spend that time in the library, so do not worry about him."

"Well then, perhaps I could join him in the library during the ball. There is nothing I would like more," Mr Bennet declared.

"My dear Mr Bennet, you may do whatever you please, and so may Mr Darcy. It is fortunate that Mr Bingley does not resemble either of you," Mrs Bennet concluded.

Elizabeth remained silent for most of the evening. So, Mr Darcy had no interest in balls, dinners, or generally in anything that most people found entertaining. Well, very likely he would not be missed. But she could not help thinking of Georgiana, wondering how difficult it must have been for her to grow up with such a haughty and aloof brother.

Around her, there was lively conversation and laughter; however, for some reason, she could not enjoy the meal as much as she might have.

Their guest left at a rather late hour, but the thrill of the evening kept Mrs Bennet awake — and her daughters around her — for another hour. She repeated many times that his request for help with the guest list for the ball was further proof of Mr Bingley's partiality for Jane.

As much as Jane tried to temper her mother's hopes and expectations, she failed, and Mrs Bennet went on until Mr Bennet declared it was late and they should retire for the night.

"You should rest and prepare for the arrival of my cousin Mr Collins. He might not be as handsome or amiable as Mr Bingley, nor worth five thousand a year, but he is certainly of equal importance, since your comfort may depend on him one day," the gentleman concluded in his usual mocking tone.

"I do not care much for your cousin, dear husband, since I have reason to believe our comfort will be well taken care of soon. I am sure Mr Bingley will not wait much longer before he secures his happiness!"

"Mama, please!" Jane interjected. "We should not expect anything from Mr Bingley simply because he has been so amiable and kind. It makes me uncomfortable to hear you speaking in such a manner."

"Hush, child. Let me worry about all that. We should go to bed now. Your father is right. We need rest to receive that despicable man tomorrow."

"Poor Mr Collins. Since he is the heir to Longbourn, he must be in possession of every flaw of character," Mr Bennet said, rolling his eyes and winking at his favourite daughter.

Elizabeth smiled at him and replied, "Papa, could it be possible that Mr Collins is a reasonable, witty man? Perhaps we shall come to like him, and he will become a friend to our family."

"Based on his letters, I doubt the part regarding his reason and wit. But he might very well become a friend to our family. After all, we have plenty of silly friends already, and there is always room for more." After that, he left before his wife had time to protest such a statement. It was already late, and the day had been too eventful for further arguments.

***

As had happened many times before, the following days proved the correctness of Mr Bennet's estimation.

Mr Collins arrived at four o'clock in the afternoon, precisely at the stated hour. He was a young man with plain features and irritating, pompous manners that mirrored his long tirades and sermons. He bowed too often and too low, paid ridiculous compliments to his 'fair cousins', which at times sounded like insults, and mentioned his noble patroness, Lady Catherine de Bourgh, in every other sentence. He had been at Longbourn for two days, and the entire family was already exasperated.

Mrs Bennet, however, started to warm towards him when he declared that he had travelled to Hertfordshire to tighten his bond with the Bennet family and also to search for a wife, as Lady Catherine had suggested. When he indicated that he would like to choose his future spouse from among his cousins, Mrs Bennet's affection for him grew. Of course, his attention immediately turned towards Jane, but Mrs Bennet informed him that she was expected to become engaged soon.

From that moment, Mr Collins moved his interest to Elizabeth, succeeding in challenging her patience and even her manners and civility. Mr Bennet was exceedingly entertained by watching his cousin chasing his favourite daughter, as he declared to Elizabeth several times, but unlike in other circumstances, she did not share his amusement. In fact, quite the opposite.

Mr Bingley called at Longbourn again and was introduced to Mr Collins. Despite his amiable disposition, even Mr Bingley became uncomfortable when faced with one of Mr Collins's long speeches, and he was barely able to say more than a few words himself.

"I was telling my cousin Mr Bennet how happy I am to have finally become better acquainted with his family. As my noble patronesses, Lady Catherine de Bourgh, often says, family must support each other. I trust the bond between us will strengthen even more if a certain event I am hoping for occurs."

Mr Bingley seemed lost as to the gentleman's meaning and glanced around, while Elizabeth averted her eyes in mortification, and Mrs Bennet displayed a broad grin of approval.

"Lady Catherine de Bourgh? Of Rosings Park?" Mr Bingley finally enquired in a desperate attempt to carry on the conversation.

"Yes, the very one. The most remarkable lady to ever live," Mr Collins said.

"What a coincidence! She is the aunt of my friend, Mr Darcy. He will be interested to know you are acquainted with his aunt."

Mr Collins seemed to stop breathing momentarily.

"Are you acquainted with Mr Darcy? Of Pemberley?"

"I am. He has been my friend for several years. More than that, he is currently my guest at Netherfield."

Mr Collins's face changed colour, and his mouth fell open in a most unbecoming way.

"Mr Darcy is here in Hertfordshire? And you believe I might be introduced to him? This is most extraordinary! I am in the happy position to be able to inform him that her ladyship was in excellent health only three days ago. If only you would do me the honour of introducing us."

The clergyman's enthusiasm seemed to leave Mr Bingley disconcerted once more, and again he cast a helpless look at Jane. But Mrs Bennet intervened energetically.

"I am sure Mr Bingley can introduce you to Mr Darcy. Just be warned that he is aloof and haughty and barely speaks at all in company!"

Mr Collins's eyes widened. "Lady Catherine always says that her nephew is an exceptional young man. If I had the good fortune of meeting him, I would never dare judge his manners, which I am sure must be the epitome of decorum."

"Mr Bingley, would you do us the honour of dining at Longbourn again tomorrow?" Mrs Bennet proposed. "And perhaps you may convince Mr Darcy to join you, so you can introduce Mr Collins to him."

The request obviously took Mr Bingley by surprise, and he needed a moment to recover.

"Indeed, sir, I would be exceedingly grateful to you for such a generous favour. I would beg you, if necessary," Mr Collins insisted.

Mr Bingley looked defeated. "Mr Collins, there is nothing to be grateful for. And please, there is no need to beg. I shall accept Mrs Bennet's invitation, and I shall do my best to convince Darcy to join me, though I cannot guarantee my success."

Mr Collins was so overjoyed by Mr Bingley's words that he was effusive on the subject until Mr Bingley bade his farewells in some haste and left with the promise of returning the next day.

***

At Netherfield, Darcy finished the letters to his solicitor, his cousin Colonel Fitzwilliam, and Georgiana but remained in the library to avoid any further distress. Bingley had called at Longbourn — again — and his sisters had vociferously disapproved of his partiality. While he did not necessarily approve of Bingley's interest in Miss Bennet, he was vexed by Miss Bingley and Mrs Hurst's malicious gossip — especially against the Bennets. Even worse, he was bothered by his own restless thoughts that centred too much around Elizabeth Bennet. He had not seen her since she had visited Netherfield, but he had found himself recollecting her pretty, sparkling eyes several times — certainly more often than those of any other woman. What was it that had captured his interest? Could it simply be her connection to his family, or should he worry that it was more?

Darcy's reflections were interrupted by the entrance of a servant, who delivered an express from Pemberley. He felt slightly perturbed as he took the letter in Mrs Reynolds's well-known handwriting and eagerly unfolded it.

At first glance, he noticed three pages — fully written — and sighed in relief, hoping he had finally received an answer to his questions. His eyes flew over the letter faster than his mind could comprehend it, and his anxiety increased with every word.

Sir,

I pray this letter finds you and Miss Georgiana in good health. Please know you both are always in our thoughts and prayers, and we count the days until we see you at Pemberley again.

It is my great pleasure to be able to answer your questions, even though the events took place more than ten years ago, and I had almost forgotten about them myself. I do remember a young girl such as you describe quite vividly. She was the daughter of a gentleman who owned a small estate, and the niece by marriage of Mrs Clarke's great-niece, Madeleine Gardiner.

Young Lizzy, I believe was her name, was around ten years old when she came to Pemberley with her aunt and great-aunt. She stayed in Lambton for several weeks and visited Pemberley on a number of occasions, but she made quite an impression in that brief time. It is one of my happiest memories during what was an unfortunate time for your family. She made Miss Georgiana laugh and roll in the grass and Lady Anne smile, which happened very rarely in those days. Lady Anne used to say that Lizzy had brought a breath of fresh air to Pemberley, and she enjoyed seeing the girls playing together.

Mrs Richmond, Miss Georgiana's governess, disapproved of young Lizzy, claiming she was too wild in her behaviour and not proper enough in her manners for her age. I dare say she was just spirited, lively, and confident, and braver than other young girls.

Her courage was confirmed the day when Miss Georgiana was thrown from her pony and fell into the lake. Lizzy immediately jumped in after her and kept her head above the water until the servants arrived to pull her out. Lady Anne was positive that Lizzy saved Miss Georgiana's life that day, though Mrs Richmond claimed there were many other servants around who would have saved her moments later.

Only God knows the truth, but that little girl jumped into the lake and grabbed hold of Miss Georgiana with more boldness and determination than many men.

I remember Lady Anne offered Lizzy a necklace as a reward for her courage. I also recollect that your father offered the Gardiners — Lizzy's uncle and aunt — a generous reward, but they declined it.

I last saw them several days before Lady Anne's tragic death, but I continued to ask Mrs Clarke about them, just as they enquired after Miss Georgiana. I am not aware whether Miss Lizzy ever met Miss Georgiana again. Miss Lizzy must be a young lady now; I hope she has not lost her spirit and bravery.

Although you did not request it, I took the liberty of contacting the late Mrs Clarke's relatives, and I attach Mr and Mrs Gardiner's direction in London in case you wish to contact them. If you do not oppose it, I would like to write to them myself too; I would be happy to have news of them.

I hope my letter has provided you with some satisfactory

answers to your questions. I hurried to send it to you, as you mentioned the matter was of some urgency. Please let me know if I may be of any more help on this subject.

A. Reynolds

He put the letter down on the desk but held it tight with his fingers, as if afraid he might lose it. His entire body was stirred by chills, while he tried to fully comprehend the letter, and eventually he read it again.

The revelation that Miss Elizabeth had been held in such affection and esteem by his mother and that she had saved his sister's life was overwhelmingly impressive. Since the details were few and unsatisfying for him, he wrote another letter, asking Mrs Reynolds for every detail. Another tormenting week would follow until he could expect her reply, and his patience got the better of him. The only way to obtain some answers sooner would be to ask none other than the heroine of the story.

He had to see Miss Elizabeth Bennet soon. Very soon.

Chapter 7

"Darcy, are you still here? Alone?" Bingley enquired a while later, entering the library.

"Yes."

"I have just arrived home. Would you like a drink before dinner?"

"A drink would be welcome. Did you have a pleasant time?"

"Relatively," Bingley admitted, handing him a glass and filling it with brandy. "I called on Colonel Forster, and then I stopped at Longbourn."

"I assumed as much..."

"Do you disapprove, Darcy? Of visiting the Bennets?"

"It is not for me to approve or disapprove of your business, Bingley. My concern is that certain actions which would raise no speculation in London might be seen differently in a small town. An apparent partiality could raise expectations that, if you are not ready to fulfil them, could cause harm. And if you are too hasty in fulfilling them, that could be hurtful too, in the future."

"I am not ignorant to your meaning, Darcy. However, I shall not deny I find Miss Bennet the most beautiful woman I have ever seen. Her nature is so gentle, her manners so sweet that I would not be afraid to fulfil any expectations in regard to her."

"Bingley, you have only just met her. You know little of her true nature and character, just as she knows little of yours. I would suggest you slow down and consider everything properly before making any decision that might make either you or her miserable."

"Your advice is too wise to argue with, Darcy. I certainly have no immediate plans to marry Miss Bennet. I am simply calling on her and enjoying her company. However, today my enjoyment was not so great as I expected."

"Was it not? Why was that?"

"The Bennets have a visitor. Mr Bennet's cousin. Apparently, Longbourn is entailed on the male line, and Mr Collins will inherit it one day. I am sorry to say, but that man is truly tiresome."

"He must be if you have declared it so. I have never known you to find anyone tiresome before."

"Well, now I do. I can only imagine how difficult it must be for the Bennets, fearing for their future if Mr Bennet should die."

"Sadly, such a thing happens in many families without an heir and financial security. It is even more pitiful when intelligent ladies find themselves at the mercy of a silly man whose only advantage is having been born male," Darcy answered. "I imagine Mrs Bennet and her daughters possess no tender feelings towards their cousin."

"I believe that is a fair statement. But Darcy, speaking of Mrs Bennet, I have a favour to ask. She has invited me to dinner again tomorrow, and she insisted that you join me. I am aware it is unlikely you will accept, but I promised I would insist upon it. Please think on it. Perhaps you might bear the discomfort for one evening."

"I do accept, Bingley," Darcy said, surprising even himself. He had been seeking an opportunity to speak to Miss Elizabeth since he had received the letter from Mrs Reynolds, and when it suddenly arrived, he embraced it instantly. The quick answer clearly shocked Bingley, who was staring open-mouthed at his friend.

"You do?" he stammered eventually. "Excellent! Thank you! How generous of you! But...to be perfectly honest, there is more to this story."

Bingley's enthusiasm embarrassed Darcy, as he knew he was deceiving his friend. He had not accepted the dinner invitation out of generosity but out of selfishness. He would do anything to discover the full truth about Miss Elizabeth's connection to his family, and to put his mind at ease.

"What more could there be, Bingley?"

"Well, Mr Collins...he is a clergyman in the parish of Hunsford, it appears. He is under the patronage of your aunt Lady Catherine de Bourgh, whom he worships."

"Oh..."

"I was imprudent enough to mention you being my friend and that you were staying at Netherfield. He became wild with pleasure and begged me repeatedly to introduce him to you. Therefore, I must warn you, if you come to dinner, you will have to bear him."

Bingley looked humbled and embarrassed, and Darcy smiled to put him at ease.

"Do not worry. I trust I am capable of tolerating the man for one evening," he said, noticing more puzzlement on his friend's face. Indeed, he would usually have avoided such an encounter, but speaking to Miss Elizabeth was his main goal for the moment.

"Good! I shall send a note to Mrs Bennet immediately. I hope you will not have a dreadful time — at least she always provides tasty meals. And I am well aware you are not fond of dining with my sisters either."

"Forgive me if at times my manners are not friendly enough towards your sisters, Bingley. I mean no disrespect. I value your friendship, and I respect your family accordingly."

"Do not worry. I am not unaware of the truth. I see that Caroline is trying to gain your attention and that she has some hopes that will never be satisfied. I have even told her so several times, but she will not listen."

"I am glad you are so reasonable as to see the truth, Bingley. I truly appreciate it."

"Then perhaps you would trust me to see the truth in

regard to Miss Bennet?"

"I promise to try. Though I know a man is wiser when his heart is not touched, and his wit often betrays him when he is in love."

Bingley laughed and gulped some brandy. "I shall not argue that I have fancied myself in love a few times — probably more than I should. But I hope I have learnt something from it."

"I trust you have, Bingley."

"Darcy, may I ask…have you ever been in love? Have you ever been unwise and unreasonable because your heart has been touched?"

"No. And I do not see it ever happening. I have always been a man of reason and self-control."

"How fortunate for you. Or perhaps I should say how unfortunate. Surely you will not consider marrying without love."

"Marriage is not part of my immediate plans, Bingley. Since you ask, I shall tell you that I do hope to feel affection for the woman I marry, but I am confident it is my reason and not my heart that will guide me towards the right decision."

Bingley shook his head, doubt written clearly on his face as he filled the glasses again, making Darcy smile.

"Bingley, I still wonder how two men can be so different and still be close friends."

"So do I, Darcy. But I am grateful it happens."

***

At Longbourn the following day, the dinner preparations were more hectic than the first time that Mr Bingley had attended. Besides Mrs Bennet supervising the cooking, Mr Collins paced around, praising Lady Catherine and sharing his knowledge about the 'remarkable' Mr Darcy, whom he looked forward to meeting.

Elizabeth was again disquieted, wondering about Mr

Darcy's acceptance. He had shown no desire to be in the company of the Bennets since they last met, yet suddenly he had agreed to dine with them. While she felt nervous, she was also determined to ask Mr Darcy more about his sister and ask permission to visit her when she next happened to be in London. Surely he had no reason to refuse her, other than his possible arrogance and superiority.

Aside from her nervousness, Elizabeth was concerned by Mr Darcy's possible response to Mr Collins's behaviour. The clergyman seemed so ridiculously in awe of Lady Catherine and her nephew that he was impossible to bear. Whether Mr Darcy would be irritated or, quite the opposite, flattered by such admiration, she could not presume, but his response would surely provide more proof of his character.

Another reason for Elizabeth's anxiety was Mr Collins's increasing display of partiality towards her. It made her highly uncomfortable, and her mother's apparent approval only made her distress grow.

At the appointed hour, the two gentlemen arrived. Mr Collins was almost bouncing on his toes, and his colour was high as he fussed with his attire and walked towards the door.

When Mr Bingley and Mr Darcy entered, Elizabeth was surprised to see Mr Darcy's gaze upon her, so insistent that she felt her cheeks heating. Greetings were exchanged, and she heard Mr Collins mumbling, while he bowed deeply.

"Mr Darcy, I am William Collins, and I have the privilege to be under the patronage of Lady Catherine de Bourgh, your noble aunt. Meeting you here, in my cousin's house, exceeds all my expectations, and I can easily call it one of the best days of my life!"

"Mr Collins, let us try to calm down. It is a coincidence that we have met, but life is full of coincidences," Mr Darcy said in a composed, low voice.

"As you wish, sir. Allow me to assure you that her ladyship was in excellent health four days ago."

"Thank you. I was not worried about my aunt's health,

as I keep a regular correspondence with her."

"Mr Darcy, Mr Bingley, let us sit and have a drink before dinner," Mr Bennet interjected. "Mr Collins, you should take a seat too, sir. You look flushed and in need of rest."

Everybody sat, and Mrs Bennet started the conversation, joined by Mr Bingley. Unlike previous evenings, Mr Collins was too fascinated by Mr Darcy to even speak, so he spent most of his time staring at the gentleman. Mr Darcy looked visibly uncomfortable, and Elizabeth's amusement grew.

Half an hour later, they were called to the dining room and, as they walked down the hall, Elizabeth was stunned to hear Mr Darcy address her in a low voice.

"Miss Elizabeth, I must take this opportunity to ask... is there any way you could grant me a few minutes of your time to talk privately? Whenever and wherever you feel comfortable."

"Is anything wrong, sir?"

"No, nothing is wrong...I have just... I must confess that after our previous conversation, I wrote to Mrs Reynolds at Pemberley, and I was shocked by the details she provided. I understand I owe you my gratitude, as well as my sister's life."

His direct address stunned Elizabeth, and anxiety delayed her response.

"That is not quite true, Mr Darcy. I remember Mrs Reynolds fondly, but her memories seem greatly exaggerated. I felt privileged to have your parents' approval and your sister's friendship for a short while. You certainly have nothing to be grateful for."

She stepped towards the dining room, and he followed her. "But...I beg you, is there a way we could speak? I do not mean to be intrusive or improper. I am prepared to ask for your father's approval for a brief encounter."

He looked serious, even grave and concerned, and there were already several pairs of eyes staring at them, so she hurried to end the conversation.

"Tomorrow morning, I shall take an early walk to

Oakham Mount. Before breakfast. If we happen to meet there, we shall have enough time for conversation."

His countenance changed to astonishment, then to contentment, and he said, "Thank you, Miss Elizabeth. I shall certainly be there."

With that, they arrived at the table and were ready to take their seats.

"Mr Darcy, would you like to sit here?" Mr Bennet said, indicating the chair to his right, while Elizabeth sat opposite him, to her father's left. "I dare say we shall have different subjects of conversation from the ladies," Mr Bennet continued.

"I would like that very much," Mr Darcy replied. As he sat, Mr Collins left his place next to Mrs Bennet and ceremoniously moved to Mr Darcy's other side, paying no attention to the pairs of puzzled and reproachful eyes.

"Mr Collins, do you not want to sit next to Lizzy?" Mrs Bennet enquired, while Elizabeth flushed with mortification and panic.

She sensed Mr Darcy looking at her, and she imagined he had noticed her horror, since she heard him saying, "In fact, there are several questions I would like to ask Mr Collins, unless Miss Elizabeth wishes for his company."

"Not at all!" she replied, so loudly that her voice sounded rude even to herself. "I mean, I would not want to deny Mr Collins the opportunity to speak to Mr Darcy," she added.

"My dear cousin Elizabeth, such generosity honours you, and I am sure Lady Catherine herself would approve of it. In fact, when I spoke to her ladyship about choosing a proper partner in life, she insisted on generosity, modesty, and demureness as the most important qualities for a clergyman's wife."

"Then I fear Lady Catherine would not approve of me at all, as all those three qualities are as far from my character as possible," Elizabeth replied. Mr Collins seemed disconcerted and confused by such a statement, while a little smile twisted

Mr Darcy's lips. Elizabeth smiled too.

"I am sure you are only being modest, Cousin Elizabeth. When you meet Lady Catherine, I do not doubt you will do everything to gain her good opinion."

"I cannot imagine in what circumstances I would meet Lady Catherine de Bourgh, Mr Collins," Elizabeth said rather harshly. "However, I assure you my statement was absolutely true, and I could be called many things but not modest."

Mr Collins was ready to add something further, but Mr Bennet interjected and filled the clergyman's glass. During dinner, Mr Collins continued to address Elizabeth and seek her attention on the few occasions when he was not engaging Mr Darcy in conversation or praising Lady Catherine de Bourgh, until finally Mr Darcy lost his patience and intervened.

"Upon my word, Mr Collins, I have known my aunt since I was born, but in my whole life, I have not heard so much praise about her as I have heard tonight from you. Even Lady Catherine herself would be overwhelmed."

"But Mr Darcy, I assure you none of it is unwarranted!" Mr Collins replied.

"Yes it is, Mr Collins. If not unwarranted, certainly excessive. Could we make an effort not to mention Lady Catherine again tonight?" he suggested, and Mr Collins's face fell.

"That would be an interesting endeavour," Elizabeth said. "Perhaps Mr Darcy could suggest a subject of conversation that interests us all." In saying that, she looked at the gentleman, and he held her gaze. It felt like a small conspiracy between them, and Elizabeth found it strangely delightful.

"My conversational skills are meagre," Mr Darcy said. "But perhaps we could speak of books or the theatre?"

"On those subjects, you had best only address me and Lizzy," Mr Bennet said. "It is fortunate that you sat near us, Mr Darcy."

"In truth, I do feel fortunate, Mr Bennet," Mr Darcy declared, and his eyes briefly met Elizabeth's again.

Two entirely different conversations were soon taking place at each end of the table; Mr Collins was somehow lost in the middle, trying to join in with one or other of the groups but failing and mentioning Lady Catherine's name again several times.

***

All in all, the evening progressed reasonably well, moving from one course to another and from one subject to another.

Darcy grew at ease with Mr Bennet and also with Elizabeth. The more he saw of her and listened to her, the more he could understand why his mother had once said she had brought a breath of fresh air to Pemberley. Her entire being was lively and witty, and her eyes — which were uncommonly pretty — drew his attention and stirred his interest more and more.

While he was enjoying his time at dinner, he also looked forward to the evening ending as soon as possible, so the morning would come sooner, and he could meet Elizabeth alone. He did not know where Oakham Mount was, but he would certainly find out. Nothing could deter him from seeing her and talking to her.

He could not guess how she felt about his request to meet and what she thought about him writing to Mrs Reynolds. She had looked rather uncomfortable at his praise and gratitude. He trusted his housekeeper, so perhaps Elizabeth did not remember her heroic gesture clearly enough.

Or perhaps she was being modest indeed, as Mr Collins had claimed and she had denied. It would have been strange if Mr Collins was right — probably one of the few occasions in his life.

Chapter 8

The wind rattling the windows woke Elizabeth abruptly. Jane was still sound asleep — they had stayed awake late the previous night, talking about the dinner and the guests. While Jane's partiality for Mr Bingley was obvious and acknowledged, Elizabeth was still unsure about her opinion of Mr Darcy.

She felt annoyed with herself for her strange responses to the gentleman that she hardly knew. She was not upset any longer and had put aside the offence at the assembly. What remained was her interest in the true nature and character of this man — Lady Anne's son and Georgiana's brother. So, he had written to Mrs Reynolds, asking about her. It was natural, even expected, but she was slightly embarrassed by how the good housekeeper had related that old story. He had sounded quite solemn when he had declared that he owed her Georgiana's life. Surely that was an exaggeration, and she was determined to clear it up as soon as possible.

Probably his gratitude was the reason for his sudden improvement in manners and his obvious effort to act civilly, almost amiably, with her family, including Mr Collins.

Regardless of the reason, for his politeness towards Mr Collins alone, Mr Darcy deserved praise. Elizabeth did not trust herself to show equal patience with her cousin, especially since the clergyman had mentioned more than once his intention of marrying and had hinted at her as his choice. Elizabeth had noticed Mr Darcy's puzzled frown several times and wondered what he was thinking. Not that she cared much; she had no intention of even considering marrying Mr Collins, which was equally hilarious and disturbing. He was perhaps a 'desirable catch', as her mother stated, but not for her.

Elizabeth was also aware that her mother would not hesitate to force an affirmative answer, should Mr Collins be so foolish as to make a request, but she was not worried in the slightest. She had her father's support if needed, but regardless, her mother would not succeed in changing her mind on such an important matter.

As the wind continued to blow, she left her bed, shivering in the chilly room. It was still dark, and the weather appeared to be against any activities out of doors. But, just as in her mother's case, it was not enough to change Elizabeth's mind.

Impatiently, she dressed and waited until the daylight broke the darkness. She put on Lady Anne's necklace, hiding it under a scarf wrapped around her neck, then stepped out of her chamber, closing the door gently.

Mrs Hill was already attending to her duties in the kitchen, and Elizabeth informed her she would go for a walk and return for breakfast.

"But Miss Lizzy, it is very cold out of doors! And the sun is barely up. Will you not have a cup of tea and take a walk later?"

"Do not worry, Hill. I shall not be gone for long. And you know I do not mind a little cold," Elizabeth replied affectionately to the kind woman who had been part of their family for more than ten years.

As soon as she left, the wind made her shiver. It was colder than she had estimated, and for a moment she even considered returning. But her curiosity and eagerness to finally speak to Mr Darcy without restraint induced her to hasten her pace. It was a rather long walk to Oakham Mount, but she hoped the exercise would help to warm her.

During her walk, the sun rose higher in the sky, and the wind dropped slightly, but the cold remained. As always, Hill was right, Elizabeth pondered. If only she had gone out after breakfast, the weather would have been warmer. But she had told Mr Darcy she would be there early in the morning, and it was better to avoid another delay to their long-awaited conversation.

Nervous and immersed in her thoughts, Elizabeth hurried to reach her destination, arriving sooner than she had anticipated. The ground was dry, the path was clear, and sunshine announced a pleasant autumn day ahead. She sat on a stump, looking around. She had seen the view so many times, yet she would never grow tired of it.

She glanced along the path, wondering from where Mr Darcy would appear. She hoped they would have time to discuss everything at length, to clarify her connection to the Darcys and to ask him more about Georgiana. If he indeed felt gratitude towards her, perhaps he could arrange for her to meet Georgiana at some time in the future, or at least write to her.

Elizabeth waited and waited; she noticed the sun had risen higher in the sky, so she knew the hour must be getting rather late. She stood up, looked around, took a few steps to better catch a view of any rider, then sat again and rubbed her hands to warm them. Slowly, her spirits lowered, and her nervousness increased. She guessed it must be breakfast time; surely he would not come. He must be enjoying a warm, tasty meal at Netherfield, while she — like a complete fool — had faced the cold and wind of the morning to meet him. How could she be such a simpleton? Yes, he had said he would be there, and she had trusted him, but he was not. She tried to find an excuse — perhaps he did not know where Oakham Mount was. But surely he could have asked one of Netherfield's servants — everybody knew it. Of course, that was if he cared enough to take so much trouble. And even if he was lost, the advantage of being on horseback would mean he had enough time to arrive — even twice. Unless something truly bad had happened, which was unlikely, he should have been there; a real gentleman would be. Such audacity, such insolence to ask her for a private encounter and then to miss it! Of course, she was not flawless. She could have suggested the conversation occur in Longbourn's library — Mr Bennet would not have opposed it. What was she thinking to make such a bad decision?

Her irritation, fed by disappointment, increased, turning into anger, and she stood up in agitation. She brushed down her gown, breathed deeply, and began the walk back, prepared to face her mother's questions about her absence — and very likely Mr Collins's comments. And it was all Mr Darcy's fault!

So lost was she in her own thoughts that she did not hear the hoofs until the rider actually appeared in her sight. She stopped; he dismounted in a hurry and almost ran towards her, while his horse, loose and free, followed him and approached her as well, causing her more anxiety.

Mr Darcy's face was red, his hair was in disorder, and he bowed deeply, speaking with haste.

"Miss Bennet, I am so happy to see you! I beg your forgiveness for being so late. I had lost any hope of finding you here still. I am so grateful to you for waiting. I deeply apologise. I took the wrong path, and then I circled around and..."

Her heart at first raced, then slowly calmed down. Regardless of the reason for his delay, he looked truly agitated and remorseful — and yes, pleased to see her.

"Mr Darcy, I am glad to see you too. I wondered what had happened that it took you so long...I am afraid the hour is late, and I cannot stay any longer. I must return home. My family will be worried."

"Of course. I understand. Then...will you allow me to escort you? That way perhaps we can also talk a little."

"Certainly," she agreed, and they set off together down the path.

She felt restless, anxious, and satisfied at the same time. He did not appear indifferent to their encounter, so she did not care much for the reason for his delay. More than his nearness, which always made her feel somehow uncomfortable, his stallion — tall, black, and impressive — following them freely, only a short distance behind, snorting from time to time, caused her more nervousness. In order to fight it, she was about to start the conversation, but he began first.

"I must apologise again for being late. I intended to come earlier, but last night I received several letters from London, and I wished to answer them immediately. I was up until the early hours, and somehow, to my utter shame, I did not awaken at my usual hour this morning. I have no excuse…"

Elizabeth laughed, still slightly nervous. "The truth is the best excuse, sir. The letters you mentioned — I hope there was no bad news? Is Miss Darcy in good health?"

He hesitated a moment. "There were some reasons for concern, specifically in regard to my sister, but she is in good health. However, I expect to return to London very soon. My presence is required."

"Oh, I see," she replied with a sudden regret that she could not explain to herself. "I am sure Mr Bingley will miss your company."

"And I shall miss his, but he knew I would not stay too long in Hertfordshire. And speaking of my sister, I must take this opportunity to thank you again."

He looked disquieted, and Elizabeth gently touched his arm briefly.

"Mr Darcy, as I told you last night, please do not imagine more than there was. I assume you already know how I came to visit Pemberley. Indeed, even as I child, I was impressed by your mother's kindness to me the moment she met me. And your sister was the sweetest girl I had known — and keep in mind that at that time I already had five sisters of my own."

She tried to sound light, but his expression was still serious.

"Yes, Mrs Reynolds told me as much. She said my mother used to say you brought a breath of fresh air to Pemberley."

Elizabeth laughed again. "As I said, Lady Anne was exceedingly kind to me. My mother would have said I probably brought noise and disorder to Pemberley. Your sister's governess and nanny surely shared the same opinion. Neither was too happy to see me around Miss Darcy."

Finally, a smile appeared on Mr Darcy's face. "Yes, I would imagine that. They were too protective towards my sister, which I fear did not help her much. But surely Mrs Reynolds did not invent that you saved her life."

"Oh, it was really nothing. I arrived at Pemberley to play with her as usual, and she was riding her pony by the edge of the lake. Somehow, the horse was spooked and threw her from the saddle. She rolled into the water, so I jumped in to help her out. There were many others there, and it was not me who pulled her from the water. Some men grabbed us both. That was all."

"But you were the first to jump into the water after her," Mr Darcy said, his expression solemn and grave. "I believe you did save her life — or at least attempt to, which was equally remarkable and brave for a girl of your age."

Elizabeth felt her cheeks burning at his too-serious praise, so she attempted to joke. "Well, I have to say there was a great benefit to my jump, since Lady Anne insisted that I should stay at Pemberley for several days. I had my own room, my own maid, and I was probably more spoilt than I have ever been before or since. And even better, I had the chance to play with your sister all day long and to speak to Lady Anne a few times."

"I am sure my mother came to love you, and with good reason. Otherwise, she would not have given you that necklace."

"I know... Even as I child, I refused to take it, knowing it was very expensive."

"It is not just its price, Miss Bennet. She was given that necklace that you now have, and she ordered one similar for Georgiana, so they might both have the same."

"Yes, she told me as much," Elizabeth replied, looking at his expression, which remained grave, and her voice changed, while a pain grasped her heart. "I asked her to keep the necklace until I was older and give it to me then. But she insisted I must take it... Sadly, she died shortly afterwards... What a tragedy! I know she was loved and cherished by so many."

"She was... We knew she was unwell. She had been ill for years, and my father had tried everything possible to take care of her. But nothing helped."

"Your father was an excellent man too. I remember people saying he was the best master and the best landlord. How painful it must have been for you and Miss Darcy to lose him too so soon."

"He was an excellent man, indeed. After my mother died, he never truly recovered. I believe he not only missed her but also felt guilty for not being able to help her more. I am not sure. He barely spoke to me of his feelings, especially since I was at school most of the time. He insisted I should educate myself in order to take over his responsibilities. I did not imagine it would happen so soon."

His voice was now heavy with sorrow, and even his shoulders seemed burdened by the weight of his feelings.

"And your sister? Has she been alone all these years?" Elizabeth asked.

"Sadly, yes. Not truly alone — she has always had people around to take care of her. All my relatives love her. She had the best teachers and possesses a great desire for improvement. She has grown up to be an accomplished and remarkable young lady. But..."

"But...?"

"She was the youngest in our family, and her nature is rather shy. She had no friends and still does not. As for me, I have been more of a father than a brother to her. She is always worried about upsetting or disappointing me, which has never happened, and I am sure it never will. But I feel something keeps her from being more open with me — from letting me know what troubles her or how I could help her..."

The conversation had flowed more easily than Elizabeth

had expected, and the honesty of their confessions could be easily sensed. She looked at Mr Darcy, seeing him in an utterly different light. Not the man she had previously known — self-confident, proud, even arrogant — but Lady Anne's son and Georgiana's brother, overwhelmed by sadness and worry, opening his heart to her.

"I am very sorry to hear that…I am sure Miss Darcy loves you. Even as a young child, she spoke with so much affection and pride about you. As did your parents."

"Thank you, Miss Bennet. Indeed, I do not doubt her affection for me but my ability to provide her with the comfort she needs and to guide her into growing more confident, trusting herself more, and seeing her own worth."

"She is still very young, Mr Darcy. She is the same age as my sister Lydia, who I dare say is too confident, in an imprudent way. Both of them need to grow. One in wisdom, patience, and education, and the other in confidence and inner strength. One must be tempered and guarded. The other probably needs a little guidance and encouragement."

"You seem to see things more clearly than I do, Miss Bennet. You possess both wisdom and inner strength."

Elizabeth felt his stare upon her, so she turned her head, meeting his dark eyes. She shivered from the same strange feeling that had troubled her previously in his presence.

"I am not sure you are right, sir. My sister Jane is the possessor of the beauty, sweetness, wisdom, and kindness in our family, though she is quieter and more restrained. I feel fortunate to have her as my eldest sister. The rest of us try to learn from her."

"I am sure no one who had the privilege of knowing you would find anything wanting in you, Miss Bennet. I dare say you are simply being too modest, as your cousin claims."

She stopped, surprised by his compliment and his attempt to improve their dispositions, which had been brought low by sadness. A little smile had returned to twist the corner of his lips.

"Mr Darcy, if you wish to be friends, you must promise to mention Mr Collins as rarely as possible and to admit that his claims about me can never be right."

"I promise, Miss Bennet. I wish to be friends if you will grant me the privilege. And I would not dare to contradict you. I have seen the daggers in your eyes when you are angry."

She laughed. It was a little forced but with pleasure and nervousness.

"Yes, I know I have daggers in my eyes, which is a major flaw of my character, as my mother has told me many times. However, I shall never forget when Lady Anne told me I had sparkling eyes. I did not even know what it meant, but her voice was so soft and gentle that I knew it must be something good."

They had resumed walking, but Mr Darcy stopped, and Elizabeth had to do the same. She faced his gaze again, and he declared with earnestness, "I heartily agree with my mother, Miss Bennet. I am sorry to disagree with your mother, but it is certainly not a flaw."

Elizabeth was uncertain how to take his words and how to handle the sensation his gaze provoked. She felt suddenly hot, and she loosened the scarf around her neck. Astonished, she felt his gloved hand grasping her arm.

"Are you wearing the necklace, Miss Bennet?"

She shivered again, feeling her cheeks burning.

"I am... I have never worn it in public before. Lady Anne said the colour of the stones would suit my temper, but I have always considered it too valuable to wear," she answered, surprised to hear her own voice trembling.

In disbelief, she watched him lift his hand towards her neck as if he intended to touch it, and she held her breath. However, he stopped only inches from her skin and lowered his hand.

"Again, I heartily agree with my mother. It does suit you very well, Miss Bennet."

A slightly awkward silence fell as they resumed walking.

When Longbourn appeared in sight a few minutes later, Elizabeth spoke again.

"Sir, will you join us for breakfast?"

"Oh no, I cannot. I am expected at Netherfield."

"I understand. You should return, then. I shall be home shortly."

"Very well. Miss Bennet, I cannot express my gratitude for this meeting and for our conversation. It meant more to me than I can say. I apologise if I burdened you with my distress."

"Please do not apologise. I am equally grateful for this encounter. I was wondering... Would you mind if I wrote to Miss Darcy? Perhaps I could cheer her a little should she be in need of some diversion?" Elizabeth asked, being certain of his agreement.

"No, please do not!" he replied hastily. She took a step back in shock, and he grasped her arm again.

"Forgive my rudeness, Miss Bennet... What I mean is that I would rather write to Georgiana first. I have not mentioned anything about you to her yet, and I would like to prepare her before she receives a letter from you."

"Yes, of course, you are right. I did not consider it properly. She might not even remember me or not want to hear from me at all."

"I doubt that very much. From everything I have been told so far, I am sure your friendship would have greatly benefited my sister over the years. I hope it is not too late..."

"Too late? What do you mean, sir?" Elizabeth asked with concern.

"Nothing in particular... I shall write to her this very morning."

"Does this mean you will not return to London as yet?"

"I shall, Miss Bennet, probably this week. But in the meantime, I shall write to her by express, and I might have her reply by tomorrow."

"Please let me know what her response is, even if she does not want to hear from me."

"I shall, I promise."

With that, he bowed, then jumped into the saddle, and Elizabeth took another step back from the horse.

"Thank you, Miss Bennet," he repeated, and she stood still, gazing after him until he rounded a bend in the path and disappeared from her view.

Walking towards Longbourn alone, Elizabeth started to feel — truly feel — the weight of her conversation with Mr Darcy and the confession he had made to her. Her heart was heavy with worry about Georgiana's answer and — to her surprise — even more so at the thought of Mr Darcy leaving and them not meeting again.

Chapter 9

Darcy rode back to Netherfield with an anticipation he had not felt for years. Earlier that morning, he had hurried to the established meeting being certain he had missed the encounter, that Miss Elizabeth was rightfully angered and offended by his delay and had left — if she had ever been there at all. Finding her and being allowed to accompany her home, having the chance to speak to her at length, had exceeded his expectations.

He knew she was genuine in her worry for his sister and in her grief for his late parents. Thinking of her warmed his heart in a strange way that he had never experienced before. The tenderness in her voice as she spoke of his mother, the light expression in her eyes when she had tried to make light of her brave gesture from ten years ago, her natural, unaffected manners, and that smile that at times brightened her entire face were simply enchanting, and he could easily understand why his mother and sister had been so readily charmed by her. Apparently, her liveliness was like a breath of fresh air, and her sparkling eyes remained unchanged, just as his mother had described them.

He was grateful for her eagerness to re-establish a connection with Georgiana, for deeper and more worrisome reasons than ensuring his sister had a friend. The previous evening, he had received another letter from Mrs Annesley and one from the family doctor, who had been fetched to examine Georgiana. Both expressed worries in regard to the girl's apparent loss of weight and pallor. Mrs Annesley related his sister's low spirits and appetite and her refusal to leave the house willingly, while the doctor mentioned that Georgiana would not allow him to thoroughly examine her, claiming she was in good health.

Furthermore, Georgiana herself had written to him again, in a forced cheerful tone, encouraging him to stay longer in Hertfordshire. He was equally hurt that his sister did not trust him enough to disclose the nature of her suffering and that she preferred him far away from her.

After reading the letters, Darcy had faced a night of distress. His first temptation had been to order his carriage and return to London immediately. But what good would his presence bring? He could not force her to accept the doctor's involvement, nor forbid her from distancing herself from other people. Wishing her the best, he could easily worsen her state. Overwhelmed by worry and unable to decide the right course of action, fearful that Georgiana might have inherited their mother's illness and be hiding it from him, Darcy spent the night restless until dawn, when tiredness had defeated him and he had fallen asleep, almost missing the encounter at Oakham Mount.

After the conversation with Miss Elizabeth, which had truly delighted him, he now saw a glimpse of hope, if it was true that his mother and sister had been so fond of the lady as a child — even if only for a short period of time. If Miss Elizabeth had saved Georgiana's life, it was unlikely that his sister would show no interest and have no desire to hear from her. Perhaps bonding with a young woman with whom she had shared happy memories would help Georgiana's spirits.

He arrived at Netherfield anxious but knowing what he must do. He attempted to avoid breakfast entirely and escape to his chamber — a plan that failed immediately. As soon as he entered, he saw Bingley was waiting for him, worried, puzzled, and claiming he was starving, as they had postponed breakfast due to his absence.

"Forgive me for not informing you. I took a ride. I am not really hungry, Bingley. I have some letters to complete this morning, so please eat without me."

"I will not have it, Darcy. You must join us for breakfast and then write your letters as you wish. I assume you will not join me in Meryton?"

"No, not today," Darcy replied, surrendering to his friend's insistence and entering the room where his sisters were waiting.

"Mr Darcy, where have you been?" Miss Bingley enquired immediately. "We expected you, and then your valet said you had been gone for some time. You gave us quite a fright!"

"I deeply apologise if that was the case, Miss Bingley. It is my habit to refresh my mind with an early morning ride, but I should have left word."

"So where have you been?" Miss Bingley continued as breakfast was served.

"Just riding around the area."

"Forgive me for saying so, but you have seemed out of spirits lately, Mr Darcy. I am almost as worried about you as I am about Charles. I trust you are wiser than him, however, and I know you have no *particular friends* in this county."

"Actually, Darcy seems quite friendly with Mr Bennet," Bingley intervened joyfully. "They share a love for books and other similar traits, some of which are not so interesting."

"Oh, hush, Charles. Mr Darcy cannot have anything in common with anyone in Hertfordshire. This is nonsense."

"Actually, Miss Bingley, your brother is not wrong," Darcy replied. "I have found some mutual interests with Mr Bennet."

Miss Bingley stared at him for a moment, then she frowned and sipped some tea, leaving Darcy content to eat in peace.

As soon as it was polite, he excused himself and hastened to the library, reflecting for a moment on what he should say in his letter to Georgiana. In truth, he was curious to know her response, and he chose his words carefully.

Dearest Georgiana,

I have some interesting news to share with you, which is pleasant and unexpected at the same time.

I might have mentioned in my previous letters a Mr Bennet, who owns an estate near Netherfield. He has five daughters, and you may imagine my astonishment when I spoke to his second eldest daughter, Miss Elizabeth, and she confessed to me that she visited Pemberley ten years ago and claimed a close acquaintance with our mother and a childhood friendship with you when you were five years old and she was ten. I was told that she has an aunt, a Mrs Gardiner, who was the niece of Mrs Clarke, our mother's seamstress. Apparently, during that summer, they visited Lambton, and Mrs Gardiner helped Mrs Clarke with some gowns for our mother — an occasion which brought Miss Elizabeth to Pemberley too.

As you may imagine, I was so intrigued that I wrote to Mrs Reynolds, and she replied enthusiastically. She gave me a highly favourable report of young Miss Lizzy, whom she claimed was a particular favourite of our mother and a dear friend of yours. Mrs Reynolds even remembered a dangerous accident when you fell into the lake and Miss Lizzy jumped in to save you. I spoke to Miss Elizabeth at length about this matter, and while she dismissed any praise for her gesture, she recollected you with genuine tenderness and apparent affection. I was impressed by how fond she seemed to be of you and of the memory of our mother, after all this time.

Miss Elizabeth told me she enquired after you many times after that summer and after our mother's tragic departure and even attempted to meet you in London. Mrs Reynolds also confirmed that Mrs Clarke sent news about our family to Mrs Gardiner in London many times. I am not certain why you never met again, but I suspect at that time, your governess, as well as some of our relatives, considered it to your benefit not to maintain such a connection.

Regardless, Miss Elizabeth still holds tender memories of you, and she expressed her desire you meet you or at least to write to you. I chose to write to you first and inform you of this coincidence, so you may decide what you wish to do.

If I may offer an opinion, I would gladly approve of a correspondence with Miss Elizabeth, whom I find to be an educated and spirited young lady with pleasant and unaffected manners and with a caring, affectionate nature.

However, the decision is entirely yours. Please do not feel obliged to proceed either way. Whatever you choose, I shall support you.

To end on an amusing note, you should not be worried that Miss Elizabeth pretends a fondness for you just to impress me, as you have mentioned on several past occasions.

Quite the contrary. I behaved rather rudely on several occasions, and Miss Elizabeth boldly but fairly scolded me. I dare say only her affection for you and our mother induced her to pardon my faults and allow me the opportunity for some friendly conversations with her.

I look forward to your reply, and please know I miss you very much.

Your loving brother,

F

He re-read the letter and was satisfied with the contents before he sealed it and asked for it to be delivered express. Then he wrote another letter to Mrs Reynolds, and only afterwards did he withdraw to his room, lying on the bed in the hope of some rest and quiet before being forced back into the company of Bingley's sisters.

***

During breakfast, Elizabeth had to answer many questions that were more tiring than the walk to Oakham Mount and back. Accordingly, she had to bear many disapproving glances, both from her mother and Mr Collins, who several times mentioned Lady Catherine's opinion about a young lady's proper manners. From her father's side, she only noticed a trace of curiosity and amusement.

"Mama, Kitty and I are going to Meryton," Lydia declared. "I have heard that Lieutenant Denny has returned from town with a friend who intends to join the regiment too. We must go and greet Denny and make the acquaintance of this new officer."

"You intend to go only with Kitty?" Mr Bennet asked, his eyebrow arching disapprovingly.

"I am sure Jane and Lizzy will come too," the girl answered hastily.

"Of course they will," Mrs Bennet interjected. "Besides, I see no wrong in you going alone either. It is only a mile each way — perfect exercise for young girls like you."

"Mrs Bennet, I see much wrong in two young girls going to meet officers, even if they are doing so with the most innocent intentions," Mr Bennet answered severely.

"Indeed, my dear cousin, I heartily agree. Young girls should not be left alone in the company of men, unchaperoned. Lady Catherine has stated as much many times!"

"Jane and I shall join them," Elizabeth declared, annoyed to hear the mention of Lady Catherine yet again.

Something else that she appreciated about Mr Darcy was that not a single time had he praised his aunt unjustly, and he had even attempted to temper Mr Collins's ridiculous veneration. The fact that he had failed was not Mr Darcy's fault, as Mr Collins seemed unstoppable.

"Very well, girls, you will all go then," Mrs Bennet concluded.

"I would rather stay at home, Mama," Mary replied, and her mother rolled her eyes.

"Do as you wish, girl."

"I believe it is my duty to accompany my fair cousins and be certain they are safe," Mr Collins stated, causing panic and distress among the girls while earning him a smile from Mrs Bennet.

Mr Bennet escaped to his library, and Elizabeth paid him a short visit before leaving for her second walk of the day.

"You look lovely, Lizzy. I am sure Mr Collins will approve of your attire."

"Papa, please do not tease me. I am already annoyed and on the verge of rudeness with Mr Collins, and I may tell him my opinion of him very soon."

"Just do not forget that he will be able to throw you out as soon as I am dead," Mr Bennet continued teasingly.

"Then you must promise you will live a very long life, Papa, as I shall never be able to pretend I enjoy your cousin's company."

"I shall do my best, child. So, are you ready for another walk, since you have only just returned from the previous one?"

"Yes... Papa, there is something I must tell you. Earlier today, I met Mr Darcy. We arranged the meeting last evening."

Mr Bennet's serenity changed to a frown.

"Did you?"

"Yes. We discussed my prior connection to his family. Apparently, he wrote to the housekeeper at Pemberley, and Mrs Reynolds made my actions appear more praiseworthy than they truly were. Mr Darcy tried to express his gratitude last night, so we discussed meeting today and clarifying everything."

"I see. And did you?"

"We did. I dare say everything is clear now. Mr Darcy seems very fond of his sister, and of course his parents. I admit it is a side of him that I very much approve of."

"I am glad to hear that. It is a small compensation for his refusal to dance with you, is it not?"

"Yes, it is a very small compensation." Elizabeth laughed.

"Well, thank you for sharing it with me. I assume you wish to keep it a secret from your mother?"

"Yes, please. I cannot bear to hear more questions or Mr Collins's opinion about my meeting Mr Darcy unchaperoned."

"You may count on my secrecy, Lizzy. Sadly, you will have to hear Mr Collins's opinion on other matters, though."

"I am aware, Papa."

"If an opportunity arises, I suggest you introduce Mr Collins to Sir William Lucas. I dare say they will enjoy each other's company."

"That is an excellent idea, Papa. I would like to call on Charlotte Lucas regardless."

"Good. I look forward to hearing all the details when you return. Now please tell your mother that I am busy, and I do not wish to be disturbed for the next few hours."

***

Never did the short distance from Longbourn to Meryton seem so long and exhausting. Alone with his young cousins, Mr Collins seemed to take the opportunity to share his opinion on everything, jumping from one subject to another and often touching Elizabeth's arm with his hand as he gesticulated. With her patience pushed beyond its limit, Elizabeth tried to remain nonchalant while wondering how it was possible that an educated man with a good situation in life could be so repulsive.

They finally arrived in Meryton, where they had the good fortune to meet Charlotte and Maria Lucas. Introductions were performed to Mr Collins, and a very short while passed until Lydia started to shout and wave, calling to their attention Lieutenant Denny and two companions, who were all approaching them.

While the lieutenant and one of his companions were familiar to Elizabeth, the other was a stranger. He was introduced to them as the new officer who had just joined the regiment several days prior — Mr George Wickham.

Only a few moments and a few polite exchanges were needed to prove that Mr Wickham was one of the most handsome men ever seen in Meryton, who had also been gifted with a pleasant figure and even more pleasant manners, a charming smile, and conversational skills matched by an attractive tone of voice.

Mr Collins was entirely overlooked, and his attempts to insinuate himself into the conversation failed until he grasped Elizabeth's arm and said loudly, "My dear cousin, you promised to introduce me to Sir William Lucas, the only titled man in Meryton, I have heard. I look forward to meeting this gentleman as soon as possible."

Elizabeth pulled her arm from his hold and was ready to reply sharply when Charlotte Lucas saved her.

"I am sure my father would enjoy meeting you too, Mr Collins. He would be pleased to see you all, gentlemen. Will you not join us at Lucas Lodge for refreshments, if you do not have other engagements?"

The proposal met with the approval of everyone, except for Mr Collins, whose expression showed his repressed anger. He clearly did not wish to be in the company of the officers a moment longer, nor to compete with them for the ladies' attention. However, the plan was made, and towards Lucas Lodge they all set off.

Chapter 10

Sir William and Lady Lucas were thrilled to welcome such special guests. The entire town had heard of Mr Collins — the future heir of Longbourn — and people were curious to meet him. Also, a new handsome officer was always a thrilling prospect for the neighbours. So, a visit bringing together both men was a matter of exceeding satisfaction to Sir William.

Mr Wickham responded to the enthusiastic reception with impeccable manners, but Mr Collins seemed to consider it all a compliment to himself, and such particular attention from a titled gentleman evidently pleased him exceedingly.

"Mr Wickham, I understand you joined the regiment recently. Did you have a previous career in the army or militia?" Lady Lucas enquired.

"No, ma'am. To be perfectly honest, joining the regiment was due to serendipity. I met my old friend Denny in London, and he convinced me how rewarding such a career could be. I must say, I am already pleased with my decision."

With that, he looked around as if he had just complimented the people surrounding him. Everybody replied with approving glances and smiles until Mr Collins interjected.

"If we are to be completely honest, a few days is hardly long enough for one to realise whether a certain career is suitable. From an early age, I knew that the church would be my choice, and I studied and worked hard to be prepared for it."

For the first time since she had met him, Elizabeth agreed with her cousin and was ready to voice her opinion. Indeed, Mr Wickham's statement seemed shallow and did not paint a good picture of the officer. To join the regiment simply because he met someone by chance meant that until that moment, he had nothing else to do. And — just as Mr Collins had stated — a few days did not make a career.

However, Mr Collins continued on the subject with growing enthusiasm, and Elizabeth's approval quickly dissipated. She had to try hard to suppress a sigh and a roll of her eyes.

"My noble patroness, Lady Catherine de Bourgh, who generously granted me her trust and bestowed upon me a living in the beautiful parish of Hunsford, always insists on the importance of thorough study and consistent effort for a man to be successful in his career."

"Unless the man is born a gentleman with connections and wealth, which ensures his immediate success without study or effort," Lieutenant Denny replied, causing some laughter.

Slightly uncomfortable, Elizabeth could not refrain from saying, "I dare say wealth and connections alone are not enough to define a man as a true gentleman."

"My dear Miss Eliza, forgive me for arguing with your statement, but wealth and connections are often enough for anything, at least in the eyes of society," Sir William answered.

"I apologise for disputing you, Miss Elizabeth, but I must agree with Sir William. I could testify with my experience over the last five years," Mr Wickham said.

"What experience?" Lydia asked, moving closer and grabbing his arm.

"Something that is not appropriate to be related to young ladies that I have only just met," he said with a smile. "It would not be gentlemanlike behaviour on my part."

"I am sure a handsome officer would always act in a gentlemanlike manner," Lydia declared boldly, and Kitty approved enthusiastically, while Elizabeth and Jane blushed in mortification.

"Lady Catherine de Bourgh has often stated that manners define a gentleman's character more accurately than a handsome figure," Mr Collins declared.

"Yes, perhaps, but a handsome figure *and* happy manners make a perfect gentleman," Lydia declared. "And speaking of perfect gentlemen, I hope you and the other officers are excellent dancers. Mr Bingley has promised to give a ball next month. He is our neighbour, you know. He is the tenant at Netherfield Park."

"Lydia, we should change the subject of conversation," Jane interjected. "It is not polite to speak of Mr Bingley's intentions in his absence. Even though he mentioned a ball, we cannot be certain of his plans until they are settled."

"Oh, I am sure Mr Bingley will keep his word. And I hope he will invite all the officers, so we can dance all night."

"Lydia, that is enough. I believe it is time to return home," Elizabeth added severely, embarrassed by her younger sister's unguarded behaviour. While the Lucases were well acquainted with Lydia and Kitty's manners, they must have made a poor impression on the officers.

"Go home? But we have only just arrived!" Lydia argued.

"My dear Miss Elizabeth, surely you cannot leave us so soon," Sir William said. "You must stay at least for a cup of tea and a stronger drink for us men."

As Charlotte and Lady Lucas added their voices to the plea, Elizabeth felt defeated and sat down next to Jane. Tea was served, and Sir William offered the gentlemen some brandy — an occasion for Mr Collins to quote more from Lady Catherine's wisdom on drinking habits. Charlotte Lucas strolled from one guest to another, making sure they were all comfortable. Lydia, Kitty, Maria, and Lady Lucas were all engaged with the officers; Sir William and Mr Collins seemed to have found a subject of mutual interest to share with the brandy.

Elizabeth heard their cousin mentioning Lady Catherine several more times and paying compliments to the hosts and their house, which sounded more like insults.

On the other sofa, Lydia continued to speak to the officers with embarrassing openness, and Kitty and Maria

Lucas seemed to copy her forwardness.

Mr Wickham continued to display the same amiability throughout the visit, encouraging the conversation; his manners were as pleasant as his smile and his figure. The more Elizabeth looked at him, the more he seemed familiar to her. His face was unknown to her, but some of his features, small gestures, a twist of his lips, and other little things stirred her anxiety. It was no use asking him whether they had met before, since he treated her as a stranger to whom he had just been introduced.

After a few minutes of reflection, she concluded that very likely she was confusing him with someone else. She focused her attention instead on Mr Collins and Sir William, who appeared to be sharing an engaging discussion, but even against her will, her eyes kept returning to Mr Wickham.

"My dear Miss Eliza, why are you so quiet today?" Sir William suddenly addressed her. "You are one of the liveliest and most spirited young ladies of my acquaintance, and your involvement in conversation is always delightful. I have barely heard you speak since you arrived. I hope you are not unwell?"

"You are too kind and too generous with your praise, Sir William. I am perfectly well, I assure you. I just felt the conversation was already engaging and animated enough, and my involvement was not needed."

"Indeed, my dear cousin, I have enjoyed my conversation with Sir William exceedingly," Mr Collins said. "Did you know that he was introduced at St James's? What a privilege!"

"Yes, I did know," Elizabeth answered, hardly concealing another roll of her eyes.

"We still have more to discuss, and I look forward to it, Mr Collins. Hopefully, you will do us the honour of dining with us at Lucas Lodge soon," Sir William said.

Elizabeth could hardly suppress her smile. Her father had been correct; only a brief meeting had been enough to create a bond between Mr Collins and Sir William. Hopefully, that friendship would keep Mr Collins away from Longbourn from time to time, making the rest of his visit bearable.

"I hope it is not our presence that has displeased Miss Elizabeth and made her quieter than usual," Mr Wickham said teasingly. "I imagine a stranger imposing his presence might be distressing for a young lady."

"Oh, no, how can you say that?" Lydia interjected. "We are very happy that we met you, Mr Wickham! Are we not, Lizzy?"

"I assure you I am not so easily distressed, Mr Wickham," Elizabeth answered with amusement. "Your presence has not displeased me at all. Quite the opposite. And since you are Mr Denny's friend, we can hardly call you a stranger."

"I am glad to hear that."

Mr Wickham's comment was surprising, but then Elizabeth realised he must have noticed her repeated glances. She had been staring at him, just as she had stared at Mr Darcy at the assembly. Apparently, Mr Wickham had better manners and was not so hasty to assume she intended to trap or chase him as Mr Darcy had, she mused, becoming more diverted.

"In fact," she continued, seizing the opportunity for some clarification, "as strange as it may sound, I have the feeling that we have met before. That is why you may have caught me scrutinising you."

Mr Wickham appeared puzzled. "Unfortunately, I do not believe we have met before, Miss Elizabeth. If we had, I would have certainly remembered you."

"Where could you have met him, Lizzy?" Lydia interjected. "Perhaps in London, when you visited Aunt Gardiner? Or have you been in Hertfordshire before, Mr Wickham?"

"We might have met briefly in London without being properly introduced," Mr Wickham agreed. "And no, I have never been to this part of the country before. In fact, I spent my childhood and most of my youth in Derbyshire."

"In Derbyshire? Does your family own an estate there?" Lady Lucas asked.

"No, ma'am. Although an excellent man, my father was only a steward. He was in charge of the management of a very large estate. Pemberley."

His statement intrigued Elizabeth, and her curiosity grew. She noticed the others were also surprised by such a coincidence.

"Pemberley? Mr Darcy's estate?" asked Mr Collins impatiently.

"Yes. I assume you are familiar with the name," Mr Wickham answered with calm and a trace of a smile. "I know Lady Catherine de Bourgh is closely related to the Darcys."

"She is, indeed! She has spoken of her late sister, Lady Anne, very often. Her daughter bears the same name."

Obviously happy to be in possession of much information on the subject, Mr Collins looked dangerously animated, so Elizabeth intervened.

"My aunt grew up in Lambton as a child. She still holds fond memories of Pemberley and calls it the most beautiful place she has ever seen."

"I certainly agree with your aunt, Miss Elizabeth. I doubt there is another place as beautiful as Pemberley."

"I assure you that Rosings Park—" Mr Collins interjected, but Elizabeth quickly stopped him.

"I assume you are closely acquainted with the Darcys, Mr Wickham."

"I am... Better said, I was. I have hardly seen any of the family or even visited Pemberley in the last five years since my parents then the late Mr Darcy died."

"Oh... May we ask why?" Sir William asked, paying no attention to Mr Collins, who was on the verge of intervening once more.

"I would rather not discuss the details. All I can say is that the late Mr Darcy loved me and supported me my entire life and even left me with the means to make an honourable living for myself. Unfortunately, the present master of Pemberley does not share his father's affection and desire to support me. Quite the opposite. He refused to honour my godfather's wish, denying me the living that he bestowed upon me."

"That we can easily believe!" Lydia exclaimed. "We all know that Mr Darcy is arrogant, proud, and insufferable, and nobody likes him!"

"Lydia, enough!" Elizabeth censured her sister severely, more and more astonished and puzzled by Mr Wickham's confession. She felt offended on Mr Darcy's behalf hearing her sister speak so ill of him, but her curiosity in regard to his connection to Mr Wickham was even greater.

Lydia's outburst had a significant effect on Mr Wickham. His countenance immediately changed, his cheeks reddening. He frowned and stood up from his chair.

"Are you acquainted with Darcy?" he asked with apparent perturbation.

"Yes, yes! More than we like!" Lydia responded. "He is Mr Bingley's friend and is staying at Netherfield. He has even visited us a few times. I do not know why Papa keeps inviting him!"

"Darcy is here? In Meryton?"

"Indeed, he is," Sir William confirmed.

Elizabeth watched Mr Wickham's face change colour again, this time to white, and his expression betrayed a mixture of feelings.

"How can it be? How unexpected indeed... What a coincidence," Mr Wickham mumbled.

"That is what I wished to tell you earlier, but nobody listens to me," Mr Collins interjected with a trace of bitterness. "I too consider it an extraordinary coincidence, about which I have written to Lady Catherine already."

"I am sure Lady Catherine was thrilled," Mr Wickham said in a cutting tone, visibly annoyed. "Do you know whether Darcy will remain long in the neighbourhood," he then asked Sir William.

"I have no knowledge of Mr Darcy's plans," Sir William

answered, appearing nervous.

"So, I do not understand... May I ask... Are you and Mr Darcy related?" Lady Lucas asked, her brow crinkled in confusion.

Mr Wickham made an obvious effort to compose himself before answering.

"No, ma'am. The late Mr Darcy was my godfather, and as I mentioned, he loved me and cared for me like I was his son — something that his actual son did not approve of and held against me. We are not related in any other way," Mr Wickham concluded, his voice bearing none of its previous amiability and charm.

While the others were still glancing at each other, he looked at Mr Denny and then addressed his hosts.

"Sir William, Lady Lucas, please accept my gratitude for welcoming me into your family so warmly. I must leave now, but I hope we shall meet again soon."

"It was our pleasure, Mr Wickham. Please know you will always be welcome at Lucas Lodge," Sir William replied, while the officers bade their farewells.

From the door, Mr Wickham glanced back, and his eyes met Elizabeth's for a brief moment. And it was in that instant, as she looked at his face, his thin lips twisted into a sad smile, but a hint of fear betrayed by the small crease between his brows and the glint in his green eyes, that Elizabeth remembered where and when she had seen George Wickham before.

The revelation stirred some deep feelings that made Elizabeth absent to everything. Memories invaded her, while she only heard pieces of conversation between Sir William and Mr Collins, then her sisters, Charlotte, and Lady Lucas speaking, and the names Darcy and Wickham reached her ears several times.

Another half an hour passed until, at Elizabeth's insistence, the visit ended. It was getting rather late, and the air had become chilly. Elizabeth's thoughts were disturbed by the chatter around her, and she longed to be home and have some rest and peace in her room to think of all that she had learnt. Whatever had happened between Mr Darcy and Mr Wickham, it sounded serious, and the little she had heard did not speak well of Mr Darcy's character. And as for George Wickham, how much and in what way had he changed since their harsh argument in the halls of Pemberley?

Their group was on its way back to Longbourn when she heard Lydia exclaiming again. Finally paying attention to those around her, Elizabeth was stunned to see Mr Wickham, accompanied by Mr Denny and Mr Pratt, approaching them.

To her increasing puzzlement, Mr Wickham moved alongside her and said, "Miss Elizabeth, please forgive my boldness. I promise I shall not bother you for more than a moment. Would you allow me a private word? I shall not detain you at all. We shall escort you towards your house."

"Yes, of course," she accepted in wonder. She could not imagine what he wished to say to her. Had he recognised her too?

Mr Collins quickly came to her other side, and she said harshly, "Mr Collins, please allow me some privacy to discuss a certain matter with Mr Wickham. You may walk with my sisters and the other officers."

Her tone allowed no argument, and whilst offended by her demand, the clergyman stepped away.

Elizabeth slowed her pace, walking slightly behind the others with Mr Wickham.

"Miss Elizabeth, I must beg your forgiveness for my awkward and un-gentlemanlike behaviour. Instead of sharing pleasant memories about Pemberley, I acted like a savage. I have no excuse other than my history with Darcy is difficult and painful. I hope to have a chance to explain it to you, especially since my current assignment forces me to cross paths with Darcy."

"Sir, there is no need to apologise to me. You certainly did not act like a savage. I confess I was intrigued by your connection to the Darcys, but you need not explain anything more to me," she said, trying to sound polite but not betray her real interest.

"I hope my past with Darcy will not forbid me from becoming a friend of your family."

"Mr Wickham, I pride myself on being able to judge my friends not by their past but by their present actions towards me."

"I am glad to hear that, Miss Elizabeth," he said, and Elizabeth tried to comprehend the reason for his interest in her good opinion and wondered for how long he intended to escort her.

Then Mr Wickham stopped, and so did the rest of their group. Still caught up in her thoughts, it was several moments before Elizabeth noticed Mr Bingley and Mr Darcy, on their horses, gazing at them. One of them dismounted, with a large smile and joyful greetings, while the other, frowning and silent, remained in the saddle, gazing at Elizabeth and her companion.

Chapter 11

The rest of the group was busy talking to Mr Bingley, but Elizabeth felt caught between the two men, the tension between them palpable. Mr Darcy's expression showed surprise, disgust, and repressed anger, while Mr Wickham seemed anxious and restless.

Mr Darcy bowed his head to Elizabeth, while Mr Wickham did the same to Mr Darcy, but his courtesy was not returned.

"We are on our way to visit Colonel Forster, and we called at Longbourn briefly," Mr Bingley explained. "Mrs Bennet informed us you were in Meryton, and how fortunate that we have met!"

"We visited Lucas Lodge and are just returning home now," Jane answered, blushing most becomingly.

"Would you like us to escort you home?" Mr Bingley asked.

"No, that is not necessary," Jane said, her voice trembling slightly. "Colonel Forster must be expecting you, and we already have our cousin with us, as well as Mr Denny, Mr Pratt, and Mr Wickham, who has just joined the regiment. Are you acquainted with him?"

"No, I am not," Bingley responded in the same joyful manner, proving to Elizabeth that Mr Wickham and his past with Mr Darcy were completely unknown to Mr Bingley.

Jane was the one who performed the introductions, and all the time Mr Darcy remained on his horse, a short distance away, as if he was undecided whether to stay or leave.

"Mr Bingley, do you intend to host a ball, as you

promised?" Lydia enquired abruptly.

"Yes, I shall, Miss Lydia! A promise is a promise. In fact, I shall speak to Colonel Forster about it today."

"Will you? I knew you were a man of your word! I hope you will invite all the officers," she continued, while Elizabeth could see Jane's face colouring from embarrassment and assumed hers looked the same.

"Of course, Miss Lydia," Mr Bingley said.

"Including Mr Denny, Mr Pratt, and Mr Wickham, yes?" Lydia insisted, turning her back to her eldest sisters in an obvious attempt to avoid their reproachful glares.

"Certainly, Miss Lydia."

"Excellent. This is wonderful! But sir, please keep in mind that now you have promised, you cannot go back on your word, even if someone might be displeased with you inviting some of the officers," Lydia concluded, and with horror, Elizabeth saw her sister glancing at Mr Darcy meaningfully.

"Lydia, enough!" Elizabeth interjected. "Mind your manners and your words, or I shall ask Papa not to allow you to attend the ball."

Such a severe outburst in the middle of the street was so unexpected that the gentlemen seemed puzzled, and Lydia looked to be on the verge of tears.

"But Lizzy, why...?"

Mr Collins attempted to speak, but Jane ended any argument decidedly.

"Lydia, enough, please! We shall continue this conversation at Longbourn. Gentlemen, please forgive us. It is late, and we must hurry home." With that, Jane curtseyed to Mr Bingley, then she grabbed Lydia and Kitty's arms and started to walk.

"We shall escort you a little farther," Mr Wickham said, and the party moved on.

Elizabeth turned her head, watching Mr Bingley standing by his horse, appearing disconcerted. Near him, still in the saddle, Mr Darcy gazed at her silently, then suddenly he turned his horse and urged him into a canter.

"Well, that was awkward," Mr Wickham said.

"Uncomfortable indeed. Mr Darcy was surely surprised to see you."

"I would say he was shocked," Mr Wickham said. "He looked like he had seen a ghost."

His tone — light and careless — irritated Elizabeth. "I would say you both looked uncomfortable. May I ask when you last met?"

"Um…a few years ago. As I mentioned, I have not been welcome at Pemberley since my godfather died."

"You did mention it, but it would still have been possible for you to have met in other places."

"I am not welcomed anywhere near Darcy," Mr Wickham continued. "Not even by those members of the family with whom I was once friends."

"What a pity… That means you have not seen Miss Darcy since she was a child?" Elizabeth asked. She remembered Georgiana claiming George Wickham was her only friend and worried how the poor girl had managed to balance her affection between her friend and her brother.

"Precisely…" Wickham replied after a brief hesitation. "She was a sweet child and very fond of me, but I have heard she has grown to be very much like Darcy in pride and arrogance."

"Has she?" Elizabeth replied, gazing at him, intrigued and doubtful. Mr Wickham's countenance changed again, and Elizabeth's irritation increased. Was he so resentful towards Mr Darcy that his rage now encompassed his young sister?

"I am surprised to hear such a claim, sir. I mean, how can a girl as young as Lydia be as proud and arrogant as a gentleman of almost twice her age?" Her reproachful enquiry seemed to disquiet Mr Wickham, and he turned his gaze towards the rest of the group.

"I shall not deny that the claim might be exaggerated. Speaking of your sister Lydia, I must thank her for her brave intervention to assure my presence at the ball," Mr Wickham said in a jesting tone. "It could be the only place Darcy and I might appear together in years."

"Mr Wickham, please be so kind as to delay your thanks for another occasion. While we would be glad to see you and all the officers at the ball, I am not particularly happy with the way my sister tricked Mr Bingley, and I would not like to encourage such behaviour."

"You are correct, of course, Miss Elizabeth. I selfishly thought only that your sister did me a great favour. Now Darcy has seen me, he will do anything to remove me from any list of guests. I might not be allowed to speak to you again if he has any influence over your father."

"Mr Wickham, whatever past dealings you may have had with Mr Darcy, I assure you they will not affect me. I am curious though — why did you wish to have this conversation with me? Why are you providing me with details of your relationship with Mr Darcy? And may I ask, why would you care if we were not to speak again? We have only just become acquainted. My opinion cannot mean anything to you."

"You are wrong, Miss Elizabeth. Your opinion is important to me. Even though we have only just met, I am impressed with your manners and your wit. And I know from Denny that your opinion does matter to the people of Meryton. Even Sir William admitted it."

Elizabeth's puzzlement only increased. She felt uncomfortable and nervous with the entire situation and longed for the solitude of her room to gather her thoughts.

"Sir William is a well-intentioned gentleman. However, he has a tendency to exaggerate. I assure you, there are few people to whom my opinion matters at all. I have already mentioned that I shall not judge your character based only on your past behaviour. If I was to do that, I would not be speaking to you at this moment."

Longbourn was only just around the corner, and Elizabeth felt relieved that they would finally separate from the officers. The entire situation with Mr Wickham was too sudden, too confusing, and simply too much.

"What do you mean, Miss Elizabeth? You would not speak to me? I am puzzled, I confess," Mr Wickham asked with apparent disquiet.

Elizabeth smiled. "Do not worry, sir. It is mostly a joke, which I have no time to elaborate on now. What I meant is that we met very recently, without being properly introduced and — obviously — without you recognising me."

Mr Wickham's frown affected his features, and his voice betrayed his worry.

"Are you speaking in earnest, Miss Elizabeth? Have we met before? On what occasion? It was related to Darcy, I assume?"

"No, not to Mr Darcy, but to his sister, Miss Georgiana Darcy."

The statement, spoken in a light voice, seemed to alter Mr Wickham's manner even more, and his gestures of nervousness became awkward. For a moment, Elizabeth assumed that perhaps Mr Wickham acknowledged his faults and his betrayal of Georgiana's trust and repented it. He certainly deserved to be tormented by regrets, even after ten years.

"Miss Darcy? But where? When? I do not understand."

"Mr Wickham, let us speak more another time. We have finally arrived home, and I am very tired. Good day, sir. It was a pleasure meeting you."

With that, she stepped away from him and grabbed Lydia's arm, ceasing any opportunity for further discussion. Lydia even suggested the officers might enter, but Jane quickly repeated a farewell and Mr Collins, happy to escape from the male rivals, bowed formally and turned, leaving the men to watch their retreating backs.

While Kitty and Lydia started to chat with their mother, relating news that they called extraordinary, Elizabeth and Jane withdrew to their room.

"That was such a tiring day... Strange and tiring," Jane whispered as they prepared for dinner.

"Strange and tiring indeed," Elizabeth admitted.

"You spoke quite a lot to Mr Wickham, Lizzy. Was there something particular you spoke of? I do not wish to intrude, but I found it puzzling since you had only just met."

"We mostly spoke of Mr Darcy. Why Mr Wickham was interested in any conversation with me puzzled me too at first. However, I then remembered that I had met him before."

"Before? When?"

"Ten years ago," Elizabeth replied, amused by her sister's stunned expression. "I shall tell you more tonight before we sleep. We should make haste — dinner will be ready soon."

***

In Colonel Forster's drawing room, Darcy felt so restless and so irritated that he barely noticed what was happening around him. He doubted his eyes and questioned his bad luck. How was it possible that the scoundrel who had disturbed his tranquillity for so many years was there? He had apparently joined the militia, and of all the regiments in the country, he happened to be in Meryton. What puzzled Darcy more was that Wickham had looked surprised to see him, but not quite as stunned as such an encounter should provoke. Had he already been aware they were both in the same place?

Even worse, what was he doing speaking privately to Miss Elizabeth? They had been walking a few steps behind the others, so they must have had something of interest to discuss. Could Miss Elizabeth be among those easily charmed by Wickham? It was possible. After all, she was young enough, and likely she lacked experience. When did she meet him? He was tempted to ask the colonel when Wickham had joined the regiment, but that would necessitate providing a reason for his interest, and he did not feel comfortable offering any.

He had agreed to accompany Bingley only to avoid

remaining at Netherfield with just Miss Bingley and the Hursts. The two sisters appeared to have a favourite topic of conversation — criticising the Bennet family — and Darcy felt less and less able to remain polite in front of their rudeness.

He grew more annoyed with every passing minute and sought a way to speed their departure, but Bingley was deep in conversation. The subject of the ball was amply debated, but for Darcy, it held no interest since he did not expect to stay in Hertfordshire till then.

Eventually, Bingley seemed to notice his restlessness and bring the call to an end, but first, he introduced one more subject.

"We have just been introduced to one of your officers — Mr Wickham. I understand he has joined the militia recently."

"Ah yes, Wickham. He is a friend of Denny and indeed only joined our regiment a few days ago. I hear he has already become a favourite with both his colleagues and the ladies," the colonel said meaningfully "I have not yet discovered in him any skills necessary for an officer, though. Thank God there is no war in Meryton!"

"Wickham is gifted with such happy manners that help him make friends easily. That he is able to keep them is less certain," Darcy interjected.

His statement startled both the colonel and his wife.

"Well, he has been a friend of Denny's for a long time," Mrs Forster said defensively.

"Have you a prior acquaintance with Wickham, Mr Darcy?"

"I have, Colonel."

"I assume your opinion of him is not entirely good. May I ask why?"

"My reasons are too personal to be shared. I am sure you will watch him carefully and will examine his behaviour so you can form your own opinion. I would be relieved to hear it differed from mine."

"I see... Well, as you said, it is my duty to watch over

my officers closely and to judge their behaviour. So far, I have no reason to distrust Denny, so his recommendation was sufficient to accept Wickham under my command."

"I am sure your trust in Mr Denny is justified, Colonel. As I said, I hope Wickham will prove worthy of your trust too. After all, men do change from time to time."

With that, he and Bingley left, but Darcy did not miss Mrs Forster staring disapprovingly at him as he bowed.

During the short ride back to Netherfield, all kinds of thoughts stormed into Darcy's head. In a cunning display of artifice, Wickham had again been successful in his plan to trick people of good, upright character. Clearly, Mrs Forster favoured him — like many other ladies — and the colonel himself did not disapprove of the scoundrel. Such opinions were only too familiar to Darcy; all too often he had seen how easily Wickham could charm his way into society.

Within him, indignation raged, almost to the point of turning round his horse and hastening to meet the man. A strong determination to deliver a blow upon that cur's countenance was growing inside him.

It was only the knowledge that doing so would expose him to ridicule and unwanted speculation about his motives that prevented him. In the delicate balance between triumph and defeat, Darcy was aware he would most certainly be on the side of the latter.

"What about Miss Bennet?" he found himself uttering almost against his will.

A sharp pain crossed his chest. Yes, he could tell Mr Bennet the truth about Wickham and ask him to keep the rascal away from his daughters. But knowing Elizabeth liked him was painful to bear regardless. The feeling was strong and disturbing, and he wondered about it, as he had never experienced it before.

Once at Netherfield, the gentlemen each hurried to their rooms to prepare for dinner. Darcy could feel Bingley's curiosity, and he expected some questions but was not prepared to answer yet. He even contemplated not attending dinner, but that would not discourage his friend's enquiries. Quite the opposite.

As soon as he entered his chamber, he noticed the letters on the table. There were three — one from his solicitor, one from his cousin Colonel Fitzwilliam, and finally the one he had waited for so eagerly from Georgiana.

That one he picked up and opened carefully, then poured himself a drink, put another log on the fire, lit another candle, and started to read.

Chapter 12

Dear Brother,

I cannot express how astonished I was by the content of your last letter.

I confess I needed to think carefully because at first, I could not recollect anything in regard to such a girl. But then, some memories returned, but except for the name Lizzy, I could not remember much. I even asked Aunt, but she did not know much either.

I hope you do not mind, but I sent an express to Mrs Reynolds myself, asking her to tell me everything she knows about Miss Lizzy. That you happened to meet her by pure chance is extraordinary indeed, and the notion that she still remembers me and has cared for me all these years is even more astounding. Please do not think I doubt her words — or yours. Quite the contrary, I am glad that you seem to approve of her. Everything you have told me about the past, as well as your description of her in the present, sounds intriguing and captivating.

However, I wonder whether I deserve someone outside the family to have held me in regard for ten years without even seeing me.

If you do not object, I would certainly like to write to Miss Elizabeth; yet, I have to wonder if she will be disappointed in me. If she knew the entire truth in regard to my flaws, I am certain she will be.

From the little you have told me, it seems she has grown up to be a remarkable young lady, which cannot be compared to my silly weakness of character. Her seeming affection for me, which has lasted for ten years, might vanish if she comes to know me.

I am eagerly waiting for Mrs Reynolds's reply. As for Miss Elizabeth's request to write to me, I beg you to decide on my behalf. I trust you know best.

Your comments about her disliking you and your rudeness I shall take as a joke, as I doubt it truly happened. I cannot see anything wanting in you, and I doubt any lady would.

I thank you for always thinking of me, and I am sending you my sincere love and regards.

Yours,

G

Darcy read the letter several times, each with heartache and sorrow. He had expected that his sister, being only five at the time, would not recollect much of her friendship with Elizabeth, but the way Georgiana disrespected herself and considered herself unworthy of a friendship was unbearable.

However, her curiosity and interest in Elizabeth were obvious, and with the information from Mrs Reynolds, it would certainly increase. He could feel her interest in the tone of the letter — something she had completely lacked recently.

That she trusted him to decide in regard to Elizabeth was touching but equally painful, as it proved Georgiana's distrust in her own judgment. His decision was made, and it seemed to be the only means to slightly lessen his sister's sadness.

Putting the missive aside to consider later, he opened the letter from his cousin and read it in a hurry.

Darcy,

I usually refrain from advising you, as you have proved yourself capable of dealing with your own business and family matters remarkably well without anyone's involvement.

However, I feel it is my right and my duty to express my opinion in regard to Georgiana, since I am her cousin and her guardian.

I visited her several days ago, and I have to say I am exceedingly worried about how pale and thin she looks. She has never been overly animated, but the little liveliness she possessed is now gone. She practises her instrument every day, but she avoids going out, even at my mother's invitation.

Mrs Annesley confessed to me that she too is concerned about Georgiana's lack of appetite and low spirits and that she has called for the doctor several times. To be honest, I do not think Mrs Annesley is enough company for Georgiana. I do admit she was an excellent choice, that she is honourable and educated and has formed a genuine attachment to Georgiana, but Mrs Annesley provides Georgiana with the same sort of companionship as my mother. They are both like caring but much older aunts. Georgiana has no friend, no one to speak to, no one to confide in. My brother's wife is closer in age but lacks the right temperament to become Georgiana's friend and confidante.

I still believe that you are the closest person to Georgiana and the one she loves, admires, and trusts the most. I am not sure why you chose to stay in Hertfordshire instead of being in London with her, but I truly believe your presence would be useful to her, even if she does not admit it.

If I can help in any way, please let me know, and I shall do everything in my power.

RF

Although the letter did not tell Darcy anything new, it increased his distress. Colonel Fitzwilliam was not a man to become easily concerned, so his words had to be taken with utter seriousness, and Darcy threw back the rest of his drink while trying to gather the composure needed for dinner.

He understood his cousin's puzzlement about him staying at Netherfield, and perhaps he was correct in suggesting he return to London. Or perhaps he should maintain the distance for his sister's comfort and instead introduce her to someone else who may be of more use to her. Someone of the right age who also possessed the nature and manners to bond with her and the desire to comfort her.

Regardless, his stay in Hertfordshire must come to an end. He would prepare for his return and inform Bingley about it. But before he left, he wished to encourage Elizabeth to begin writing to his sister.

Also, should she happen to be in London, Elizabeth could visit Georgiana. Her presence would certainly benefit Georgiana, of that he had no doubt. Even without their prior acquaintance, he became more and more certain that Elizabeth could help his sister fight her turmoil, dislike, and disrespect for herself.

However, Darcy now faced a new obstacle that had to be removed. The gentleman who had caused Georgiana's grief and crushed her spirit was there, claiming a new career in the militia, and everyone apparently approved of him. It was this matter that he needed to take care of first, without delay. That required an immediate discussion with Elizabeth, and probably with Mr Bennet too, which he planned for the following morning. He considered taking another early morning ride to Oakham Mount, hoping to meet Elizabeth, but he abandoned the idea. The matter was too important to leave to chance.

After a dinner with no appetite and little patience for Miss Bingley and Mrs Hurst's irritating criticism of everybody in the neighbourhood, followed by a sleepless night filled with more disturbing dreams than rest, Darcy woke up at dawn realising the matter might be more urgent than he had previously estimated, and his sister in greater need of companionship, comfort, and protection than he had initially believed.

He was still in such a state of perturbation when he and Bingley called at Longbourn the next morning, immediately after breakfast.

***

"So, Lizzy, who is this Mr Wickham your sisters have talked about incessantly since yesterday? He sounds so perfect that he already irritates me," Mr Bennet said. "Besides, I find it puzzling that he chose to share his past misfortunes with your youngest sisters. That is enough to question his judgment."

"Do not worry, Papa, he is far from being perfect. At least I believe so. I have heard varying reports of him, and I do not know him well enough to fix his character. I have some past knowledge of him and some recent observations to add to his own claims."

"Past knowledge? Have you met him before?"

"I have. Ten years ago, when I stayed in Derbyshire with my aunt. As for his past dealings with Mr Darcy, in fact he started sharing it with me, and the others overheard it."

"Did he remember meeting you before?"

"Not at all, Papa."

"In that case, sharing his past with you was equally improper. To him, you were a stranger, no more trustworthy than Lydia or Kitty."

"I agree. I admit being intrigued that Mr Darcy could hold a grudge against Mr Wickham without good reason. If you do not mind, I shall speak to Mr Darcy about Mr Wickham next time we meet."

"If Mr Darcy agrees to speak to you, I shall certainly not oppose it. But are you sure it is appropriate for you to interfere?"

"I observed Mr Darcy was deeply affected by their meeting, but the gentlemen's business is their own. My concern is in regard to Miss Darcy. I felt uncomfortable about how Mr Wickham spoke of Georgiana. He sounded resentful of her, and I cannot forget how he took advantage of her when we were young. If only for all the benefits he gained from his connection to her family, he should mind his words about her."

"Dear Lizzy, I have to say this is too much drama for me, and it is giving me a headache. Do as you wish, as I intend to finish my book. By the by, I have already completed the one you brought me from Netherfield. I should return it to Mr Bingley."

"You can do so now, Papa. I see Mr Darcy and Mr Bingley approaching. Oh dear, Mr Collins is already on the drive ready to greet them. Let us hope they will not run away when they see him," she joked, trying to conceal her sudden blush and the baffling racing of her heart.

Elizabeth and her father entered the drawing room moments before the visitors were introduced.

The guests were received with pleasure by Mrs Bennet and her daughters and with obvious partiality towards Mr Bingley. Mr Darcy was welcomed with politeness and restraint, and he responded in the same manner. While Mr Bingley took a seat between Mrs Bennet and Jane, Mr Darcy chose to accept Mr Bennet's invitation to join him in the library. Mr Collins looked disconcerted, as he was disregarded by both parties. He rose to accompany the gentlemen to the library, but Mr Darcy suddenly requested privacy, claiming he had a private matter to discuss with Mr Bennet.

With a look of confusion, Mr Collins sat on the sofa next to Elizabeth, much to her despair. Paying little attention to her cousin's speech, she wondered about the private matter between the two men. She had rarely seen her father so interested in being in the company of another man, except for her uncle Gardiner. Since she knew that her father was not impressed by Mr Darcy's situation in life, she assumed there must be something the two of them had in common, despite their obvious differences.

As in their prior meetings, the Bennet ladies and Mr Bingley were talking about the ball.

Mr Collins seemed interested and declared that such entertainment organised by an honourable gentleman was by no means disagreeable to a clergyman.

"Dear Cousin Elizabeth, I look forward to dancing with you and all my other cousins. May I ask why you are so quiet today? Your opinion is truly missed."

"There is not much left to say on the subject, so my opinion can bring no value to the conversation, Mr Collins. Now please excuse me, I must see whether my father needs my assistance."

"Your assistance?" Mrs Bennet intervened. "Why on

earth would he need your assistance, Lizzy?"

To avoid answering, Elizabeth pretended she did not hear the question and left the room. She hesitated to disturb her father, but her curiosity was too strong, and returning to the drawing-room was not appealing, so she breathed deeply and knocked on the library door.

The invitation to enter came after a brief delay, but when she stepped in, her father welcomed her with a large gesture.

"Lizzy, how fortunate that you are here. Mr Darcy and I were just talking about you."

"I am sorry you could not find a more diverting subject," she replied, casting a glance at Mr Darcy, who looked as serious as ever.

"As always, I enjoy your teasing, my child, but you should sit down, as the matter is very serious."

Elizabeth looked at Mr Darcy again, then at her father. Both men wore a frown which supported Mr Bennet's statement.

"What is it, Papa?"

"I shall actually let Mr Darcy tell you, since it is his proposal, and it is addressed to you. I confess I was surprised when I heard it, and you will probably be the same."

With another glance at Mr Darcy, Elizabeth finally sat.

"What proposal could it be, Papa."

"Do not worry, he does not intend to propose marriage to you. That is a pleasure you should probably expect from my cousin."

"Papa!" Elizabeth cried, mortified by such an improper, poor attempt at a joke. "Surely it cannot be something too serious, since you are not serious at all," she scolded him.

"Forgive me, Lizzy. I shall move into the corner by the window with my glass and my book and let Mr Darcy explain everything to you."

He did so while Elizabeth turned to Mr Darcy, intrigued and still flustered from her father's jesting.

"Miss Bennet, I shall start by saying that I have received

a letter from my sister, and she is as thrilled as I expected by my encounter with you and the prospect of her meeting you too. In truth, she does not remember much about your time together, since she was very young, but she has glimpses of recollections and a dear wish to renew your acquaintance."

"This is wonderful news, Mr Darcy!" Elizabeth answered with genuine delight.

"I believe so too. My sister does not have many friends… in fact, she shows no desire to make new acquaintances, and except for her companion, Mrs Annesley, and our relatives, she rarely sees other people. I truly believe that your friendship will be of great help to her."

"To me too, I assure you! Just yesterday I wrote to my aunt again and expressed my hope for such news. I shall write to Miss Darcy even today, before dinner!"

While Elizabeth rejoiced in the news, she could see Mr Darcy's frown had not abated, and he cleared his throat before continuing.

"There is more that must be said, and my proposal — or I should say my plea to you — still has to be expressed."

"Please speak freely, Mr Darcy. After you have brought me such happy news, you may ask me anything." She tried to sound lightly to encourage him.

"You have asked me more than once whether Georgiana is in good health. She is — there is nothing that the doctor has found while examining her, except for…how should I put it? A lack of liveliness and self-confidence. She spends most of her time practising the pianoforte and finds little enjoyment in anything else."

"You sound rather worried, Mr Darcy. More worried than your description would suggest. After all, my sister Mary also finds little enjoyment in anything but her study and practice. We are all different."

"True. But there is more, and I cannot voice it properly. What I mean is that, while she has never expressed such a wish, I am certain Georgiana needs the company of someone closer to her age, someone she can confide in, someone who can support and guide her with affection and patience. Apparently, neither an older brother nor an aunt or cousins, not even her teachers or Mrs Annesley are capable of accomplishing such a thing."

Elizabeth listened to him with growing concern; his expression spoke of deeper reasons for worry than his words voiced.

She tried to guess his meaning, but she felt so overwhelmed by the effort that she waited for his proposal with uncertainty.

"The more I have come to know your nature and your character, Miss Bennet, the more I have become convinced that you are the only one who might help my sister find what is missing in her life. I wish only to know that she is healthy, safe, and happy, and I fear I have failed. This is why I am asking — I am begging you — to continue the friendship that started ten years ago, not only through correspondence but also in person. To stay with her for a while, so she can learn from you what her teachers could not teach her and to enjoy that sort of intimacy which her present companion cannot provide."

Elizabeth glanced at her father, noticing he was watching them, while she tried to fully comprehend Mr Darcy's request.

"You wish me to go to London to be your sister's companion?"

"No. She has a companion. I wish you to be her friend. To be the same Miss Lizzy that Mrs Reynolds mentioned in her letter and my mother was deeply fond of."

Elizabeth gulped at the lump in her throat. She stared at Mr Darcy in shock, barely able to reply.

"You flatter me, sir, and I am not certain I am worthy of your trust."

"I have complete confidence in you, Miss Bennet. Please believe me. I have given this matter much consideration in the last few days, and I fully understand it will be a significant effort which might disturb the comfort of your family."

"That would not be an issue, sir. I would do anything for Miss Darcy if she needed and wished for my help. I could go to London and stay with my uncle and aunt for a while and visit her often if that is agreeable to you."

"Anything you want would be agreeable to me. However, to be honest, I was considering that, after becoming reacquainted with Georgiana, you may like to move in with her, to live with her, so you can be with her all the time. However, I understand that might be inconvenient for you, so I shall be grateful for anything you decide."

Elizabeth could not conceal her astonishment and looked at her father quizzically again.

Under usual circumstances, the chance to meet Georgiana and spend time with her would have been enough to make Elizabeth exceedingly happy, and she was tempted to accept immediately. However, that would mean she had to go to London and stay in Mr Darcy's house, which immediately increased her anxiety.

Even more disquieting, Mr Darcy's voice, his eyes, and his entire countenance proved that he was truly begging, and that betrayed the depth of his concern and the gravity of Georgiana's situation.

A cold shiver of apprehension ran through her. He had said the decision was hers, but that was not entirely true.

"Mr Darcy, meeting your sister again is something that I have hoped for more than ten years. I shall write to my aunt and make the arrangements for my travel to London. But first, I must talk to my father. He will decide what should be done."

"Of course. That is why I took the liberty of addressing your father first. I must return to London at the end of this week, but I shall wait for news from Mr Bennet. Please allow me to make the arrangements for your journey to town. I could send you my carriage, and perhaps Mr Bennet might travel with you. Also, if you wish for one or more of your sisters to join you, that would also be agreeable. Furthermore, whilst she is living in my house at present, my sister also has her own establishment, close to mine, so if my presence is a reason for concern, please know you can move to a different residence with Georgiana and Mrs Annesley…"

He became more and more animated as he spoke, while Elizabeth and Mr Bennet glanced at each other.

"Mr Darcy, now that you have Lizzy's acceptance, let us discuss further details over another drink while my daughter returns to the drawing room."

"Of course, Mr Bennet," Mr Darcy replied, and Elizabeth stood up, ready to leave.

"For the time being, I would suggest that, except for the three of us and perhaps Jane, everyone else be told that Lizzy is going to London to visit her uncle and aunt. I shall write to my brother and sister to conceive a little plan."

"Thank you, Mr Bennet. I am sorry to give you so much trouble."

"Do not mention it, Mr Darcy. I must consider whether I am to travel with her or if she takes one of her sisters. It depends on how soon you expect Elizabeth to meet your sister, as everyone is obsessed with this ball now."

"Of course, I hope to see Miss Elizabeth in London as soon as possible, but you and she will choose the time."

Before she left, Elizabeth felt the urge to ask the question that had bothered her for the last two days. She knew it was not entirely proper, but it might affect her final decision, and since he would leave soon, she might not have another chance to address it.

"Mr Darcy, you mentioned your sister has no friends at all. However, I remember that even in her childhood, she was very fond of George Wickham, who is here in Meryton, as you know. I understand you have not allowed him to see her lately, but perhaps his presence might entertain and amuse her."

At the very mention of the name, Mr Darcy's face pinched and paled, his eyes narrowed, and his lips pressed together as though trying to prevent an outburst.

"I assume Wickham has already told you some of his complaints against me, Miss Bennet. I assume he told you that I denied him a living…"

"He did…but it is not my business to interfere in gentlemen's affairs. I was only thinking of Miss Darcy's pleasure in meeting an old friend."

"George Wickham is nobody's friend unless he has something to gain from it. He did see Georgiana a few months ago, in the summer, and he betrayed her trust and abused her affection, as he always does with everybody who allows him to. His actions only added to her present unfortunate state and made her lose the little faith she had in people."

Elizabeth's heart ached, and an odd fear enveloped her, again sensing that Mr Darcy's statement hid something deeper and more painful. She suddenly remembered Mr Wickham claiming he had not seen Georgiana for many years, and his effrontery irritated her. Could he have taken her for a fool and lied to her so boldly?

"Lizzy, it is time you returned to your sisters," Mr Bennet said, dismissing her. "Let everybody know I am not to be disturbed until I have completed my business with Mr Darcy. In fact, I shall lock the door to avoid any interference."

"Very well, Papa," Elizabeth replied, walking towards the door, still shaken by the gravity of everything that had happened in such a short time.

"Miss Bennet!"

Mr Darcy's voice startled her, and she turned to face him. He walked towards her, and to her disbelief, he took her hand for a moment and bowed over it.

"Thank you, Miss Lizzy," he said, adding so much meaning to that simple sentence that she quivered again, feeling that her hand, which he had just released, was burning.

Chapter 13

Darcy and Bingley dismounted in front of Netherfield and handed their reins to a servant.

"You spent quite a lot of time with Mr Bennet, Darcy. Upon my word, I would have never imagined you two having so many mutual interests to talk about."

"We do, in fact. And to be honest, we employed our time better than talking about the ball or listening to Mr Collins's nonsense."

"I assumed as much. Speaking of Mr Collins, I noticed he pays particular interest to Miss Elizabeth. I believe Mrs Bennet encourages him. He might intend to propose to her."

"Mr Collins is without sense. He is so infatuated that he is confident in her reception of his addresses. If he does propose, he might suffer a well-deserved rejection."

"How can you be so certain that he will be rejected, Darcy? I do agree that he and Miss Elizabeth are completely ill-suited, and I doubt she would be happy if she married him, but he is a desirable enough match. I doubt many women with such an uncertain future would reject him, and probably many parents would force their daughters into such a marriage."

"I am quite confident Miss Elizabeth will reject him, Bingley, and that Mr Bennet would never force her into anything."

"My goodness! How can you be so certain, Darcy? I am curious because you barely know either of them."

"I know them well enough. Mr Bennet has already teased me about marrying his daughter, and Miss Elizabeth called it a very bad joke. I am rather certain she would reject me too if the situation arose — and I dare to be so bold as to call myself slightly more attractive than Mr Collins."

They were already in the house, walking towards the drawing room, when Bingley stopped in utter astonishment.

"I do not understand what you mean, Darcy. Did you speak to Mr Bennet and Miss Elizabeth about marriage? Are *you* mocking *me*?"

"No, no, Bingley. It was just a joke. A poor one, as I already mentioned. I shall explain more to you tonight, after dinner. I trust you will be able to keep what I tell you to yourself. It must not be disclosed to anyone just yet."

Bingley blinked repeatedly, a frown between his eyebrows, staring at his friend and struggling to comprehend his bewildering response.

"You have me even more confused, Darcy!"

"I imagine as much. I promise all will be clear after we talk tonight. Now please excuse me, I have some letters to send immediately. My valet will start packing my luggage. I shall return to London the day after tomorrow."

"What? You are leaving? Why? When will you come back? What about the ball?"

"My friend, the ball is the least of my concerns. I am sure it will be even more successful without my presence. Regardless, I cannot stay longer. I am needed in London."

"I have some business in London too, but I thought to go after the ball."

"You should follow your plans, Bingley. If I may be of any help, let me know. However, I am confident that you are perfectly capable of achieving your goals by yourself," Darcy declared, then hurried to his room, leaving behind a still-dumbfounded Bingley.

He did have to write important letters — one to Georgiana, informing her about his return, and one to Colonel Fitzwilliam. But Darcy also wished to be alone and reflect on his discussion with Mr Bennet and Elizabeth. All in all, his mission had been successful. Mr Bennet was even more generous and more considerate than Darcy had expected, and he was willing to somehow deceive his family in order to provide Elizabeth with the opportunity to be close to Georgiana. The final arrangements sounded quite perfect for all parties involved due to Mr Bennet's wisdom and willingness to help. For that, Darcy was deeply grateful and ashamed of his arrogance in misjudging the Bennet family at the beginning of their acquaintance.

As for Elizabeth, her affection for Georgiana was proved once again, revealing more qualities that made her worthy of admiration. Not a trace of doubt remained for Darcy that Elizabeth — *young Lizzy* — was the answer to his prayers and the means to support his sister's recovery and improvement.

The only shadow over their understanding was Wickham. That impertinent scoundrel had already insinuated himself near Elizabeth and her sisters and had begun poisoning Darcy's name. He wondered what he could have said to Elizabeth — and to others. He certainly had not mentioned the Ramsgate incident, since Elizabeth had suggested his friendship might comfort Georgiana. What an outrageous notion!

Darcy realised that, if she ended up agreeing to live with Georgiana, Elizabeth should be informed about the failed elopement. Perhaps he should tell her immediately, but he did not feel either brave or composed enough for such a confession.

The more he thought of it, the more he reached the conclusion that it was his duty to warn Elizabeth and Mr Bennet about Wickham. Perhaps they would dismiss his advice, just as Colonel Forster had, but it was his responsibility nevertheless.

He sealed the letters and closed his eyes, contemplating the future. If everything went according to plan, Elizabeth might live in close proximity to him for a while. As soon as he gave that thought proper consideration, he became distressed, even tormented.

While that was precisely what he wished for, the picture of her being around day after day overwhelmed him. Her company, her nearness, although delightful, was also disquieting. He was certain Elizabeth's presence would be a significant addition to Georgiana's life, but how she would affect his, he was incapable of estimating yet. Besides, he did not matter much. Georgiana's well-being was his priority, and Elizabeth seemed the best suited to provide for it. As for the rest, he would solve it in due time.

***

"Lizzy, close the door," Mr Bennet asked when Elizabeth entered the library at his request. "Before your mother calls us to dinner, let me tell you briefly what I have arranged with Mr Darcy."

"Very well, Papa. You should know that Mama is already curious, and so is Mr Collins. They questioned me rather insistently."

"Yes, well, they will remain unsatisfied, I suspect. Do you wish to attend the Netherfield ball?"

"No, not necessarily, Papa. I would rather go to Georgiana as soon as possible."

"Good. Then I shall write to my brother Gardiner. I shall go to London with you Monday next, and as soon as we arrive, I shall notify Mr Darcy. He will come to call at Gracechurch Street. Then you and I, and your aunt — who was previously acquainted with Lady Anne Darcy — will call and meet Miss Darcy. And from there we shall take it one step at a time."

"Very well, Papa."

"You may tell Jane the truth, and Mr Darcy said he would inform Mr Bingley. I shall tell your mother and everyone else that I have some business in London, and I am taking you with me. I shall also mention briefly that Mr Darcy is helping me with some of my affairs."

"I feel uncomfortable that we have turned a childhood

friendship — something that is nothing to be ashamed of — into a secret," Elizabeth said.

"It was, in fact, my suggestion, Lizzy. Since we are not certain yet how things will turn out — whether you will succeed in renewing your friendship with Miss Darcy or not, whether you are invited to stay with her or not — it would be a tedious, vexing task to be able to explain your mother, Mr Collins, Sir William, and many others how you know Miss Darcy, why Mr Darcy asked you to visit her, and then, if things go wrong, to provide further explanations. It is easier not to mention anything for now, and if all goes well, you may say that you met Miss Darcy in London and befriended her. Simple and easy."

"Your reasoning makes perfect sense, Papa. We shall proceed as you suggest."

"Good. Mr Darcy has indicated that he will cover all your expenses — which was expected of course. He mentioned that, if you and Miss Darcy agree that you will stay with her, you will have the same pin money for the duration of your visit."

"What?" Elizabeth cried, feeling her cheeks burning with anger and affront. "Does Mr Darcy intend to pay for my friendship?"

"Calm down, Lizzy, and lower your voice. Resume your seat, please. My child, you are too hasty in judging people and situations, and at times you fail to use your reason. May I ask, if you happen to go to the opera or theatre with Miss Darcy, as her friend, what will you wear in order to not feel embarrassed? You will be watched and judged by people in her circle. Will you purchase one dress and one pair of shoes and wear them everywhere? Or will you wear one of your old gowns? I would gladly pay for everything if I could afford it. But I cannot. So, should I borrow money from your uncle? How should we resolve this dilemma?"

As her father continued to question her, Elizabeth's discomfort increased as the situation became clearer.

"Papa, I..."

"You what, Lizzy? I find Mr Darcy's assurance that you will be treated equally to his sister fair and appropriate. My child, you must promise me to think twice before you speak and take offence only when there is some to be taken."

"I am sorry, Papa, but I shall never agree to take Mr Darcy's money under any circumstances."

"I doubt he intends to pay you, Lizzy," Mr Bennet replied, rolling his eyes with apparent annoyance. "I rather assume he will make arrangements for purchases for both you and Miss Darcy. To me, this is a detail of little significance. Let us not waste more time over it, shall we?"

"Yes, sir."

"Good. Now let me catch my breath for a moment before the conversation with your mother. I need to write to my brother Gardiner too, so he receives it tomorrow."

For the second time that day, Elizabeth left the library confused, unsteady on her feet, and uncertain of her wishes. She was relieved and happy about leaving for London soon; the plan devised by her father and Mr Darcy sounded reasonable, except for the regrettable and embarrassing realisation that Mr Darcy would pay for her expenses. Of course, she intended to have no expenses at all; however, as her father had pointed out, that was unreasonable. So far, that was the only part of the entire scheme she did not approve of, and it ruined her disposition.

As her mother and sisters were preparing for dinner, Elizabeth found the time for a delicate discussion with Jane.

Her sister expressed many doubts and worries about Elizabeth's departure, regrets about Elizabeth not attending the ball, as well as concerns for Miss Darcy's health.

"Lizzy, I hope we shall at least be together for Christmas. I shall miss you so much!"

"You may come to London too, Jane. I am sure Aunt Gardiner will be happy to have you. And, if I am invited to stay with Georgiana, Mr Darcy said any of my sisters — or all of them — could join me at any time. He is a brave man to make such a suggestion," Elizabeth joked.

"Mr Bingley mentioned he might go to London after the ball," Jane said shyly.

"Well, that would be a perfect time for you to come to visit Aunt Gardiner too! And perhaps by then, you will have some more news in regard to Mr Bingley."

"Lizzy, do not tease me. Please do not assume more than there is. Mama is already doing that so often that it frightens me. Hoping for too much might cause great disappointment too."

"Forgive me. I shall speak no more on this subject, but you must promise to write to me often."

"And I pray you will not be disappointed when you meet Miss Darcy again, Lizzy. I know you hope for so much in regard to that encounter. I do not want you to suffer."

"I am confident I shall not suffer because of Georgiana, Jane. Although I have not seen her since she was a child, I trust our reunion will not disappoint either of us."

"What about Mr Darcy, Lizzy? Will you live in the same house as him?"

"I am not sure yet. He said Georgiana has her own house, and we may live separately from him, if necessary. To be honest, there are still things that worry me in regard to Mr Darcy. Nevertheless, I know he wishes the best for his sister, and he has been quite considerate to me and Papa in this arrangement."

"Did he mention anything about Mr Wickham?" Jane asked shyly.

"He did because I enquired. Now, I only have a few more questions to address to Mr Wickham to determine which of them lied to me."

"But Lizzy, is it wise to interfere in their past dealings?"

"No, and I shall not do that. I am not concerned about their dealings with each other but about their actions and claims to me," Elizabeth uttered, only a moment before Lydia entered and summoned them to dinner.

Chapter 14

The following day, early in the morning, Elizabeth woke up with a terrible headache. She had barely slept at all, anxious about the plan which still contained so many uncertainties. The true state of Georgiana's health and her response to their meeting were worrisome; furthermore, she expected opposition from Lord and Lady Matlock, as well as from Colonel Fitzwilliam, about whom Mr Darcy spoke often. There was also her mother's response, which could be good or bad. Fortunately, the decision belonged to her father, and he would certainly not break his promise to Mr Darcy.

Another subject for reflection was Mr Wickham and his relationship with Georgiana. She clearly remembered how the young George had taken advantage of the affection of a five-year-old girl and induced her to lie and steal on his behalf. Could he have perpetuated this vice over the years? Was it possible that he was still taking money from her, and Mr Darcy had discovered it? Was this the reason he had been denied the living? She was determined to find out more from Mr Wickham when — and if — she saw him again before her departure.

As Jane was still soundly asleep and there was no chance of Elizabeth finding more rest, she dressed and went for a walk. It was not full daylight yet; the air was cold, and the ground was covered in frost, and her shoes slipped at times. She walked carefully, looking down at her feet.

Out of habit, she unconsciously took the path towards Oakham Mount, remembering her encounter with Mr Darcy. It seemed so long ago, although only a few days had passed since then. Her relationship with him had utterly changed, though she had not completely sketched his character yet. His arrogance and improper pride were faults that he had admitted and attempted to amend, but there was still more of his character that remained hidden. And, despite his friendship with her father and even with her, she still felt somehow uncomfortable and anxious in his presence. Her mind turned to him more than it had ever done to any other man, and that was probably due to his connection to Georgiana, Elizabeth concluded.

After the first turn of the path, near a small grove, Elizabeth was surprised by the very object of her musings walking absently, his horse following him. Noticing her, he greeted her in a composed manner but with a hint of joy in his eyes that she did not miss.

"Miss Bennet! I am truly glad to see you."

"Mr Darcy!" Again, nervousness and a quiver along her spine bothered Elizabeth. No other man had caused such feelings before. "I did not expect to meet you here, sir."

"I have come for a last morning ride. Tomorrow, I intend to depart for London."

"Were you admiring the view? It is lovely, though not quite as beautiful as Pemberley."

"Aside from the view, which I admit is lovely, I confess I hoped to meet you. It was an unrealistic expectation, but in the end, I was fortunate."

His voice was friendly and gentle, and there was a small trace of a smile on his lips. Another shiver made her avert her eyes.

"If not for poor sleep and a headache, I had no intention of walking this morning. It is a fortuitous meeting but not at all unpleasant."

"I am relieved you think so, Miss Bennet."

"Is there anything particular that you wish to speak to me privately about, sir?"

"No. Only to thank you for sacrificing your time for the

benefit of my sister and me."

"Mr Darcy, please do not speak of sacrifice. I hoped we had clarified that it is my pleasure and my wish to see your sister again. And speaking of clarification, there is something particular I wish to speak to you about."

He raised his eyebrows in obvious surprise and interest. "Please do so."

She lowered her gaze and rubbed her hands together, her discomfort growing.

"My father mentioned to me your offer to cover my expenses if I were to live with Miss Darcy. Please know there is no need. I do not wish for there to be a monetary arrangement in a matter of affection." She felt her cheeks burning and became irritated with her own silly response.

"Miss Bennet, I completely agree. We should not mention any monetary aspect, and I apologise if this subject upsets you. However, I strongly believe that you should be treated equally if you come to stay with Georgiana as a friend — as a sister. I know she will insist on this. As you will see, my sister and I do not discuss money either. While she has her own means to live comfortably, it is a responsibility that I have assumed since our father died, and I shall continue to do so until the day she marries. There are some establishments where she holds an account, and the bills are sent to me afterwards."

"Yes, but…"

He took another step closer and gently touched her arm.

"Miss Bennet, I am begging you one more time — let us not discuss this any longer. In truth, there is another subject that requires our attention, and I have been struggling with how and what to tell you in order not to betray my sister or deceive you."

"Dear Lord, this sounds frightening. What can you possibly mean? Has something happened since yesterday?"

He released her arm and moved a step away, glancing around as though he was avoiding her scrutiny.

"No, not since yesterday. I am afraid it is something from much longer ago that has had a great influence over Georgiana. It regards George Wickham."

"Oh..."

"Miss Bennet, I can only imagine what he told you about me — my cruelty in denying him a living, my jealousy of him, and other sorts of falsehoods. Please know that he was generously compensated for that living on the day he told me he had no intention of entering the church and wished to pursue another career. Sadly, I learnt many years ago that Wickham's pleasant manners are the opposite of his true character, and that honesty and honour are two traits he mostly lacks."

"I am sorry to hear that. I know your father held him in regard and wished to provide him with the means to succeed in life. Is that not true?"

"It is true. My father loved him dearly. He supported Wickham at school and wished him to have the best education. He enjoyed his company and accepted his outward displays of gratitude as proof of affection. Wickham's actions were not known by my father but easily discovered by me, since I have caught him unguarded many times. Still, I hoped he would see his faults and improve himself since he was still very young. But my father died five years ago without knowing his godson's faulty character."

"That is so sad... One can hardly believe that Mr Wickham's appearance of goodness might be so deceitful! People in Meryton have already come to like him."

"I imagined as much. Miss Bennet, since you barely know me either, I understand your doubtfulness. If you need proof, my cousin Colonel Fitzwilliam has witnessed all my dealings with Wickham. I also have the written settlements..."

"No proof is needed. I do not doubt your claims, Mr Darcy."

"Thank you. I am relieved that my father did not suffer the disappointment of discovering the truth. Especially since Wickham became accustomed to a life of deception and dissipation."

"I admit this description does not come as a surprise to me, sir. I witnessed some of this behaviour during my short stay at Pemberley. Of course, Mr Wickham does not remember our prior meeting. I hoped he had changed since then."

Mr Darcy looked truly surprised. "Did you?"

"Yes...I am not sure if you know, but he was taking advantage of Miss Darcy's affection. He...asked her to steal things from him and give him her money..."

Darcy's eyes widened and anger darkened them.

"I was not aware of that!"

"I confronted him at the time, and I threatened to tell Lady Anne or Mr Darcy. We had quite a fight, as I remember it, but we were both very young. Sadly, things turned out for the worse in the next few days, and then your mother died. I only met him again a few days ago, and it pains me to know he has not changed in essentials."

"He has not. He tried to take advantage of Georgiana's affection and deluded her in the worst way, with no remorse that she was the daughter of his godfather."

"What a horrible, horrible man!"

"Yes...Miss Bennet, as I told you earlier, there is more that you should know before deciding whether you wish to renew your friendship with Georgiana. There is something no other soul knows, except me, my sister, and Colonel Fitzwilliam, who is her other guardian, but I completely trust that you will keep the secret. And, if you still agree to meet my sister, I would ask you to not reveal this conversation to her either. Hopefully, she will trust you enough to confess it herself."

He looked deeply troubled, and Elizabeth's heart ached again; it was her turn to gently touch his arm in a reassuring gesture. A painful, frightening suspicion slowly grew inside her, so horrible that she did not dare admit it.

"Mr Darcy, I hope that by now you understand that

meeting Miss Darcy again has been one of my dear wishes for many years. Nothing could alter my desire. As for this secret that seems so hurtful to you, I would rather hear it only when and if your sister herself wishes to reveal it to me. Till then, let it be buried."

He only nodded in agreement, and then he gently took her gloved hand from his arm and briefly touched his lips to it.

"Thank you," he whispered, and she nodded in return.

Elizabeth felt her voice quiver when she replied, "I must return home now, sir."

"Yes, of course. I shall call at Longbourn later, to bid farewell to your family. You should know that I told Bingley in confidence about your former friendship with Georgiana and your visit to London."

"I told my sister Jane, too. I believe they are both trustworthy."

"I fully agree."

"Mr Darcy, one last thing. You are a man of wealth, means, and power. You should not allow anyone to hurt your sister out of consideration for the past."

"I shall not — never again. As for Wickham, I admit I have purchased some of his debts. He is entirely at my mercy now, and I could throw him into debtors' prison at any time. I have only not done so because Georgiana begged me not to."

"I am relieved to hear that. But should not Colonel Forster and the people of Meryton be warned against him?"

"I have already mentioned it to the colonel, but both he and his wife seem to favour Wickham. I also intend to speak to your father. As for the others, I wonder whether they would trust my word against Wickham's."

"Probably not," she admitted. "However, I still have some unfinished conversations with Mr Wickham, and I intend to complete them."

"Please do not give Wickham cause to hold a grudge against you, Miss Bennet. I fear he is capable of the worst if he fears his well-being is in danger. Wickham is my responsibility, and I assure you I shall watch him carefully. It is a gentlemen's affair and a rather disturbing one."

Slightly irritated, Elizabeth was tempted to reply that he was surely not watching Wickham so carefully since he had been unaware the man had joined the regiment. If Wickham had hurt one of her sisters in the way she feared he had hurt Georgiana, Elizabeth was certain she would have done anything to punish him.

As though he was reading her mind, Mr Darcy continued.

"I have been perhaps too forgiving with Wickham, but this is a fault that I shall remedy."

"And you should. And do not worry, sir, I shall not intervene in gentlemen's affairs. Any discussion I might have with Mr Wickham will be based on my own experience only. Now forgive me, I must hurry to Longbourn. Good day."

"Good day, Miss Bennet. I shall see you again later."

With hasty steps, she walked away. The icy sensation inside her grew stronger, as well as her fury against Mr Wickham. Did he dare? Was he capable of such an abomination as to seduce his godfather's daughter? Mr Darcy's insinuation, and his misery and pain while mentioning it, all suggested such a horror.

As she entered the house, she was startled by the recollection of her sisters Lydia and Kitty being completely enchanted by Mr Wickham. Although her sisters could offer the scoundrel no advantage, no benefits, the danger was palpable to her, and suddenly, the disturbing gentlemen's affair became her concern too.

***

Breakfast was filled with Mr Collins's chatter, which Elizabeth succeeded in disregarding.

While she was pleased by the encounter with Mr Darcy and touched by their heartfelt, honest conversation, she was still disquieted by mixed feelings for him, tormented by Georgiana's situation, and nervous about her time in London. But most of all, she was eager to see Mr Wickham again. Also, that very day she planned to speak to her father at length about that man.

In the afternoon, Mr Bingley and Mr Darcy called at Longbourn again, bringing the news of Mr Darcy's departure. Although they showed deep regrets, Mrs Bennet and her youngest daughters were mostly relieved, as they admitted later on. The absence of the proud, aloof gentleman would ease their interaction with other gentlemen, including Mr Bingley and the officers.

Mr Collins took the opportunity to praise Mr Darcy and Lady Catherine several more times and expressed his hope of seeing Mr Darcy again when he visited Rosings Park.

Like the previous day, Mr Darcy spent most of the time with Mr Bennet and only took a brief farewell from the others. Although she knew they would meet again soon, Elizabeth felt unsettled by Mr Darcy's departure, and she could see he was not completely at ease either. They shared not a single private moment, but the early encounter was satisfying enough to pave the way for future meetings.

Eventually, the two gentlemen left. Only then, with a drink in his hand, did Mr Bennet reveal to his family that he had some business in town and would have to travel soon, taking Elizabeth with him.

After a moment of silent confusion and wordless puzzlement, an uproar of voices followed, Mrs Bennet's being the loudest of all.

Mr Bennet finished his drink unperturbed, shrugging at Mrs Bennet's opposition to Elizabeth missing the ball and her lamentations of Mr Collins not being able to dance his first set with his fair cousin. To all of this, Elizabeth listened silently, only exchanging a few glances with Jane.

Eventually, the master of the house stood up, still holding his glass.

"I shall allow you to complain as much as you like. You must know, though, that I am unmoved, and my plans are not to be changed. In five days, at the end of the week, Lizzy and I shall leave for London. My brother Gardiner has already been informed and is expecting us."

Chapter 15

"Mama, Kitty and I shall go to Meryton," Lydia said after breakfast. "We shall call on Maria Lucas and visit Aunt Phillips."

"You will not go alone," Mr Bennet intervened unexpectedly. "I shall approve it only if one of your older sisters accompanies you."

"But why, Papa? We have been walking to Meryton since we were small, and we are ladies now!" Lydia replied in disbelief.

"Precisely because you are young ladies, and it would not do to wander alone through a town full of officers." Mr Bennet held firm to his decision, much to his daughters' annoyance.

Elizabeth knew the argument was the result of Mr Darcy's confession in regard to Mr Wickham's character and her own doubts expressed to her father the previous evening.

"I need to go to Meryton too, Papa," she said conciliatorily. "I need to purchase new gloves and a bonnet for travelling to London. Will you join us, Jane?"

"Yes, I shall, Lizzy."

"Then it is settled. As long as Lizzy or Jane accompanies you, I have no objections," Mr Bennet concluded.

"I promised to call at Lucas Lodge too," Mr Collins interjected. "And, if I may be so bold, I would gladly watch over my fair cousins. Lady Catherine always says that I am trustworthy in regard to proper behaviour."

"I am sure you are, Mr Collins. If you go with my daughters, I shall certainly be even more at peace," Mr Bennet declared genuinely. Mr Collins's face glowed with pride as he completely missed the true meaning of that statement, while the girls all sighed in exasperation.

"Mr Bennet, I also need a private meeting with you," Mr Collins continued. "Since you and Cousin Elizabeth leave for London soon, the matter has become rather urgent."

Elizabeth panicked, glancing at her father, who waved his hand in a gesture of dismissal.

"I shall make time for a private meeting either later today or tomorrow morning, Mr Collins. For now, I must review some papers and write some letters. You should go to Meryton, as planned. Mrs Bennet, would you not like to join the girls and visit your sister? I shall gladly ask John to prepare the carriage."

"That is an excellent idea, Mr Bennet," the lady accepted joyfully, bringing a smirk to Mr Bennet's lips.

Even for the short distance to Meryton, the Bennet carriage was small and uncomfortable, and Elizabeth decided to walk back home, accompanied by Jane.

She was appalled by the notion that Mr Collins might speak to Mr Bennet with the intention of asking for her hand. The proposal itself was not worrisome, as it could have only one outcome, but the scandal that her rejection might arouse just before her departure disquieted her.

Their party first stopped at the Phillipses', and their aunt, alone at home, was happy to welcome them.

"How lovely that you came to visit me, Sister! I see Mary stayed at home again. You should do something with that girl, or else she will remain a spinster with no friends! I am glad to see Mr Collins, though."

"And I am exceedingly happy to see you again, Mrs Phillips! How could I not be since we are practically family?"

"Indeed, sir. I am sorry my husband is not at home to offer you a drink. I am afraid you will have to be content with the ladies' company."

"Is Mr Phillips not at home?" Mrs Bennet interjected before Mr Collins had time for another long reply.

"No, Sister. He went to meet a gentleman who is apparently in search of an estate near Meryton. Another solicitor from London recommended Mr Phillips to assist in the transaction."

"A gentleman? Where does he come from? Who is he?"

"I do not have knowledge of such things. I shall find out more as soon as Mr Phillips returns."

"How thrilling! I bet he is young like Mr Bingley. But what if he is married? Or ugly?" Lydia asked until her mother silenced her.

"Hush, silly child! Did you not hear that Mrs Phillips does not know? I am sure she will tell us as soon as she has news."

"Lady Catherine is always reserved and cautious when someone new arrives in the neighbourhood. Her ladyship is very careful in judging people! Even I needed a while before I gained her trust."

"We are cautious with strangers too!" Mrs Bennet responded. "My brother Phillips is an excellent solicitor and a good judge of character."

"I am sure that is true, madam. But my young cousins' readiness to approve of a man based on his appearance could be dangerous," Mr Collins continued, his sensible remark surprising Elizabeth.

The conversation continued between Mrs Phillips, Mrs Bennet, and Mr Collins; Lydia and Kitty soon lost their patience. They drank a cup of tea, then they expressed a wish to take a stroll. Their intention to look for the officers was transparent, but their mother readily agreed. Elizabeth, as well as Jane, immediately followed the two girls.

"Lizzy, you said you wanted to buy a new bonnet. Let us go now. I might find something for myself too," Lydia suggested.

"I need a bonnet also," Kitty seconded her.

"Dear Lord, shall we ever be free from Mr Collins? If he does not leave soon, I shall leave home so as not to be forced to see or hear him again," Lydia said.

"He is so dull!" Kitty admitted. "And he always has an opinion about everything! So tedious! Mary is the only one who listens to him — she should marry him!" She laughed.

"Kitty, you should not jest at Mary's expense!" Jane censured her. "Nor about our cousin."

"But I only spoke the truth, Jane," the girl defended herself. "Oh, look Lydia — there is Mr Denny and Mr Pratt! Let us go and greet them."

"I hope I shall dance with both of them at the ball! And with Mr Wickham! And I wonder what this new gentleman looks like. Oh, I must absolutely ask Mr Bingley to invite him to the ball too!" Lydia said, the impropriety of her words matching her loud, unguarded voice.

"Lydia, please mind your manners before the officers hear you," Elizabeth tried to temper her. "You will not ask Mr Bingley anything, certainly not in regard to a strange man! What is happening to you? Do not upset Papa further, or you might not attend the ball at all."

"How could he know unless you tell him? I hope Papa will stay in London and not return for the ball," Lydia said. "He has been very severe with us lately, and so have you, Lizzy!"

"Severe? That is the last word I would use to describe Papa, Lydia. It is his duty to take care of us all and our reputations. Keep in mind that in other families, the younger daughters come out only after the older are married."

"Dear Lord, that would be a disaster! To stay at home until you and Jane marry? Do not even mention such a thing to Papa! I would rather die!"

"Lydia!" Elizabeth scolded her, as the officers were approaching.

"Is Mr Wickham not with you?" Kitty asked moments later, much to Elizabeth and Jane's mortification.

"He should be arriving soon," Mr Denny replied. "I believe he was talking to Miss Mary King and her uncle. Colonel Forster and Mrs Forster are also with them. Look, they are just coming."

Indeed, from around the corner, a large group with the colonel and his wife, Mary King and her uncle, as well as Mr Wickham appeared.

"My dear Mrs Forster, I am so happy to see you!" Lydia cried.

"Likewise, dear Lydia. To be honest, I missed you. Life has been rather dull lately. Thank God I have Wickham and Denny and Pratt to amuse me."

"I have found life dull too! I look forward to seeing you! You are the prettiest and most elegant and joyful woman in the entirety of Hertfordshire!" Lydia declared, not caring that the remark might sound offensive to her sisters as well as to Mary King.

"How nice of you to say so, Lydia. We are about to have a small tea party. Will you join us? And you should call me Harriet. After all, I am only a few years older than you."

"How funny it sounds to call you that when you are a married lady!" Lydia said. "I would love nothing more than to come to your party. Lizzy, Jane, can we?"

Kitty almost jumped with joy, supporting her sister, but Elizabeth took Lydia's arm gently, though tightly. "I am afraid that is not possible. We are visiting our aunt, together with my mother and our cousin. We are expected to return soon."

Lydia and Kitty both argued vehemently, and Mrs Forster kept insisting, creating an embarrassing situation, which was surprisingly interrupted by Mr Wickham.

"Miss Elizabeth, would it not be possible for you all to come for a cup of tea? Perhaps for half an hour, to satisfy your sister and Mrs Forster's desire for each other's company? I shall gladly go and inform your mother of your whereabouts and beg her to pardon the change of plans." He was smiling charmingly, his voice low, friendly, and insinuating, and he looked at Elizabeth directly while he pleaded with her.

"To be honest, I would also be delighted to continue the intriguing conversation we started a few days ago. That is if you are still willing to talk to me."

Elizabeth glared at Mr Wickham, trying to control her ire. He was addressing her with a familiarity that made her cringe, especially since the others immediately enquired about the nature of that *intriguing conversation.*

"Mr Wickham, since my aunt's house is only a few steps away, I shall go and ask for my mother's permission," Elizabeth said.

"Lizzy, just do not let Mr Collins come too, or else he will ruin everyone's disposition!" Lydia cried after her, causing a peal of laughter from the group.

Trembling with anger and shame, Elizabeth entered her aunt's house and, as she feared, Mrs Bennet immediately granted her acceptance. Furthermore, she declared they must stay at the party until she came to fetch them.

Mr Collins, also as anticipated, tried to join her, but Elizabeth had already lost her patience and replied that the invitation was only for the Bennet sisters, and they would not stay more than an hour.

Rejoining the group in the street, she was received with overjoyed cries. Elizabeth agreed to spend an hour at the Forsters', and they all walked together. She was in no disposition for such a gathering, but she was too tired and ashamed to argue with her sisters in public. Lydia and Kitty's manners were outrageous indeed, and the fact that Mrs Forster seemed to approve of them did not comfort her much.

As they were approaching the colonel's house, another encounter delayed them. Mr Phillips climbed down from a large carriage, followed by a gentleman with an elegant appearance, fashionable and obviously expensive clothes, and a confident posture that complemented his handsome features very well.

An introduction was impossible to avoid, and the stranger was presented as Mr Andrew Ross, who declared himself pleased to make everyone's acquaintance but said little else except the usual pleasantries.

Despite several attempts, Mr Ross did not allow himself

to be drawn into the conversation, but he mentioned that he would remain in the neighbourhood for a while.

"Do you have any relatives in Hertfordshire, Mr Ross?" Mrs Forster enquired.

"No. But I hope to have my own house rather soon. My wife is much more inclined to spend time in the countryside than in town."

"Wife?" exclaimed Lydia, her eyes widening at the mere mention of the word. "See, I told you. Mr Ross has a wife. How utterly tedious."

Mr Ross turned an angry red, and Lydia found herself the recipient of numerous disapproving glances.

Mr Phillips cleared his throat before resuming the conversation.

"I hear you are staying at the inn."

It is unacceptable for a gentleman to stay at the inn for more than a couple of nights," Mrs Forster declared. "Is it not, my dear?" she addressed her husband.

"My dear, what seems unacceptable to a lady, for a gentleman might be perfectly acceptable, even enjoyable," the colonel answered. "Men find amusement even when there is a lack of comfort," he said with a wink to the other gentlemen.

"I invited Mr Ross to be our guest for the duration of his stay in Meryton," Mr Phillips interjected. "We are sad that he prefers the solitude of the inn."

"Mr Phillips's invitation was very kind and much appreciated. However, I do not wish to intrude, and as the colonel mentioned, I am not much bothered by the lack of comfort. I have found my stay at the inn to be a diverting change and perfectly agreeable for a few days."

"Well, sir, if you wish for more diversion and some amusement, you may always join my officers for a game of cards and a drink," Colonel Forster said.

"Thank you, Colonel. I shall certainly accept such an invitation. Now please excuse us. Mr Phillips and I still have some papers to look over, so we must leave you. It was a tremendous pleasure to make your acquaintance. Ladies, gentlemen, have a good day."

Mr Ross took his leave in the company of Mr Phillips. His status as a married gentleman had rendered him somewhat less captivating than he might have been had he been unattached. Soon his presence was altogether forgotten.

While refreshments were served, Elizabeth was sitting near Jane, restless, with little interest in Mr Ross but glancing at Mr Wickham frequently. He was the man who held her attention; while she had been reluctant to attend the impromptu party, she knew it might be the last opportunity to speak to him before her departure. She was too impatient to wait, too curious to feign disinterest in him, but not bold enough to approach him when he was surrounded by Mrs Forster, Lydia, and Kitty.

Eventually, Mr Wickham stood, and meeting Elizabeth's gaze, he walked towards her. She rose too and, holding his gaze, forced a smile.

"Miss Elizabeth, I hope you will not trifle with me any longer," he said when he was standing in front of her. "You must tell me the circumstances of our first meeting. I have hardly slept at all since we last spoke."

"I doubt that my words had the effect of keeping you awake, Mr Wickham," she said, smiling.

"They did. And I feared I might never know the answer. I have learnt that Darcy has visited your family several times, and I assume he has said nothing favourable of me. Since he is a friend of Mr Bingley, the logical conclusion was that you would refuse to speak to me again."

"You are quite hasty with your conclusions, Mr Wickham. I have already told you that I form my opinions on my observations. Besides, you might be surprised to learn that Mr Darcy has said nothing worse of you than you have said of him."

"I am glad to hear that," he said, looking uncertain about how to take her words. "So, will you tell me, then?"

"I shall. May I ask first, when did you see Miss Darcy last? I know you mentioned it, but I do not recollect." Elizabeth tried to speak in a light, composed tone. He seemed determined to seek the information he desired, but so did she. Her last question brought a shadow of worry to his face, but he concealed it behind a smile.

"Georgiana? Um…I am not certain. A few years ago…"

"Only a few years ago?"

"May I ask why this is important to you, Miss Bennet?"

"Because I am trying to sketch your character as accurately as possible, Mr Wickham."

"How intriguing. May I ask what has been your progress since we last met? I doubt you have found anything good, considering the source of your information."

"I have not made much progress. I am trying to balance the universal good opinion of you with the fact that you seem unwilling to provide me with accurate answers."

"This is a harsh accusation, Miss Bennet. May I ask what I have done to deserve it?" His serene countenance and light tone differed from his words.

She smiled in anticipation of his response.

"Mr Wickham, I am just a lady, and therefore I do not interfere in gentlemen's affairs. Your business dealings with Mr Darcy are not my concern. But I happen to know, beyond a doubt, that you have seen Miss Georgiana Darcy this year. Quite recently in fact. Since I doubt your memory has betrayed you, I must question the reason behind your denial of that meeting."

She felt that her voice had become sharper and experienced a slight satisfaction when he paled.

"Um…this is…I am not…I assumed such information was of no real interest to you."

"Even if that was the case, did you believe that a dishonest response was appropriate? That is a peculiar choice, I dare say."

"I believe a man is entitled to discretion when he wishes

it. May I ask what you know of my recent encounter with Miss Darcy?"

"I know what I need in order to complete my sketch, Mr Wickham, based on my own judgment, as I promised when we met last week," she said, her smile broadening while his expression darkened even more.

"I am sorry you disapprove of me, Miss Bennet. I truly wished to be friends, and your good opinion was important to me. Nothing will convince me that Darcy had no influence in your judgment."

Elizabeth took a moment to compose herself. They were in a room full of people where everybody was talking and laughing while the two of them were carrying on a distressingly serious conversation.

"Mr Wickham, I am not trying to convince you of anything. And I can understand it is easier for one to blame another person for their own faulty behaviour. If one lacks the desire to examine one's own decisions and actions, one might not expect any improvement."

"Miss Bennet, I am sorry to sound disrespectful, but I have heard such a lecture many times from Darcy himself. I am in no disposition for more repetition," he replied, his confidence apparently returning.

"I have no right and no wish to lecture you, Mr Wickham. I understand you dismiss anything coming from Mr Darcy. However, you said your godfather always loved you and treated you as his son. Have you ever wondered what he would have to say if he witnessed the growth and success of his beloved godson?"

"I...I am afraid this is not your concern, Miss Bennet."

"Apparently it is not yours either, Mr Wickham. And in order to clarify everything between us, I shall tell you about our prior meeting."

She paused, looked him in the eyes, and brought back the smile to her lips as he watched her, obviously intrigued.

"It was at Pemberley, ten years ago. I was a visitor there.

Perhaps the mention of my jumping into the lake to pull Georgiana out of it might refresh your memory. I remember you, as you were watching as she almost drowned. Just as well as I remember you asking her to steal things for you. It was during that time that you were much loved and supported by the late Mr Darcy. Perhaps I should have told him, as I intended, despite the fact that you called me a servant and assured me he would never believe me over you."

Mr Wickham's astonishment was now complete, and he stared at her, standing still, blinking, holding his breath.

"But that was in the past, when we were all foolish children," he said with barely supressed anger.

"Yes, indeed we were. But we are not foolish children now," Elizabeth concluded. "Mr Wickham, what matters is what we grew into and how much each of us improved. I hope you agree with me at least on this, Mr Wickham."

Mr Wickham's face twitched, but before he could reply, he was interrupted.

"Wickham? What are you doing here? What are you talking to Miss Elizabeth about so seriously? Come, we need you. We want to play cards!" Mrs Forster intervened, grasping Mr Wickham's arm.

"Please do not count on us, Mrs Forster," Elizabeth said. "We should leave soon. My mother might come to summon us at any time."

"Oh, let us worry about that when she comes," the young lady replied, taking Mr Wickham with her. He did not look back, nor did he attempt to speak to Elizabeth again, only casting some dark glares at her whilst he smiled charmingly at his other companions.

Elizabeth resumed her place near Jane, while the others took seats at the tables. Another hour passed until Mrs Bennet finally arrived. Mr Collins immediately joined the conversation. Relieved that her mother had arrived, and loyal to her earlier decision, Elizabeth took her farewell and, together with Jane, returned to Longbourn on foot, allowing the cold autumn breeze to cool her face and her mind.

Chapter 16

Darcy bore the relatively short journey from Hertfordshire to London with difficulty. Accustomed to travelling frequently, over long distances, the journey gave him a strange discomfort. He had informed Georgiana of his return, but he was still concerned about her reception. It was as though his presence tormented her, and she tried to avoid being near him, which he struggled to understand.

After a brief reflection, he had to admit that the weight that burdened his chest was not only caused by the upcoming meeting with his sister but also by his departure from Elizabeth. The more he thought of it, the more he was forced to accept that Elizabeth Bennet and her sparkling eyes had stirred some deep, strong, and disquieting feelings inside him — ones he had not felt for anyone else.

That realisation was worrisome for many reasons.

First, as enchanting and worthy of admiration as she was, he had never contemplated marriage to a woman with a situation in life so much below his own. To him, she seemed to possess everything he had ever wanted in a woman, and her image was vivid in his mind every moment of the day and night. However, it was not entirely his choice but also a matter of his responsibility to his family that would directly influence Georgiana's position in society too.

As much as he enjoyed Mr Bennet's company, the gentleman was far from Darcy's usual circle, as Lady Catherine would say. He needed to think carefully and examine everything with a clear mind to be certain of his wishes and the actions that would follow. Then, if his reason reached the same conclusion as his feelings, he had to discover Elizabeth's feelings and desires in regard to him. And only then, if they were in accord, would he decide on the best course of action, in order to expose Elizabeth, Georgiana, and their families to as little turmoil as possible.

But he would allow himself no actions — not even thoughts or dreams — that might be considered improper for as long as Elizabeth was under his protection, perhaps even in his house, for the purpose of supporting Georgiana. He had begged Elizabeth and Mr Bennet to agree to his plan, and he had promised to them and to himself to provide her with all the comfort, care, and protection she deserved. He could examine his feelings and contemplate actions, but nothing would happen whilst she was under his protection.

When the carriage stopped in front of the house, he stepped down, eager yet anxious. Mrs Penfield, the housekeeper, greeted him and welcomed him inside but managed to add little else before he left her presence in search of his sister.

With his coat and hat on still, he moved towards the drawing-room, where Georgiana could usually be found at that hour, when suddenly she appeared in the hall with Mrs Annesley behind her.

"Brother, you are home," she said in a small voice, and Darcy needed a moment to soothe the claw in his chest so he could reply while wondering at how pale and thin she looked after only one month.

The dark circles around her blue eyes revealed her tiredness and lack of sleep.

"I am home and very happy to see you, dearest," he finally said, embracing her gently, barely feeling her small body in his arms.

"Mrs Penfield, what time will dinner be ready?" Darcy asked as he walked along the hall with his sister holding his arm. "We shall eat together in the dining room. Mrs Annesley, please join us. Richard might come too. He knows I shall be home tonight."

"Of course, Mr Darcy. Dinner will be served whenever you are ready."

"Thank you. I only need a little time to change."

"I shall be in the music room until you return, Brother," Georgiana said, and Darcy nodded, then exchanged a glance with Mrs Annesley.

"She looks very ill," Darcy whispered as soon as the girl left. "I should have returned sooner."

"She barely eats at all, sir. And I believe she sleeps very ill too."

"We should fetch the doctor. I shall send for him."

"Mr Darcy, the doctor has seen Miss Darcy several times and found no signs of visible illness. Besides, his presence upsets her further."

"What do you suggest instead, Mrs Annesley? To do nothing and let my sister take a turn for the worse?"

"I have no suggestions, Mr Darcy. I am only telling you what I know," the woman said humbly. "I am here to help Miss Darcy to the best of my abilities."

"Of course... Forgive me, Mrs Annesley. I did not mean to imply otherwise. I thank you for your loyalty to my sister. I shall take care of everything from now on. Besides, I have reason to believe that soon Georgiana will have reason to improve her disposition."

"Oh, I am glad, sir."

"As am I. An old friend will come to visit her, and I am confident it will be useful to her. We shall discuss it more after I confirm all the details with Georgiana."

"What details, Brother?" the girl enquired, startling him. "Forgive me for interrupting you. I changed my mind about practising."

"I am glad you did. I have something to tell you," Darcy said with a gentle smile, while Mrs Annesley left to allow them privacy.

"You have not changed your clothes yet, Brother."

"Not yet, but I shall do so immediately. I have one small but excellent piece of news."

"Do you? How lovely! I also wished to ask you about Miss Elizabeth Bennet, but we can discuss that later."

"The excellent news is in regard to Miss Elizabeth Bennet, dearest. She is to come to London with her father in a few days, and she has expressed a desire to see you."

The lady's eyes brightened instantly, then a shadow fell across them.

"She has?"

"Yes. I hope you are as eager as she is. In truth, I would love to have a friend who had not seen me for a decade yet still cared for me," Darcy said, putting a smile and some enthusiasm into his voice. However, Georgiana remained thoughtful.

"I am grateful for her interest. I just hope she will not be disappointed in me."

Darcy took his sister's hands. "I must confess I told her this worry of yours, and she looked at me like I was a lunatic. She told me there is nothing and nobody that would alter her affection for you. And you see, my dear, I really believe her. Miss Elizabeth is not someone who expresses dishonest opinions."

"Very well, then. Would you tell me more about her? And when will she arrive? Is she to come here?"

"I shall tell you everything you wish to know during dinner. I hope you do not mind Mrs Annesley and Richard hearing too?"

"Not at all. Brother, are you pleased that Miss Elizabeth will come to visit me?"

Darcy kissed the young girl's hand. "I am very pleased indeed. Let me go and change my clothes now. There is more that I must tell you, but it can wait until tomorrow morning."

***

The reunion with Colonel Fitzwilliam was a happy event, as always. Aside from his affection, loyalty, and care for both Darcys, the colonel was a man with amiable manners and an easy nature that made him a favourite among his acquaintances as well as those who had just met him.

He listened to Darcy's narration about his time in Hertfordshire and asked some questions about the Bennets, especially Elizabeth.

While he answered diligently, Darcy was surprised to feel a warmth growing inside him and a smile that kept twisting his lips.

Even just talking about Elizabeth had a stronger effect on him than most of the other ladies he was acquainted with, and that notion was equally thrilling and frightening.

"Mr Bennet's cousin is Lady Catherine's clergyman? That is so amusing!" the colonel said.

"Less amusing than you assume. The man has something to say about Lady Catherine every other minute," Darcy replied.

The colonel laughed. "Lady Catherine certainly loves that. And, from everything you have said about Miss Elizabeth's wit and boldness and manners, Lady Catherine would surely despise her."

"I cannot argue with that," Darcy admitted.

"I am sure Lady Catherine will not despise Miss Elizabeth!" Georgiana intervened. "Why would she? Miss Elizabeth sounds charming!"

"That is precisely why, my dear." The colonel laughed again. "I look forward to meeting this person who has made such an impression on you all."

The evening progressed in a pleasant way, and then Mrs Annesley retired for the night. Darcy struggled for a little while with the confession he still needed to make to his sister and his cousin, wondering whether he should do it separately or to both, and whether he should delay it in order to not distress Georgiana more or reveal it right away.

"What is troubling you, Darcy? You barely heard what I said," the colonel asked.

"In fact, there is something that occupies me," he admitted after another moment of hesitation. "Perhaps I should have waited for a better moment, but I owe you both the consideration of the truth."

"What is it, Brother?" Georgiana whispered.

"This sounds rather ominous, Darcy. Do I need another brandy?"

"You probably do, Cousin. I discovered that George Wickham has joined the militia," he said, heartbroken as he saw Georgiana turning pale and clasping her hands together.

"Has he? Well, that is precisely what the militia needs," the colonel said sarcastically.

"There is more to tell, unfortunately. He has joined precisely the regiment that is encamped in Meryton. Near Bingley and the Bennet family."

"Now that is a terrible coincidence. The scoundrel seems to stick to you like a disease," the colonel said, then turned to Georgiana. "Forgive me, my dear, I do not want to pain you more. I know your father loved him, my own parents thought highly of him, even I was friends with him for a while. He deceived us all. Now I would gladly break every bone in his body—"

"Richard, let us speak calmly and mind our words," Darcy interrupted him. "It was merely information that I wished to provide you with. It does not affect any of us."

"Brother, have you spoken to him? What will you do?" the girl enquired shyly.

"My dear, I promised you I would not take any measures against him, provided he keeps his side of the bargain and does not bother any of us again. I hope you know I always keep my promises."

"I know... Does anyone know that George... Is Miss Elizabeth aware that...?"

"The people of Meryton know what Wickham told them — that he was our father's godson and that I was a cruel man and disloyal son and denied him the promised living," Darcy explained. "If you ever want to tell Miss Elizabeth anything else, the decision will be yours. But I am confident it has no significance to her in regard to your friendship."

The young lady nodded, and both men noticed she was on the verge of tears. She remained in their company only for a few more minutes, then apologised and withdrew for the night.

"I would gladly break every bone in Wickham's body too," Darcy burst out as soon as Georgiana left. "Or at least throw him into debtors' prison."

"I wonder why you do not. You waste your patience on that undeserving rascal."

"Yes, even Miss Bennet asked me why I was so lenient with him," Darcy declared.

"Miss Elizabeth Bennet? Have you spoken to her about him?"

"Yes. Wickham spread his falsehoods, and she asked me for my side of the story. I told her the truth."

"The entire truth?"

"Not quite. It was a rather odd conversation because she remembered Wickham had been a friend to Georgiana when they were young. Naturally, I had to explain that Wickham had deceived and hurt Georgiana. There was no need for more, but I suspect she guessed the nature of Wickham's deception."

"She likely did, if she is as clever as you described her."

"It is somehow ironic that she apparently met Wickham when she visited Pemberley and remembered him taking advantage of Georgiana even then, by asking her to steal small things for him. Georgiana was only five at that time. Miss Lizzy confronted Wickham back then, and I am worried she might confront him again."

"Well, well. The more I learn about her, the more I am certain Miss Elizabeth is my kind of lady."

"No, she is not, Richard," Darcy replied so severely that the colonel stared at him.

"Richard, although I do not question your honour, and I am sure Miss Elizabeth is perfectly capable of protecting herself, I must tell you I shall not allow even the smallest joke or teasing if it shows any sign of impropriety or disrespect. She will be my sister's guest, under my protection, and I am responsible for her."

"Come, Darcy, you are being serious. I should be offended by your assumption. Do you truly doubt my behaviour?"

"I do not doubt you, Richard, but there are times when you are not careful enough with your words. You must admit it."

The colonel gazed at Darcy intently, and his eyebrow arched in challenge.

"I do admit it. But are you aware that you betray significant and unusual interest in this Miss Elizabeth?" The colonel leant back, amused, sipping from his glass, and Darcy's reply made him almost fall from his seat.

"I am aware, Richard. However, we shall not mention it again as long as Miss Elizabeth is my sister's guest. The earlier warning of treating her with caution and consideration was meant not just for you but also for me."

"So...Darcy, you do admit it? Your interest in Miss Elizabeth, I mean?"

"I do — to you only, and I trust your secrecy. Now let us change the subject."

"Change the subject? Very well. Let us plan how we can punish Wickham!"

"Richard, I believe we have had enough brandy for one evening. Speaking of brandy, you would like Mr Bennet's, I am sure. You would certainly like the gentleman himself too. He excels in teasing and mockery, so you would make a good match."

"Your interest in both Miss Elizabeth and her father

frightens me, Darcy. And no, I certainly have not had enough brandy. In fact, I need another drink. When did you say Mr and Miss Bennet will arrive? I must go with you to meet them both."

Darcy rolled his eyes and filled his cousin's glass one more time. There was not much to be done with Colonel Fitzwilliam.

***

At Longbourn, the day before Elizabeth's departure was as agitated as she expected, and the worst that she feared, happened. Immediately after breakfast, Mr Collins insisted on a private meeting with her.

"My dear cousin Elizabeth, as you will leave tomorrow, and I cannot return to Rosings Park without accomplishing my mission, this meeting has become urgent and cannot be postponed."

In sensing the ridiculous intent on Mr Collins's part, Elizabeth attempted an immediate refusal, but her mother insisted and almost pushed her inside the drawing room, closing the door behind her.

She remained standing, while he moved around her.

"My dear cousin, as much as your modesty and demureness demands you feign ignorance, I am sure you cannot be unaware of the reason for this meeting."

"Mr Collins, I assure you I am neither modest nor demure, and I try to refrain from making assumptions. With all due respect, I assure you there is no subject that requires privacy between the two of us."

"Indeed, you are wrong, Miss Elizabeth. As I disclosed at the beginning of my visit, I came here with more than one purpose. And the one that I should have probably mentioned first was Lady Catherine's advice on finding a wife. I believed it only fair to start my search among my cousins, in order to compensate for the pain of losing your home as soon as your father dies."

"Mr Collins, I beg you to stop before placing both of us in a horrible and ridiculous situation. Let me state clearly that anything you wish to ask me, my answer will be no, and anything you would like to propose to me will receive a rejection. I have no doubts that, if Lady Catherine knew me, she would disapprove of me enough not to wish to see me often. Whatever she advises you to do, I am certainly not the choice to satisfy her demands!"

Mr Collins looked dumbfounded, confused, slowly becoming panicked, and kept gulping and blinking repeatedly, so Elizabeth had time to continue.

"Sir, let us tell my family that you only wanted to talk to me to wish me a safe journey and pleasant stay in London. And since I shall leave tomorrow and be gone probably for a long while, you have time to extend your search and to wisely select in such a way as to please Lady Catherine."

"But...but...this is..."

"This is the best way to handle a delicate situation. I shall leave you now, and I pray for a happy resolution to your quest."

She left in a hurry, and in the hall, she bumped into her mother. Mrs Bennet ran after her, asking what had happened.

"Nothing happened, Mama. Mr Collins and I agreed that I am lacking in many ways, and Lady Catherine would never approve of me."

"What? How? What are you talking about, Lizzy? Did he propose to you?"

"No, Mama. Now excuse me, I must talk to Papa and then to Jane."

"Lizzy! Lizzy, come here!" Mrs Bennet continued to scream, while Elizabeth entered the library.

Mr Bennet briefly raised his eyes from his book and peered at her over his glasses.

"Is it done?"

"Yes, Papa."

"Will Mr Collins come to complain to me?"

"Unlikely. But Mama surely will. Her nerves must be greatly affected."

"I have grown accustomed to Mrs Bennet's nerves over the last twenty years, so I know how to manage them. Are your trunks ready?"

"Yes, Papa. Please, please, before we leave, speak to Mama and Lydia and Kitty one more time and warn them about their behaviour around the officers. I have already tried to, but they paid me no attention. I know Jane will be here, but she cannot manage everything by herself."

"I shall talk to them, Lizzy, but I anticipate little success. Regardless, you know I shall only stay a few days in London. I intend to return just after the ball. I trust no tragedy will occur in a week."

"I hope not, Papa."

While they spoke, they expected Mrs Bennet to appear at any moment, but it did not happen. Instead, Lydia came to announce that Mr Bingley and Charlotte Lucas had arrived to take their farewell from Elizabeth and Mr Bennet, so for another hour the family was busy entertaining guests.

Mr Collins was sitting in a corner, angry, resentful, silent, glaring at Elizabeth from time to time.

When the visit ended, Charlotte Lucas embraced Elizabeth, then she addressed Mr Collins with an invitation from Sir William. Mr Collins, as though he had taken a breath of fresh air, immediately accepted, informing the Bennets that he would likely not return for dinner.

Mrs Bennet panicked and was ready to hold him by force, but Mr Bingley declared that he would remain for dinner, if possible. Obliged to choose between the two gentlemen, Mrs Bennet found enough satisfaction in Mr Bingley's presence and reluctantly watched Mr Collins leaving with Charlotte, barely repressing her anger. She assured Elizabeth that they would discuss the matter further as soon as she returned from London, and Elizabeth agreed.

That evening, Mr Collins did not return, his absence contributing to a pleasant dinner and to quite some open sighs of relief.

The next morning, at dawn, Elizabeth and Mr Bennet left Longbourn, on a journey whose conclusion neither of them could anticipate.

Chapter 17

Since she was a child, visiting the Gardiners had been one of Elizabeth's favourite times of the year. For as long as she remembered, her uncle Edward Gardiner had been the second most important man in the world to her, and she loved and trusted her aunt Gardiner with all her heart. Since the first Gardiner child was born, Elizabeth's attachment to the joyful, warm house in Gracechurch Street had grown every year.

However, that journey was different from any others before, and while she missed her relatives and was eager to see them, her heart and her mind were filled with images of another house — one she had never seen but made her heart pound.

The object of her speculations was Georgiana, and as the carriage approached London, her thrill increased, as well as her nervousness. The reunion with Miss Darcy caused Elizabeth to fret almost as much as the prospect of seeing Mr Darcy again, though for different reasons. Reasons that were still uncertain to her.

"I have a peculiar feeling about this journey," Mr Bennet said unexpectedly. "It should be a mere visit to my brother Gardiner, but it feels different."

"It feels different to me too, Papa. I cannot believe I shall finally see Miss Darcy again after ten years. Unless Mr Darcy has changed his mind, either of his own will or forced by his relatives, who have kept me away from Georgiana all this time."

"Let us not turn it into a drama, Lizzy. Things were different back then. You were very young. Nobody cares about children's opinions, especially when they are five or ten. Mr Darcy sounded very decided when he suggested this visit. He does not appear to be a man whose decision might be easily altered. And if he is, we may return to Longbourn at any time."

"Of course, Papa. I find myself being unreasonable lately, as I tend to imagine the worst. My nerves seem to resemble Mama's."

"Heaven forbid! If that is true, I might leave you in London for a long time."

Elizabeth smiled at the seriousness in her father's tone.

"Speaking of Mama, I am uncomfortable knowing she was upset with me when I left. I cannot imagine she put so much hope in me marrying Mr Collins. It was an absurd expectation."

"No quite so absurd, if we are to speak honestly, Lizzy. Many young ladies in your position would be pleased to receive a marriage proposal from my cousin. And many fathers — wiser than me — would have insisted upon it. I know you are too clever and too independent to marry such a man, but he is not an undesirable husband. I hope neither of us will come to regret the decision."

"Papa, this is a subject not even worth mentioning. I am not arguing about Mr Collins being a desirable husband. He is just not for me, and I shall never regret that. I wonder how long he will remain at Longbourn. He did not seem bothered by your leaving."

"I wonder too. I expected he would leave when we did, but he seemed determined to follow his plan. He might fear returning to Lady Catherine before he finds a wife. Perhaps he will propose to another of your sisters. Mary seemed to admire his sermons," Mr Bennet concluded, whilst Elizabeth wondered whether he was serious or not.

"Papa, have you instructed Mama to supervise Kitty and Lydia? Especially in regard to the officers?"

"I have, my dear. I confess I even asked my brother Phillips to watch over them from a distance. But let us be reasonable — there is an upcoming ball. I imagine all the girls in Meryton are looking forward to the ball and dancing with the officers."

"Lydia and Kitty behave with less decorum than other girls," Elizabeth replied meaningfully. "It might affect their future, in more than one way."

"I thoroughly believe Lydia and Kitty are too young, too silly, and too poor to catch any man's interest."

"Except if the man is a scoundrel who would secretly pursue a girl for dishonourable reasons…"

"Even so, Lizzy. A scoundrel will always choose a more… discreet, obedient, and quiet object for his pursuit, if you take my meaning. I understand you are particularly concerned about that Wickham fellow. But being in Meryton, among our family and friends, and considering his position as an officer in the regiment, I doubt he could be a danger to anyone."

Mr Bennet's voice and behaviour were too relaxed compared with Elizabeth's worry, yet she could not say much more, as her father changed the subject. In the late autumn, the day was short, and soon the sun lowered to the horizon. Before darkness fell, the carriage arrived safely on Gracechurch Street.

The Gardiners received them with their usual joyfulness; Mrs Gardiner and the children immediately embraced Elizabeth, while Mr Gardiner welcomed them warmly.

In the middle of exchanging greetings, Elizabeth startled, dumbfounded, as she noticed the astonishing presence of Mr Darcy, waiting silently some distance away. She stared at him, locking his gaze for a short, yet intense moment, enveloped by a strange nervousness, trying to say something and hoping he would speak first.

"Mr Darcy! What a lovely surprise! I did not expect to find you here, sir!" Mr Bennet uttered, saving the moment.

"Mr Bennet, Miss Bennet, welcome! I am so glad that you arrived safely. That is the reason I disturbed Mr and

Mrs Gardiner with my presence," Mr Darcy replied, stepping forwards.

"How kind of you to wait for us. I would have wagered that you did not know where Gracechurch Street was," Mr Bennet continued with a hint of humour.

"Mr Darcy has visited us before," Mr Gardiner said. "His company is a great pleasure."

"I am sure it is. It is a pleasure for us, too," Mr Bennet continued, while Elizabeth chose to remain silent.

"Will you join us for dinner, Mr Darcy?" Mr Gardiner asked.

"Unfortunately, I must decline. In fact, I shall leave immediately. It is rather late, and my sister is waiting for me. But I hope we shall dine together soon. If you choose a date, I shall gladly arrange a dinner."

"It depends on my brother Bennet," Mr Gardiner said. "We have no fixed engagements except with our children."

"Very well, then. We may speak more on this subject when Miss Bennet calls on my sister."

"I would like to go tomorrow if that is agreeable to you," Elizabeth finally interjected. "I confess I am rather eager for this meeting."

"Tomorrow would be perfect," Mr Darcy answered, and their gazes met again. "My sister and I are also eager for this reunion."

"I would prefer to accompany Lizzy," Mr Bennet said.

"Of course, sir. You are all welcome," Darcy addressed the Gardiners too.

"I shall remain at home with the children. They are a handful for our maids. But my husband may join my brother and my niece," Mrs Gardiner offered.

"Thank you. We look forward to your visit," Mr Darcy responded with a bow, then took his farewell again.

Mr Gardiner showed him out, while Mrs Gardiner invited everyone to dinner. The children were placed on a separate table, and the conversation returned to the subject of their mutual astonishment.

"How come Mr Darcy was here?" Mr Bennet addressed the question that bothered Elizabeth too.

"He said he wished to know you had arrived safely, as he said," Mrs Gardiner replied. "I understand your amazement. I would have never imagined Mr Darcy visiting my home. The first time he came to introduce himself, I was shivering like a simpleton."

"I assume he is truly worried for his sister and wishes to be sure Elizabeth will visit her soon," Mr Gardiner added, as he returned. "All in all, he is quite a pleasant fellow. Unexpectedly amiable, considering his situation and our brief acquaintance."

"I agree. I find him pleasant, too," Mr Bennet replied. "Some considered him arrogant and haughty, but he is my sort of man — smiling and talking just as much as necessary, well-educated, and fond of books. I need nothing else from a man."

"He sounds like my sort of man too," Mr Gardiner said. "Lizzy, I heard that your first impression of him was not so favourable."

"My first encounter with Mr Darcy might be called challenging. Neither of us showed our best behaviour, but I hope both of us have improved in civility since then."

"He told us he was rude to you, which I find rather difficult to imagine," Mrs Gardiner said. "He looked utterly miserable while confessing his faulty behaviour, which I admit to finding diverting, considering he is the master of Pemberley, and men in his position rarely apologise or even admit their flaws."

"Once we clarified our misunderstandings, Mr Darcy proved to be a perfect gentleman," Elizabeth admitted. "His worry for his sister might have added to his friendliness, though."

"Speaking of that, my dear, Mr Darcy gave the impression that you might help Miss Darcy in some way. Which is strange, as he mentioned the doctor found no real illness that could have altered her state or could be healed. I wonder what is truly wrong with Miss Darcy, and I fear Mr Darcy has put too much faith in her improvement once she sees you."

"From the little Mr Darcy revealed to me, I suspect it is not so much an illness but a lowness of spirits. I understand her to be very timid, withdrawn, even fearful of everything around her."

"Which might be explained by the losses she suffered at such a young age," Mrs Gardiner added thoughtfully. "I know she was always a delicate child. That is why Lady Anne was so pleased when Lizzy befriended her. To lose her parents so early, with no brothers or sisters of her own age, with only a brother who was probably more like a father burdened by all sort of responsibilities, she must have suffered in silence and solitude. Poor girl."

"With that, I can certainly help her," Elizabeth said confidently. "I shall visit her tomorrow, and I shall allow her the liberty to choose how our acquaintance progresses. If she needs a trustworthy companion, I may be one for her."

"Mr Darcy mentioned something about a dinner party before you return home, Brother."

"Let us not make further plans yet. We shall see how things unfold tomorrow and decide accordingly," Mr Bennet answered. "Now we should finish dinner and rest. I, for one, am exhausted from the road."

Dinner ended rather early, and Mr Bennet withdrew for the night. Elizabeth remained in the drawing room, talking for some time with her aunt. She was disquieted in regard to the following day, although she had no particular reason for it. After all, it was a mere call, with no obligations on either side.

Her thoughts again spun between Georgiana and her brother.

The unexpected encounter with Mr Darcy, although brief, had a strong effect on Elizabeth; while the surprise was not unpleasant, she felt overwhelmed and grateful that he had left so soon. Strangely, he had seemed comfortable, even familiar with the Gardiners, and even more surprising, he had called on them twice. Probably he wished to meet Mrs Gardiner, who had been remotely connected to his mother — there could be no other explanation.

Even after an hour of conversation and two cups of herbal tea, Elizabeth still could not sleep. She forced herself to lie still, hoping for some rest and trying to imagine how she would feel in Mr Darcy's house.

***

Although the family was gathered around for a rich breakfast, only the children seemed to have a healthy appetite. Elizabeth barely listened to the conversation, anxiously counting the minutes until they would leave. She had dressed with much care and arranged her hair as prettily as she could manage. She chose to wear the necklace from Lady Anne, hoping Georgiana would consider it a tender reminder of the past.

During breakfast, she brushed her fingers over the necklace several times, with a strange feeling, as though wearing it had placed additional responsibility on her.

Eventually, Mr Gardiner ordered the carriage, and together with Mr Bennet, they began the journey towards the place that had been in Elizabeth's thoughts for so long.

"I look forward to your return. I cannot remember when I was last so eager for news," Mrs Gardiner said.

Her aunt's unusual agitation increased Elizabeth's even more. She was relieved when the horses begin to move and argued with herself, trying to overcome her emotions. Why on earth would she entertain such strong and restless feelings for a mere visit? What was happening to her?

After a while — too long for her eagerness, too short for her anxiety — the carriage finally stopped. Mr Gardiner was the first to step out and Elizabeth the last. All three of them stared at the house — large and impressive, just as they expected — exchanging glances as they climbed the steps to the front door.

Before they had time to knock, the door opened and Mr Darcy appeared, welcoming them with less composure than they expected from him.

Two servants took their coats, while Mr Darcy enquired about their journey and escorted them forwards. Elizabeth glanced around, barely having time to notice what was around her. She hoped to see Georgiana directly, probably together with her companion; but the elegant drawing room they entered was empty, except for a couple of maids arranging some refreshments on a silver tray.

Mr Darcy dismissed the servants and invited them to sit. Mr Bennet and Mr Gardiner made themselves comfortable, whilst Mr Darcy still appeared slightly disconcerted.

"Mr Bennet, Mr Gardiner, may I offer you a glass of brandy? Miss Bennet, would you like some tea? It is terribly cold, is it not?" Mr Darcy addressed them, looking mostly at Elizabeth. She observed that he had noticed the necklace, and his scrutiny of her skin made her quiver.

"Yes, it is cold," she answered. "I would love some tea, thank you. But should we not wait for Miss Darcy to join us?"

Mr Darcy's eyes tentatively met hers as he held a cup which he was ready to offer her. Mr Darcy's willingness to serve her, her father, and her uncle was an image she could hardly accept.

"No, we...my sister...she... I deeply apologise, but my sister is not feeling well this morning," he finally mumbled. "I am afraid she cannot entertain guests. I beg your forgiveness for making you travel all the way here. I fear you will have to be content with my company alone."

His struggle and distress were apparent, and a slight tremble of his fingers could be noticed as he put down the cup. Embarrassment, anxiety, and regret were all visible on his face.

"Miss Darcy is ill? Yesterday you mentioned she was

waiting for us," Elizabeth insisted.

"Yes, I was under the same impression. Only this morning...she did not join me for breakfast, and Mrs Annesley informed me earlier she was unwell."

"Has the doctor seen her?" Elizabeth continued the enquiry that made Darcy obviously more uncomfortable.

"Yes. There is nothing of immediate concern, but he recommended she should stay in bed and rest. I apologise on her behalf and mine."

"We are very sorry to hear that," Mr Bennet said. "And there is certainly no reason to apologise, Mr Darcy. Do not make yourself uneasy."

Mr Gardiner nodded in approval, and Elizabeth hesitated briefly. Then, barely minding her words, she stood up and declared decidedly, "Mr Darcy, I do not wish to sound disrespectful, but I would like to see Miss Darcy. Even if she is in her room."

Darcy stared at her, confused, while Mr Bennet threw a reproachful glare at her, which Elizabeth chose to overlook.

"As I said, she is not prepared for guests. She has not left her chamber today."

He was standing too, facing her, only inches away. Elizabeth looked at him, daringly holding his gaze.

"Mr Darcy, we agreed that my visit might be beneficial for Miss Darcy. I came to see her hoping she was in good health. Now that I find out she is ill, how can I leave without seeing her? I must speak to her, if only for a few moments."

"I... This is quite unexpected. I might send a maid to ask her. I do not wish you to place yourself in an unpleasant situation, Miss Bennet."

"You would not, sir. Do not send the maid, just please take me to her room. I know my request is inappropriate, but it is heartfelt. Please trust me."

"Lizzy, I believe you have insisted enough!" her father interjected. "Mr Darcy must decide what he believes to be right."

Although Mr Bennet's voice was strong, Mr Darcy seemed to pay him no attention, and he answered Elizabeth.

"I do trust you, Miss Bennet. I only fear you might be disappointed. I wish the best for my sister and for you."

"So do I." Elizabeth smiled at him. "Do not worry that her refusal might upset or offend me. I promise you that will not be the case. If my presence is disagreeable to her, if she rejects me, I shall leave without hesitation."

Her smile was bright and broad, as opposed to Mr Darcy's frown. He hesitated for another long moment, glanced at their other two companions, and then, with apparent reluctance, his eyes returned to Elizabeth again.

"Very well, Miss Bennet. I shall escort you to my sister's apartment. Please excuse me, gentlemen. I shall return shortly."

He invited Elizabeth to accompany him, and without consideration for her gesture, almost regretting it a moment later, she took his arm. He lowered his eyes, but she only looked straight forwards, and they climbed the stairs to the first floor. Elizabeth was so anxious of her bold request as well as being alone with Mr Darcy, on his arm, in his house, that she noticed nothing else around her.

They stopped in front of a door, and she withdrew her hand, waiting. He knocked, waited until a voice invited him in, and only then did he enter. Elizabeth followed him, and with her heart racing from emotion, she saw an elegant woman of middle age staring at her, while Mr Darcy spoke in a low voice.

"My dear, I know you are unwell, but Miss Elizabeth Bennet is here. She has come a long way to meet you, and she insisted on seeing you, if only briefly."

A gasp, more like a deep sigh, could be heard, and as Darcy turned to her, Elizabeth caught a glimpse of Georgiana, sitting up in bed, her back resting against pillows, her hand covering her mouth in an expression of extreme surprise.

With her hair loose over her shoulders, the young lady looked so thin and pale that Elizabeth could hardly suppress her own gasp.

She took another step forwards, struggling to smile, while she said, "Georgiana, I do not believe you remember me. I am Lizzy Bennet. I have longed to see you for more than ten years, and I am happy that it has finally happened. Will you see me for just a few moments? Please?"

The girl turned even paler, her lower lip trembled, and her eyes seemed to moisten with tears. She cast a desperate look at her brother, who forced a little smile of reassurance.

"Forgive me. I am not dressed to entertain guests." The girl formed a weak apology.

Elizabeth approached the bed, while Mr Darcy took a step back, allowing them space. Unconsciously, Elizabeth touched her necklace, waiting at the edge of the bed.

"I am not a guest, and I do not wish to be entertained. I only want to spend a little time with you. May I?" Elizabeth continued gently. The young lady appeared resigned and glanced at her companion, who immediately invited Elizabeth to sit down.

"May I sit here?" Elizabeth asked Georgiana, indicating the side of the bed.

Surprised, the girl looked disconcerted by such a request, but she agreed.

"Please do...if you prefer to."

"I do, thank you," Elizabeth replied. Only then did she steal a glance at Mr Darcy and noticed him watching in disbelief.

"My dear, may I return to the other guests while you speak to Miss Bennet?" he enquired. Georgiana nodded and he continued, "Miss Bennet, do you mind?"

"I do not mind at all, Mr Darcy. Quite the opposite," she assured him. As he left, all three ladies glanced at the door. When it closed, Elizabeth looked at Georgiana, and their eyes met and locked. She smiled widely, hoping it would conceal her worry. Seeing the girl from such a short distance, she perfectly understood all Mr Darcy's concerns and his desire to do anything possible for Georgiana's well-being.

"I am very happy to see you at last, Miss Darcy," she repeated, trying to break the deep, heavy silence.

Chapter 18

Leaving his sister's apartment, Darcy stopped in the hall, torn between his duty to attend to his guests and his worry in regard to what was happening behind the closed door.

After their separation, his reunion with Elizabeth was as pleasant as it was disturbing. His feelings — profound and disquieting — provided the final evidence that his relationship with Elizabeth had overstepped the boundary of friendship, at least on his side. Of her feelings, he was uncertain, but he did not allow himself to reflect much upon it, since he had decided to take no action. Courting Elizabeth while she was meeting with his sister was unthinkable; besides, he was not even certain he wished to. Any display of his sentiments would imply a prior decision to pursue her to the altar. As powerful as his admiration for Elizabeth was, and as strong as his affection for her grew, as much as he respected her father, there were still some significant objections to such a union.

Considering the distressing situation with Georgiana, an action that could arouse conflict and more turmoil within the family was the last thing Darcy wanted. Besides, he was uncertain of Elizabeth's feelings too, though he assumed she would not reject a marriage proposal from him. It was not arrogance but common sense — that, Darcy did not doubt. But such reflections were in vain, as his feelings and desires in regard to Elizabeth were of little consequence at that time.

He leant his ear towards the door, listening, but nothing could be heard.

A day prior, he had been content seeing Georgiana animated about Elizabeth's visit. She seemed to look forward to it, giving him evidence that his little plan had been correct.

Earlier that morning, Georgiana's lack of spirits and her refusal to meet the guests had hurt and disappointed him. He had sent for the doctor but suspected it was not an illness that had changed Georgiana's mind but her poor disposition and usual reluctance to meet strangers.

He felt embarrassed and guilty towards Elizabeth and her father and feared they might be offended. Regardless, he did not even consider disrespecting his sister's wish, until Elizabeth decided otherwise, taking both of them by surprise.

Darcy would never have imposed upon anyone who had expressed a desire for privacy. He knew Georgiana had been stunned, even panicked by Elizabeth's impromptu appearance, and even to him, it was a bold action that broke the rules of decorum.

What convinced him to accept that questionable encounter was Elizabeth's determination and her genuine concern for Georgiana. He was impressed by her statement that she did not need to be entertained, nor would she be offended by a rejection.

Such devotion for someone she had not seen in ten years was uncommon and touching.

Also astonishing was Georgiana's readiness to accept Elizabeth's presence, despite its impropriety. There was something in Elizabeth's manners, her expression, and especially in her eyes that seemed appealing to all the Darcys, he mused, while finally returning to his other visitors. Still doubtful, he prayed that the reunion behind the closed door would not harm any of the ladies dear to his heart.

Mr Bennet and Mr Gardiner were waiting, restless and obviously worried. He assured them all was well momentarily, then invited them to the library for another drink.

***

Very soon, the silence became awkward; Georgiana

looked at Elizabeth with penetrating blue eyes shadowed by a sadness that was almost palpable.

"I am sorry that you found me in such a horrible state. I am sure I look terrible," she whispered.

"Not at all," Elizabeth replied. "You look just like me or my sisters when we are unwell or tired after a sleepless night. Except we are grumpier," she joked.

"You have more sisters?" the girl enquired.

"Yes, four sisters."

"Oh yes, my brother mentioned that to me..."

"Miss Bennet, would you like some tea?" Mrs Annesley intervened politely.

Elizabeth glanced at the lady, then at Georgiana.

"That would be lovely, but only if you and Miss Darcy will have some too," Elizabeth said. "Mr Darcy told me you did not eat breakfast."

"That is true. Miss Darcy has not eaten at all," Mrs Annesley replied with affectionate reproach.

"I felt unwell, and I was not hungry," Georgiana whispered, lowering her eyes.

Elizabeth caught Mrs Annesley's pained expression, so she instantly decided to continue to be bold.

"I confess I hardly ate anything at all. I was so eager to see you today that I lost my appetite. Tea would be lovely. Even a little something to eat, if possible?"

Georgiana seemed positively shocked, but Mrs Annesley became more animated.

"Of course, anything you like, Miss Bennet. I shall go to the kitchen to order it immediately."

The lady was ready to leave when Elizabeth called to her.

"Mrs Annesley, anything you order, please request enough for all three of us. I have no intention of eating alone."

"Of course, Miss Bennet!"

As soon as Mrs Annesley left, Elizabeth turned her gaze towards Georgiana.

"You have grown up to be so beautiful, but I can still

remember the little girl I met ten years ago at Pemberley," she said, putting the warmth from her heart into her voice.

"I am sorry, I do not remember you," the girl answered. "Mrs Reynolds told me about you... She wrote me two letters and explained everything. I do remember something...but I do not recognise you."

"That is understandable. You were very young, and I am sure I have changed a lot in ten years. Do you remember this?" Elizabeth asked, leaning forwards so the girl could see her necklace. Georgiana moved closer until she could see properly.

"I remember it! I have one almost the same, only the stones are a different colour."

"I know. Lady Anne told me as much when she gave it to me," Elizabeth said.

"It happened when you saved me from drowning, did it not? I might have died without your intervention. Mrs Reynolds told me that."

"Mrs Reynolds is giving me too much credit! There were many other people there taking care of you. I am sure someone would have intervened immediately. I just happened to see you and jumped in the water first. It might have been because I was a wild child. My mother always reminds me of that, and it is not praise."

They were now so close to each other, only inches separating them. Relieved that Georgiana seemed to accept her presence instead of rejecting her, Elizabeth smiled again with her whole heart. Suddenly, the girl sighed.

"I do remember you! Not your figure, but the way you look at me!" she whispered.

"I am glad you do," Elizabeth answered, gently touching the girl's hand. "And I am glad you have not sent me away yet. I know my unexpected entrance distressed you."

"I do not wish to send you away. But I was distressed to see you. I did not imagine you wished to see me, considering my situation..."

"I have longed to see you for ten years. I wished to see

you and know you were well, and even more so when I found out you were ill."

"Thank you. You are very kind," the girl replied in a weak whisper. "If you only knew... I do not deserve your kindness. I wanted to see you too, but if you knew more about me, about my terrible behaviour, you would not wish to be near me at all."

The small voice, burdened with sadness that seemed overwhelming for the girl's thin body and frail strength broke Elizabeth's heart. She could feel the dismay in Georgiana's voice, and for a moment, grief made her helpless and speechless. Her only thought was that she could finally understand Mr Darcy's anguish.

However, that moment passed soon, and Elizabeth's spirits rose, whilst affection and care pushed her into acting as her heart induced her, with little regard for decorum.

"I do not want to sound disrespectful, but I dismiss such a statement. I can see you are suffering, but I cannot imagine the reason for it. A young lady like you, so sensible, so well educated, so loved by her family and always guarded by a companion, could not have many occasions to behave so wrongly as you suggest. Even if you did, any mistakes at your young age cannot be given too much significance and are certainly easy to remedy."

"But I did! I made a terrible mistake, which deeply hurt my brother and my entire family. I am only telling you this because I want to protect you from being associated with me and suffering the consequences."

Georgiana's grief and the words that seemed to burst out as if they had been kept imprisoned for too long, added to Mr Darcy's prior confession and strengthened Elizabeth's worst suspicions.

"Miss Darcy, I see you are tormented, and you probably assume the situation is worse than it is. You should know that my youngest sister is your age, and she behaves badly at least three times a day. Unlike you, she could not care less." She struggled to sound light, but the girl was not amused.

"You should trust my word, Miss Bennet. It would be safer for you if you leave now. I thank you for taking the trouble to visit me. I do not wish to repay your kindness with harm."

Elizabeth stretched out her hand to hold the girl's. She startled at the touch and withdrew a few inches.

"Miss Darcy, if you are giving me the choice, I have no intention of leaving. I came to see you, to renew our friendship if possible. Friends are not together only in times of happiness, only to be entertained. I have come to be at your side if you will allow me. I shall leave if you want me to, but it will be against my desire, and that would hurt me indeed."

Elizabeth's decided statement clearly stunned Georgiana. In disbelief and silence, she seemed torn and fearful about how to reply. Then, with a little gesture that appeared of great difficulty to her, she stretched out her own hand and touched Elizabeth's.

"I do not want you to leave, Miss Bennet. But it would not be fair to allow you to stay," she whispered. Then her words were choked by tears falling down her pale face. Heavyhearted, Elizabeth put aside any prudence and moved closer on the bed, placing her arms around the girl and embracing her tightly. Georgiana froze, as if she did not know what to do other than to allow the tears to burst out, to free her soul from the burden of hidden suffering. Elizabeth stroked the girl's hair gently, wondering, fearing to imagine what had caused such devastating grief.

Neither of them heard the door opening and Mrs Annesley entering together with Mr Darcy, nor noticed the two staring at them with astonishment and panic.

"Miss Bennet? Georgiana? What happened?" Mr Darcy asked, and his strong voice, although soothed by concern, startled the two friends.

Georgiana immediately withdrew, as though she was ashamed of her weakness, and turned her head to wipe her eyes.

"Nothing happened. We were just sharing memories and were a little bit overwhelmed by our emotions," Elizabeth explained, trying to conceal her own tears. Her eyes met Mr Darcy's for an instant, and she was certain he understood more than her reply revealed.

"We brought some food and some tea," Mrs Annesley said. "The master was so kind as to help me carry the tray. I shall put it here, on the table."

"And I have come to tell Miss Bennet that her father and uncle wish to leave in an hour," Darcy added.

"Oh...so soon?" Georgiana sighed.

"It does seem too soon," Elizabeth admitted, smiling reassuringly at the girl. "Mr Darcy, if my father and uncle need to leave and I wish to stay longer, would there be a way for me to return to Gracechurch Street later?"

Her question brightened Georgiana's face, and Mr Darcy's expression also softened.

"Of course, Miss Bennet. If your father approves, I shall place a carriage with a footman and a maid at your disposal to use as you please. You may stay as long as you wish."

"And there is also a room prepared for you on this floor, next to my chamber, if you wish to rest or to stay overnight," Mrs Annesley said, trying to sound helpful.

Although that had been the plan from the very beginning, the notion of staying in Mr Darcy's house disquieted Elizabeth for a moment, as neither of them had expected it to occur so quickly. She dared cast a glance at him; he was gazing at her, waiting.

"Could you stay?" Georgiana asked with equal hope and fear in her eyes.

After another brief silent exchange with Mr Darcy, Elizabeth smiled at the girl.

"I shall speak to my father and ask for his approval immediately. There is nothing I would like more than to stay," she agreed.

"Will you not eat first? The tea and the soup will get cold," Mrs Annesley caringly offered.

"If you do not mind, I shall speak to my father first. It should not take long," Elizabeth said.

"I shall show you to your father, Miss Bennet," Mr Darcy offered, leading her to the door. When she was ready to leave, Georgiana called to her.

"Miss Bennet? Will you return?"

There was so much sadness in that plea that Elizabeth felt cold shivers down her spine.

"Of course I shall. But only if you call me Elizabeth. Or Lizzy, if you prefer, as you called me before," she jested, and a little hint of mirth lit in Georgiana's blue eyes.

"I shall wait for you…Lizzy," the girl replied, a trace of a smile twisting her lips as she wiped the last of the tears from her face.

Mr Darcy opened the door and held it, and Elizabeth left, glancing back towards Georgiana.

In the hall, the two of them stood still, gazing at each other for a long moment.

"Miss Bennet, do you wish to stay? I do not want you to feel forced to do something against your will," Mr Darcy said.

"You must not worry, sir. Everything I am doing is according to my wishes, and I accepted the invitation with all my heart. Do *you* wish me to stay, Mr Darcy?" she enquired, her gaze locked with his.

"With all my heart, Miss Bennet," he said, the corners of his mouth twisted in a small smile as he mirrored her answer. "I cannot express how grateful I am to you."

"Then do not speak of gratitude, Mr Darcy. You have already done it too many times," she continued. "Please take me to my father. I promised to return before the tea and soup get cold."

And yet, he remained still another moment, then took her hand and briefly brought it to his lips, bowing his head in a gesture of thankfulness.

"Thank you," he repeated in complete earnest, then offered her his arm and hurried towards the library.

Chapter 19

Mr Bennet's approval was readily granted, although his surprise at how quickly things had progressed was obvious.

"Papa, please ask my aunt to send me some clothes as soon as possible. I am not certain how long I shall stay, but I shall send word as soon as I have news."

"Miss Bennet—" Mr Darcy interjected, but she silenced him with a friendly yet determined smile.

"Mr Darcy, I am aware of your arrangement with my father, but Miss Darcy does not appear in a disposition to go shopping or to attend any events that might require new gowns. For the time being, please allow me to proceed as I consider appropriate."

He looked confused and agitated, then lowered his eyes with obedience.

"Of course, Miss Bennet. Please know that, for as long as you are my sister's guest, this is your home in all respects. Also, Mr Bennet, as well as Mr and Mrs Gardiner, may come to visit at any time they wish. I hope they will."

"Thank you, sir. For now, my only concern is Georgiana's comfort. I shall return to her now. Papa, I hope you will not return home immediately?"

"Not at all. I need to stay long enough to avoid that ball, or otherwise your mother will drag me to it."

It was only a few minutes until Elizabeth returned to Georgiana's room. Climbing up the stairs, she remembered Mr Darcy's words about it being her home. She knew he was only saying so for politeness, yet a slightly unsettling feeling enveloped her.

By the time she entered, she found Georgiana seated in an armchair near the fireplace, a warm blanket round her shoulders. In front of her was a small table, with two more chairs waiting. At Elizabeth's entrance, the girl's face brightened with relief.

"I took the liberty of making a little arrangement so we can eat more comfortably."

"That is perfect, Mrs Annesley. Let me help you with the dishes," Elizabeth replied. They filled three bowls of soup, poured some tea, and set out cold meat, bread, and fruit, then both sat down with Georgiana.

Elizabeth's attention returned to the young girl, and she immediately noticed that she was wearing the twin necklace. They shared a smile, and Elizabeth said, "The sapphire is perfect for you, Georgiana."

"And the rubies for you, Lizzy," the girl said shyly.

"Lady Anne was too generous with me," Elizabeth said. "I am not sure I am worthy of her gift, but I do love it."

"I am sure you are, Lizzy. My brother believes so too."

Elizabeth felt her cheeks burning. "Mr Darcy is too generous to me too," Elizabeth responded, wondering when Mr Darcy had made such a statement to his sister.

The atmosphere suddenly became heavy with emotions and brought a moment of silence.

"We should eat. The soup will get cold," Mrs Annesley suggested.

"I am not very hungry, but it is pleasant to sit here with you," Georgiana confessed.

"I am very hungry, but I intend to only eat as much as you do," Elizabeth responded.

Georgiana gazed at her, puzzled.

"That is unfair. I usually eat very little," she whispered.

"My dear Georgiana, when you know me better, you will see I am not fair at all when it comes to my friends' well-being. I must warn you that I shall use any schemes to see you feeling better and healthier," Elizabeth answered, causing Mrs

Annesley to give a little smile of satisfaction.

"Oh…" the girl murmured.

"And even worse, now you have invited me to stay, I shall not be easily sent away, even if you want me gone," Elizabeth added with teasing determination.

"I do not wish to send you away," Georgiana replied with a trace of panic.

"I am glad to hear that, because I would like to stay for a while. My only concern is that, if you keep up these eating habits, I might be starved to death!"

Mrs Annesley let out a chuckle, and even Georgiana smiled.

"I would not wish that," the girl admitted while tentatively sipping some soup. Elizabeth smiled too.

***

The small meal proved to be successful. At Elizabeth's constant nagging, Georgiana tasted everything. Not more than a few bites, but Mrs Annesley's repeated glances of surprise revealed that it was more than usual.

After they finished eating, Mrs Annesley offered to show Elizabeth her room. Georgiana encouraged her, claiming she would like to rest for a little while also, so Elizabeth agreed.

While she returned to the bed, Elizabeth and Mrs Annesley exited quietly. They needed only a few steps to reach the other door, which Mrs Annesley opened.

Elizabeth glanced around only briefly; the room was almost as large as Georgiana's bed chamber, with elegant furniture, a generous bed with crisp sheets, and several pillows.

It was rather cold, a sign that the fire burning lively in the hearth had only recently been started.

"The master had this room prepared, in case you wished to stay, Miss Bennet. However, if you prefer a larger one, there are several guest rooms and two apartments. Mr Darcy said you may choose whichever you want."

"This one is perfect. I shall only need it for sleeping. Otherwise, I prefer to spend my time with Georgiana."

"Did you bring a nightgown with you, Miss Bennet? If not, Miss Darcy has several new ones which I believe would fit you well."

"That would be lovely, thank you. I brought nothing with me, as I did not expect to remain from the first day. But... Mrs Annesley, all is well, except...may I ask you more about Georgiana's state? You have been with her all this time. Could you please help me with more details? What is wrong with her? What did the physician say? What is the nature of her illness?"

"I have been with her almost every minute of the day, Miss Bennet, yet there is not much more I can tell you except what I assume the master has already related to you. I have been Miss Darcy's companion since August, after her former one was dismissed."

"Yes, I know that. Mr Darcy confessed he was very pleased with your service and attachment to Georgiana."

"I am glad to hear that, but I doubt my abilities to be of use to Miss Darcy. She is so sweet and gentle, and kind, and yet she seems so distant most of the time that I wonder if she does not trust me or does not like me. I am glad you are here, Miss Bennet. I hope you will succeed where I have failed."

"I would not agree with such a conclusion, Mrs Annesley, and I would certainly not say you have failed. Something has affected Miss Darcy's health in recent months. She would not tell me what, but I am certain you are not to be blamed for it. She might be more open with me because of our past meetings."

"I pray she will, Miss Bennet. Let me know if you need anything else for your comfort."

"There is nothing else, thank you, Mrs Annesley. I assume you are very tired. I believe you should rest now, since I intend to keep Miss Darcy company myself."

"Oh, I could not…"

"Please do so. There is no use having both you and Georgiana exhausted."

"You are very considerate, but I shall ask Mr Darcy first."

"Of course. Now I shall return to Georgiana," Elizabeth concluded.

After the conversation, she was torn between relief that there was no specific illness affecting Georgiana and concern that the reason for her distress remained hidden. She decided not to enquire further until the girl was willing to open her heart.

Elizabeth returned to Georgiana's chamber and sat in an armchair, watching the girl sleeping, while thoughts and emotions surrounded her.

Everything had unfolded so quickly that she had no time for proper consideration. However, her father and uncle would leave soon, and she would be left alone with Georgiana. In Mr Darcy's house.

That knowledge was disturbing in ways she had never felt before. No, she was not worried about being in a man's house. Mr Darcy was not the sort of man one needed to fear in that way. Her concern was her own exhilarating feelings, her nervousness at knowing she was under his roof. Those sentiments were strong and disquieting, and she could not — or dared not — explain them. She struggled to dismiss those musings and scolded herself for being such a simpleton. Her only reason for being there was to take care of Georgiana, and she should be content that the girl had accepted her so readily.

A soft yet heart-breaking cry startled Elizabeth, and she hurried to the bed; Georgiana seemed caught in a terrifying dream, sweating, moving frantically, incoherent words flying from her lips.

Elizabeth shook her gently, calling her name quietly at first, then more loudly, until the girl woke up, looking around in obvious agitation. Elizabeth held her hands tightly, while Georgiana rose to sit.

"Lizzy?" she whispered.

"I am here. What happened, my dear?"

"I thought I was dreaming of you..."

"You look so frightened," Elizabeth said, stroking her hair. "Is it so because you dreamt of me?" she teased her.

"No...not because of you."

"It sounded like a terrible dream."

"I think I have dreamt of you before, Lizzy. When I was younger. Mrs Richmond — my governess — used to tell me it was only a dream... Now I see you were real..."

"Very much so, my dear. Would you like a drink?"

"Yes please... Mrs Annesley?"

"I asked her to go and rest. She was very tired also."

"Thank you. I know she is exhausted because of me—"

As they spoke, a knock on the door interrupted them, and Mr Darcy entered. His gaze fell on them, followed by a little frown.

"May I enter?" he enquired softly.

"Please do, Brother," Georgiana answered. Elizabeth noticed the girl met her brother's gaze only for a moment, then averted her eyes.

"Miss Bennet, I have come to tell you that your father and uncle have left. Mr Bennet will return tomorrow and bring your belongings. I shall send my carriage for him."

"Thank you, sir."

"It is almost dinner time. Will you join me for dinner downstairs?" he continued. Elizabeth looked at Georgiana, who seemed disquieted.

"Lizzy may go, but I am not hungry. In fact, I ate earlier. I am sorry, Brother," the girl said apologetically.

"We thank you for the invitation, Mr Darcy, but we shall not come downstairs tonight," Elizabeth replied. "However, we would like something to eat, if possible. I am still hungry, and Georgiana promised me she would always keep me company while I am eating," she said, smiling meaningfully.

A trace of a smile appeared on his lips too. "Of course,

Miss Bennet. You only need to ring once, and a maid will come to attend you. And...Miss Bennet, are you pleased with your chamber?"

"Very much so, Mr Darcy."

"If you wish, there are other larger ones, even on this floor—"

"Mrs Annesley told me," she interrupted him. "But the one I have is perfect. Thank you for choosing it."

Their gazes locked briefly once more, then he bowed and left.

"Your brother seems very fond of you." Elizabeth turned her eyes and smile at Georgiana. "He always speaks highly of you and is very proud of your accomplishments."

"My brother is too good to me. I do not deserve it," Georgiana answered in a low voice. "He has no reason to be proud of me. I am not worthy of his affection."

"I am certain that is not true, my dear. But I shall not argue with you again on this subject. Not today, and not before dinner," Elizabeth concluded, keeping her smile, although the girl's sorrow was like a knife in her heart.

"It is true. He knows the faults of my character, and he is still kind to me. I am so ashamed when I am around him. And you... If I would only dare to tell you..."

"Georgiana, let us speak no more of such things tonight. You should know you can tell me anything when you are willing to. As for faults of character, just wait to hear about mine. And about your brother's, if I may be so bold as to mention it."

The young lady's eyes widened. "My brother's? Fitzwilliam is a man without fault," she stated decidedly, and Elizabeth laughed.

"He might be without fault to you, just as you are without fault to him, my dear. But you cannot deny that he is haughty and arrogant with strangers, quite impolite at balls and parties, and refuses to dance even when gentlemen are scarce and more than one lady is in want of a partner,"

Elizabeth concluded, her eyebrow arched in challenge.

After another moment of hesitation, Georgiana put her hand to her mouth to conceal a chuckle. "I cannot deny it," she admitted, and Elizabeth laughed again.

Mrs Annesley returned shortly, and dinner was ordered for all three of them. Elizabeth was pleased that her efforts to raise Georgiana's spirits were not in vain. There were several moments when the girl seemed to forget the grief that burdened her soul and allowed herself to be amused by her companions.

Late in the evening, Mr Darcy came again to wish them a good night, and not long after that, Georgiana began to show signs of exhaustion. She assured both Elizabeth and Mrs Annesley that she was well and needed no help, asking them to retire to their own rooms, which they eventually did, even though both were reluctant to leave her.

Alone in her bedchamber, Elizabeth felt restless. She changed into the borrowed nightgown, which fitted her well enough, and climbed into bed, tired after the previous agitated night and eventful day but not enough to sleep. She got up again and looked through the window at the view of the street. There were torches burning and carriages passing; the sky looked serene, with stars and a bright moon. It was probably very cold. Her room was warmed by the glowing fire, but she still felt a hole of ice in her stomach.

She considered writing to Jane to calm herself, but there was no paper or ink. Nervousness made her thirsty, and only then did she realise there was nothing to drink in her room.

Wrapping the robe around her, and holding a candle to guide her, Elizabeth exited the room in search of a maid. She remembered the route to the library, and there she went, hoping to find the desired paper and pen too. With the hour so late, the house was silent and dark. Her steps sounded loud and strange.

Elizabeth stopped in front of the library door and pushed it carefully. The room was also dark; only the fire was still burning steadily. She walked towards the wooden desk — Mr Darcy's desk! — and immediately she noticed a pile of paper, as well as a pot of ink and some pens. For a moment, she even considered sitting on *his* chair and writing the letter at *his* desk, but her galloping heart changed her mind. Furthermore, she realised that taking some paper and a pen without asking permission would be unacceptable. She only dared to pour herself a glass of wine, sipped it, and turned to leave when a voice halted her.

"Miss Bennet?"

The surprise startled her. She dropped the glass and the candle on the floor. Fortunately, the carpet was thick and soft, and the glass survived, but the candle was extinguished. Elizabeth leant down to pick it up, and so did Mr Darcy. As they crouched, they almost collided, and she stumbled. His strong arm grabbed her, then he rose to standing, pulling her up with him.

"Miss Bennet, why are you here? Are you unwell? Has something happened to Georgiana?" he asked, his voice laced with panic.

Shame put a lump in her throat.

She shook her head. "I am perfectly well, sir. I apologise for disturbing you. I came to find a drink...and I wished to write to Jane. I thought I could find some paper in here," she mumbled, looking everywhere except at him. In the dark room, lit only by the fire, her heart was racing wildly.

He immediately lit two candles on the desk, and her face was in full light as he gazed at her.

"Forgive me for not considering it earlier. I shall send paper and ink to your room. As for a drink, the maid certainly forgot it. There is no reason to leave your room in the middle of the night. You only need to ring and ask for whatever you need."

"Yes, I know...but I did not wish to disturb anyone just for a little wine. I am sorry I still disturbed you..."

"You did not disturb me. I only feared the worst when I

saw you here. And there are several servants who are on duty at night, so it will be no bother for anyone."

"Oh…" She felt silly, as she only thought of Hill and John, who worked hard every day and needed rest at night. Surely the servants in Mr Darcy's house could not compare.

"Miss Bennet, would you like some tea or hot milk to help you sleep? Or a little bit of port, perhaps?"

She smiled, finally gaining some composure, although her cheeks were still warm.

"No, thank you. Only a little wine. Please, have a glass with me. If you would like to, that is."

"Would you like some paper and ink, too?"

"If you do not mind."

"Quite the contrary. A maid will bring you everything you need."

"Thank you," she repeated. Their gazes were still locked, and neither of them broke away.

"It is cold and very late. Not a proper time for a conversation," he finally said. "You should return to your room now, Miss Bennet. I shall send a maid with everything you need."

"Yes, of course," she replied, her cheeks burning again. How silly of her to venture out like that in the middle of the night. What if a servant had seen her alone with the master in the library? She had not even considered that, but he had. He was very careful to preserve his good name and his reputation, whereas she had acted carelessly.

"Good night, Mr Darcy."

"Good night, Miss Bennet. And…"

"Yes?"

"No, nothing… We can talk more tomorrow, in the daylight."

With those words, he dismissed her. He only took a few steps to accompany her to the door but kept a significant distance between them. He opened the door for her, as she had the glass in one hand and the candle in the other. For only an instant, they were so close that their bodies brushed against each other. The silky nightgown glided against her skin like a tentative caress. She hurried her steps, hoping that he would not notice her heated face nor hear her heart beating.

She did not turn her head at all, but she still felt his gaze upon her.

***

Darcy remained at the door, gazing at Elizabeth as she walked away, the fabric of the nightgown dancing around her figure. It was the first time he had seen her with her hair loose, falling over her shoulders. He had dreamt of her thus but did not dare admit it even to himself.

He was grateful she had left before she had noticed his perturbed state of mind. He returned to his seat, filled a glass of brandy, and opened the window widely, allowing the freezing air to cool his senses.

Chapter 20

Arriving in her room, Elizabeth needed a moment to catch her breath. She shivered and, assuming it was from the cold, sat in a chair near the fire, rubbing her hands.

Shortly after, a maid knocked and entered, bringing her several more candles, paper and ink, and some wine. As she was leaving, the maid reminded her once again that she only needed to ring for anything she might want.

Elizabeth thanked her, and as soon as she was alone again, all kinds of thoughts returned to trouble her. To avoid them, she began writing to Jane, which employed her time for more than half an hour. Afterwards, she decided to check on Georgiana before she finally tried to sleep.

She entered with infinite care, but a mere glance was enough to notice Georgiana turning her head towards her.

"What are you doing, my dear? Still not sleeping?" Elizabeth asked, moving closer. Even in the weak light of the fire, she observed the tears in the girl's blue eyes.

"Georgiana, what happened? You have been crying!"

"It is nothing. Do not worry. Just another dream."

"If these dreams prevent you from sleeping and make you unwell, I shall worry about them," Elizabeth said, climbing into the bed. Georgiana seemed surprised but did not argue.

"You look tired yourself, Lizzy."

"I am. But I shall stay with you until you fall asleep again. Do you mind?"

"Mind? No...but you should cover yourself. It is cold," Georgiana said, and Elizabeth pulled the blankets over herself, then arranged them around Georgiana.

"Your hands are so cold, my dear. I shall put another log on the fire," she said and left the bed again, only to return moments later.

"You are so kind to me, Lizzy."

"I am not the only one, my dear. Is your brother not kind to you? And Mrs Annesley?"

"Oh yes, they are. Fitzwilliam is the best brother one could hope for. And Mrs Annesley is the perfect companion. And all the servants who take care of me. They always have, since I can remember. But you are kind in a different way. I do not know how to explain it…"

"I am just happy to be here, Georgiana."

"And I am happy to have you here, Lizzy. Very happy. And my brother is happy too."

To that, Elizabeth said nothing, only stroked the girl's hair.

"You should sleep now, my dear. It is very late."

Although silence fell in the room, broken only by the sound of the crackling fire, it took some time until Georgiana finally appeared to rest. Relieved, Elizabeth decided to stay only a moment longer, to be certain the girl had fallen asleep. But against her will, tiredness defeated her too, and she fell into a deep sleep that lasted until dawn.

***

Darcy woke up early, as was his habit, even though his sleep had been less restful than usual. The brief encounter with Elizabeth had stirred his senses in a way he had never before experienced. If he had been free to do so, he would have asked her to sit, would have enquired how she was feeling, how she had fared since he had left Netherfield, how she felt about Georgiana — anything to start a little private conversation simply to have her near him. But he was not allowed to do that. He had been careful about any gesture, any breath that might jeopardise her reputation while in his house. It was a delicate enough situation that a young woman was living in a single man's house, even if she was Georgiana's friend and Mrs Annesley was there as a chaperon. Elizabeth certainly did not need to worry about more gossip to repay her kindness.

His valet helped him prepare for the day, but he was still lost in his thoughts. Mr Bennet was expected to arrive around noon, and that was the perfect opportunity to take Elizabeth and her father on a tour of the house.

Darcy went down to his library, asking for coffee. Lately, he had developed a habit and a fondness for that drink, which apparently had the power to compensate for poor sleep; at least that was the claim of his cousin Colonel Richard Fitzwilliam, Darcy mused with a smile to himself. Until meeting Elizabeth Bennet, and before that low-life Wickham's scheme with Georgiana, he had rarely needed anything to keep him awake and attentive to his duties.

The first meeting of the day was with his housekeeper. She came to ask for the day's requirements and to provide him with a report of the previous day.

"Have you provided a maid for Miss Bennet?"

"Yes, sir."

"We are obligated to provide Miss Bennet with the same comfort as any member of the family. She is a gentleman's daughter and the closest friend of my sister."

"Of course, sir."

"Please be warned that one evening soon we shall host a dinner party. There will be likely ten to twelve people in attendance. I am not certain when and if it will truly occur."

"We can make preparations for such a small party at any time, sir."

"Good. That will be all for now." He hoped that Georgiana would agree to have a family dinner with only Elizabeth's relatives and probably Colonel Fitzwilliam. However, the chance was small considering his sister refused to even have dinner or breakfast with him alone.

With concern and some strange anticipation, Darcy left his library to pay his morning visit to Georgiana. Except that, starting that morning, he would see Elizabeth too — a notion equally pleasant and distressing.

When he knocked and entered, he only saw his sister and Mrs Annesley, which caused him a slight — and unreasonable — disappointment. They greeted him, and he noticed there was a little more colour than usual in Georgiana's cheeks.

"Miss Bennet has gone to dress for the day," Mrs Annesley explained before he enquired.

"Lizzy was here the entire night," his sister added. "I had a bad dream, and Lizzy was concerned and stayed with me until I fell asleep again. She is so kind to me!"

"It seems you slept better than usual, for you look rested," Darcy said with a smile.

"Miss Darcy even ate quite well yesterday. Miss Bennet has a way of making us do as she asks. She is quite persuasive, which is commendable," Mrs Annesley added.

At that moment, Elizabeth entered, and on seeing Darcy she stopped in the doorway. She held his gaze for a moment, then averted her eyes.

"Good morning, Miss Bennet. Mrs Annesley was just praising your power of persuasion. I hope you slept well?"

"My power of persuasion is what my mother calls obstinacy and stubbornness and does not find it praiseworthy," Elizabeth replied with a nervous smile. "I did sleep well, thank you, sir."

"I told my brother that you watched over me the entire night," Georgiana added.

"I do not deserve any credit for that. My intention was to retire to my chamber, but apparently, I fell asleep too. Mrs Annesley woke me this morning."

"I hope both of you rested well," Darcy said. "Miss Bennet, your father will arrive later, and I would like to take both of you on a tour of the house if you agree. Perhaps Georgiana might join us?"

Elizabeth smiled in approval, but Georgiana paled.

"Oh, forgive me, Brother, but I would rather remain in my room. Please show Elizabeth the house by yourself."

"Of course, my dear. May I hope you will join me at least for breakfast?"

"No yet. Perhaps tomorrow?"

"As you wish. My dear, there is something else I want to discuss with you. Before Mr Bennet returns to Hertfordshire, I would like to invite him and Mr and Mrs Gardiner to dinner. They are lovely people, and I know they wish to be acquainted with you. Richard might attend too."

Georgiana's eyes widened, and her face became even paler. She looked at Elizabeth, then back to Darcy.

"That would be lovely, Brother. I wish to meet them too," she whispered.

"I shall leave you now, ladies. Have a good day." He bowed and left.

***

Elizabeth scrutinised her friend with careful attention. She felt Mr Darcy had somehow forced his sister into accepting the dinner invitation, but perhaps it would be helpful for the girl. She knew her father, uncle, and aunt were loving and considerate people with no pretensions to make the girl uncomfortable.

"Oh, I forgot to ask Mr Darcy about my letter to Jane. I wrote it last night, and I would like to send it to Longbourn."

"Would you like me to take it to the master? I am going downstairs," Mrs Annesley offered. Elizabeth hesitated a moment. In all honesty, she would prefer to speak to Mr Darcy herself, but the chills she felt at that thought warned her against it.

"Yes please, Mrs Annesley. I shall fetch it in a moment."

Several minutes later, Elizabeth found herself alone with Georgiana. The young girl's anxiety was so obvious that she could not refrain from addressing it.

"My dearest, forgive me if I intrude, but may I ask why you are avoiding your brother? I know how fond he is of you, but you act as if you loathe his presence."

The straightforward enquiry left the girl dumbfounded, her tearful expression revealing a profound distress which made Elizabeth regret her imprudence.

"I do not loathe my brother! Why would you assume that? I love him dearly, and I am grateful every day for his affection and support!"

"Georgiana, please forgive me for upsetting you! Your distress seems so deep that I would do anything to bring you some comfort."

Elizabeth stretched out to grasp the girl's hands, and Georgiana did not withdraw.

"I know you mean well, Lizzy."

"I am just trying to understand what pains you, what frightens you so much that it has affected your health and your spirits."

"It is certainly not my brother, Lizzy! But you are right, I do wish to avoid his company, because…"

"Yes?" Elizabeth asked gently to encourage her.

"It is I who hurt him! And I am afraid I shall hurt him even more. That I shall ruin his name and his entire life. He is a man of honour, and I do not know how he will live if… And my cousins, my uncle and aunt…all will be hurt and devastated."

Emotions overwhelmed her, and she began sobbing, while Elizabeth embraced her, puzzled and helpless. A few minutes passed with Elizabeth only holding her and stroking her hair, while the girl kept weeping. The door opened quietly, and Mrs Annesley entered, then stopped in shock. Elizabeth silently gestured to the lady to leave, as she was sure Georgiana had not seen her.

When she seemed to calm a little, Elizabeth handed her a handkerchief to wipe her face.

Heavyhearted and fearing rejection, Elizabeth breathed deeply and gathered the courage to speak.

"Georgiana, I realise we only met again yesterday after so many years, and I promised to wait patiently until you are ready to tell me what bothers you. But I cannot do that. I can no longer bear witnessing your sorrow and your brother suffering on your behalf while fearing the worst, without trying to help in some way. I do not wish to sound disrespectful to your grief, but I cannot imagine what you could possibly have done to cause the devastating outcome you imagine. A lady of your age, with your situation in life, watched by a permanent chaperon, could not do something evil even if she wished to! It simply cannot be!"

With every word, Elizabeth's agitation grew, and her voice became more insistent, even demanding. Georgiana's torment was apparent, but Elizabeth was determined not to allow the girl to fall back into her silent turmoil.

"My brother fears the worst? What worst?" Georgiana whispered fearfully.

The question took Elizabeth by surprise.

"What worst? He is frightened that you are sick from some strange illness, that you do not trust him, that he has failed you as a brother, and probably much more. A tragedy even. And now that I have seen you, I understand him. Please, my dear, tell me what tortures you so. I promise not to betray your secret to any living soul. Or to tell your brother. Or Mrs Annesley or one of your relatives. But you cannot keep it buried within yourself any longer, or it will break you completely!" Elizabeth pleaded.

After the loud and agitated outburst, a heavy, deafening silence followed, with the two ladies staring at each other wordlessly, barely daring to breathe.

"I do not dare tell my brother or Mrs Annesley," Georgiana finally spoke, pale, her lips and voice trembling. "And certainly not my relatives. My cousin Richard is aware of some... He is my guardian, together with Fitzwilliam, did you know?"

"I did."

"If you wish, I shall tell you. As I said yesterday, you deserve to know, so you have time to distance yourself from me before it is too late."

"I shall never wish to distance myself from you, my dear. But I do wish you to tell me. Please!" Elizabeth begged once more, holding the girl's hands again.

Georgiana nodded and cleared her throat, taking a deep breath, then started speaking.

Chapter 21

"This dreadful situation began this past summer when I spent a month in Ramsgate." She paused for a moment, averted her eyes in shame, and sighed. "I forgot prudence and decorum and what I owed to my family. I forgot the consideration due to my brother and...I decided to elope..."

Elizabeth was prepared for the worst; hearing the girl's confession, she almost sighed in relief. She immediately remembered her discussion with Mr Darcy in Hertfordshire. The name that had not even been mentioned sprung into her head, and rage built inside her.

"I am sure you are shocked and appalled, and I deserve your harshest judgment," Georgiana said.

"I could never judge you. And I am not appalled. I am simply astonished. You are so young, and you are chaperoned all the time. I wonder at how you met someone and such a plan was formed."

"It was... He was an old friend. I did not meet him there. I have known him my entire life. I spent my childhood with him, under my father's protection."

"I see..."

"I have always been fond of him. I always had very few friends. As a child, there was only one constant friend who was always by my side."

"May I ask who he is?" Elizabeth asked, although she knew the answer.

"He was almost ten years my senior, and he was my father's godson. We shared the same name."

"George Wickham?"

Georgiana could barely utter the words. "Do you know him?"

"I met him when I was at Pemberley, ten years ago. I even had an argument with him. And I met him again recently."

"I did not remember you meeting him as a child. But my brother told me he had joined the militia, in Meryton, so I assumed you knew him."

"I do. And I must admit I had another argument with him."

"My brother does not like George. He never did. Papa used to say Fitzwilliam was too good and responsible a man, and he expects perfection from himself and from others. He said he disapproved of George because he was too different from him. But Papa loved him."

"I am more concerned about your well-being than George Wickham's character now, my dear. Would you not tell me what happened in Ramsgate?"

"George happened to be there at the same time, and I was so happy when we met! He visited every day, he took me on long walks on the beach, we spoke of our childhood and of my father. He was so kind and so understanding, and it was so easy for me to talk to him. He always knew how to make me feel comfortable."

Another pause challenged Elizabeth's patience. George Wickham's vicious plan was clear, but somehow, Georgiana seemed not to blame him still.

"I felt so happy with him, and he made my days joyful. I was grateful that he wasted his time keeping me company instead of joining his friends. I missed him when he was gone, and he used to write me little notes, to which I replied with eagerness," the girl confessed with a sad little smile.

"I knew he had no career yet, and he told me my brother despised him for that, but many people struggle to find a profession that suits them. And..."

"Yes?"

"I felt so much affection for him, and he confessed he

was in love with me. That he had wished for a chance to speak to me, but he knew my brother would not allow it. And he said the only chance for us to be together was to elope, because the fear of a scandal which would hurt his name and his family would convince Fitzwilliam to accept him."

Georgiana's voice became more and more agitated, and Elizabeth struggled to keep her composure. It was apparent that the young girl's feelings had not subsided, and she held no grudge against Wickham, although the scoundrel's scheme was all too transparent.

"May I ask, where did you two meet to carry on these conversations? How did your companion allow it?"

"Mrs Younge and George were good friends. I discovered that in Ramsgate."

"How fortunate a coincidence for him," Elizabeth replied with repressed anger. "May I assume you eloped and were caught?"

"We did not..." the girl replied, and Elizabeth frowned. "My brother arrived unexpectedly a day prior to the elopement. He had missed me and came to see me. I could not go through with the elopement, knowing how much I would hurt him. I could not bear seeing him suffer and facing shame because of me. Therefore, I told him. I had to choose between betraying my friend and betraying my brother..."

Tears interrupted the confession, and Elizabeth embraced the girl to comfort her.

"I imagine your brother was upset," Elizabeth said a while later.

"He was. Not with me, with George. He waited for him that evening, and they had a horrible fight. He dismissed Mrs Younge too. I thought I would die of pain..."

"My dear, I am so sorry for all the torment you had to suffer."

"Fitzwilliam said some hurtful things about George, and he implied it was only a scheme to benefit from my dowry. He must have been right. After all, why else would George love someone so plain and dull as me?"

"While I cannot say your brother was wrong, I must dismiss your question. You are one of the most accomplished women I have ever known. You are beautiful, well educated, kind, with a sweet and generous nature. Everyone who knows you adores you!" Elizabeth said with all honesty, which made her voice a little too loud.

The girl shook her head in doubt, so she continued.

"But even if his affection for you was genuine, for a man of that age to convince a girl ten years his junior, almost a child yet, to elope with him — that is unacceptable! Instead of making a living, proving himself worthy of you and capable of supporting a wife, Mr Wickham tried to take the easiest road, to gain a comfortable position for himself without much trouble! Just as he always has!" Elizabeth burst out without much consideration for her words.

"As he always has? What do you mean, Lizzy?"

"My dear, I do not wish to pain you more, but you probably do not remember, and perhaps it is better to know the truth. I mentioned an argument I had with George Wickham when I was at Pemberley. I caught him asking you to give him some money and to steal something for him. And you were only a child of five then! I am sure he did that many times."

The girl's eyes opened wider, and a sigh escaped from her lips. "That was not... I know he meant no harm. They were only small things that no one missed around the house. George had very little money. His father earned a good wage, but Papa said his mother spent too much. I helped him..."

Elizabeth gently stroked her hair. "Your entire family helped him, my dear. I believe that was the problem. He always obtained what he wanted by deceiving others. When I confronted him, he claimed nobody would believe me because his godfather loved him and trusted him."

"Oh..."

"I am sure he did the same with your brother too. I understand Mr Wickham was given a good education. But to no avail, since he chose not to use it to further himself."

"My father told me to take care of George when he was gone. He said Fitzwilliam demanded more than George could give, and that was why they were always in disagreement."

Elizabeth struggled to repress an eye roll, as she did not want to upset the girl even more.

"Georgiana, please help me understand. The elopement did not occur. Your brother settled things with Mr Wickham in some way. Then why all this turmoil and suffering? Why do you believe you will hurt your brother and your family? What scandal do you fear? It is all over now. Mr Wickham is forced to keep the secret. He cannot reveal his plan to elope with you! That would be devastating for what is left of his reputation. I hope he will work to be worthy of his new career as an officer."

Georgiana gazed at Elizabeth, and the pain in her eyes was heart-breaking.

"There is something that nobody knows...except for George and Mrs Younge. I told nobody else..."

"Would you not tell me, please? If there is more, I am here to help."

"You cannot help me, Lizzy... It is so shameful that nobody can..."

"Still, I am begging you to tell me."

Several long moments passed until the girl could continue.

"A few days prior to the engagement, we dined together. Me and George and Mrs Younge. We had such a wonderful time. I played the pianoforte, and George turned the pages for me... then I felt suddenly dizzy, I could not stand or sit... I had to go to sleep, and I do not remember how I got to my room, but I woke up the next morning...and...George was there, in my bed..." she whispered with the last of her strength.

"Oh!" Elizabeth gasped against her will.

"Yes... George told me I insisted on him staying with me. That he agreed because he knew we would be married soon. I did not remember anything at all... Not a single moment.

Mrs Younge knew too. She said she would not be surprised if I were to be with child after that night. And that it was good that we would be married so soon before anyone noticed. Then my brother came the next day and..." Georgiana started to cry again, all her pain coming out in her tears.

Elizabeth was left helpless and speechless, lost as to what she could say.

"And are you with child?" she dared whisper.

"I believe so. I must be. I feel ill all the time and cannot eat anything. And I am always dizzy. I know a little about how women feel... Mrs Annesley told me that her niece was very ill when she was with child."

"Does Mrs Annesley know?"

"Oh no! She received a letter from her sister some time ago, and I asked for details."

"And the doctor could not be certain of your...situation? I know he examined you several times."

"I did not tell the doctor either! How could I? He would have told Fitzwilliam! He only listened to my heart and took some blood and gave me some tinctures. Even George told me I looked different, so it was probably apparent to him."

"George Wickham? Did you see him again?"

"Yes, several times, while I walked with Mrs Annesley in Hyde Park. He barely said a few words to me, as Mrs Annesley did not know who he was. I told her he was an old acquaintance. Then I avoided going to Hyde Park entirely."

"Does your brother know that?"

"He does not. Why would he? I am sure it was a mere coincidence. There are always hundreds of people in Hyde Park! Once he was alone, once with some friends, once with Mrs Younge. But that was a few months ago, at the end of the summer."

Elizabeth stood up impatiently, taking a few steps while she tried to put her thoughts together. She did not believe such meetings could be a coincidence, but what concerned her more was Georgiana's grief and the best way to soothe it.

She looked at the girl, then took a few steps, rubbing her forehead with her fingers. If Georgiana was with child, there was no other way than to inform Mr Darcy. Such a secret could not be buried.

"I understand your distress, Lizzy, but I am still happy that I told you. I know it is difficult for you to be near me now, and I promise I understand if you wish to leave."

"Leaving you is the furthest thing from my mind, my dear. I am trying to think what the best way forwards might be. I cannot allow you to suffer another moment longer. Even if you are with a child, there must be a solution."

She stopped and looked at the girl, who was sitting up in bed, her head leaning against the pillows.

"My dear, you were in Ramsgate in July? Four months ago?"

"At the end of June. Five months ago. There are four more months until…"

"You cannot suffer such distress for four more months! I know little about such things, but I remember my mother and my aunt Gardiner when they were with child. You certainly do not look as they did."

"I do not know much either, Lizzy. I have been so unwell since then. I have all the signs… I avoided my uncle and aunt so they would not notice. And Lady Catherine. If she finds out…"

"Let us calm ourselves for a moment. I understand you do not wish to speak to your relatives. But would you not want to talk to someone knowledgeable and trustworthy who cares for you and will respect your need for secrecy? Someone who may know the truth?"

"I would… That would be the physician, but he has been in our family service for many years. I would die of shame if he knew."

"I am not talking about the physician but of my aunt Gardiner. The one who brought me to Pemberley and who was so fond of your mother!"

Georgiana's astonishment was now complete. "Mrs

Gardiner? But—"

"My aunt has four healthy children. She would know. If only you can trust her enough to give her all the details, she might know better than a doctor. Once we know the true situation, we can decide what to do next."

"Lizzy, I do not know... How could I reveal something so horrible to a stranger? I would always be ashamed in her presence. And she might demand you leave me immediately, in order to distance yourself from the scandal."

"My dear, I am starting to become so annoyed with you for repeating this nonsense that I truly might leave you!" Elizabeth said with determination and a trace of jest. "Enough of this! Please consider carefully whether you are able to speak to my aunt. If you are, I shall write to her and ask her to come and visit shortly. All will be done with the utmost discretion, and I trust we shall put an end to the misery, doubts, and speculations."

Elizabeth resumed her place on the bed, while Georgiana fell into silent thoughtfulness. They were suddenly interrupted by a knock on the door, and Mr Darcy entered. Seeing him, Georgiana turned pale. Elizabeth became uncomfortable also, which only drew his attention to her.

With unease, he greeted them again and said, "Miss Bennet, your father has just arrived. Mr and Mrs Gardiner are with him too. They are expecting you whenever you wish to come downstairs."

Georgiana gasped, then suddenly covered her mouth with her palm. Elizabeth caught her breath for an instant and then held Darcy's gaze.

"Thank you, sir. I shall be down immediately. If Georgiana agrees, I might bring my aunt to greet her. She has longed for an opportunity to see Miss Darcy again."

Mr Darcy bowed and left, leaving the two ladies alone again, staring at each other.

"I do not wish to hurry you, Georgiana. I can ask her to call another day."

The young lady breathed so deeply that it sounded like another sigh.

"Do whatever you think is best, Lizzy. I trust your judgment more than mine."

Chapter 22

Elizabeth hurried down the stairs in such a tormented state of mind that she almost stumbled. Georgiana's story itself — although painful and disturbing — did not come as a complete surprise to her. She had some prior suspicions from the day of Mr Darcy's confession about Mr Wickham in Hertfordshire.

More frightening than the attempted elopement planned by a vicious, disgraceful man was the turmoil and the fear that had grown inside Georgiana's heart, like a poisonous weed that had suffocated her spirit. The girl's good heart, very similar to Jane's, prevented her from seeing the whole truth — as depraved as it was. Elizabeth had no doubt that it had been an elaborate scheme, designed by Mr Wickham with the involvement of Mrs Younge, in order to trap Georgiana and her dowry, which must be considerable. Being Mr Darcy's brother-in-law was something that Mr Wickham had likely never dreamt of, but he had not taken the trouble to attain that goal through honourable means and hard work. Why would he, since he had already gained so much in his life by deception and disloyalty?

As for Georgiana being with child, Elizabeth did not dare speculate. She thanked the Lord that Mrs Gardiner was already there. She should know what to ask and what to look for in order to discover the truth. Regardless of its nature, the truth was better than the dreadful doubts that had tortured the girl for so long. At least they would know what to expect and have a little time to attend to the circumstances in the best possible way.

She found her relatives in the drawing room with Mr Darcy, engaged in a surprisingly friendly discussion. She greeted them and sat for a moment, preparing her excuse to take her aunt away.

"How is Miss Darcy today?" her father enquired.

"She is a little better," Elizabeth answered hesitantly. "In fact, she has expressed a desire to see Aunt Gardiner, since she is one of the very few people who spent time with Lady Anne during her illness."

As she spoke, Elizabeth saw Mr Darcy's frown of surprised disbelief, but she pretended not to notice it.

"Oh, that would be wonderful indeed!" Mrs Gardiner exclaimed. "I would be honoured and delighted to meet Miss Darcy if she wishes it."

"She does. If the gentlemen do not mind, we shall go upstairs."

Mr Darcy approved the scheme with a nod, his puzzlement obvious in his stare that followed them.

In the hall, Mrs Gardiner expressed her joy one more time.

"Aunt, there is something very important that I must speak to you about before you meet Georgiana," Elizabeth said urgently. "We shall go to my chamber first, to speak privately for a few moments."

"Of course, my dear. You sound very worried! Is something wrong?"

"Something is terribly wrong, and I hope you will help us resolve it," Elizabeth confessed as they entered her chamber.

"Aunt, there is something of extraordinary importance I must ask your advice about. I trust your secrecy and your wisdom, and I must beg you not to share this with anybody, including Papa and my uncle. Georgiana will grant you her complete confidence — something she has not dared to do with her own relatives."

"My dear, now I am really scared. Stop warning me and let me know what is happening!"

With a few hesitant words and in a trembling voice, Elizabeth related the story, ending with the request she must make of her aunt.

"Dear Lord, what a despicable man! When you wrote to me asking about Mr Wickham, I did not imagine such a horrible character! Poor Mr Darcy would be devastated to know how his godson has turned out."

"He probably would, but at this time I care little about anyone but Georgiana and her peace."

"Let us go and see her. But my dear, I believe you should only stay until she grows at ease with me, then leave us alone. She will be more comfortable answering my questions in complete privacy."

"Very well."

With tension burdening them both, they knocked and entered Georgiana's apartment. The girl was fully dressed, and Mrs Annesley was there. After a brief introduction, Georgiana kindly asked her companion to leave.

Mrs Gardiner sat on the indicated chair, and for a moment, she and the girl exchanged some glances.

"You have inherited Lady Anne's beauty, Miss Darcy," Mrs Gardiner said. "From a hundred young ladies, I could have guessed you were her daughter without hesitation."

"Thank you, Mrs Gardiner," Georgiana whispered, lowering her eyes.

"I imagine it is difficult for you to see someone you probably do not remember here in your room. I know I am a stranger to you, but please know Lizzy and I have kept you in our hearts all these years."

"Lizzy told me. I am so grateful to you both."

"Dearest, I have told my aunt about your situation," Elizabeth interjected. "Please do not hesitate to speak to her openly. If you agree, I shall leave you two alone and will wait outside the door."

"Oh...yes, it is probably the best," the girl agreed after a moment of panic and hesitation.

"I shall be in the hall if you need me," Elizabeth assured her again with a smile and a gentle embrace. She closed the door behind her and then leant against the wall, taking a deep breath and rubbing her temples to ease her headache. It was still morning, and she had only been in Mr Darcy's house for a day and a half, but it felt as long as a month.

She put her ear to the door but could hear nothing from inside. The sound of footsteps startled her only when they were very close, and she found herself facing Mr Darcy's dumbfounded stare, matching the frown between his eyebrows.

"Miss Bennet? What are you doing here?" he asked. His voice seemed to echo in the heavy silence. Shocked, Elizabeth impulsively tried to quiet him by pressing her palm over his mouth. As he was speaking, his moving lips were parted, and her fingers brushed over it. The sensation of his warm breath on her skin was so powerful that it burnt her, and she instantly withdrew her hand, while thrills overwhelmed her entire being. Abashed, she averted her eyes, and in doing so, she missed Mr Darcy's gesture of licking his lips after her touch and his own embarrassment at realising it.

Knowing he deserved an explanation, Elizabeth took a few steps away, and he followed her. She rose onto her toes, and he lowered his head to better hear her whispers.

"Georgiana is talking to my aunt. Privately. And I do not wish to disturb them."

Mr Darcy's look of astonished puzzlement only increased.

"Alone? Without you?"

Hoping he had not noticed that his nearness in the middle of the empty hall had made her warm and shivery at the same time, she continued.

"She spoke to me too. But she needs a mother figure, for advice and guidance which I cannot provide."

"But…"

"Please do not worry, sir. I trust my aunt with my life.

She would never betray a secret."

"I do not doubt Mrs Gardiner. I just wonder why my sister chose to speak to her since they are barely acquainted."

"Sometimes it is easier to confide in a stranger than your own relatives, as much as you love them."

"That I can understand," he admitted. "Even I have confessed things to you that I have kept secret from my own family."

"I am glad you did," she replied. They were now close enough to feel the warmth of each other's unsteady breathing, which made both dizzy. It was Mr Darcy who took a step back to increase the distance between them.

"I shall leave you now unless you require my presence."

"I do not. I shall stay here to watch the door until they call for me."

"Thank you, Miss Bennet. In less than two days, you have succeeded where I have failed for so many months."

"You are too severe on yourself, sir. A young girl can more easily open herself up to a friend close to her age than to her much older brother whom she loves and admires."

"Will you tell me what is happening?" he enquired with apparent disquiet.

"Only if and as much as Georgiana allows me to. However, I promise I shall do everything in my power to soothe her distress and to see her improve."

"That is all I hope and pray for," he admitted. He looked at her with lingering gaze for another moment, appearing undecided and uneasy, until he found his words again.

"My cousin Colonel Fitzwilliam has arrived, and he is looking forward to making your acquaintance. Perhaps you could join us?"

"As soon as Georgiana completes her conversation with my aunt, I shall see how she feels. My plans for today depend on her."

"Of course. Thank you."

He turned to leave when Elizabeth grabbed his arm.

"Mr Darcy?"

"Yes?"

"Please stop thanking me, sir. Every time I speak to you, I fear you will thank me again," she teased him.

"I shall try since it is your wish. But I cannot promise, since I am truly, deeply thankful to you, Miss Bennet."

With that, he left. Elizabeth watched him depart, then she looked at her fingers that had pressed over his mouth. Since he was gone, she had time to recollect that moment and realise she had touched the inner part of his lips and even his tongue for an instant. That thought was disturbing, in a pleasant, mortifying way that made her quiver and feel ashamed of herself. She just hoped he gave no importance to her silly action and forgot it as soon as it occurred. It was truly nothing; only her being a simpleton caused her to be so affected by an innocent — though improper — gesture.

***

To Elizabeth, the waiting was torture; her worry for Georgiana mixed with her torment regarding Mr Darcy. As much as she tried, she could no longer deny the strength of her feelings for him, nor dismiss them. He had never shown her anything but the utmost respect. Except of course for his disapproval of her appearance, which was clearly expressed at the Meryton assembly the first time they met. It was absurd for her to imagine anything more than a mere friendship with Mr Darcy, which he had already kindly offered to her and her family. Any other feelings she might have entertained had to remain buried.

Eventually, the door opened, and Mrs Gardiner appeared. Her aunt's serene expression soothed some of Elizabeth's distress.

"You may enter, Lizzy."

She did so and found Georgiana on the same chair, at the small table near the window. Mrs Gardiner took a seat;

Elizabeth sat too, hoping for explanations she did not dare ask about.

"So, my dear, I shall repeat what I have already told Miss Darcy. I am not a physician, and I cannot claim medical knowledge, but I have carried five children, including one I tragically lost before she was even born. I have also witnessed your mother and other friends carry and give birth to several healthy children. I would say that it seems impossible to me that Miss Darcy has been expecting for five months. At this stage, a child should already be moving inside its mother, and a woman's body undergoes several obvious changes, even if she is exceedingly thin."

Elizabeth watched both her companions, too fearful to be overjoyed at such good news, especially since Georgiana was as silent and grave as usual.

"Mrs Gardiner said it cannot be," Georgiana repeated in a whisper. "I do not doubt her, but I find it so hard to believe…"

"I can understand that. Therefore, I have offered Miss Darcy the chance to obtain a second opinion. Might you ask Mr Darcy to allow you two to visit me? I shall invite my physician, Dr Talbot, to come and kindly ask him to examine my niece who has recently married and come to visit me in London. Dr Talbot has been our doctor for more than ten years. He cannot possibly be wrong."

"That would mean deceiving Mr Darcy," Elizabeth said thoughtfully.

"Only in regard to the doctor's examination," Mrs Gardiner admitted. "You will visit me, and we shall have a cup of tea together. In that, you are telling the truth."

"Am I not deceiving my brother already, Lizzy?" Georgiana whispered. "I would rather do as Mrs Gardiner suggests as soon as possible. But I shall not tell Fitzwilliam about visiting your aunt, or else he will want to join us. I shall ask him for the carriage so the two of us can take a ride around London. I am sure he will agree."

The girl sounded so animated that it surprised

Elizabeth.

"Now that I have a chance to discover the truth, I cannot wait any longer, Lizzy. I never before imagined ever talking to anyone about my suffering, and here you are — both of you listening and supporting me. Please help me to end this uncertainty, Lizzy."

"Very well," Elizabeth agreed after some more reflection and doubts. She felt somehow disloyal to Mr Darcy, but in the end, his purpose in bringing her to his house had been to help Georgiana. All her actions were serving that goal.

"However, we must tell Mr Darcy that we visited my aunt, at least when we return home. I do not wish to have the coachman inform him and reveal our deception."

"Of course, Lizzy. Forgive me for placing you in such a delicate situation. Thank you both," Georgiana said tearfully.

"I must leave you now," Mrs Gardiner declared. "I shall wait for you tomorrow or the day after tomorrow. In the meantime, I shall inform Dr Talbot about the upcoming arrival of my niece, so he will be prepared."

"I shall walk you out," Elizabeth offered.

"Elizabeth, you may stay downstairs for a while. I shall rest a little," Georgiana suggested. The girl looked exhausted, but her countenance was brighter than before, and the little smile on her lips seemed genuine. The light of hope was tentatively dissipating the shadow of grief.

Elizabeth walked arm in arm with Mrs Gardiner, and she finally dared to ask what had taken place in Georgiana's chamber.

"I have not the smallest doubt that she is not with child, Lizzy. However, her state is worrisome. My greatest fear is that she has inherited Lady Anne's illness."

"Their physician has examined her many times and has dismissed such a supposition. I believe it is only the torment, the suffering, the shame that has damaged her health and her spirits all these months."

"If so, that Wickham man together with that Mrs

Younge should rot in jail, if not worse! My assumption is that Miss Darcy has not even...you know. From the answers I received from her in regard to that night, to the state of her clothes, her discomfort, her recollections...I suspect he only pretended to have shared her bed in order to scare and shame her and force her to accept the elopement. And Mrs Younge must have been an accomplice!"

"Dear Lord, could he have been so cruel to her? To allow her to be tortured by doubts all these months? And he even 'happened' upon her in Hyde Park a few times! I am sure he did that on purpose too."

"I fear it is very likely. Eloping with a young woman out of reckless love and passion is one thing. But the cruelty of such a plan is entirely different, and he must be severely punished!"

"I hope he will be! In such case, Mr Darcy must show no mercy."

"I agree, my dear, but it would be delicate to reveal such a discovery to Mr Darcy. Regardless, Dr Talbot's examination will confirm the truth."

In the drawing-room, the first thing Elizabeth observed was Mr Darcy's dark gaze upon her. She struggled not to look at his face, in order to avoid a single glimpse of his lips, which she could still feel against her fingers.

Fortunately, the presence of the new gentleman — Colonel Richard Fitzwilliam — proved to be joyful and entertaining. Within a few moments after the introductions, the colonel proved to be an amiable man with impeccable manners, friendly and unassuming. He declared he had heard so much about Elizabeth and the Gardiners and looked forward to knowing them better.

The conversation flowed easily, and Elizabeth found herself pulled into it. However, Mr Darcy remained silent and withdrawn, and although she rarely dared to meet his eyes, Elizabeth felt his stare on her all the time.

When the Gardiners and her father left, Elizabeth

excused herself and returned to Georgiana. She found Mrs Annesley there, and they entertained themselves for a few hours until Mr Darcy came to see them.

Georgiana welcomed him and invited him to sit with a liveliness that puzzled him.

"Brother," the girl addressed him after a short while, "I have a great favour to ask you."

"Of course," he replied, his puzzlement evidently increasing.

"Tomorrow I would like to spend some more time alone with Elizabeth, to better know each other. I am sure Mrs Annesley will not mind. Would you be so kind as to have a carriage prepared for us, so we can take a ride around the town?"

The request seemed to stun both Mr Darcy and Mrs Annesley, leaving them speechless and dumbfounded. Mr Darcy glanced at Elizabeth, but she could hold his gaze only for a moment, enough to notice his complete astonishment.

"Certainly," he finally replied. "You may ask for anything you want, my dear. I am exceedingly happy to hear you wish to go out. But are you sure you do not want Mrs Annesley or even me to join you?"

"Oh no, there will be no need. The coachman will suffice for such a ride. Lizzy and I shall share memories and talk about the past, that is all."

"Very well..." Darcy agreed, though Elizabeth could hear the reluctance in his voice.

"Thank you," Georgiana whispered. She stretched out her arms to embrace him, which seemed to complete his utter disbelief.

Elizabeth easily understood Mr Darcy's puzzlement. Georgiana's state had changed so much from earlier that day, that it would have surprised anyone. Mr Darcy was worried as much as astounded, that was obvious, and he looked at Elizabeth in search of an explanation that she was not ready to provide yet.

"Will you join me for dinner tonight?" he eventually asked Georgiana.

"Not tonight. But I have great hopes that I shall do so tomorrow. I hope you do not mind."

"As you wish, my dear. Mr Bennet will return home by the end of the week, so I have planned a dinner in two days. I trust you will feel well enough to attend that too."

"I shall, Brother," the girl promised, and only Elizabeth understood the slight uncertainty that was still present in her voice.

Several minutes later, Mr Darcy left, and they did not see him again that evening. Elizabeth had dinner with Georgiana and Mrs Annesley, then retired to her chamber.

She rested in her bed with her eyes closed, reflecting on the extraordinary events of the day and worrying about tomorrow.

As she was falling asleep, at the edge between reality and imagination, the last question she tried to answer was how Darcy's lips would feel on her skin if he willingly touched it. The thrill she felt followed her deep into her dreams and troubled her sleep till morning.

Chapter 23

The following morning, Elizabeth found Georgiana already fully dressed and prepared for their day out. Dark circles around her blue eyes proved that the girl had not slept well; it was no wonder, considering the tormenting day ahead of them, a day which could make the difference between turmoil and tranquillity.

Elizabeth had spent a restless night too, partially due to her worry for Georgiana and partially due to her anxiety in regard to Mr Darcy.

That day was to be a turning point. She had not mentioned to Georgiana Mrs Gardiner's suspicions that Mr Wickham had only pretended to have shared her bed in order to force the elopement. From his many deceptions, she could not decide which would hurt Georgiana the most. Regardless, after the meeting with Dr Talbot, all would be revealed clearly.

Georgiana invited Elizabeth and Mrs Annesley to join her in keeping her brother company at breakfast.

Their appearance was clearly a surprise to Mr Darcy, who hurried to welcome all three of them and immediately ordered more food and tea.

"You look lovely, my dear!" he addressed Georgiana. "And you also, of course," he said quickly, turning to Elizabeth and Mrs Annesley. "I am just content to see my sister in better spirits."

"So am I, sir," Mrs Annesley admitted. "And I agree, Miss Darcy looks beautiful."

"Do you intend to go shopping too?" he enquired.

"No, not today. When we do that, we shall certainly take

Mrs Annesley with us," Georgiana replied. "Today, I only wish to take a long ride with Lizzy. That is all."

"Only not too long, please, as it is very cold," Mr Darcy suggested. "I have asked for some blankets and hot bricks to be placed in the carriage for you."

"Thank you, Brother."

"Please do not worry, Mr Darcy. Regardless of how long the ride is, I shall take care of Georgiana," Elizabeth promised.

"I did not doubt that for a moment, Miss Bennet. My concern was both for my sister and for you. I would not wish either of you to catch a cold," he replied.

Elizabeth felt silly as her cheeks heated.

"By the by, Miss Bennet, I have some news too. I invited your father and uncle to accompany me to my club, but we did not establish a clear date. Earlier today I received a note that we could meet this afternoon. My cousin the colonel will join us. Tomorrow we shall meet again to discuss some affairs with my solicitors, so we have everything completed by the time your father returns to Longbourn."

"Oh, how kind of you!" Elizabeth exclaimed in genuine surprise. Such favours to her father, although certainly done in return for her assistance in Georgiana's case, were of much importance. "Thank you, sir," she added in all seriousness.

"There is no reason to thank me, I assure you. Also, I have just received a letter from Bingley. He is eagerly anticipating the ball, and he says that your sister and your mother have been very helpful with suggestions for dishes for supper."

"How lovely." Elizabeth smiled. "I assume Mr Bingley's sisters were not equally pleased with their suggestions."

"Bingley's sisters are rarely pleased, but after all, he is the master of Netherfield," Mr Darcy replied, returning the smile.

"Mr Bingley is one of the kindest, most amiable people I have ever met," Georgiana interjected.

"He truly is," Elizabeth agreed. "He also spoke very highly of you."

"Georgiana and Bingley are the only people I know of whom everybody speaks highly," Mr Darcy declared, then added, "No, that is not true. I have heard nothing but praise of Miss Bennet and Miss Elizabeth too."

Elizabeth laughed openly. "You are very generous, Mr Darcy. In regard to my sister, I believe that is true, but in my case, we both know at least two, even three people who have criticised me more than once."

"Three?" he enquired, amused by their little conversation.

"Yes, two on numerous occasions, and one at the Meryton assembly."

Instead of being diverted, his smile vanished; he looked at Elizabeth apologetically, and she assumed he was recollecting their first meeting that seemed to have taken place many months ago.

"I am just teasing you, Mr Darcy," Elizabeth said to put him at ease. For a little while, their gazes were locked, and neither noticed their companions also observed their little puzzling exchange.

Immediately after breakfast, the carriage was brought round to the front door. Elizabeth and Georgiana were accompanied by the coachman and another servant. Inside, they sat on the same bench; two blankets, soft and warm, were waiting.

Darcy escorted them to the coach, watching attentively as they were settled.

"It is cold indeed," Georgiana agreed. Her brother placed one blanket around her, tucking it in carefully to be sure she was protected. Then, he entered the carriage, and before Elizabeth had time to say or do anything, he addressed her.

"Miss Bennet, may I?" At her confused nod, he then wrapped her in the blanket, as he had done with his sister. Although the gestures were similar, the sensations were disturbingly different, though each struggled to conceal it.

Even through the blanket, Elizabeth could feel his

touches that made her instantly warm, and her cheeks flushed.

When he completed the task, he looked at Elizabeth for a moment before he climbed down into the freezing air.

"I believe all is ready now. I wish you a relaxing day, just as you desired."

"Thank you, Brother," Georgiana answered, her voice filled with more gratitude than he could surely understand.

When the carriage began to move, Georgiana looked at Elizabeth, who returned the gaze, adding a reassuring, comforting little smile.

The carriage rolled towards Hyde Park, entering and riding through it for a little while. It was cold, not appropriate for a long ride, but no weather could affect Georgiana's newly found determination. She looked like once she had seen a light and a chance to escape from her cage of torment, she was determined to follow it.

"I still cannot believe that I might return home without this fear," Georgiana whispered. "I wonder what the doctor will say. What if he recognises me?"

Elizabeth grabbed her hand.

"Even if he does, he will certainly keep the secret. But how could he? You are not out yet, nor have you attended such places where you could have met. And even if you had, I doubt he would remember you. You should not worry."

After several minutes of riding in Hyde Park, Georgiana asked the coachman to take them to Gracechurch Street. The loyal servant was obviously puzzled and reluctant to obey such an unexpected request.

"We are going to pay a surprise visit to Miss Bennet's aunt Mrs Gardiner, who called yesterday. We shall have tea with her while my brother meets Mr Gardiner and Mr Bennet at his club."

The explanations seemed to put the servant at ease. But neither Elizabeth nor Georgiana felt calm, and they spent most of the long ride in silence, looking out of the windows.

Mrs Gardiner received them with her usual openness

and led them inside. The children were with her, and they immediately surrounded Elizabeth, claiming her attention.

"I shall send a maid with a note to Dr Talbot. He knows we need his help — only the hour was undecided. And I shall order some tea while we wait."

Georgiana looked so uncomfortable that her torment could have easily been judged as pride and hauteur from being in a place so below her situation in life. She spoke a few words to the children and took a few sips from her cup of tea.

"Dr Talbot is an excellent physician. He served in the army years ago, and his situation in life is very good. Yet, he chose to remain in this part of London, where his family has lived all their lives. He has a son who has been successful in trade and has partnered with my husband in some affairs."

Georgiana nodded again, sipping more tea, obviously paying no attention to the details. When the doctor finally arrived, she startled and almost dropped her cup.

Dr Talbot entered and greeted them. He barely remembered Elizabeth, whom he had not seen in several years, and declared they had caught him at the perfect time, as he had an appointment later that afternoon. Without further delay, Mrs Gardiner led him to a guest room; Georgiana, pale, her lips and hands slightly trembling, took Mrs Gardiner's arm and went with them. Elizabeth remained behind to entertain and watch over her cousins, her chest tight with worry for her friend.

It took almost an hour — which felt even longer — until the three returned. As she resumed her previous seat, the turmoil was apparent on Georgiana's countenance, but why, Elizabeth could not speculate. Mrs Gardiner offered Dr Talbot a drink, which he accepted. He enquired after Mr Gardiner, then made a comment about the club he used to attend; he finished his brandy in some haste, then took a joyful farewell and left.

Once alone, Mrs Gardiner sat on the sofa with Georgiana, while Elizabeth cast puzzled glances at them.

"Dr Talbot confirmed my suspicions," the lady said. "To

be honest, I had no doubt that he would. There was no room for uncertainty."

Elizabeth looked at Georgiana, who seemed on the verge of tears.

"So…all is well?" she enquired.

"Very much so," Mrs Gardiner replied.

"We should return home now," Georgiana whispered. "It is getting late, and I do not want to upset my brother even more."

"Of course. Children, come and say good-bye, then wait for me in your room," the lady requested in a composed yet determined tone.

As they all walked towards the door, Georgiana struggled to speak.

"Please forgive me for leaving so quickly. I do not… I cannot express how grateful I am. Nobody has ever done such a thing for me. How can I ever repay your kindness?" Her voice was strangled by tears, and Mrs Gardiner was barely concealing her own emotions.

"Nonsense, Miss Darcy. I have truly done nothing! Do not even think of it. Let us only remember this day as you calling on me."

"You have a lovely house," the girl said politely.

"I would hope so, although I am sure you noticed nothing of it. Perhaps another opportunity will arise soon."

"Yes. Most certainly…" Georgiana kept thanking her while entered the carriage. Elizabeth only thanked her aunt with a smile.

"We shall meet again in two days. Mr Darcy was so kind as to invite us for dinner. He suggested I could take the children too, but since I know them better, I am not decided yet. Now hurry home, you have a long ride across London."

The carriage started to move; the cold was sharper, and Elizabeth wrapped the blanket around Georgiana, then covered herself in the other one.

She looked at the girl, hoping for a glimpse of relief and

perhaps a smile; instead, Georgiana started to sob, a heart-breaking cry from the bottom of her heart. Elizabeth embraced her silently, caressing her hair and allowing her to ease her soul from the long-lasting turmoil.

It was already getting dark when the carriage approached their destination.

"Lizzy, would you please tell Fitzwilliam?" Georgiana pleaded, making Elizabeth panic.

"Tell him what?"

"He will ask where we have been. I believe he deserves to know why I have distressed him all these months. But I cannot tell him myself..."

For the first time, Elizabeth was tempted to refuse the girl's request. How could she possibly discuss such a matter with Mr Darcy?

"What exactly should I tell him, my dear? It is a very delicate matter to discuss with a gentleman who is almost a stranger to me..."

"I am aware, and I am ashamed for causing you more trouble. Tell him as much as you want in order to put his mind at ease. Please! He does not deserve to suffer a day longer."

"Very well...I shall see what can be said," she reluctantly agreed.

"I am so exhausted, Lizzy. I am looking forward to sleeping. I could sleep for so long..."

"You will rest and get healthier now, my dear. I shall take care of this."

"There is something more I must tell you. The last thing..."

"What is it?" Elizabeth enquired with returned worry.

"When I left for Ramsgate, Mrs Younge suggested I should take some extra money with me. Now I understand it was a scheme that had been planned for a long while. I took the money from my brother's study. Later on, I gave it to George when he said he wished to prepare for our elopement."

"How much money?"

"More than five hundred pounds...and a brooch and bracelet my mother gave me. He said he would keep them to remind him of me until we were together. I had no courage to tell Fitzwilliam."

"I do not believe Mr Darcy would mind about any amount of money if he knew you were safe and sound."

"I hope not. I am so sorry to put this burden on you, Lizzy."

And I am so sorry I cannot strangle Mr Wickham and that Younge woman with my own hands, Elizabeth mused to herself. To Georgiana, she smiled and assured her she had no reason for worry.

Chapter 24

The carriage stopped in front of Mr Darcy's house, and the coachman opened the door. It took a while for them to unwrap themselves from the blankets and for Georgiana to wipe her eyes and arrange her bonnet. When they finally stepped out, the cold winter air made them shiver.

As they approached the door, it opened, and Mr Darcy appeared, his handsome face transfigured by feelings Elizabeth could only guess. Behind him was Mrs Annesley, her countenance darkened by worry.

"Georgiana! Miss Bennet! Where on earth have you been?" Mr Darcy burst out. "Are you hurt? What happened? I was about to go searching for you around the town!"

His voice was louder and harsher than Elizabeth had ever heard it, and he allowed them no time to reply.

"Are you hurt? Either of you?" he repeated as they entered the house.

"We are not hurt, Brother," Georgiana whispered. "All is well."

"Well? You left after breakfast and have been gone all day!"

"We went to visit Mrs Gardiner. It was my wish and my request. Tom and John only obeyed my commands."

Mr Darcy's puzzlement was complete, betrayed by his wide eyes.

"Visit Mrs Gardiner? But why did you not tell me? You cannot deny something happened. I can see you have been crying! You are pale and look ill!"

"I am not, I assure you, Brother. All is well," the girl

repeated. "Please excuse me now. I am very tired, and I must sleep. Lizzy will tell you everything."

"I shall help you to your room, Miss Darcy," Mrs Annesley offered, gently taking her arm.

There were several servants gathered in the hall, including the housekeeper, and Mr Darcy's eyes flickered towards them. He bit his lip, then took a deep breath.

"Miss Bennet, I would be grateful to you if you would come and speak to me whenever it is convenient for you. I shall be in my library." He turned to the group of servants. "I believe it is time for everyone to resume their duties. Standing around in the hall cannot be a task assigned to all of you."

His fragile composure was clear, and the servants immediately disappeared. He continued to talk to his housekeeper.

"Mrs Penfield, I am sure my sister and Miss Bennet would like a hot meal and a bath. Please make sure they are properly attended to."

The housekeeper nodded and excused herself, but Elizabeth stopped her.

"Mrs Penfield, a moment, please. Mr Darcy, I apologise for the distress we have caused, but I assure you Georgiana needs nothing but rest at present. She will sleep, and all will be well. If she needs anything else, Mrs Annesley is there. As for me, I would rather speak to you now to put an end to this unsettling situation."

"Should I bring some tea and soup to the library?" Mrs Penfield offered.

"Yes, please," Darcy replied. "Have Stevens bring in the tray," he added while leading Elizabeth along the hall.

Once they entered, he left the door slightly ajar for propriety's sake and invited her to sit in a large chair by the fire. His torment was apparent, and he paced the room in an attempt to calm himself.

"I apologise for acting so savagely," he began. "It might sound irrational, but I imagined the darkest scenarios. My sister has never been gone for such a long time without me knowing her exact whereabouts. Her desire to ride alone with you sounded alarming to me in the beginning. I could feel something was wrong. I am only requesting honesty, Miss Bennet. Have you truly been to visit Mrs Gardiner, or is my sister hiding something from me?"

His perturbation induced her calmness, knowing she had the answers which could soothe his distress.

"Both are true. We did visit my aunt, and we did hide something from you, sir. That is precisely why we did not reveal to you the purpose of our ride."

He stared at her, incredulous and apparently hurt, while she continued.

"I can imagine you feel betrayed. I deeply apologise for upsetting you, but not for our actions. They were necessary in order to put an end to Georgiana's turmoil. And yours."

He stopped, frowned, and kept staring at her.

"Would you be so kind as to take a seat, sir? This is a most delicate and distressing conversation for me. One that I have never had before with any man. I shall try to be honest, but there are some disquieting details that I cannot express freely," she said, averting her eyes while her cheeks burned.

He hesitated briefly, then fetched a chair and placed it opposite her, at a safe distance but close enough to increase their mutual anxiety.

"Since I arrived, I have struggled to understand what caused the alteration of Georgiana's state. Her illness was real, though your physician declared her body was healthy."

She paused and he waited. There was a knock at the door and Stevens entered with the tray. Mr Darcy took it, placed it on the table, and dismissed the man.

"Fortunately, I discovered the truth early enough ease her turmoil," Elizabeth continued. "And yours too, since one of her main obsessions was that she had ruined your peace of mind and would destroy your good name and honour."

"I see..." he said, standing up again. "I assume she

revealed to you the attempted elopement. I hoped she had put the entire story behind her, that she could forget it. It was prevented without any harm coming to her. Why would she be concerned about my name and honour? My concern is her well-being, far above any other considerations."

"You considered it over. To her, it was only the beginning of a devastating torment."

"But why? How?"

Elizabeth paused again. "May I have some tea, please?"

"Yes, of course. Allow me to pour a cup for you," he offered hastily. In an obvious hurry, he filled a cup and passed it to her. It was hot, and only then did she realise her fingers were cold. She took the cup, and in doing so, their fingers touched. The warmth spread inside her from that touch to her entire core.

She took a sip, then gathered herself enough to continue.

"Mr Wickham's scheme with that Mrs Younge was more devious than you probably know. I have reason to believe they conspired prior to arriving in Ramsgate. It was an elaborate plan to induce Georgiana to mistake childhood affection for romance and agree to elope with him. Furthermore…"

"Yes?" Mr Darcy enquired, his anxiety clearly growing and his expression displaying the mix of feelings storming inside him.

"He…one evening they…during a dinner, they probably intoxicated Georgiana and…"

"And?"

"They led Georgiana to believe she had spent the night with Mr Wickham," Elizabeth said, her voice barely a whisper.

"Oh…" he said, the subject clearly affecting him as much as her. "That is why…"

Elizabeth shook her head. "There is more. They convinced her she might be with child. Therefore, they had to elope and marry…"

Again, embarrassment caused her to pause, and he only replied with another. "Oh."

"When you arrived unexpectedly, Georgiana could not bear to pain you, and she confessed to the elopement. But since then, she has lived with the fear of the shame she would cause your family if she had a child."

"Dear Lord," he uttered, pacing around. He rubbed his forehead, cast a few glances at Elizabeth, and finally spoke again.

"Even if that was the case, I would not have allowed her to spend her entire life with such a low life of a man. Even if she had a child, we would have found a way. She is certainly not the only one who..."

Elizabeth nodded.

"So, she is not... This is why she said all is well?" he enquired.

"No... Yes... I only found out yesterday, and since I have no knowledge of such matters," she confessed, hiding her face in mortification, "I asked my aunt's advice. She was quite certain it was not the case. But Georgiana was still doubtful, so today we visited my aunt, who asked for the assistance of her physician. He was told Georgiana is my aunt's niece, newly married."

"I see," he said, though he looked dumbfounded, confused, hurt, restless. "This is why you planned this secret visit..."

"Yes. We could not have revealed the reason, until we knew the truth."

"All these months...she could have been saved from so much suffering if she had only confided in me."

"It is not a matter one would speak to an older brother about, sir."

"Indeed. One would need a friend — a sister — to support her in such circumstances. My sister was fortunate to have you. We both were fortunate to have you, Miss Bennet, though I am aware you have done everything for Georgiana."

Something in his voice touched her heart deeply.

"Not only for Georgiana, sir. I am fortunate too, for

having a friend like her. And like you."

Another small pause, and then she continued.

"Equally disturbing is that the two scoundrels convinced Georgiana to give them some money, as well as a brooch and a bracelet. She knows you will be upset about her foolishness, and rightfully so, but she was so young and innocent that she was an easy victim for those predators. I truly cannot fault her."

"I care little about the money. My father and I were foolish enough in the past to give much more to Wickham for one reason or another. I cannot fault her for that either. Much more important is that she has tortured herself for such a long time…"

"Mr Darcy, forgive my boldness, but I believe some strong measures must be taken against both Mr Wickham and Mrs Younge. Considering their deception, the money and the jewellery Georgiana gave them was nothing but robbery. Forgive me. I can see you are calm and composed, as you should be, but I am becoming more enraged by the minute."

"I am neither calm nor composed at all, Miss Bennet. I am just repressing my anger in order to protect you from witnessing it. Strong measures will be taken. You may judge me as you please, but I am a resentful man. I might forgive an offence against myself but not the suffering caused to a loved one. Especially my sister."

"I am glad to hear that. I know this sounds very unladylike, but I am truly glad."

He smiled at her. "Thank you for sharing my torment, Miss Bennet. And thank you for telling me the truth. I can imagine how difficult it must have been for you."

"It was difficult, but not as bad as I feared. Somehow you eased my burden. Of course, I suspect tomorrow I shall die of mortification remembering the nature of our conversation," she tried to jest.

"You have no reason to be embarrassed by anything you said or did, Miss Bennet. Quite the opposite. I promised not to thank you again, yet, I have already done so. So, I shall only repeat what my mother once said. You are a breath of fresh air in our lives, Miss Bennet. You have helped us breathe again."

Instead of denying it, she simply replied, "I wish nothing more than to see you and Georgiana breathe and smile freely, Mr Darcy."

"Will you stay longer? Now that everything seems to be resolved?" he enquired.

"Would you like me to leave?" she asked in surprise.

"No! Not at all…quite the contrary…I would wish you to never leave. But it is not my desire that matters — only yours."

"Oh…" she answered, not knowing how to take his powerful statement. "Then I would like to stay. I do miss my mother and my sisters, but I would dearly like to spend more time with Georgiana if you do not mind."

"I would by no means suspend any pleasure of yours, Miss Bennet. In this case, the pleasure is mine. Please let me know how I can make your stay more comfortable."

He sounded serious, even grave, and she felt shivery, although she was not cold any longer. To conceal her unease, she attempted to joke.

"I would like something to eat, if possible. I am truly hungry."

"Of course! How silly of me! I shall ask for dinner to be delivered to your room. Is that convenient?"

"Certainly," she agreed, puzzled. "I shall speak to Georgiana and Mrs Annesley, to see if they would like to come downstairs for dinner. If not, I may come, if you do not mind," she said. Her suggestion clearly surprised him, and his reply was delayed, as if he did not know how to answer. She felt her face burning with shame for such boldness, which obviously had not pleased him.

"I would be happy for you to join me for dinner of course. However, if Mrs Annesley and my sister prefer to remain in their rooms, I may order dinner in Georgiana's apartment, as usual. I fear that the two of us dining alone might cause rumours and speculation among the servants."

"Oh...how silly of me...I apologise for such a lack of consideration. I must be tired since I neglected to see the impropriety of my suggestion."

She got up from her seat, turning to leave. She felt like a simpleton and was ashamed to imagine what he thought of her.

She startled when she felt his hand on her arm.

"Miss Bennet, I must ask, even if my question is improper. Would you like to dine with me?"

She barely dared to meet his gaze, struggling to find a reasonable and proper answer. However, she was indeed too tired to think it through.

"I would. Since our conversation had become so easy and comfortable...I thought we might continue it during dinner. I did not consider that it might affect your reputation."

He was still holding her arm when he answered.

"Miss Bennet, there is nothing I would like more than to spend time with you, either at dinner or in conversation. Besides my gratitude for what you have done for my sister, I cannot remember enjoying anyone else's company as much as I enjoy yours. My concern is not for my reputation but for yours. As long as you are in my house, under my protection, my duty is to guard my actions."

"Oh..." she whispered, still puzzled, barely comprehending the meaning of his words.

She lifted her eyes and met his gaze one more time. This time she held it for a longer moment. Her heart was racing, as his closeness made her dizzy.

"It has been a long day. I believe it would be better if we had dinner in Georgiana's apartment, as usual. Hopefully, from tomorrow, such a habit will change."

"I look forward to it, Miss Bennet," he answered. Against her will, she noticed the slight movement of his lips and remembered the sensation of the touch from the previous night.

To her equal pleasure and distress, she saw him taking her hand in his and bowing his head so he could press a brief, barely felt kiss on her palm — so quick that it felt unreal.

"Your eyes are truly sparkling, Miss Bennet. Good night."

"Good night, Mr Darcy," she answered, withdrawing her hand and stepping away, still dizzy and confused by his kiss and his last statement.

Chapter 25

It had been the worst in a row of sleepless nights for Darcy. His conversation with Elizabeth, instead of soothing him, had increased his distress, turning it into rage. The notion that two people in whom he and his father had put their trust had plotted to take advantage of and then torment Georgiana on purpose was unbearable. How much grief, pain, fright, and shame must have been in Georgiana's poor soul for as many months, and how devastating it must have been to not be able to share her secret or seek support from anyone.

Yes, in the end, Georgiana would have realised that she was not with child, as she feared. But several more months of turmoil in her precarious state could have destroyed her health entirely.

The thought that his sister did not trust him — or anyone else in their family — enough to share her burden was also disturbing for Darcy. Mrs Annesley had proved to be an excellent woman so far. However, after Mrs Younge's betrayal, it was understandable that Georgiana felt reluctant to trust another companion so soon.

While he pondered the gratitude he owed to Elizabeth and Mrs Gardiner, he mused again over his despicable manners towards the Bennet family at the beginning of their acquaintance. Nothing he could do would be enough to compensate for his behaviour. The conclusion was simple: his mother's favourites — Elizabeth and her aunt — were the only ones capable of remedying the damage caused by his father's favourite, Wickham. Fate certainly had a peculiar sense of irony.

Of Elizabeth, he tried not to think too much; his body and his heart were already defeated and enchanted by her. Therefore, he tried to at least keep his mind clear. He had been bold and barely proper in the brief private encounters with her; he had to control himself better. That was only in regard to Elizabeth, of course; when it came to Wickham and Mrs Younge, he intended to show no restraint.

"Mr Darcy, for how many people should we arrange the breakfast table?" the butler enquired.

"For four people," he replied. "I am not certain yet, but I hope my sister and her companions will join me."

"Very well, sir."

"Please have this note delivered immediately to Mr Dodge. I wish to speak to him as soon as possible."

"Of course."

As soon as the man left, Darcy moved to his library. It was his habit to have a brief morning meeting with his housekeeper; with the dinner party the following evening, he needed to be certain everything was prepared accordingly. He found himself strangely concerned with a mere dinner for family, and he knew his nervousness was due to his wish to have everything perfect for *her*.

***

Despite her restlessness, Elizabeth slept better than she had in quite a while. She hurried to prepare for the day, then went to Georgiana. The girl met her with a little smile, fully dressed, her hair elegantly arranged. She was very thin, and her gown had become too large for her. She still looked pale, and there were dark circles under her eyes, but her smile was genuine and bright.

"My dear, you look lovely!" Elizabeth embraced her.

"You are too kind, but I know I look better than yesterday since I feel so much better. Did you have a chance to speak to my brother, Lizzy?" she enquired shyly.

"Yes. We spoke last night. It was a brief conversation,

but both Mr Darcy and I were happy with it," she answered meaningfully since Mrs Annesley was present.

"Would you come with me to talk to him?"

"If you wish, of course," Elizabeth responded.

"Shall we have breakfast with Mr Darcy?" Mrs Annesley interjected. "I believe he is expecting us."

"Yes, he has waited for me long enough," Georgiana said, grabbing Elizabeth's arm as all three of them walked downstairs.

When they entered, Mr Darcy was already at the table. He stood to greet them, an expression of surprise and delight on his face.

"Dearest, I am so happy to see you!" he said, embracing his sister. "You ladies look beautiful this morning. I am happy to see you all," he added. Although she knew it was mere politeness, Elizabeth felt her cheeks colour again.

It was the first time they had sat together at a table, and Georgiana took the chair to her brother's left, with Mrs Annesley sitting next to her.

"Miss Bennet, will you sit here, opposite Georgiana?" Mr Darcy offered the position to his right.

"It is perfect, thank you," she replied, feeling warm as he held the chair for her.

Dishes were being brought in when suddenly the door opened, and without an announcement, Colonel Fitzwilliam entered.

On seeing the party assembled, his eyes widened in disbelief, and a grin spread over his face.

He hurried to Georgiana and leant in to embrace her tightly.

"My dear, what a joy to see you! You look so pretty! A little too thin, a little pale, but pretty nevertheless! Ladies, I am delighted to see you too."

"Cousin, will you join us for breakfast?" Mr Darcy offered.

The colonel seemed to hesitate a moment, looking at the

table.

"Colonel, would you like to sit next to Mr Darcy? I can move to the next chair," Elizabeth offered.

"Move? Not at all, Miss Bennet. I shall stay for a little while, and I am perfectly comfortable here, next to you," he said. Then he looked around the table again and repeated, "I am so happy to see you all!"

"So are we, Richard," Mr Darcy replied. "May I ask what you are doing here so early?"

"I have come to talk to you. About the dinner tonight and some other issues. I might be a little late for dinner. I am not sure yet, but it is possible since I have another earlier assignment."

"Thank you for informing us. Would you like to go to the library to discuss the other issues, or can they wait until after breakfast?"

"They can wait. I do not wish to ruin your appetite. Nor Georgiana's! I am truly happy and so grateful to see she has left her room."

"We are all grateful," Mrs Annesley interjected with gentleness. "Miss Bennet truly performed a miracle in regard to Miss Darcy's health. And it took only a few days. It seems her presence was the perfect medicine," she said, ending with a trace of unease.

"While I do agree, I must say we have all appreciated your care for my sister all these months, Mrs Annesley," Mr Darcy answered, clearly understanding the lady's distress.

"Oh, yes!" Georgiana added. "I could not hope for a better companion, Mrs Annesley. But, you see, Lizzy has been my friend since I was a little girl, and I was so happy to meet her again. She could help me in a way no one else could. But that does not make your support and affection any less valuable."

The praise seemed to touch Mrs Annesley deeply, and she seemed on the verge of tears.

"Thank you. How lovely of you to say so. I assure you, it was my only desire to see you recover and your health improve."

"I know that, and I apologise for all the trouble I have caused you," the girl replied.

"Well," the colonel interjected cheerfully, "you ladies all deserve a reward. I know my mother and sister — my brother's wife — often reward themselves after a success. Some new gowns, maybe? Perhaps some jewels too? Anything you want! I feel very generous since I am offering Darcy's money," he declared, causing everyone to laugh.

"An excellent idea," Mr Darcy said. "I strongly suggest some shopping, whenever you ladies wish."

Georgiana looked at her two companions enquiringly.

"If I may choose a reward, I would rather take a walk in the park. But if it would be too tiring for you, even a ride in the carriage would do."

The colonel's puzzlement was apparent.

"You prefer walking and riding over shopping? That is rather singular!"

"Miss Bennet is certainly different in many ways from most ladies her age," Mr Darcy said. "We have to thank her for that."

"You are all too kind and too generous with your praise, if that was praise. My mother has always disapproved of my inclinations," Elizabeth said, trying to conceal her nervousness behind a tease. "I admit I love spending time out of doors."

"Then you should definitely ride, not walk," the colonel said. "It might be too cold on horseback, so the carriage would be the best choice."

"Riding a horse would not be for me in any case." Elizabeth laughed. "I greatly admire horses from afar. When they are too close, they make me nervous."

"You do not ride, Lizzy?" Georgiana enquired, surprised. "I cannot imagine you being afraid of horses. I cannot imagine you being afraid of anything."

"And here is another undeserved compliment," she jested. "I did learn to ride when I was a child and even enjoyed it. But then, something happened. I do not even remember what it was that caused me distress and distanced me from horses until I gave up on them entirely."

"I have loved to ride since I was very young," Georgiana admitted. "My brother taught me. I cannot even remember when I was given my first pony."

"I heard your first pony gave you some troubles when you were five, and Miss Bennet had to save you from the lake," the colonel interjected.

"True! I barely remember that day. Everything is hazy in my mind, but Mrs Reynolds wrote to me about it."

"As I said, we must thank Miss Bennet for many things," Mr Darcy added, while Elizabeth attempted to disagree again.

"If the ladies do decide to take a walk in the park, I would suggest they take the carriage there. They may walk as long as they like, and when they are cold, return to the carriage," Mr Darcy suggested. Georgiana had not given her acceptance yet. She had barely left the house in the last two months, and Elizabeth knew she was still fearful of exposing herself to the crowd. However, she eventually agreed, though reluctantly.

Breakfast ended, and the ladies went to prepare for the ride. It was planned to be short, since they needed to return to prepare for that evening's dinner.

**

Darcy and the colonel retired to the library to continue their conversation.

"I could not believe your note that said things had been settled," the colonel said. "How? In what way? And how on earth did Miss Bennet convince Georgiana to leave her room and even go out of doors? We failed for months!"

"There are some particular details that I shall reveal to you, but the most important is that Georgiana trusted her more than any of us."

"You know, I asked my mother why Miss Bennet and

Georgiana had not seen each other for ten years. She did not particularly remember either."

"Georgie's governess at the time was opposed to it, Mrs Reynolds said. She did not consider the niece of a man in trade to be good enough company for my sister and did not approve of her manners."

"Her manners? She was ten years old!"

"I find it ridiculous too. But she was quite strict about the behaviour of young ladies. Instead of being grateful that Miss Bennet saved Georgiana from drowning, she called it 'a wild display of impropriety'."

"That is ridiculous and stupid."

"It is. I only learnt about it recently, from Mrs Reynolds's letters. By the way, although she did not say as much, I assume that Miss Bennet's fear of horses began when she saw Georgiana falling from her pony. Unlike my sister, she was old enough to recollect the moment and for it to make an impression on her."

"Very likely," the colonel agreed. "Lady Anne deservingly approved of Miss Bennet, and so did your father, did he not?"

"He did. But my mother died shortly after that, and my father cared for little else. My sister's governess made most of the decisions regarding my sister, some of which I did not agree with, although they were well meant."

"Mother said that Lady Catherine was there one day in London when Mrs Gardiner tried to speak to Georgiana. She chased the woman away and forbade her from attempting any further contact with Georgiana."

"I did not know that, but I find it easy to believe. Lady Catherine always approved of the governess's severe style of education, which was completely unsuitable for a young girl like Georgiana. Mrs Gardiner did not mention anything of the sort, probably out of common sense and decency. By the way, we have Mrs Gardiner to thank as much as Miss Bennet in regard to Georgiana."

"Do we? How is that?"

"Prepare yourself to hear things that I never imagined speaking of," Darcy said. "But as Georgiana's guardian, you have the right to know. And as my best friend, you deserve the confidence of such a story."

"This sounds awfully distressing, and I am only calm because I saw Georgiana was well. But wait, before you start, I need a brandy," the colonel declared.

Sometime later, when Darcy had completed his narration of the events of the last few days, he revealed the reason behind Georgiana's suffering. The colonel never interrupted him, but when he had finished, he was almost suffocating with anger. While he was well aware of all the particulars of the elopement and Darcy's previous dealings with Wickham, the added details enraged him beyond his control.

"I cannot believe it! Poor Georgiana, to suffer alone for all these months! This is worse than outrageous! You should shoot Wickham, Darcy! Not to death, but enough to suffer daily in his pathetic life! And that wretched woman too!"

"I shall not shoot him, but he must suffer indeed. And Mrs Younge too. I have requested a meeting with Mr Dodge, and I shall ask him to discover her whereabouts, then I shall have a private meeting with her."

"Good. And Wickham?"

"I have already purchased some of his debts, so I must find a way to use them against him."

"How? Throw him into debtors' prison?"

"I could do that, but he would then lose his position in the regiment too. I want him to suffer more than Georgiana did and not have a moment of peace but not to lose his income. I want to respect my father's wishes as much as possible, even though Wickham betrayed him. I know it sounds difficult to understand."

"It does. I never understood my uncle's partiality for that scoundrel. He was a wise man in every other situation except that."

"I long ago ceased to judge his choice, Richard. Now, I must think of a way to take revenge on those two scoundrels. I am ashamed of myself for being so resentful, but I cannot help it."

"Why would you be ashamed? I am proud of you, and I look forward to hearing what you decide. And Darcy?"

"Yes?"

"What about Miss Bennet?"

"Miss Bennet? What do you mean?"

"I do not wish to be disrespectful, but I have seen the way you look at her. There is more than gratitude and friendship there. I am sure you will deny it, but you must give it careful consideration."

"I have no wish to deny it," Darcy replied, and the colonel's eyes widened. "However, my main concern is to ensure Miss Bennet feels comfortable and safe while she is my sister's guest."

"Well, well... This is a shock indeed. A pleasant one, but still a shock. Although I have only just met her, I can understand your preference. And what of Miss Bennet? Do you know her opinion of you?"

"The beginning of our acquaintance was unfortunate, mostly due to my behaviour, and I can safely say she loathed me for a while. In time, her opinion of me improved, but I assume it was mostly due to her discovering who I was. Lately, she has been a loyal friend to me and Georgiana. I do not dare to speculate more."

"I see... Well, well, this is unexpected," he repeated. "I do not wish to speculate either, but I believe if you did decide to pursue Miss Bennet, you would have a hard time explaining it to Lady Catherine and even to my family. As supportive as they might be of Miss Bennet as Georgiana's friend, if you were involved, their opinion might differ."

"Richard, if such a moment did come to pass, Lady Catherine's or anyone else's opinion, except for that of Miss Bennet herself, would matter little to me. Please let us leave the subject for the time being. I must think of Wickham and Mrs Younge now."

Chapter 26

Hyde Park was crowded, despite the cold weather. The carriage crossed it at a slow pace, much to Elizabeth's enjoyment, as she took great pleasure in watching the scenery and the people pass. Almost an hour later, the coachman stopped, and they stepped out; all three shivered at the same time, some from the cold, some from emotions.

"This is where I used to walk with my brother when I was younger," Georgiana indicated, grasping Elizabeth's arm.

"I have always loved Hyde Park, although I have only had the chance to visit it a few times. Something about it is so appealing to me," Elizabeth said.

"I confess it intimidates me," Georgiana admitted. "I love the colours of the flowers in the summer, the lake, the old trees...but it is so large and always so crowded. At every turn one may meet an acquaintance..."

"You may meet an acquaintance, but I am certain that I shall not." Elizabeth laughed. "None of my family or friends spend much time in Hyde Park. But speaking of size, is not Pemberley also very large and grand and intimidating?"

"Not to me. It is my home, and I love every inch of it. And there is no danger of meeting someone you do not want to."

Although the conversation was carried in a light tone, Elizabeth could feel Georgiana's grasp tighten on her arm; the girl was obviously still scared by the prospect of an encounter with certain *undesirable acquaintances*.

"I look forward to seeing Pemberley, after everything I have heard of it," Mrs Annesley said.

"My aunt used to say Pemberley was the most beautiful

place she had ever seen. I remember being happy there, but I was a child, and I confess I remember few details," Elizabeth replied.

"Would you come to Pemberley in the summer, Lizzy?" Georgiana asked.

"My dear, I do not know. I have not discussed my plans for the summer with my father or with your brother. I do not even know where I shall be for Christmas," she answered with a teasing smile.

They walked for a little while; the weather was sunny but cold, and Georgiana was still holding Elizabeth's arm tightly. Suddenly, her grip loosened, and the girl's voice became animated.

"Look, Fitzwilliam is here!"

Elizabeth felt momentarily disquieted, watching Mr Darcy approach them. Her heart was suddenly racing. She prayed she appeared more composed, or she would make a fool of herself.

"Brother, how lovely to see you here! We did not expect you."

"My meeting did not take as long as I expected, and I thought a little exercise would be beneficial. It certainly suits you well, from what I see."

His eyes were mostly resting upon Elizabeth as he spoke, and she found she could not look away from him either.

"Should we take another stroll before we return home? I suggest you rest a little before dinner," Darcy proposed.

Georgiana took Elizabeth's arm again, claiming her company. Since the path was too narrow for all four of them to walk together, Mr Darcy and Mrs Annesley took a few steps back, walking behind them.

Minutes later, a carriage stopped next to them, and a woman's voice called cheerfully, "Mr Darcy! How lovely to see you, sir! We have not seen you since last summer."

The door opened, and a young woman, elegant in a fashionable gown and with a confident air, stepped down, stretching out her hand to Mr Darcy. Immediately behind her, another woman of a similar age followed, while a third, an older lady, remained inside.

"Lady Emmeline, Lady Isabella, Lady Campbell, I am delighted to see you."

"And so you should be, Mr Darcy!" Lady Campbell replied. "You have been missed and enquired after many times. Colonel Fitzwilliam can confirm this."

"I do not need any confirmation, as I do not doubt your words, madam. I thank you for your care. I have been well. Mostly out of town with business."

"Now that you have returned, you must promise that we shall see you more often," Lady Emmeline demanded. "Keep in mind there will be many balls and parties around the new year. We shall look after you!"

"I cannot make any promises, considering my plans are not fixed yet. But I wish you a wonderful time, with the most enjoyable parties," Mr Darcy offered politely.

"Is this your little sister?" Lady Campbell interjected again. "She is all grown up now! Is she out already? I have not seen her in society at all."

"My sister is still young yet, and she has expressed no desire to be out," Mr Darcy replied, while Georgiana was gripping Elizabeth's arm.

"Well, she should, any time now. She is exceedingly pretty but looks rather timid. Is that her companion, whose arm she is grasping?"

"This is my sister's friend, Miss Elizabeth Bennet. And this is my sister's companion, Mrs Annesley." Mr Darcy performed the introductions.

"I have never seen Miss Bennet before. Do you live in town, Miss Bennet?" Lady Campbell continued the enquiry with obvious curiosity.

"No, ma'am. My father's estate is in Hertfordshire."

"You are just visiting London?"

"Yes. I am visiting my uncle and aunt. And Miss Darcy,

of course," Elizabeth explained. While Georgiana seemed disconcerted and Darcy impatient, she was rather amused by being the object of interrogation. The ladies' interest was obviously in Mr Darcy, and she was only an annoyance to them.

"Hertfordshire? And how did you happen to befriend Mr Darcy's sister?" Lady Emmeline asked with slight harshness in her tone.

"Miss Bennet has been my sister's friend since their childhood," Darcy interjected, his own voice having a sharp edge, a clear sign of his irritation. "Miss Bennet is also a family friend, and my parents were very fond of her. I am afraid it is too cold for a longer conversation. We must beg you to excuse us. It is time for us to return home."

Without allowing time for further discussion, Mr Darcy bowed to the ladies and then directed his party back to the carriage. Less than half an hour after the encounter, they were all back home, and only then did Georgiana seem to relax.

"It was cold, but the exercise was refreshing," Mrs Annesley said while helping Georgiana out of her coat. "I shall order some tea, and then I believe it would be best for Miss Darcy and Miss Bennet to rest, as Mr Darcy suggested."

"I shall be in my library," Mr Darcy said, and the ladies withdrew to their rooms.

Elizabeth found herself slightly anxious after the walk, and she realised it was due to the meeting with the three ladies. Not because their treatment of her was rather rude but because of their clear interest in Mr Darcy. A mother and two daughters chasing an eligible man was nothing unexpected, Elizabeth mused with a smile to herself. And yet, it troubled her, though she could not truly understand why. Her response to Mr Darcy and all those around him was increasingly disquieting, and she realised — and feared — only one explanation was possible. She was falling in love with Mr Darcy. No, that was not entirely true. She had already fallen in love with him, and she needed all her strength to mind her behaviour and keep her composure so she would not make a fool of herself in front of him or Georgiana.

In order to distract her mind, she began reading Jane's letter again, trying to amuse herself. Mr Wickham's name was too often mentioned; however, apparently his partiality had already moved on to Mary King.

Jane also revealed her anticipation of the ball and Mr Bingley's regular visits to Longbourn. What really shocked Elizabeth was the news that Mr Collins had proposed to Charlotte Lucas, and she had accepted. Elizabeth had always praised Charlotte for being wise and well-mannered; how she could agree to marry a man she had only met a few days prior was a mystery. The need to secure her future, which was probably what had induced Charlotte into the engagement, was not enough for Elizabeth, and she felt bitterly disappointed in her friend. Several minutes of reflection later, Elizabeth admitted it was presumptuous on her part to judge Charlotte's actions. She had no right to think ill of her choice. There was only sadness in knowing how slim the chances had been for Charlotte to find a husband truly worthy of her.

***

Darcy sipped from his coffee, looking absently at his papers. Earlier, he had been visited by Mr Dodge and requested he complete a thorough investigation into Wickham and Mrs Younge's present situations. He needed to know their dirtiest secrets to decide how to act. In all honesty, he felt uncomfortable with his savage desire for revenge, but he could not dismiss it.

Meeting Georgiana and Elizabeth in the park had had a calming effect on him. Although pleased to see his sister finally out of the house, his interest had been mostly in Elizabeth, and every glance, every smile from her warmed his heart. For a moment, he was tempted to invite her to walk back with him, while Georgiana and Mrs Annesley returned in the carriage. He knew she would have enjoyed the walk, but it would have been a bold gesture, causing rumours and speculation, just as had happened with Lady Campbell and her daughters. He amused himself, wondering how it was possible that he remained indifferent to any attentions from Lady Emmeline and other women, while just thinking of Elizabeth caused such thrills inside him.

With such thoughts, he prepared for dinner, The first to arrive was Colonel Fitzwilliam, with whom he had a drink in the library until he was informed the ladies were waiting for them in the drawing room. He took a moment to admire Elizabeth before he greeted them. She was wearing a pale-yellow muslin dress, simple yet very flattering to her figure. Both she and Georgiana were wearing matching necklaces, offering the colonel a perfect subject to start the conversation and engaging both Elizabeth and Georgiana in it. Mrs Annesley, as well as Darcy, watched silently.

Soon enough, the other guests arrived. Mrs Gardiner explained the children had been left in the care of the maids; having them travel back and forth across town in such weather would have been too tiring.

"They were perfectly happy to stay at home without their mother's strict supervision," Mr Gardiner added as Darcy escorted them towards the dining room.

Mr Gardiner and Mr Bennet were invited to sit either side of Darcy, for easier conversation. The colonel was delighted to remain with the ladies, and the conversation resumed while the first course was served.

The dishes, the arrangements, all were a little too much for a mere family dinner, Darcy mused while watching his guests. He had requested it to please Elizabeth.

Georgiana seemed comfortable enough, although still timid; Mrs Annesley actively participated in discussions, showing more wit and knowledge than Darcy had had the chance to witness before. Mr and Mrs Gardiner, as well as Mr Bennet, were delightful company, but most enchanting to him was the expression of joy on Elizabeth's face and her lively eyes sparkling every time she looked at him.

As the evening progressed, the guests accepted an invitation to stay overnight.

"If I return home tomorrow, Mrs Bennet will compel me to go to the ball, I fear," Mr Bennet said.

"Well, you may claim a cold," Mr Gardiner offered.

"I really cannot understand why you despise balls so much," Mrs Gardiner said. "You may at least amuse yourself watching others."

"Well, I am sure Mr Darcy understands me," the gentleman said. "I would be amused if I could withdraw to the library whenever I want, otherwise it is dull and tiresome. Hiding in the library is not such a bad idea after all. I shall ask Mr Bingley to give me the key."

"I am sure he would be happy to oblige," Darcy interjected. "Nobody uses the Netherfield library, so you should be quite safe there."

"I am surprised to find someone else who dislikes balls as much as Darcy," the colonel said. "To me, there are few things more enjoyable. What is not to like?"

"I notice most officers favour balls and parties. It must be because ladies are usually charmed by the uniform," Mr Bennet said.

"You are probably right." The colonel laughed. "I assume you do like balls, Miss Bennet."

"I confess I do. In a small town like Meryton, we have few other entertainments."

"I hope Georgiana will not take after Darcy," the colonel said. "My mother is looking forward to preparing her coming out party. That is, if Darcy does not marry before then and his wife takes over the task."

Georgiana looked suddenly pale, and Darcy felt embarrassed; he cast a quick look at Elizabeth, who looked amused and slightly flushed.

"I do not need a coming out party," Georgiana

whispered, and her obvious discomfort induced the others to change the subject.

***

After dinner, the colonel asked for some music, but Georgiana declined. She apologised to the guests and withdrew to her room. Considering it was her first gathering in a long time, nobody opposed it. Elizabeth accompanied her to her apartment and helped her prepare for the night.

"I hope you will not leave soon, Lizzy," she whispered. "I shall miss you dearly. I wish you would never leave, but I know that is not possible."

Elizabeth kissed the girl's cheek and stroked her hair.

"Let us not worry about that, my dear. I shall stay for as long as you need me."

Georgiana finally climbed into bed and, covered in blankets, fell asleep while Elizabeth was still watching. Before she exited, she put another log on the fire and looked back at the girl. With surprise and distress, she admitted having the same thoughts as Georgiana but did not dare to voice them. As much as she missed her sisters and her mother, she did not want to ever leave either, but she knew that was not possible.

Elizabeth returned to the others in the drawing room, and the first thing she noticed was Mr Darcy's gaze upon her. The gentlemen were enjoying a glass of port and the ladies a cup of tea. The conversation focused on Derbyshire and Pemberley. With great delight, Mr Gardiner informed her that Mr Darcy had just invited the entire family to spend a month at Pemberley in the summer — news that sent chills down her spine and made her cheeks burn. The entire family for a month? Was their new friendship enough reason for such courtesy? Was the invitation proof of his gratitude for Mrs Gardiner's involvement in Georgiana's case? Or could he have another reason — one she feared to even consider?

It was close to midnight when everyone withdrew to

their rooms. Unlike Elizabeth, the others were hosted in the guest wing, so Elizabeth found herself in the hall leading to her chamber with only Mr Darcy. They had found no time to speak much in person that evening, and certainly it was not the most proper time or place to do so now, and yet she spoke.

"Thank you for your generosity towards my family, sir."

"That is a strange sentence from someone to whom I am indebted for life," he said, smiling. "Of the two of us, I am the only one allowed to speak of gratitude, Miss Bennet."

"That is rather arrogant of you, sir, to forbid me from speaking of something I wish to," she teased him back, while she felt her cheeks burning.

"I would by no means suspend any pleasure of yours, Miss Bennet. Yet, in this matter, I must insist, even if you call it arrogance."

"Considering you are the master of the house, I shall not argue with you. But are you sure you meant your invitation? Having my entire family at Pemberley, with my parents and my sisters as well as my four young cousins, might be a daunting task even for you."

"I am sure. Besides, you may not remember many details, but Pemberley is a large enough place to provide entertainment but also privacy for many people," he continued in the same light tone.

"Please note that I have warned you," she joked.

Her lips, slightly parted, curved into a playful smile, a feeble attempt to disguise her unease. She was mortified to discover that she held a secret desire for Mr Darcy's lips to meet hers in a kiss. Elizabeth could not help but feel a sense of dismay at the intense want. Her left hand grasped the folds of her gown, and she took two measured steps backwards.

Mr Darcy stood in perfect stillness, his countenance betraying no hint of emotion. Elizabeth found herself captivated by his presence, unable to supress her curiosity. Were Mr Darcy's thoughts aligned with hers? She felt the tension, and a shiver thrilled her entire being. She remembered the touch of his lips on her skin and hoped — or rather feared, she was not certain any longer — it might happen again. Uncertain of her own desires, she only curtseyed gracefully and said, "Good night, Mr Darcy. I am quite content to be here."

With that, he stepped away and walked towards his apartment. Elizabeth needed a moment to recover before she opened the door to her chamber.

***

The following morning, chatter and laughter filled the house as the party gathered for a very early breakfast. Georgiana seemed more at ease than the previous evening, and her newfound contentment and improved rest had started to brighten her countenance. Elizabeth and Mr Darcy were less talkative though, and they mostly spoke to others, their eyes barely meeting.

Afterwards, Elizabeth embraced her father, wishing him a safe journey. Mr Bennet looked a little more emotional than she expected, and that made her embrace him even tighter as she demanded he wrote the moment he arrived home.

Mr Darcy left the house together with his guests, informing everyone he would return in the afternoon. Elizabeth remained with Georgiana and Mrs Annesley, in a sudden silence that felt strange and heavy. Her companions clearly shared the same sensation, and Georgiana accepted Mrs Annesley's suggestion to practise the pianoforte for the first time in many weeks.

Chapter 27

Elizabeth and Georgiana, under the watchful eye of Mrs Annesley, played the pianoforte for a while. Within minutes, Elizabeth understood that Georgiana's skill was far superior to her own at the instrument, so she was content to turn the pages for her.

After a reluctant beginning, the young lady seemed to relax, and her passion was revived. Elizabeth and Mrs Annesley sat and admired her talent and flawless execution. So captivated were all three of them that they did not notice the guests observing them with great interest from the door.

"My dear, what a joy to hear you playing again!" a voice interjected when Georgiana had finished. Three pairs of eyes turned to stare at the elegant woman accompanying Colonel Fitzwilliam. Georgiana and Mrs Annesley immediately stood up, and so did Elizabeth.

"Aunt!" Georgiana hurried to greet her. "Have you been waiting long? Forgive me for not seeing you!"

"Do not worry, my child. It was a pleasure to just watch you perform. You look lovely! I cannot believe the improvement from the last time I saw you. Lovely indeed!"

"I told you as much, and you doubted me," the colonel interjected in a light tone.

"I feel better, Aunt," the girl replied. "Please allow me to introduce to you my friend, Miss Elizabeth Bennet. Elizabeth, this is my aunt, Lady Matlock."

"Miss Bennet, I am truly happy to meet you! I have heard so much praise of you. Considering your visible influence over Georgiana, none of it seems undeserved."

"Lady Matlock, it is an honour to make your acquaintance," Elizabeth said, curtseying. "I am sorry to contradict you, but I certainly do not deserve praise in regard to Georgiana. I am simply enjoying her company and her friendship."

"How lovely of you," Lady Matlock said, dismissing her modesty. "Come, let us sit. Tell me a little more about yourself, Miss Bennet. Oh, you have matching necklaces! I assume this is the one Anne gave you."

"It is," Elizabeth said.

"We all know about the incident, and I am grateful for your bravery. Now tell me, how are you enjoying London so far? When do you plan to return home? How is your family?"

"I hope Lizzy will not leave any time soon," Georgiana whispered. "She has not seen much of London since she arrived, as she has been taking care of me."

"Well, we must correct that," the colonel interjected again. "I am more than willing to take you, Miss Bennet, and Mrs Annesley to see anything you would like. There is also a play people are speaking of, if you like to attend the theatre."

"Indeed," Lady Matlock approved. "And since you are feeling so much better, I plan to host a little party. Miss Bennet and Mrs Annesley will be invited too."

"Oh…" Georgiana sighed, instantly paling. "I do not feel well enough for parties…or for the theatre. It is too crowded… but Lizzy may go if she wants to—"

***

"Go where?" Darcy interrupted them as he entered the room and greeted his aunt.

"We were talking about Georgiana leaving the house more," the lady explained. "Richard offered to escort her and her companions wherever they want to go. He mentioned a play at the theatre. And I am planning a small party for her."

"My dear aunt, we are grateful for your care and

considerate intentions, but I would kindly ask you to not make any plans for us," Darcy responded politely. "I am thankful to see my sister's health improving, and I am doing my best to provide her with anything she wishes, including opportunities for entertainment. She still needs to recover her strength before considering parties or the theatre."

"I am sure you are doing your best, Darcy, but you are not the best example for leaving the house more," his aunt teased him. "I fear Georgiana might also be influenced by your dislike of gatherings and parties, not to mention balls, which are so enjoyable to other people."

"I enjoy gatherings too, Aunt. I am not a savage. As you surely know, I am a faithful admirer of the theatre and opera. I also enjoy parties, even balls when the company is to my liking."

"You surely are too fastidious in regard to balls. They are only meant to amuse you, not to be taken in earnest," the colonel declared.

"Speaking of enjoyable company, I heard you met Lady Campbell and her daughters yesterday. They have been enquiring after you for quite a while."

"Yes, we met them," Darcy replied sternly. He felt uncomfortable opening the subject in the presence of Elizabeth.

"Lady Emmeline is one of the most eligible women in London at present. Very handsome, highly accomplished, well educated, a title attached to her name, and a reasonable dowry. And she has a peculiar inclination towards you. I cannot understand why you keep refusing to call on them. Or have you changed your mind in regard to Anne?"

The colonel seemed to wish to add something but remained silent.

Darcy's anxiety increased.

"Dear aunt, I cannot believe we are debating such a subject in the presence of Georgiana and Miss Bennet. Surely we can find a more proper subject."

He felt embarrassed as he tried to guess Elizabeth's thoughts, and he cast repeated glances at her. His family's insistence that he find a wife had been bothering him for years but never so badly as that moment.

Watching Elizabeth at that very moment, his thoughts became as clear as crystal.

Although no stranger to the company of ladies, just like any other man of the world of eight-and-twenty, he had never felt real passion, attraction, desire so powerful that it would burn one's soul. He had pretended to understand the meaning of love but had never experienced it.

More importantly, he had never desired to marry a particular lady, although he knew his duty and his responsibilities required it. Never had his heart been touched before. Until he encountered Elizabeth.

He looked at her.

He could see Elizabeth seemed disquieted too and wondered at the reason for it. Was she simply uncomfortable, or was she bothered by the subject? Could she be a little jealous? If she was, that might signify she held him in some regard. Did she, or was he simply entertaining unreasonable hopes?

Lady Matlock looked displeased with his scolding.

"Well, Georgiana must be involved in the family's concerns. She is already at that age. As for Miss Bennet, since she is an old friend of the family, I am sure she wishes nothing but the best for you. If I sounded impolite, I apologise. It was certainly not my intention. However, you should decide soon."

"Aunt, I am kindly asking you again to change the subject. In regard to deciding, I might follow in Richard's footsteps. He is three years my senior," he concluded, trying to sound light in order not to upset anyone.

"That is true. However, you cannot compare with me, since it is universally agreed that you are a man with no faults and impeccable conduct," the colonel mocked him in return.

Lady Matlock did not look amused.

"I shall not continue this argument. For the present, I am just happy to see Georgiana much improved and to have met Miss Bennet. That should be enough for one day. My dear, if I may be of assistance to you in any way, please do not hesitate to tell me," the lady addressed her niece with warm gentleness.

"Thank you, dear aunt. Mrs Annesley and Lizzy are here. I need nothing else," Georgiana said with a small yet bright smile.

"You must come to have tea with me one of these days," the lady continued. "Bring Miss Bennet with you, of course. Your uncle is curious to meet her too."

"I shall."

"You also need some new gowns. You are taller and thinner compared to last winter. I shall make an appointment with Madame Yvette."

"Oh no, that is not necessary, Aunt. Perhaps later," Georgiana answered with apparent anxiety.

Some tea and pastries were brought in. Lady Matlock remained for another half an hour. She enjoyed a cup of tea, talking mostly to Elizabeth and Georgiana, with Mrs Annesley rarely intervening and Darcy and the colonel enjoying their drinks.

**

Although she only meant well, Lady Matlock was rather intrusive in her enquiries to Elizabeth. However, Elizabeth kept her composure and felt more amused than annoyed.

While she did feel Lady Matlock's behaviour was slightly superior and presumptuous, Elizabeth was not offended by it. She recognised the lady's concern for her niece and nephew and could not blame her for it. However, the discussion about Mr Darcy's decision to marry distressed her exceedingly. Lady Campbell and her daughter had seemed very interested in the handsome bachelor; she also seemed to be on friendly terms with Lady Matlock, since she had immediately informed her about the meeting in the park. And Anne? Who was Anne? Lady Catherine's daughter?

After Lady Matlock and the colonel left, Georgiana let out a sigh of relief. Elizabeth smiled, as her feelings were similar.

"I hope Lady Matlock did not make you uncomfortable, Miss Bennet. She loves us dearly, but she has the tendency to impose her own way upon everybody. Strangely, my uncle is the same. I often wonder how they manage between them," Mr Darcy said.

Elizabeth smiled again; Mr Darcy had the same tendency, only he had tempered it lately.

"We all like to have our own way, except not all of us can impose it," Elizabeth answered.

"Perhaps. I for one admit to being guilty of such a charge," Mr Darcy declared. "Have you played the pianoforte, by any chance?"

"Indeed, Miss Darcy and Miss Bennet practised," Mrs Annesley said enthusiastically. "It was a delight to listen to them."

"Georgiana played. I mostly admired her," Elizabeth added. "My skills are so poor that I did not want to ruin her performance."

"That is not true, Lizzy! You play very well. Perhaps you need to practise a little more," Georgiana added in earnest.

"Then you will have to teach me, since I have never taken the trouble to practise consistently," Elizabeth admitted with another laugh. "That is why I do not excel in anything."

"I strongly disagree about that, Miss Bennet," Mr Darcy interjected. "No one admitted to the privilege of knowing you can think anything wanting."

Elizabeth stared at him, their eyes locking for a moment. He seemed serious, and his statement sent chills down her spine. Such praise in front of his sister was disquieting as much as it was pleasant.

"Both Darcys are too generous to me. I fear I might

become accustomed to it," she joked.

"Both Darcys love you dearly and are grateful to you. Are we not, Brother?"

Georgiana said genuinely and innocently. Her eyes were indeed bright with affection, but her honest yet naïve statement stunned both Mr Darcy and Elizabeth, and turned one pale, the other red-faced.

"We certainly do," Darcy admitted after a brief hesitation, and Elizabeth's hands trembled with both anxiety and exhilaration. She was not a simpleton — she understood that the profession of love was innocent and without any strong meaning, but still, it affected her greatly.

"Thank you…both…" she whispered.

"Now excuse me. I have some letters to write. I hope I shall have the pleasure of your company at dinner?" Mr Darcy asked.

"You will, Brother," Georgiana answered, and he removed himself from their presence with some haste.

***

The little indiscretion caused by Georgiana's statement of affection left both Elizabeth and Darcy disconcerted and uneasy, and they needed a little time to get over it.

That evening, the ladies joined Darcy for dinner; they did the same for breakfast the next morning and every day that followed.

Elizabeth spent most of her time with Georgiana and Mrs Annesley. Darcy was always there, only to provide them support and comfort, without imposing his presence on them. He longed to see Elizabeth first thing in the morning and last thing at night. His sleep remained restless and full of dreams of Elizabeth, but he preferred that sort of thrill over any proper rest. As long as she was there, near him, he was content. Fulfilled. Although she had been there only for just over a fortnight, he dreaded even imagining not having Elizabeth in his home. Even though he still struggled to keep a fair distance from her and to act with nothing but friendship, his heart knew better.

He noticed that she was growing closer to him too. They became accustomed to reading together in the library, with or without Georgiana present, or he assisted while they practised the pianoforte.

They discussed — and often argued over — books or the theatre, politics and war. They both enjoyed heated debates and mutual teasing, much to Georgiana's amusement.

They played chess, something they discovered they had in common, and their skill was evenly matched. For the first time in a long time, open laughter sounded in Darcy's house.

He accompanied them to visit the Gardiners, and they spent almost an entire day in Gracechurch Street. He also joined them in Hyde Park and took them to visit Lady Matlock, where Elizabeth was introduced to Lord Matlock, as well as his eldest son, the viscount, and his wife. At Lady Matlock's insistence, an appointment was made with Madame Yvette, which Elizabeth accepted with even more reluctance than Georgiana. Darcy simply mentioned that he would 'settle things' with Madame Yvette accordingly after their purchase, and the matter of payment was closed without further embarrassment on Elizabeth's part.

***

From Hertfordshire, Elizabeth received notice that her father had arrived home safely, and everyone was in good health. A more detailed letter arrived from Jane three days later, containing details of her sister's pleasure in the ball and a faithful narration of it; although more discreetly expressed, Jane's increasing attachment to Mr Bingley was also obvious.

Her letter also contained news of Mr Wickham.

Lydia and Kitty are upset too, as Mr Wickham, whom they favoured, seems to be continuing his attentions to Mary King. Even though we know Mary very well and have the highest opinion of her sweet nature, that is not enough for Lydia, Kitty, or Mama, who are all most put out. I hope you are as happy as you hoped in London, Lizzy. Papa brought us the extraordinary news of Miss Darcy's recovery, and please know we shall continue to pray for her.

The knowledge that Mr Wickham was still pursuing Mary King was worrisome. With his character still unknown in the community, with his deceptive skills and wish for an easy living, Mr Wickham was free to scheme to deceive honourable people and naïve girls, and that Elizabeth could not allow. With the letter in her hands, she went in search of Mr Darcy and found him in the library. She knocked, and he called to her to enter, but she remained at the door until he came to open it. Even then, she felt shy entering; she had not been alone with him, not even for a moment, in quite some time, and she felt equally thrilled and anxious about a private encounter.

He seemed somehow uneasy too but invited her inside.

"Miss Bennet? Is something wrong?"

"No. I mean yes, perhaps. I have come for your advice, and I do not wish to trouble Georgiana more."

Handing him the letter, she briefly explained the problem. Mr Darcy looked as concerned as she had expected.

"Please have a seat, Miss Bennet. What would you like to do next? After our last discussion in regard to Wickham, I hired Mr Dodge — a man truly proficient in ferreting out secrets and acting with the utmost discretion and efficiency. He has the assignment of discovering anything that can be used against Wickham and Mrs Younge."

"Oh. And has he been successful?"

"Yes. I have received some satisfying information so far, but nothing surprising to me. I agree that Miss King's uncle needs to be warned."

"I believe the same," Elizabeth said. "I am sorry to expose him, but if Mr Wickham has genuine affection for Mary and honourable intentions, he must prove his worthiness."

"I agree. However, I am still waiting for Wickham to prove his worthiness in anything. I shall write to your father too. He is the right person to assist me in this matter."

"Very well. I shall leave you now. I do not want to bother you any longer. I know you have more important things to do," she said, standing up. He rose to his feet too.

"You never bother me, Miss Bennet," he said seriously, his eyes locking with hers. "And nothing is more important than you."

Another thrill ran down her spine. She averted her eyes, too nervous to hold his intense, dark gaze.

"Please forgive me, I do not wish to embarrass you. And you must not worry. I would never say or do anything that might make you uncomfortable. I have been trying very hard from the day you entered this house, and I apologise if I have not always succeeded."

He looked apologetic and remorseful, and she struggled to understand his distress.

"Mr Darcy, I shall not deny that at times I feel uncomfortable in your presence, but it is not your fault, sir. You have been nothing but gentlemanly in your words and actions since I arrived here. Even long before that. My unease is not due to something you have done, and it is certainly not unpleasant."

"Miss Bennet, I...I am not sure what to make of your words, and I am afraid of assuming something that is not there."

They were standing, facing each other, a short distance apart, both overcome with emotions that neither dared express.

"Then perhaps a thorough clarification is in order, sir? To avoid further miscomprehension and embarrassment?" she suggested with a boldness that astonished and frightened her, as she realised it might cause irreparable harm if it was misplaced.

His stare expressed doubts and hesitations, mixed with fearful hopes and repressed feelings hidden for too long.

His lips moved to speak, but his words froze when the door was opened suddenly.

Dumbfounded, they both turned to see Miss Caroline Bingley, leaning against the wall, staring at them in apparent shock.

"Eliza Bennet? How is this possible? What on earth are you doing here? You are the last person I expected to find here!" Miss Bingley finally uttered, her eyes wide and her hand on her chest.

Mr Darcy stepped towards her, his anger at being interrupted barely concealed.

"Miss Bingley, what a surprise. Miss Bennet has been living with us for a while now, as my sister's guest. I would rather ask what you are doing here, without invitation or notice?"

His voice was sharp, at the edge of politeness, and his resentment could be easily heard. Miss Bingley gulped a few times, her mouth open in a gasp.

"I shall return to Georgiana. She must be waiting for me. I shall leave you two to clarify your mutual surprise," Elizabeth said with a satisfaction she could not control seeing Miss Bingley's increasing despair. When she passed by, she added with amusement, "It is lovely to see you again, Miss Bingley."

Elizabeth felt ashamed of herself for rejoicing in the lady's distress. Only for a brief instant, though. Then the tumult of thoughts invaded her mind, wondering what would have happened if they had not been interrupted.

Chapter 28

"I do not understand. Eliza Bennet has been here all this time?" Miss Bingley asked, her tone laced with confusion.

"Yes. She is my sister's guest, as I mentioned."

"But…how? How can they be friends?"

"They have been friends since their childhood. It is a long story, and one I am sure my sister or Miss Bennet would share with you. May I be of some help to you at present, Miss Bingley?"

"I wished to ask for your assistance in a delicate matter, since Charles is about to do something foolish that will ruin his life. But I can see I have come to the wrong place."

"No, indeed. In regard to Bingley, you may apply to me at any time. What has happened? Is your brother in town too?"

"No. He should have come, but he said he would write to you instead to help him with his business. I believe he intends to propose to Miss Jane Bennet — something we have feared for weeks now. I warned him that such a connection would be a disaster for him, and I hoped you would advise him likewise. But I see now that you approve of the Bennet family more than I imagined. This is quite shocking!"

Miss Bingley's voice was now angry, and she was mumbling, while Darcy struggled to understand her.

"Miss Bingley, it is not for me to approve or disapprove of anything that your brother has decided. It is a matter of consideration and respect to trust his wisdom. And yes, I do approve of the Bennet family. As a matter of fact, Miss Elizabeth saved my sister's life, both in the past as well as recently."

The shock widened Miss Bingley's eyes, and she stared wordlessly for a long moment.

"I cannot understand what is happening! Saved her life? Where did all these stories come from? You have always acted strangely around Eliza Bennet, and things seem to have gone from bad to worse! I am as worried for you as I am for Charles!"

"Thank you for your concern, but I assure you it is not necessary. Now please forgive me, I am expecting an important visitor soon."

With that, he dismissed Miss Bingley, who still needed a moment to gather herself enough to leave.

The unexpected visit left Darcy amused as well as unsettled. His thoughts immediately returned to Elizabeth, wondering what would have happened if they had not been interrupted.

He could not help but smile to himself. His relationship with Elizabeth was growing stronger every day, not only through Georgiana but between the two of them too. It brought him a sort of exhilaration that he had never known before. In only a fortnight, her presence in his home had become so much a part of his life — of himself — that he dreaded to think of the moment when she might leave.

Miss Bingley's visit made Darcy think of his friend. He was probably ready for the most important step in his life and did not have his sisters' approval. Only a short while ago he would probably not have had Darcy's approval either. For a long time, Darcy had been unaware of the real meaning of joy and happiness. Elizabeth had shown him his faults and brought out feelings that had been buried deeply inside him. Her smile and sparkling eyes had brought liveliness to his life as much as to Georgiana's. And peace. A long-desired peace that he had feared he had lost and would not find again.

Mr Dodge arrived at the expected hour, and Darcy received him in the library, with the door locked. Darcy offered the man a drink and poured one for himself.

"Mr Darcy, I think I've managed to find out some

interesting information. You already know that Wickham is in Meryton. Apparently, he left London with debts of over two thousand pounds. I've sent a man to enquire discreetly within his regiment, where I suspect he's run up further debt. As for the Younge woman, she still owns the building in Edward Street, and she's renting it out. She inherited it from her mother. It's always full of people, but reports say she's not good at managing the money."

"I see. And the jewels?"

"I've located them. Fortunately, there are very few places in London where such valuable pieces might be sold. I was told one item was brought by a woman and the other by a man."

"I suspected as much, Mr Dodge. I shall give you the money to retrieve them. I do not wish to expose my family to any rumours."

"Of course, Mr Darcy. May I be of service to you in any other way?"

"For the time being, your investigation of this matter has been quite satisfying. Keep me informed about anything more that might arise."

"Very well. I'll fetch the jewels and bring them to you as soon as possible."

After the man left, Darcy sipped from his glass, reflecting on what he must do next. With Georgiana recovering in health and in spirits so wonderfully with Elizabeth around, his initial fury and need for revenge had calmed, allowing him to use his reason. Christmas was quickly approaching, and he knew he had enough reasons to be grateful and let go of the resentment that was burdening him.

Although he was in no way willing to forgive those two poor excuses for human beings, he was able to ponder his actions.

Just like Mr Dodge, he also suspected that Wickham had accumulated further debts in Meryton. After all, he had been in the regiment for about three months — enough time to expose his real character.

With that thought in mind, he remembered that he had a letter to write to Mr Bennet and one to Bingley, enquiring about the latest news from Hertfordshire.

Elizabeth and Darcy encountered each other on several occasions during the day as they went about their business in the house, and each time, a slight awkwardness was palpable between them. They both sensed the importance of their early encounter in the library, and of the moment wasted by the sudden arrival of Miss Bingley. But neither of them had the courage — or the opportunity — to speak of it.

***

Several more days passed in Darcy's house, with life continuing peacefully and pleasantly, with daily activities that varied from eating together to conversation, walks, and rides in the park, business appointments, and performing music, sharing witty conversations and sometimes heated arguments. It felt like a blissful family life, a notion equally enchanting and dreadful, as it was meant to come to an end one day, sooner rather than later.

Thoughts and struggles troubled Darcy's days and nights. He had long understood and accepted that Elizabeth was the woman perfectly suited to him, the woman he had waited for and had lost hope of ever finding. Any reservations he had against her or her family seemed ill-grounded now, even ridiculous, and he was ashamed of himself for ever considering them.

Of his feelings and wishes he had long been certain. But Elizabeth's feelings and desires were of more importance to him.

As friendly as she was to him, he could not be sure if her feelings were for him as a man or for Georgiana's brother.

If he would dare to speak to her, to confess his admiration, his love, his hopes, she might receive his declaration with joy and pleasure. He could be even bolder and propose marriage, and she might accept him. They could be engaged by Christmas, which would be the answer to his prayers and the fulfilment of his dreams.

But what if she felt only friendship for him and such a confession would embarrass her? She would surely not stay longer in the same house as him, so he would hurt both her and Georgiana. Even worse, what if she were to accept a marriage proposal from him only for Georgiana's sake? That thought was the most hurtful and stopped him from attempting any action. He would simply enjoy her nearness, keeping her and Georgiana company whenever he had the chance, without imposing his presence.

As promised, Lady Matlock took the ladies shopping and almost forcefully ordered two new gowns for each, claiming they were necessary in the event of a party or even a night at the theatre. Such an event, though, was unlikely to occur soon.

Despite an obvious improvement in her appearance and spirits, Georgiana declared her reluctance to attend any gathering, including a dinner at the Matlocks, and especially the theatre or the opera, where she would be exposed to public scrutiny. Lady Matlock tried to insist, but Darcy stepped in, carefully protecting his sister's privacy. She felt happy at home, with Mrs Annesley and Elizabeth and short visits from the Gardiners or the Matlocks. For Darcy, her wish was his command, and he fully supported her.

"Brother, there is something I want to speak to you about," she said one morning before breakfast.

"What is it, my dear?"

"It is about Lizzy...Elizabeth...I would like to buy her a gift. I know you will be generous with everyone, including Mrs Annesley. But for Lizzy, I want something special."

Darcy smiled at the mysterious glimmer in his sister's eyes.

"Do you have something in mind?"

"I do... The necklace that mother gave her suits her so well. Could we possibly find some earrings or a bracelet to match it? I want to give her something from me to add to Mama's gift, to remember me when she leaves." The girl became emotional, and Darcy frowned.

"I believe that is a wonderful idea, my dear. The necklaces — both of them — were custom-made, but I shall try to find something as close as possible."

"Thank you."

"Georgiana, what do you mean by Miss Elizabeth leaving? Has she mentioned something?" he asked with some distress and a sudden lump in his throat.

"No…she said she would stay as long as I need her. But I know she is missing her family very much. She received a letter from her sister Jane yesterday, and I saw tears in her eyes."

"I see. She was indeed very close to her family, especially Miss Jane Bennet."

"Yes. And she mentioned to me that every year the Gardiners travel to Longbourn for Christmas. I know you invited Mr and Mrs Gardiner to dine with us at Christmas, and I should be happy to see them again, but I feel like I have broken up their family to my benefit," she whispered, her voice getting weaker.

"You are too severe on yourself! How can you say such a thing? I am sure Miss Elizabeth would be upset if she heard you. Besides, my dear, even if…when she returns home, you will forever be friends, will you not? You may meet and visit whenever you want!"

"I would like to ask her to come to Pemberley for the summer if you approve of it," the girl said, and Darcy's heart raced.

"You know I approve of her. Why would you doubt it? When it comes to Miss Elizabeth, you do not even need to ask for my approval. Besides, I have already invited the Bennets and the Gardiners to join us in Derbyshire next summer. I spoke to Mr Bennet and Mr Gardiner when they came to dinner."

Georgiana smiled with gratitude and wiped her eyes.

"I know I am speaking like a selfish simpleton, but I wish she could stay with me forever. I wish she never had to leave," the girl said with a sigh.

"So do I," Darcy replied from the bottom of his heart, the words flying from his lips before he had time to stop them.

Georgiana's blue eyes widened in surprise, and her lips parted in astonishment, revealing that he had said too much in just one unguarded sentence.

"My dear, as I have said from the beginning, it is my goal to make you and Miss Bennet as comfortable as possible," he said abruptly, with a sharpness in his voice that clearly did not deceive Georgiana since she was staring at him with a searching expression. "I shall look for the jewellery right away and will inform you about my progress," he concluded.

"Thank you. Brother, there is something else I wish to speak to you about if I may..." she continued hesitantly.

"Of course. Anything."

"About George," she whispered timidly, barely daring to look at him. He waited for her to speak further.

"I know you are angry with him and Mrs Younge. And you want to punish them...but I wish only to forget about them and about my own foolishness. Perhaps if not for them, I would not have met Lizzy again. I am upset, but I do not want to cause you more trouble, especially at Christmas time..."

Darcy embraced her and gently placed a kiss on her hand.

"Do not worry. I am not as angry as I was, my dear. I must punish them, though. I shall not have it any other way. I am not as generous as you are. But trust me, it will not cause me any trouble. Please do not worry about it any longer."

"I do worry, Brother."

"I know." He smiled affectionately. "Now let us go. We are surely expected at breakfast."

When they entered the dining room, they found Mrs Annesley talking to Elizabeth. At their entrance, a smile touched Elizabeth's lips and eyes, and Darcy did not dare guess for whom it was meant.

But he did know without any doubt what gift he could offer Elizabeth to make her happy. So he smiled too, his eyes locking with hers briefly.

Chapter 29

To Elizabeth, the time spent in Mr Darcy's house was a curious blend of sweetness and sorrow, with happiness as well as painful distress.

Her friendship with Georgiana had enhanced her life, and in less than a month, they became bonded by a friendship unlikely to ever be broken. Her only fear was how that relationship would continue if — when — Mr Darcy finally married. Since she had accepted her growing attachment to Mr Darcy, there were occasions when she wildly hoped that he might return her feelings, and he might propose to her. Becoming his wife and Georgiana's sister was such a wonderful dream, but she forced herself to push it aside in order to avoid the grief of disappointment.

She had met the Matlocks and Colonel Fitzwilliam several times, and they all treated her with politeness, even friendliness. But she knew all too well that none of them imagined that she might be anything else more than Georgiana's friend. Also, she had heard Mr Darcy's engagement to his cousin Anne de Bourgh spoken of several times — a report that Georgiana dismissed as being false.

"Lady Catherine has spoken of their engagement since I was a child. I even asked Fitzwilliam about it. Anne is very sweet and quiet and gentle, and I would not mind having her as a sister. But my brother told me he is no fonder of Anne than our other cousins, and he has no intention of marrying her. He said he told Lady Catherine so too."

"I cannot blame your aunt for wishing to marry her daughter to such an honourable man as Mr Darcy. Any mother would want that," Elizabeth replied.

"My brother is fond of Anne, and I am sure he will always help and protect her. I know many gentlemen enter into arranged marriages, but he does not seem inclined to do so."

Elizabeth rejoiced in the relief she felt at such news, which, in the end, could mean nothing to her; Mr Darcy might not be considering marrying his cousin, but he would still seek a wife from his circle and with similar wealth and connections.

Christmas was approaching, and Elizabeth's distress was deepened by being away from her family — for the first time ever. She knew such thoughts were childish; after all, both she and Jane could have been long married by their age and far away from their family. Yet, she could not help pining for her happy past while fearing and praying for the future.

She especially missed Jane and their long, meaningful conversations. If Jane were there, she might have confessed to her that she had fallen in love with Mr Darcy, and very likely Jane would have doubted her words. Who would not? Even she was astonished and puzzled by such a drastic change from the night of the assembly, which was only two months ago.

Jane, on the other hand, seemed happy in the letters that she wrote to Elizabeth. Mr Bingley was still a regular visitor at Longbourn and had chosen to remain at Netherfield, even though his friend and his sisters had left. There could not be a better indication of what the future held for Jane. Despite Miss Caroline Bingley's apparent disgust at finding Elizabeth in Mr Darcy's house, which showed that she — and very likely Mrs Hurst too — were completely against a possible connection between their brother and the Bennets, Mr Bingley seemed firm in his decision and steady to his purpose.

The rest of the reports from Jane indicated to Elizabeth that things had not changed much.

Even Kitty and Lydia's partiality for the officers remained the same; especially for Mr Wickham, who seemingly had turned all his attention towards Mary King.

As much as she tried to control her resentment,

Elizabeth's anger towards that man turned into a hatred that she had never felt for anyone. She had found no opportunity to speak to Mr Darcy about his plans for that scoundrel; she could not open the subject in the presence of Georgiana, and Mr Darcy avoided any private encounters with her. She hoped that her father had warned Colonel Forster as well as Mary King's uncle regarding the danger of having Wickham around.

Four days prior to Christmas, Elizabeth was invited to the drawing room, where she found Mr Darcy alone. The moment she entered, his intense stare made her quiver, and her knees shook. The drawing room door was left wide open so they could be seen and avoid an improper situation. Still, his closeness and the feeling of being alone with him made her unsettled.

"Miss Bennet, please sit down. I have just received these letters. Two are for me, from your father and from Bingley. This one is for you, from your sister."

He handed her the letter, and she took it hesitantly, fearing and hoping she might touch his fingers. She did not, though, as he carefully withdrew his hand.

"Thank you. I confess I am a little jealous, sir. My father has written to me only once, but he seems to maintain a diligent correspondence with you."

"I have not opened Mr Bennet's letter yet, but I am sure it contains mostly dull reports of business. You have no reason to be jealous, Miss Bennet," he said teasingly. A little smile revealed his dimples, making her quiver again. He was certainly referring to her last statement, but she felt like he was guessing her thoughts.

"Regardless, I trust you will find a reason to forget any jealousy when you read your sister's letter," he added, his smile turning mischievous.

"I am sure I shall. I always love receiving news from Jane."

"I dare say her latest news will be particularly enjoyable," he insisted. Elizabeth peered at him, puzzled, until comprehension struck her.

"Oh! How wonderful! I look forward to reading it."

"I imagined as much."

"I suspect Mr Bingley shared some news in his letter, too. I hope it did not displease you, Mr Darcy?"

"Not at all, I assure you. In fact, aside from your friendship with Georgiana, few things have given me more pleasure."

Although his statement was innocent, something in his voice, as well as his declaration of pleasure, made her anxious. She needed a moment to calm herself before she replied.

"If you do not mind, I shall go and read my letter now."

"Of course. If you wish to reply to your sister, please bring me the letter. I shall be sending my responses to Hertfordshire too."

"Thank you, I shall." She took the missive and left, almost jumping for joy; the desired outcome had occurred, and Mr Darcy had indicated as much.

She finally unsealed it and read with her own eyes, amused that Jane's writing sounded more muddled than ever. Happiness could be felt behind the lines, as well as nervousness. Jane revealed that Mr Bingley had proposed only the day before, and Mr Bennet had given his blessing.

> *Dearest Lizzy,*
> *I cannot believe one can be so happy!*
> *I can barely breathe from the fear that it is only a dream, and I shall wake up, making it disappear.*
> *Now I only pray that you will feel equal bliss very soon!*

Elizabeth folded the letter with a tender smile; even in her most joyful moment, Jane was still thinking of her. There was no better sister, nor better person. Only Georgiana was close to Jane in nature and kindness of the heart. Her sister's engagement was certainly the best present she could receive for Christmas but also enhanced her longing to be at Jane's side at such an important moment in her life.

After the ladies spent a joyful afternoon of shared news and planning for a Christmas dinner party, Mr Darcy joined them. Only a few hours had passed since he had teased her, conveying the most delightful surprise, but Elizabeth noticed his expression was dark, and the frown had returned between his eyebrows. Georgiana had clearly noticed too, and worry was also visible on her countenance as she asked what had happened.

"Only some business, my dear, do not worry," he answered. "I shall be gone for the rest of the day, and I might be away tomorrow too."

"Gone? Where?" Georgiana insisted with apparent panic.

"As I said, only some business. I came to inform you, but I am begging you to not be worried. There is no reason," he answered. He cast repeated glances at Elizabeth, but his eyes did not rest on her for long.

"I have instructed Mrs Penfield that Miss Bennet has the authority to make any decision in the house as much as you do. I hope you do not mind."

"No, of course not. But Brother, you speak like you will be gone for days! Will you not give us any details?"

He cast another glance towards Elizabeth and reluctantly answered, "A friend has asked for my help in an urgent and very important matter. It might be resolved within hours, or it might take a few days. I could be home tonight, but it will be very late, and I shall go to my room directly and likely leave in the morning before you wake up."

"But is it dangerous?"

"No, not at all," he responded, then he gently embraced his sister and said good-bye. Before he left, his eyes caught Elizabeth's for only an instant. ·

Mrs Annesley tried to calm Georgiana, whose worry was still evident despite her brother's assurance. Elizabeth stared at the door absently; the way Mr Darcy had tried to not look at her alarmed her, and concern pushed her to act imprudently.

"Forgive me, Mr Darcy told me to give him the letter I have written to Jane. I must ask him what I should do with it," she offered and ran down the stairs before the other two had time to question her rather silly explanation. Catching her breath, she found Mr Darcy in the library, ready to depart. At her entrance, the surprise was obvious in his expression.

"Mr Darcy, forgive me. I must ask...I can see you are more worried than you wish us to believe. May I ask what has happened? I saw you were looking at me like I am somehow involved..."

He looked around, hesitating. They were alone, and she was only inches away from him.

"Fortunately, the matter is not of immediate concern to you, Miss Bennet, but it is somehow related to you. An hour ago, I received another letter from Mr Bennet. He asked for my help on behalf of a friend. It seems that scoundrel Wickham eloped last night with Miss Mary King. Apparently, they have gone to Gretna Green. Her uncle is devastated and has gone after them with his sons and Colonel Forster."

Elizabeth's shock was such that she gasped for air and sat down heavily in the nearest chair. Mr Darcy, who was about to leave, brought her a glass of wine and sat next to her.

"He had the audacity to elope with Mary? A girl who has a family to protect her? Mary's uncle and cousins will shoot him, as he deserves! That man has lost not only his mind but also his decency! Poor Mary!" Elizabeth mumbled, still confused.

"I barely remember Miss King and her family. But your father asked for my assistance, and I shall help them find him. After all, Wickham is my responsibility," he said in earnest.

"Surely you are joking, sir! How can you take the blame for such an occurrence?"

"Quite easily, I am afraid. I did not take proper measures against him to avoid such a situation."

"I strongly disagree, sir. Sadly, not only Mary King but

other girls might have eloped with Mr Wickham, regardless of what you said. Including my sisters Lydia and Kitty. Our good fortune was our lack of dowry and connections," she said, trying to joke to conceal her embarrassment.

"That might be true, yet I still feel that I failed to do my duty."

"So, are you going to Gretna Green now?"

"Not at all. I believe it is likely they journeyed to London first, at least for a short time while Wickham gathers some funds to travel to Scotland. I suspect where they might be, or at least who knows of his whereabouts."

"Mrs Younge?"

"Probably. Miss Bennet, I cannot stay any longer. I must leave you now."

"Of course. I apologise. How silly of me..."

He put on his hat and coat, but Elizabeth turned from the door.

"Mr Darcy, are you going alone? I cannot imagine where you are bound, but I imagine such a place might be dangerous for a gentleman like you..."

"I have no intention of being a gentleman, Miss Bennet. Not this time," he replied sharply, his voice heavy and his resentment apparent.

Then he took her hand to his lips, only for an instant.

"Miss Bennet, thank you for coming to talk to me. Please do not worry. You have no reason. Trust me."

"I do trust you, Mr Darcy. And I do worry," she whispered. Their glances locked for a moment, and then he bowed and left.

***

Mr Darcy's departure left Georgiana and Elizabeth in a state of complete distress; however, only one of them dared to voice it, although both felt it equally strongly.

Since Mr Darcy had not requested her secrecy and because she had promised complete honesty to Georgiana, Elizabeth made a controversial decision and revealed the truth. She immediately regretted her decision, as the news affected her friend deeply, despite the girl's struggle to conceal her turmoil.

Mrs Annesley, ignorant of her charge's past history with Mr Wickham, could not understand Georgiana's response. However, Elizabeth understood only too well and blamed herself for her thoughtlessness.

That evening, only Elizabeth and Mrs Annesley dined. Georgiana had some soup and then retired to bed early, claiming she wanted to sleep. Mrs Annesley followed soon after, and Elizabeth moved to her room, then back to the library, trying to read. She intended to wait up for Mr Darcy, but she knew it would be foolish. He might not return at all, and even if he did return in the middle of the night, he would surely not want to speak to her. But she would at least be at peace knowing he was safe.

**

Darcy collected Mr Dodge on his way to Mrs Younge's boarding house. When he first received the note from Mr Bennet, he had felt disbelief mixed with uncontrollable anger. Not for a moment did he presume Wickham had any feelings for that girl, Mary King. Mr Bennet's mention that the girl had a dowry of ten thousand pounds, and the suspicions he had already run up more debts in Hertfordshire, were enough reason to explain the elopement. Which enraged Darcy even more.

That scoundrel had dared to deceive another honourable young girl and her family and betray his colonel and his fellow officers, and Darcy took it as a personal affront. One he was not willing to accept without repercussions.

The carriage stopped in front of Mrs Younge's building, and Darcy climbed down, asking Mr Dodge to remain inside. He asked for the proprietor, and ignorant of his identity and hoping for some business, she appeared. Seeing Darcy, she almost fainted, but he pushed the door open and entered. A servant tried to intervene, but the woman asked him to withdraw.

"Mr Darcy... I certainly did not expect to see you, sir. What brings you to this part of town? May I be of some help to you? May I offer you a drink?"

"Mrs Younge, I do not have more than a minute to waste with you. I shall only tell you this — I have discovered the extent of the deception you wrought on my sister. Everything! Including the scheme with Wickham spending the night in the house and you two stealing the jewels and selling them for your benefit!"

The woman took a step back. "I did not steal anything! Miss Darcy gave them to Wickham of her own free will! He said we should sell them afterwards. You did not ask for them back, and Wickham assumed he could keep them! It was not my fault!"

Darcy showed his disgust with a grimace, while he stepped towards her and spoke further.

"Mrs Younge, I trusted you with my sister's safety, and you betrayed me in the worst manner. This, I cannot forgive and forget. Just as I shall not forgive or forget that you caused my sister pain and grief. I shall have no peace until I exact my revenge."

The woman's eyes widened, and she took another step back. She was now standing with her back to the wall, with Darcy only inches away.

"I do not understand...what revenge? I have done nothing. Wickham forced me to—"

"Spare me your abominable lies! I have witnesses and papers that show you sold jewels that belonged to my sister. Unless you have proof that she willingly gave them to Wickham, I can easily throw you in prison this very night. This very hour. I imagine spending the winter there is not a pleasant prospect."

The woman was pale and shivering, and Darcy wondered whether she might faint. Not that he would care at all.

"But…I have not…I do not understand…why now? It has been many months…"

"Why now? Because I want to. Because I wish to amuse myself. You see, Mrs Younge, sending you to prison is my diversion. Of course, you are entitled to a trial, and I look forward to you bringing proof to dismiss mine. Whenever you want."

"I do not want to, sir! It is all a horrible misunderstanding. I beg you to tell me how I can atone for my errors. I did nothing to harm Miss Darcy!"

"If you repeat these lies to me, I shall have you arrested this very day. You did quite a lot to harm my sister. On purpose. She trusted you, and you sold her!"

"I did no such thing!" she cried. "I did not—"

"Enough! I do not believe a word you say! I assume you purchased this building with the money from my sister's jewels. If I take you to court and ask you to repay the value of the jewels, you will lose your building and your business. You will starve on the streets!"

"Mr Darcy, you cannot…I shall not—"

"Mrs Younge, keep quiet and listen to me carefully. I have enough proof against you to have you in my hand. I can throw you in prison any time I want. I may let you be poor and in debt whenever I please. Today, tomorrow, next year… I have men who are constantly watching you. You cannot escape me. You cannot escape my revenge. You may only pray that it will not happen too soon. My revenge will touch you one day, and you have nothing else to do except wait and pray!"

Darcy knew his voice was frightening, and as never before, he felt satisfied. He had never threatened anyone in his life, but he felt no remorse. The woman was trembling — barely breathing from fright. Instead of feeling sorry for her, he recollected Georgiana's months of suffering.

That woman must spend at least five months in terror and apprehension. And still it would not be enough, since Georgiana had been innocent, and that woman was guilty to her bones.

"I am sorry," the woman whispered. "I cannot understand how it happened. It was not my fault—"

Darcy interrupted her again.

"Do not cry. I care little for your tears after witnessing my sister's for so long. I shall not take any measures tonight. I might do so tomorrow, next week, or next month, or whenever I am in a poor disposition. You will never know. You can only pray for the best and fear the worst."

With that, he took a step back, giving her some space, while the woman kept whispering, "I am sorry...it was not my fault..."

"I shall give you the chance to prove to me you do feel a trace of remorse," he said, and the woman looked up, her eyes wide with sudden hope. "I want to know where Wickham is," he said calmly, and Mrs Younge's hands trembled until she clasped them together.

"If you deny seeing him, you will only enrage me more. I know he has come to London with a young woman. If he is here, I want to know where."

"He is not here... I had no spare rooms..." she mumbled.

"I am sure you know his whereabouts. I shall wait in the carriage for half an hour. As you will see, I am not alone but with a man of the law. It depends on you what I shall do next," he concluded, then he left. Glancing back, he saw the woman collapse onto the bed, and he felt no contrition. For a moment, he wondered whether he could ever relate that discussion to Elizabeth and whether she would approve of his behaviour.

Chapter 30

Darcy poured himself another cup of coffee. He had a terrible headache, due not only to the lack of sleep but also to the anger and frustration, from which he could not escape. It was early morning but still dark, and he had just arrived home. He was too tired to even go and change, simply slumped in the armchair. A knock on the door drew his attention; somehow, even before his eyes proved it, his heart suspected it was Elizabeth.

She took only a step into the room, then waited. He stood up and stretched out his hand, inviting her in. He knew he should not be alone with her in the library, in darkness lit only by the fire and a few candles. But her presence comforted and calmed him, and he could not reject it.

"I am well aware that my presence at this early hour is improper," she whispered, as though guessing his thoughts. "I promise I shall not stay long. I only came to see how you are."

"Miss Bennet, then please stay. I most certainly do not wish you to leave."

His voice, tinged with tiredness and melancholy, reached her. Her countenance momentarily betrayed her unease at hearing him sounding rather defeated. She deliberated for a moment and ultimately resolved to occupy the seat across from his desk, waiting for his next words.

"You woke up early," he said.

"I slept little. I waited to... I saw your carriage through the window and came to enquire..."

She seemed embarrassed, and he felt a thrill of joy imagining she had been waiting for him, looking out of the window.

"I am sorry you were distressed. Would you like some coffee, Miss Bennet?"

"No, thank you, sir. I want to know...do you have tidings? Did you find them?"

"Yes, I found them. It was not even much trouble."

"Truly? Does Mary's uncle know? And Colonel Forster?"

"I sent a man to search for them last evening. They should be on their way back to London by now."

"How fortunate for them to have your assistance! Without you, they would not have been found in time."

"Sadly, it does not even matter. Mary King, who is of age, refused to hear any reason. She is determined to marry Wickham, regardless of his faults and his debts."

Elizabeth covered her mouth with her hand.

"Poor, silly Mary! I have known her since she was a child. I did not expect her to be so naïve and allow herself to be so easily deceived. He will marry her only for her dowry, and she will be miserable for the rest of her life. How can she not see it? Could she have been blinded to the truth by her love for such a man?"

Darcy sipped the last of his coffee. "Love may cause blindness, I suppose," he replied hoarsely, glancing at her. "However, I do not think that is the case. I spoke to Miss King privately and tried to convince her to return to her family. I told her he was a deceptive man with significant flaws of character who would do anything for a comfortable life. I told her that he had previously attempted to elope with other women of means."

"And?" Elizabeth asked.

"She said she suspected as much. She said she knows she is not a handsome woman and has little to recommend her except her fortune. That she would never be able to marry better than Wickham and expected to be considered a spinster soon. She is determined not to lose the opportunity to enjoy herself."

With each word, he became more uncomfortable, while Elizabeth blushed in mortification.

"She said that? Mary King? I can hardly believe it."

"You can imagine my surprise. It is not the sort of statement one would expect from a young woman in peril. However, she was determined to stay with him. I could not take her away her until her relatives returned. I felt she was fully aware of her actions and the consequences of them. She even mentioned that nobody could change her decision."

"This is quite a shock," Elizabeth replied. "Not only the elopement but her behaviour too."

"I saw that nothing could be done. As a last resort, I mentioned his debts that I have purchased and that I could throw him in jail. She begged me not to do that. She said she would purchase them from me, but she cannot afford such a sum since she will have to cover his present debts. Any help I offered, she seemed to have a reason to reject. Undoubtedly, it was not a sudden elopement. She had thought of it for some time."

Elizabeth's eyes widened in disbelief.

He poured himself another cup of coffee and she gasped, stretching her hand over the desk to touch his.

"You are hurt!" she exclaimed.

He shivered, not from the pain but from the overwhelming thrill of her tender touch.

"It is nothing, really. Only the consequence of my private conversation with Wickham..."

She stared at him; their eyes locked. A little embarrassed smile appeared on his lips; only hours ago he was wondering whether to tell her. And now they were talking, unrestrained, alone, her tentative fingers touching the back of his hand.

"As I said, I did not act like a gentleman, and I have not accomplished much except for locating them. I allowed Wickham to aggravate me, and I lost control. I am not proud of myself."

"Well, I am," she replied, much to his surprise. "And

judging by your hand, I dare say you accomplished something important during your private conversation. I know a lady should not agree with fighting, and I know you do not need my approval, but you have it nevertheless," she ended with a teasing smile, which widened his too.

Without much consideration, he covered her hand with his other one.

"You are wrong, Miss Bennet. Your approval means everything to me," he said hoarsely.

Silence fell over them as they sat in the dark library with the fire burning, two candles lightening their faces, and her hand imprisoned between his. Her fingers moved gently, brushing against his bruise, but she did not withdraw them.

The sound of the door opening startled them. Each pulled back, increasing the distance that separated them. From the door, Georgiana looked at them, stepping inside hesitantly.

"Oh, please forgive me for interrupting! I could not sleep. I heard you had returned."

"Do not worry, my dear. Please come in," Darcy invited her, offering her a chair next to Elizabeth, who was flushed from embarrassment.

"I was just telling Miss Bennet what happened. Please take a seat. I shall order some refreshments, so we can speak at length."

She sat, looking at Elizabeth. "I am sorry I retired so early last night. I was a little distressed," Georgiana whispered. "You look tired, Lizzy."

"I am perfectly well, dearest. Except I have not slept at all."

"You both should rest," Darcy said protectively. "I am afraid there will be quite a lot of upheaval in the house today. I am expecting Mary King's relatives to arrive."

For the next half an hour, Darcy repeated parts of his story for his sister's benefit, avoiding the details about Mary King's statement, which were unsuitable for a young lady like Georgiana. To Elizabeth, he could open his heart; he felt like she was his equal in understanding and judgment, even in her belief that it had not been wrong for him to punch Wickham. With her, he could be completely honest. He was speaking to his sister, yet the thrill of Elizabeth's touch was still stirring him inside. Such a deep sensation from a brief touch he had never felt before, nor had he ever imagined it.

Before noon, the search party finally arrived, and Darcy offered them food and drink, which they refused with thanks, as they were all in a hurry to retrieve Mary. Darcy chose not to reveal his conversation with the young woman, except for mentioning that she had refused to join him at his house.

Colonel Forster was enraged and threatened to punish the culprit. The uncle still held hopes that Mary would return home — something that Darcy knew to be unlikely, but he could not shatter the man's hopes. He accompanied the men to the location where they would find the two fugitives and would likely face a hurtful disappointment.

***

Elizabeth spent some time with Georgiana, to be sure the girl was not too affected by recent events. Surprisingly, Georgiana showed strength and calmness. She admitted to being hurt, disappointed, and sad, but she felt even worse for Mary King, whom she considered a victim of Mr Wickham. Since they were both tired, each retired to their rooms, as Mr Darcy had suggested. Despite lying in her bed, Elizabeth found little rest. Neither her body nor her mind could find peace with the stirring sensation she felt inside her.

Her last interlude with Mr Darcy, alone in the library, had been different from the others in a gratifying yet perturbing way. Unlike in the past, when he had insisted on propriety, this time he had invited her to stay. He had opened his heart to her and related to her much more than he had later told Georgiana. And then his hand covering hers had been such a delightful feeling that her heart still raced at its recollection.

They had been once again interrupted, but she did not regret it. Georgiana seemed so perfectly suited to be with them, on any occasion, that her presence was always a blessing.

When silence returned to the house, Elizabeth fell asleep, still wearing her day clothes, defeated by the previous night's tiredness. She was startled later on by the sound of shouting, and she jumped from her bed. She only had time to take a quick look in the mirror and brush her fingers through her hair before she hurried downstairs.

In the hall stood a lady she had never seen before — a tall, large woman, wearing an elegant gown, carrying a cane, and displaying an air that suggested anything but amiability. Her self-importance was apparent, and her features — which might once have been handsome — were twisted in a frown.

At Elizabeth's entrance, the lady's eyes narrowed, and before Elizabeth even had time to greet her, a shout shook the walls.

"Miss Bennet, I presume. The country nobody who made my nephew lose his mind! Well, it is good he is not here, so we can talk properly! Come with me to the drawing room this instant!"

Elizabeth was stunned, glancing around at the servants, who were watching from a discreet distance.

"Forgive me, madam, there must be a misunderstanding," Elizabeth replied harshly. "I shall certainly not go anywhere, and neither will you before you introduce yourself. Mr Darcy is not at home, and I shall not allow strangers in his house!"

The woman's eyes widened, and her lips narrowed.

"I am no stranger, young lady! Do you know who I am? I am Lady Catherine de Bourgh, his aunt! His mother's sister, which makes me his closest relative. I can go wherever I want in this house. Come with me. I must speak to you!"

The lady walked away decidedly, and Elizabeth had no other choice but to follow her. The lady was everything she expected from Mr Collins's description.

"You will pack your things and leave today! You have no business being here. You have already embarrassed yourself and your family by spending weeks in a man's house!"

Elizabeth felt a lump in her throat from anger and mortification. Such horrible accusations, coming from nowhere, left her speechless for a moment — long enough for the lady to continue.

"You must know your arts and allurements will fail. He might be entertained by you for a while, but he would never marry someone so below him in every possible way. Besides, he is already engaged to my daughter!"

Finally, Elizabeth found her voice, trembling with anger.

"Lady Catherine, this is either a misunderstanding or a ridiculous, mean, and vicious attack with no grounds. In such a case, I shall defend myself by walking away from this laughable argument. You must excuse me now."

"I shall not excuse you! Misunderstanding? Have you not been in his house for weeks now? Have you not lied to everyone in your town by telling them you were staying with your uncle? Do you have no shame? It is no wonder Mr Collins chose another woman to marry! You hoped to marry better, but you will make a fool of yourself!"

"It seems someone misinformed you, madam! It was done either from stupidity or from malice, but it could not be further from the truth. I have come here for Georgiana, with no intention to marry anyone!"

"You make me laugh! For Georgiana? How could you have even known Georgiana? Such a ridiculous pretext! And Darcy! Bringing a woman into the house and imposing her on his sister. He must have lost all his sense and decency!"

"You have said enough, Lady Catherine. Your accusations are beyond sense and decency, and they deserve no consideration." With her entire body trembling with devastating embarrassment and repressed anger, Elizabeth walked to the door, but the woman grasped her arm.

"Not so hasty, if you please! You must tell me if you are

engaged to my nephew or not!"

"I must not tell you anything, but since I am fond of truth and decency, I shall answer. I am not, nor have I ever spoken to Mr Darcy about any engagement. This is absurd!"

The woman's voice dropped a little.

"And will you promise me you will never become engaged to him?"

"Such a request is ridiculous, and my absence from your company is long due, madam," Elizabeth replied, pulling her arm from the lady's grip. But the woman grasped it again, and Elizabeth struggled not to simply push her away, as she deserved.

"Lady Catherine, release my friend this instant!" a small but strong voice demanded from the door. Georgiana Darcy was there, with Mrs Annesley, the housekeeper, the butler, and Mr Darcy's valet behind her.

Lady Catherine stared at her niece, obviously surprised by the intervention. A moment was enough for Elizabeth to escape her grip and step towards the door.

"Please leave and return when Fitzwilliam is at home," Georgiana continued. The effort of confronting her aunt was obviously too much for the girl, but she did not abandon it.

"Your friend? You poor, naïve little thing!" the lady laughed jeeringly. "You are aware of nothing in this world, and you should not make a fool of yourself further. You have been nothing but a pawn in an indecent scheme planned by your brother and this woman!"

"Lady Catherine, you are making a fool of yourself, and you should know that the whole household is laughing at you. This is Elizabeth Bennet, who has been my friend since I was five years old. The one who saved my life when I almost drowned. The one whom my mother loved dearly, and you probably forbade from seeing me! The one who, with the exception of my brother, is the most important person in the world to me, and I would do anything to protect her!"

Although her voice was softer and weaker than the

woman's, the girl's speech roused Lady Catherine's interest enough to silence her and to increase her scrutiny with a trace of disbelief.

"You have offended my friend, and I expect you to apologise to her," Georgiana requested.

"Apologise to her? Never! She is nothing to me! She is nothing at all, just a country nobody! And you have no right to address me in such a way. I am your mother's sister!"

"I wonder what my mother would say of your behaviour, Aunt! Your accusations against Elizabeth are as ridiculous as your claim of an engagement between Fitzwilliam and Anne — something which everybody laughs at, including the two of them," the girl continued. The statement shook Lady Catherine so deeply that her face changed colour several times. Elizabeth feared she would respond violently, and she moved in front of Georgiana.

Mrs Annesley was on Georgiana's other side, while the housekeeper, the valet, and the butler stepped in front of the girls, as a barrier against any attack.

Lady Catherine's fury grew to such a height that it left her speechless, and she only banged her cane, cursing.

"Lady Catherine," the butler interjected calmly, "the master is out, and I have to follow Miss Darcy's directions. It is my duty to do so. Therefore, I would kindly ask your ladyship to leave. I shall certainly inform the master of your visit, and I am sure he will call on you soon."

While his voice was calm, he took another step closer, and so did the valet. The prospect of being carried out was obvious even for the lady, and she pushed the men away, then stormed out of the door.

Behind her, the servants removed themselves in silence.

Georgiana was holding Elizabeth's arm tightly, and together they moved to the sofa, followed by Mrs Annesley.

"I am so sorry, Lizzy...so sorry," the girl whispered tearfully.

Elizabeth forced a smile. "Do not apologise, my dear. You

were extraordinarily brave and strong. I could not be more grateful and prouder of you!"

"Your friendship gave me strength, Lizzy. And I only spoke the truth. Except for Fitzwilliam, you are the most important person in the world to me!"

"Thank you, dearest. Now please excuse me, I need to rest a little. I have barely slept since yesterday," Elizabeth replied, trying to conceal the tremble in her voice. She felt drained, exhausted by the mortification of such a dreadful offence being thrown at her in public.

Georgiana accompanied her to her room, and once there, Elizabeth entered and gently closed the door behind her. She needed time away from anyone, including her best friend.

As she lay in bed, she had to admit to herself that Lady Catherine was not entirely wrong; although the accusations were ill-grounded, her thoughts and hopes in regard to Mr Darcy were real. And she felt guilty for her feelings and for exposing Mr Darcy and Georgiana to such horrible rumours. With tears rolling down her cheeks, she understood it was time for her to return home.

Chapter 31

Darcy entered the house, his only desire to sleep for several hours before enjoying a peaceful dinner with Georgiana and Elizabeth. The matter with Wickham was still not entirely resolved, with some details remaining to be discussed, but as he estimated, Miss King had not been swayed from her decision. Therefore, after hours of arguments, tears, and shouting, the family had no other choice but to accept the unwanted engagement.

Colonel Forster had refused to allow Wickham to return to his regiment or to offer any recommendations for another assignment; therefore, the scoundrel had to be given a new way to earn a living. Fortunately, Miss King's family had many connections among wealthy tradesmen in London, and Wickham's future was decided.

Darcy's only involvement was to take the entire party to his solicitor's, where, against Wickham's will, a strict settlement was signed and sealed with witnesses.

With amusement and self-satisfaction, Darcy mused that the scoundrel had found his match. Behind her plain figure, Miss Mary King hid a strong character which admitted no opposition. Between her requests, her uncle and cousin's visible guns, and the colonel's threat with accusations of betrayal, Wickham had no choice left. Even better, the settlement set out expectations for his behaviour towards his future wife, and breaking it would send him to prison for all his debts.

Darcy saw Miss King as perfectly capable of letting her uncle send her husband to prison if he wronged her in any way. He anticipated relating all the details to Elizabeth and entertaining her with the unexpected chastisement of the scoundrel who had tried to dishonour a young lady for his own gain.

In the hall, not only the butler but also his valet and Mrs Penfield were waiting for him, with worried expressions and lowered gazes.

"What has happened?" he asked abruptly.

"Sir, there is something... Lady Catherine de Bourgh came to see you. You were out, and she spoke to Miss Bennet and Miss Darcy," the butler mumbled.

Darcy frowned for a moment, cold shivers of panic running down his spine. "Where is my sister? And Miss Bennet?"

"They are both in their rooms, resting. Miss Bennet instructed us not to disturb her. She was very tired," the housekeeper explained.

Tiredness turned into a headache that cut across his temples, and Darcy went to the library demanding that his servants follow.

"Close the door," he told his valet. "Now tell me what happened."

"Sir, I—"

"Mrs Penfield, please! I am too tired and too angry to have patience. I sense something wrong happened, and I want to know every detail of it. Every single detail. Every word. Speak!"

He could not even stand while the three, with reluctance, revealed to him the dreadful, horrible argument. With horror, he heard of his aunt's accusations towards Elizabeth and with pride listened of his sister confronting their aunt, of whom she had always been frightened.

His head was spinning; after his anger towards Wickham and Mrs Younge, and his annoyance with Miss Bingley, now his rage overstepped the limit. His aunt had acted the worst of all, her resentment hurting Elizabeth.

"When Miss Darcy told Lady Catherine that everybody laughed at her for her insistence on the engagement between you and Miss de Bourgh, the lady seemed to wish to hurt her. I had no other choice but to ask her to leave. I know I was impolite. I went beyond my duty. I am ready to accept the consequences," the butler said.

"You carried out your duty most excellently," Darcy said. "All of you did, and I thank you for your loyalty. I appreciate the honesty of your narration. I hope there is no need to explain that my aunt's accusations are as false as they are ridiculous."

"Sir, such an explanation is not necessary. We deserve no thanks. I was devastated to see Miss Bennet so hurt, and I am sorry we could not protect her," the housekeeper said with apparent emotion.

"It is my duty to protect my sister and her friend. Which I shall do immediately. Mrs Penfield, if my sister or Miss Bennet wakes up, please inform them I shall return shortly."

He left the house again; the cold air of winter and the wind blowing in his face refreshed him. He hesitated between going to Lady Catherine's townhouse or to the Matlocks' and chose the second. Regardless of her whereabouts, he would find his aunt and settle the matter with her.

As soon as he entered the Matlocks' residence, he heard Lady Catherine's irritated and irritating voice.

He followed it before the servant had time to announce him and pushed open the door, finding the colonel, his parents, Anne, and her mother in the middle of a heated conversation.

"Darcy, here you are!" Lady Catherine exclaimed. "How fortunate, as we were just talking about you. Come, sit. Let me tell you about the abominable manner in which I was treated by your sister, your servants, and that woman who, for some inexplicable reason, lives in your house. Georgiana's impertinence is outrageous! I have never suffered such an offence, and I insist you take the most severe measures!"

Darcy looked at his other relatives — who seemed quite distressed — and at Anne, who was silent and pale. To her, Darcy nodded in a friendly gesture before he responded, struggling to temper his rage.

"Lady Catherine, I have no intention of sitting. And I have not come here to listen but to speak. You have embarrassed me — and Anne! — many times over the years, but today you overstepped any boundaries of decorum. Whilst I hold Anne in affectionate regard, I am ashamed that you are my aunt."

Lady Catherine gasped for air, and her eyes opened wide in shock.

"Excuse me! What are you talking about, young man? Have you lost your mind?"

"I am talking about you breaking into my house and offending my sister's guest, the same one who saved Georgiana's life twice. You offended her with all the servants as witness. Furthermore, you accused me of bringing a woman into my home for a dishonourable purpose and imposing her on my sister against her will. How dare you!"

"Do not be ridiculous. How could I have known who she was? Miss Bingley wrote to me about a woman living in your home, and I questioned Mr Collins, who had heard a different report. What should I have assumed, especially since I found the woman in your house?"

"You should have minded your own business, as you never do!" Darcy shouted in such a way that all the ladies gasped, and even the colonel and the earl stood up and tried to calm him. Yet, he was too tired to mind his words, so he took a few steps away and continued.

"It is not for you to question me or my life. You have hurt and embarrassed poor Anne with this ridiculous pretence of an engagement, which everybody has laughed at. You should know once and for all that I shall always take care of Anne, but I shall never marry her!"

"How dare you, ungrateful boy! It was your mother's desire as much as mine—"

"Oh, stop this nonsense, Catherine," the earl intervened.

"You and Anne spoke a few times as a joke about your children marrying. Darcy is right. You have taken this foolishness too far. You should apologise and be done with this unfortunate situation."

"Apologise? Me? Never! Not in a hundred years! You have all lost your minds, and I suspect it is that woman's fault!"

"I have no intention of forgiving you, Lady Catherine," Darcy answered. "However, I must thank you. You see, I have long admired Miss Bennet, but I have never dared to confess my feelings to her, as I was uncertain of hers. I have never treated her other than with the utmost respect as my sister's friend, but I would probably not have gathered enough courage to speak to her so soon without your intervention."

His words had an extraordinary effect on the others, who were all staring at him with either disbelief or amazement.

"However, due to your actions, I shall have to apologise to her on your behalf. And I shall take this opportunity to reveal my admiration to her. Furthermore, if her response encourages me to do so, I intend to propose to her this very evening," he ended calmly.

"You will not do that! You would not dare!" Lady Catherine cried.

"Darcy, let us not be hasty," the earl interjected. "Let us ponder all this with reason and wisdom."

"Uncle, I am not being hasty. I have pondered over this more times than I can count. As I said, the only reasons that prevented me from addressing Miss Bennet were that she is my sister's friend and guest, and I did not want to embarrass her, and also that I was uncertain of her opinion of me. Now please excuse me. I must leave."

He turned to walk away, while Lady Catherine and the earl called after him. Reluctantly, he stopped and added, "If Miss Bennet does me the honour of accepting my marriage proposal, it will be a great blessing to me. I do not expect you to approve of it, and I understand this comes as a shock to you all. You are entitled to your opinion. I understand such a marriage will affect our family relationship. As long as you treat Miss Bennet politely, I shall respect your decision. However, I shall cut all ties to anyone who ever offends Miss Bennet again."

He bowed again and exited the house with a huge sense of relief. Now, he could finally return home, to Georgiana and to Elizabeth.

***

When he entered his house, the scene that met him was most disturbing: his sister was alone, waiting for him, her face betraying the signs of profound distress, such as he had not seen in more than a month.

"My dear, why have you been crying? You look very ill! Did something else happen while I was gone?"

"Brother, Lizzy wants to leave. She said she cannot stay any longer... Mrs Annesley is helping her pack her luggage—"

"I shall speak to her immediately," he said, hurrying up the stairs with Georgiana barely keeping pace with him. A sharp claw was gripping his chest, and he took a moment outside her door to catch his breath.

"My dear, I wish to speak to Miss Bennet alone," he said. Georgiana seemed a little bit surprised. "I do not wish to disturb her with my presence, so please enter and ask her if she would speak to me privately."

The girl nodded, knocked, and entered. Darcy waited in the hall, time passing painfully slowly. Finally, when the door opened again, Georgiana appeared, together with Mrs Annesley and a maid.

"Lizzy said you may enter," she whispered.

"You may wait here. It will not take long," he replied, loud enough that the maid could hear too. The last thing he needed was more rumours about him and Elizabeth.

He found her sitting on a chair near the small table by the window.

She looked at him; her eyes, burdened by sadness, had

lost their sparkle, and no trace of a smile touched her lips, pressed together in an obvious attempt at fighting tears.

He asked permission to sit, and she granted it silently.

"You look tired, sir," she whispered.

"My tiredness is nothing compared with your sadness, Miss Bennet. I shall not even beg your forgiveness. The circumstances are beyond apologies, and I shall never be able to remedy the turmoil you have been through."

"There is nothing for you to remedy, sir. Please do not distress yourself with further blame which does not belong to you," she said with a glimpse of teasing in her voice.

"You wish to leave?"

"I do...I feel it is time. Georgiana has grown stronger, and her health is completely recovered. I shall write to her often—"

"Georgiana has improved in spirits and in health because of you. We cannot ask you to stay against your will, but she will not be the same without you. Neither of us will."

"Staying would not be against my will. Quite the opposite. I simply must leave."

"I understand you are upset with us, with the entire family. And with good reason."

"Oh, please, do not say that. I have already begged Georgiana not to assume such a thing. I am not upset with either of you. Why would I be? The time I have spent here has been some of the happiest of my life."

"And of our lives," he added, a little pause following his words.

"May I ask...if you are not upset with us, why do you want to leave now? You must not fear — Lady Catherine will never bother you again. I have settled things with her in a way that will never allow such an incident to occur again."

"I am not afraid of Lady Catherine." She smiled bitterly. "The only reason I did not treat her with the harshness she deserved was my consideration for her as Lady Anne's sister. Otherwise, she would have heard more from me."

She looked a little more at ease as the conversation progressed.

"Miss Bennet, I trust you more than almost anyone else I know, and I know you would not deceive me. If you want to leave to return to your family, that would be understandable. I shall make the arrangements for you to travel safely to the Gardiners' or to Longbourn. But if you wish to stay, please do not go, whatever the reason might be..."

***

His hoarse voice made Elizabeth tremble; he spoke so tenderly, so protectively. His expression was so affectionate that it made her heart melt.

Or perhaps that was only what she hoped to see, to respond to the feelings inside her.

"My staying here could be more damaging than helpful to you and to Georgiana. And perhaps to me too. If such rumours reached Lady Catherine in Kent, they surely have spread among my family and friends as well. I was foolish to overlook the danger when you warned me about it from the very beginning."

"No rumours have been spread. It seems Miss Bingley, in an act of rage, wrote to my aunt, and she questioned her clergyman, then drew her own conclusions."

"Oh..." Elizabeth sighed. "Yes, Caroline Bingley. She found us that day, and she imagined... What an imprudent lady! What pains me the most is that Georgiana was exposed to such dreadful accusations. I was so ashamed that she could imagine that... Even if she doubted me, how could your aunt assume such horrible things about you?"

"My aunt is the most unreasonable woman one could imagine. And Miss Bingley is not far removed. I owe her my opinion on this matter."

"Perhaps. But let us be honest and reasonable and treat the situation with calm," Elizabeth said. "You knew such rumours might arise, and I disregarded them. It was my fault. I should not have come to your library that day…or any other day. As much as I enjoyed talking to you, my imprudence might harm your reputation and mine. This is why I must leave before more damage is done."

Elizabeth had calmed her distress somewhat, and speaking to Mr Darcy put her more and more at ease. On the contrary, she saw Mr Darcy's countenance become graver, his voice lower, and his gaze darker.

"Miss Bennet, I cherished every moment I spent with you — alone or with others. Every time I was in the library, I hoped you would come. Every time I heard steps in the hall, I was startled and prayed it was you. I longed to see you first thing in the morning and last thing at night."

Elizabeth stared at him, listening with amazement, wondering about the meaning of his words, not daring to accept her comprehension.

"I have not been honest or reasonable for a long time in regard to you. I have struggled to conceal my feelings and remain silent to protect you from a confession I feared you might not wish to hear. My struggle was in vain, and my disguise caused more harm than the truth would have. With complete honesty and all fears aside, I must tell you how ardently I love and admire you."

The tumult of feelings that overwhelmed Elizabeth took her breath away and silenced her. With his every word, her heart raced as she struggled to keep her mind alert, although she felt dizzy with perturbation.

"Perhaps this was not the proper time to speak. Perhaps I was wrong not to remain silent and have only added more to your distress. I cannot judge clearly enough to decide what is best. Your wishes and feelings are the most important to me, but my love is so selfish that it cannot be repressed any longer."

"You were not wrong, Mr Darcy. Your silence would have added much more to my distress than your words did. If I say little, it is because I feel too much, and I still do not dare to be sure of your meaning. I am still not certain if I understand you clearly. I am not even certain that this moment is real or just a dream meant to comfort me."

"You have always understood me quite well, Miss Bennet. If I did not express myself clearly enough, allow me to do so now. I shall simply ask: Would you do me the honour of becoming my wife, dearest, loveliest Elizabeth?"

He moved closer and knelt in front of her, waiting. His soul, freed from the burden of the belated confession, waited for her answer.

Elizabeth was still tearful, and words still betrayed her. His handsome features were now brightened by pure delight; she gently touched his face and cupped it with trembling hands. He turned his head so he could place a soft, lingering kiss in each of her palms.

"Yes, Mr Darcy. You must know my answer is yes. You must have known it for a long time now," she whispered. Then slowly, she lowered her face so that their lips met in a sigh of shared love that soothed any prior turmoil.

"I believe I did know, but just like you, I did not dare to be sure of it," he answered, his lips claiming hers again, this time more daring, with no remaining doubts or fears.

Chapter 32

The evening after the proposal passed truly like a dream for Elizabeth and Darcy, as well as Georgiana. For the first time she and her brother could remember, Miss Darcy yelled, cried, and jumped with joy.

Since they did not have Mr Bennet's blessing yet, only Mrs Annesley was informed about the engagement, the news being kept secret from the servants.

Despite his deep tiredness, Darcy immediately wrote to Mr Bennet and to Mr Gardiner by express, then he decided to move to Georgiana's house — only minutes away from his — that very minute. Considering the engagement, he found it inappropriate to spend another night in the same house as Elizabeth, so he sent his valet to make the arrangements.

Another note was sent to Colonel Fitzwilliam, to inform him about his new residence, then Darcy bade his farewells to the ladies and left. By the time he arrived at the house, the colonel was already there. Despite him being completely exhausted, Darcy had dinner and several drinks with his cousin, sharing the news and discussing the events of that extraordinary day.

Elizabeth and Georgiana barely slept at all, even though both were exhausted after the most challenging couple of days. The girl's joy was so profound that it almost exceeded Elizabeth's.

Only several hours had passed since Lady Catherine's horrific visit and Elizabeth's decision to leave, and her turmoil had turned into bliss. With Darcy's profession of love in her mind and the taste of their kisses — more than one! — on her lips, she was enchanted, thrilled, and dizzy with gladness and gratitude.

She intended to write to Jane but was too tired even for that. She counted on the letters Darcy had already sent; despite everything that had occurred in the last two days, despite not sleeping at all, he seemed to never be too tired to do what was right. He was surely the best of men — and soon he would be hers, she mused with exhilaration and thrilling anticipation.

The morning after the engagement was a day prior to Christmas. Darcy returned to the house early in the morning; the moment she woke up, Elizabeth felt he was there, and she hurried to the library. Unlike other times, he locked the door behind her and wrapped his arms around her in an embrace that placed her where she belonged — near his heart.

"I have missed you so much," he whispered to her, allowing her no time to respond before he kissed her passionately. Sometime later, they finally found the strength to speak coherently and discuss their plans in a reasonable manner. But not for long, as another kiss and the many others that followed interrupted them again.

During breakfast, Mrs Annesley and Colonel Fitzwilliam joined them, the colonel displaying his usual large smile and a special greeting for Elizabeth, together with his congratulations.

The colonel did not stay long, but he was expected to join them for a Christmas dinner party, together with the Gardiners. Around noon, after she had written to Jane, Elizabeth went to the library to take the letter to Darcy for posting. She found him there with Georgiana. At her entrance, both stopped what was a seemingly intimate conversation.

"Lizzy, there is something I wish to tell you," the girl said with apparent solemnity, and Elizabeth was worried for a moment.

"I have something for you. I wanted to give it to you for Christmas, but I confess I have no patience to wait."

With obvious delight, the girl handed her a velvet box,

which Elizabeth took reluctantly.

"My dear, I do not need any presents," Elizabeth said.

"I know you do not need it, but I really need to give it to you, Lizzy. It is something from me, to add to what you already have from my mother," the girl whispered.

With trembling fingers, Elizabeth opened the box and gasped, while tears moistened her eyes. A pair of earrings and a bracelet of gold set with rubies, an almost perfect match to her necklace, were shining in the box.

"My dear Georgiana, this is too much," she whispered, embracing the girl.

"Allow me to put your bracelet on," Darcy offered, taking her hand and caressing her wrist. Georgiana chuckled and averted her eyes. Elizabeth also put on the earrings, glancing at her image in the mirror. From behind her, the two Darcys were smiling at her with a love of a different kind but equal depth and strength.

"I have nothing to give you," Elizabeth said, glancing at them both.

"You have given me my life back, Lizzy," Georgiana said. "Now and ten years ago."

"I have something for you too, Elizabeth. It was prepared a few days ago, but it has not been delivered yet," Darcy said.

"A few days ago? Before our engagement?"

"Yes. It should be here any moment."

"I do not need any more presents, Fitzwilliam. I truly do not."

"I know," he said, kissing her hand. "I hope you will enjoy this one, nevertheless. Georgiana, could we have some music?"

The glances exchanged by brother and sister showed Elizabeth they were together in the little scheme.

She ceased any opposition, allowing herself to be spoilt by their attention, and followed them into the music room. Georgiana played while Elizabeth and Darcy listened, her hand resting in his. His right hand was still bruised, and she caressed it lovingly, wondering about how their lives had changed in the last few days.

The peaceful moment was interrupted by the sound of a carriage, and Darcy stood up immediately, excusing himself. Elizabeth assumed the gift was being delivered. Curiosity led her to follow Darcy, with Georgiana only steps behind her.

Footsteps could be heard, and when the door opened, with amazement and rapture, Elizabeth saw her family gathered at the entrance. She glanced at Darcy, who was watching her with an expression of gratification, then at Georgiana, who was only smiling. If previously she had fought sad tears, the tears of joy were impossible to stop as she embraced her sister and parents.

"Please come in. It is very cold," Darcy invited them, while Mrs Bennet and her daughters admired the house. Behind them, Mr Bennet and Bingley, less rapturous, greeted him.

"I cannot believe you are all here! But how is it possible? Mama, I know you do not travel during the winter."

"My dear, I never have since you were born," Mrs Bennet answered while maids came to their aid. "But when your father told me that you were staying with Mr Darcy, as his sister's companion, and he had invited us to stay in his house until Twelfth Night and would send his carriage for us, I told Mrs Phillips and Lady Lucas and Mrs Long, and all three of them almost fainted from surprise! So, I had to come if only to annoy them."

With her mother's every word, Elizabeth's astonishment increased, and she kept glancing at Darcy, whose smile of contentment widened. He had invited her family to stay in his house. All of them. How was it possible? Did Georgiana know of this? She was still smiling, though timidly in the face of that gathering of strangers. It sounded like a plan had been made days before Lady Catherine's visit. Darcy had done it for her, before he knew she returned his feelings, before their engagement. He had prepared that thoughtful gift for her out of his generous love.

Darcy introduced his sister to the Bennets, and Georgiana greeted each of them with care and friendliness, although in a timid voice.

"I wish to say that Lizzy is not my companion, she is my best friend," Georgiana added daringly.

"How kind of you to say so, Miss Darcy," Mrs Bennet replied. "You look so pretty and elegant! I hope my Lizzy is not too wild for you — she always had the tendency of doing only what she wanted."

"She is the perfect friend for me, I assure you," Georgiana responded.

"Please allow a maid to show each of you to your rooms," Darcy interjected, and the ladies responded with rapturous cries. "Mr Bennet, if it is acceptable to you, sir, you may join me in the other house, my sister's, where I live at present. Or you may stay here. There are plenty of rooms."

"My dear Mr Darcy, all I need is a warm room to sleep in and a library to hide myself as often as possible. It might be in either house," Mr Bennet answered.

Amidst the din, Elizabeth realised her family had not received the news of her engagement. If they had, her mother's rapture would have been heard from Derbyshire. She allowed Darcy to handle the matter, while she accompanied her mother and sisters upstairs. She decided Jane would share her room, as they did at Longbourn, since both missed each other and had much to share after a month of separation. Lydia, Kitty, and Mary were sharing a large guest apartment with two bed chambers, while another apartment was offered to Mrs Bennet.

Darcy took Mr Bennet to the library for a drink, and Bingley left to return to his own house.

After several hours of rest, the ladies were given a tour, during which time they had more chances to admire the house and express their amazement.

A rich and elegant dinner was prepared, much to Mrs Bennet's satisfaction, and Mr Bingley returned to join them, sitting next to his betrothed.

"Lizzy, what do you say about Jane's engagement to Mr Bingley? Is it not the most wonderful thing?"

"It is, Mama, and well deserved for them both. I have rarely met two people so good in nature and so perfectly suited to each other," Elizabeth answered, glancing at the pair affectionately. In her heart, she knew there were two other people in the room even better suited, and Darcy's glance told her he had guessed her thoughts.

"I never imagined I could be so fortunate and so happy," Bingley declared.

"Everybody in Meryton agrees that Mr Bingley is the perfect match for Jane," Mrs Bennet interjected. "Even Lady Lucas, although I know she is dying of envy."

"Lizzy, may we go shopping on Oxford Street?" Kitty asked. "I do not know where it is, but Maria Lucas told me Sir William mentioned it. You surely must know it."

"I have only been shopping once since I arrived in London," Elizabeth answered. "But yes, we may go wherever you want."

"Lizzy, by the by, I forgot to tell you! Do you know Mr Wickham eloped with Mary King? What a silly thing for him to do. She is so plain, and her face is full of freckles. She might have ten thousand pounds, but surely he could have done better!"

Elizabeth quickly glanced at Georgiana, who looked rather amused.

"Mr Wickham is known for his imprudent actions," Mr Bennet interjected. "Let us not ruin our appetite with talk of such annoying things."

"Speaking of annoying things, Mr Collins has returned," Lydia said. "Oh, my Lord, if I have to listen to him one more time, I swear I shall die of tedium!"

"You are not alone, my dear," Mrs Bennet said. "Mary, let us not forget to write to my sister Phillips tomorrow. Now that we are gone, she must be tired of hearing only about Charlotte

Lucas's engagement."

With such subjects of conversation, some amusing, some embarrassing for Elizabeth, the evening passed. The long, tiring journey sent all the ladies to their rooms soon after dinner. As it was already late and cold out of doors, Darcy decided to remain in the house. With the new arrangements, his presence was not a danger to propriety. He and Mr Bennet spent more time in the library, where Elizabeth found them later on. With a long look at Elizabeth and an excuse to Mr Bennet, Darcy left, allowing father and daughter some privacy.

Dizzy from the brandy and from the good news, Mr Bennet embraced her tenderly and congratulated her.

"My dear Lizzy, I am lost for words. I confess I still cannot believe this is true! Please tell me that you are happy. I know you respect Mr Darcy, and with good reason. But do you truly love him? Are you not marrying for gratitude or for friendship with his sister?"

"I do love him, Papa. I have loved him for a while, but not even I dared to dream he might propose to me. I learnt he had loved me since we were in Hertfordshire, but he did not dare say a word."

"Well, I am glad to hear that. And relieved. Of course, I gave Mr Darcy my blessing. He is the kind of man to whom I would not dare refuse anything, regardless."

"Papa!" Elizabeth laughed. "I hope you did not give him too hard a time! He is truly the best man I have ever met. Including you," she jested, kissing his cheek.

"Well, I should hope so, my dear. I am not much of a catch. I always prayed you would find a husband better than me in every way," the gentleman answered in earnest. "So far, both you and Jane have succeeded. I have only one requirement, for you and for Darcy. Allow me to tell your mother about this engagement whenever I find it appropriate. I know I shall have no peace for days after such news."

"Very well, Papa," she agreed, embracing him lovingly. Outside the library, Elizabeth found Darcy waiting, leaning against the wall. With no words, her eyes locked with his in the relative darkness, and she rose onto her toes, cupped his face with tender hands, and lowered his head for a kiss more meaningful than any expression of gratitude.

***

On Christmas Eve, Darcy's house was fuller than he could remember. With the Bennet family, the Gardiners — and their four children — Bingley, and Colonel Fitzwilliam, there was little room to spare around the table. Bingley's sisters were not invited, as Darcy had confessed to his friend about Miss Bingley's shameless intervention.

Georgiana was still restrained, sitting between Elizabeth and Mrs Annesley. She had spent some time with Elizabeth and Jane and spoken a little to the other sisters, but there were too many people whom she had just met for the first time for her to feel comfortable.

The acknowledged betrotheds smiled at each other, spending all their time together. The unknown pair only exchanged glances and smiles over the table.

Once the dinner ended, all moved to the drawing room for drinks.

"I have to say, this is the best Christmas I have ever had!" Mrs Bennet declared. "Mr Darcy, I cannot apologise enough for believing you were arrogant and unpleasant when I first met you. I hope you can forgive me."

"Those times are long forgotten, Mrs Bennet," he offered generously. "Besides, your opinion was based on my actions, and I have only myself to blame."

"Oh, how generous of you to say that! And to have all of us in your house! And with Jane engaged to Mr Bingley. Upon my word, one cannot imagine a better Christmas!"

Mr Bennet sipped from his glass, a mischievous smile on his face that both Elizabeth and Darcy noticed.

"Mrs Bennet, now that you mention it, there is

something I have to tell you."

"Mr Bennet, I know you always like to tease me, but there is nothing you can say to ruin my evening!" the lady said, sipping a little from her sherry.

"I have no intention of ruining your evening. Quite the opposite. I might make it even better."

"Better? I cannot see how you could improve perfection, Mr Bennet!"

"Well, allow me to try proving you wrong, my dear Mrs Bennet. Mr Darcy, hold my glass. There is something I must share with my wife!"

***

Longbourn, February 1812

On a cold yet sunny day, the entire neighbourhood was gathered in front of the church to witness the most unlikely and astonishing event: the wedding of Miss Elizabeth Bennet to Mr Fitzwilliam Darcy.

Their wedding day was shared by Miss Jane Bennet and Charles Bingley, but that couple gave nobody any concern or surprise, since they were the perfect match, and their marriage was long expected.

Those two weddings followed two others: Charlotte Lucas to Mr Collins and Mary King to the former officer George Wickham. Whilst marriage seemed to have benefitted Mr Collins and his wife so far, of Mary King and her husband there was little news, since both had left Hertfordshire and were now residing near Bath. Rumours said that Mr Wickham was working as a clerk to one of Mary's distant uncles. The once handsome and admired officer was soon forgotten, especially since gossip about his flaws of character had reached the neighbourhood.

At the present wedding, among the attendees were Mr Darcy's sister, with her companion, and his cousin the colonel. Also, unexpectedly, Miss Darcy seemed to be on friendly terms with the younger Bennet sisters, Mary, Kitty, and Lydia.

On Mr Bingley's side, there was only his eldest sister, Louisa Hurst, and her husband — who were not on friendly terms with anyone.

It was universally admitted that the Bennets were the most fortunate family that ever existed in the neighbourhood — something that Mrs Bennet had agreed with since the Christmas evening when her husband had given her the extraordinary news of Lizzy's engagement to Mr Darcy.

Two months had passed since then, and Mrs Bennet still feared it was only one of her husband's tricks. Only when the wedding service was over could she breathe easily.

After the ceremony, the entire party left for Netherfield, except for Mr and Mrs Darcy, who were expected in London, Mrs Bennet explained to all her friends.

"You must understand that my Lizzy will now have responsibilities according to her new position in society that you and I cannot even imagine," she told Mrs Phillips, Mrs Long, and Lady Lucas. "It is one thing to be married to — let us say — a clergyman, or even to a rich man like Mr Bingley, and completely another thing to be the wife of Mr Darcy, who owns the largest estate in Derbyshire. He has a fortune as great as an earl, you know. By the by, did I mention that his uncle is an earl and so was his grandfather? And he has invited us to stay at Pemberley for the whole summer!"

Nobody could contradict Mrs Bennet in her claims, as in truth, nobody could imagine how it would be to be the wife of a man like Mr Darcy.

Only Elizabeth knew. After she bade farewell to her family and friends and the carriage door closed behind them, her husband's arms embraced her tightly, and he claimed her lips for a long kiss — the first one of their married lives.

There was no business awaiting them in London, except for a week of blissful privacy to start their life together. Georgiana had decided to remain in Hertfordshire and return to London later, with the Gardiners, to allow her brother and new sister time to themselves.

"I hope you will not find it dull with me alone, Mrs Darcy, after being in the midst of your friends and family. I am known for not being a pleasant nor an entertaining man," he teased her.

"Not to mention arrogant and haughty, Mr Darcy. And not fond of dancing or parties," she replied, her fingers tantalising his face.

"True. Yet you cannot blame me, since you knew all this long before I proposed to you. And still, you married me."

"I did know all this long before I fell in love with you, sir. And still, I did," she answered, her lips touching his daringly, while his arms held her even tighter.

Pemberley, April 1812

The carriage drove at a slow pace through Pemberley Park, surrounded by beauty that was hard to describe. While Mrs Annesley loudly expressed her admiration, Elizabeth was silent, only holding her husband's hand. She was wearing Lady Anne's necklace and the earrings and bracelet from Georgiana. Her husband's presents to her did not need to be exposed.

After two months of exquisite felicity in London, they were finally going home — to Pemberley, the place to which all were bound by long-lasting memories.

The place she had carried in her heart for more than ten years seemed even more beautiful to Elizabeth, perhaps because now she saw it as his home. Their home.

She glanced at her husband several times with her eyes filled with emotions, and he tenderly kissed her hand. Her heart was racing, filled with past memories and present happiness, as well as promises for the future.

The carriage stopped in front of the house, and Darcy helped his wife, his sister, and her companion out, holding his arm around Elizabeth's shoulders. She looked at him again, her eyes sparkling and her face beaming.

A short distance away, Mrs Reynolds, the housekeeper, ran to greet them with her arms open. Georgiana embraced her, and then the housekeeper stopped in front of Elizabeth, covering her mouth with her hand.

"My dear girl, it's you! It's really you, and you are back at Pemberley! You have changed so much, but I remember your eyes!"

Then she immediately minded her words and curtseyed, bowing her head.

"Please forgive me. I forgot myself. Welcome to Pemberley, Mrs Darcy, and please receive my warmest congratulations on behalf of myself and the entire household," she said ceremoniously.

Elizabeth embraced her with genuine affection, tearful with emotions.

"I have not forgotten you, Mrs Reynolds, and there is nothing to forgive in your loving reception. I have so many fond memories of you."

"Come, let us enter," Darcy suggested, placing his arm around his wife again. "Elizabeth has returned to Pemberley, and she will never leave it. We shall have a lifetime to share old memories and make new ones, as we are all home, together."

Elizabeth's heart swelled with joy as her beloved husband spoke the words she had longed to hear. "Indeed, my dearest, we have at last arrived home," she replied with a smile. "Together."

ANDREEACATANA